CAMINO MAGGIE

TEEN REBEL SERIES

JOY LLEWELLYN

This book is a work of fiction, though the story follows the Santiago de Compostela Camino Francés 1,000-year-old pilgrimage route.

Cover designed by Wicked Whale Publishing
First edition, 2019.

Llewellyn, Joy,

Camino Maggie/Joy Llewellyn, pp 344

Summary: After getting caught breaking into her aunt's store, Maggie's punishment is an 800 km hike in Spain with her aunt, a youth counsellor, and three other young offenders. Who knows where boys, betrayals, and blisters might lead her?

ISBN: 9781999276805

Tamarack Journey Publishing
4741 Bosun Way
Pender Island, BC
Canada, V0N2M2
www.joythierryllewellyn.com

To the eternally playful, sometimes challenging,
and always adventurous man
who introduced me to the first
of what have become many
Camino hikes together.
Evan, je t'aime.

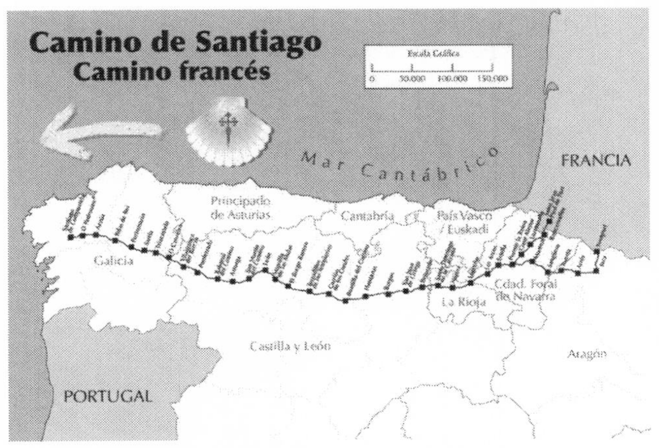

(iStock, Photitos2016)

1

MAGDALENE'S HEARTH

I knew I was doing something stupid when the smart part of my brain yelled, *Stop!*

I had this jab of conscience just as Tony began to shake his head frantically, making his curly hair swing from side to side. I turned and looked at him in growing panic, but still found time to think, *Man, he's cute!*

Tony stopped moving but continued supporting my arm. He leaned forward as though ready for a 100-metre dash, and was barely visible in the darkened alley, his black jeans and black hoodie blending into the shadows. "Keep still!" he hissed.

It would have been easier for me to do what he asked if he hadn't let go of my arm and if my right leg wasn't already through the open window.

I tilted forward and without him to hold me steady I floundered. I grabbed the window ledge, at the same time listening to my boyfriend—*ok, my wannabe boyfriend*—disappearing down the alley. The rest of my body followed my leg, and I fell through the window in a tumble of khaki pants and jean jacket.

My landing on the wooden floor was painful and loud.

Should have signed up for those gymnastics lessons my mother was always pushing me to take.

"Tony!" I called out in a whisper that echoed in the alley outside. All I heard was the sound of quickly fading footsteps. A light flashed on, making me squint.

An angry male voice behind me yelled, "Stay where you are! Don't move a damn muscle!"

I've never been very good at doing what people told me to do. I darted around the man, dashing ahead of him and down the hallway I knew led to the display room and the front door. The hall was dark, but the glow of the storefront lights helped me see where I was going.

Why were the lights even on? Tony had said he'd timed things and the guard wouldn't be here.

I knew the windows of the second-floor apartment were dark because we'd checked them when we arrived. I was the one who had told him the owner, who lived above the store, was out for the evening. The whole building had looked empty, just like it was supposed to be.

The guard's footsteps were getting closer. I dashed into the large front room with its empty shelves that usually held New Age books, crystals, Tibetan healing bowls, and incense.

My body suddenly lurched backwards, the guard's hand clutching my jacket.

"I said, don't move!" He slammed me down on the hardwood floor. There was a loud "crack." I knew parts of my body would hurt tomorrow, especially after he stuck his knee into my back. Lying there I had a view of taped boxes and cloth dust covers and caught a whiff of the scented candles that were always lit when the store was open for business.

This guy had seen too many action movies. He may have been

only a minimum wage security guard, but that didn't stop him from whipping out a pair of handcuffs and roughly locking my arms behind my back. It hurt, though he was surprisingly efficient about the whole thing.

"Shit, take it easy, man!"

He wasn't listening, and his excitement was audible when he called 911 and said breathlessly, "Albright Security Guard Jason Nickle calling from Magdalene's Hearth corner of Almont and Schooler I've caught a B&E! One got away I need backup!"

"Let me guess, your code name is 'Wolverine' or 'Bond,'" I said.

"Shut up!" He shoved me up against the wall and spent the next 10 minutes pacing. He could hardly contain the anticipation of his Moment of Glory. When the police came, I was almost sorry for him. The cops barely gave him a nod.

They took me in handcuffs to the police station. They walked me passed a desk where tattooed men leaned against the wall and a woman in a very short skirt slouched on a bench. A skinny guy was puking into a wastebasket in the corner. Once the cops had my name and address, they put me in a room with metal chairs and a dented table. *I wasn't going to lie, why bother?*

I ignored the chairs and sat on the table, flexing my newly freed wrists. My legs, arms, and butt were sore and bruised. I wasn't sure if I'd been more banged up by the fall into the store or when the guard had slammed me down on the floor. When I tried to assume the Sukhasana yoga position I'd learned from my BFF Janie, my right leg wouldn't bend. So much for being flexible. I started doing meditation deep breathing.

I snorted. *Who was I kidding?* I was trying to seem cool and uninterested in case there was someone on the other side of that mirror, like in the movies. In truth, I was a jumbled mess of tightened stomach and clenched jaw. I put my hand up to my left eye and tried to stop it twitching.

I started quietly chanting a mantra, something else I learned from Janie: "Breathing in, I calm body and mind. Breathing out, I smile." I'd only joined the Meditation group because Janie, the founder and president, threw great parties. I repeated the words over and over but was aware of the cold metal table under my jeans and the occasional yell from the hallway.

On top of the party attraction, everyone in the meditation group got to go on what Janie convinced the social-sciences-jerk-teacher were "important spiritual and political field trips." We'd been to hear people like Jane Goodall and that guy who won that medal at the last Olympics. The talks were supposed to help us "see the world in a broader sense" and discover our "life passions."

There were advantages to going to a private school. The teachers wanted us to be knowledgeable about the rest of the world. Or as knowledgeable as 16- and 17-year-olds wearing this year's designer clothes and driving Range Rovers could be.

The last field trip I'd taken with Janie's group had been to see the Dalai Lama, who was funnier than I'd expected. When he said, "My religion is kindness," he smiled in my direction. I'd blushed. I never blush. I agreed with him on one point though. "In the practice of tolerance, one's enemy is the best teacher," he told us. That sounded like he knew my mother, but then he ruined it by talking about forgiveness, which got pretty boring. I started helping Janie with her Sudoku.

I stretched my arms and linked my fingers trying to unkink my sore back. It would've been more comfortable to sit on a chair, but I thought I'd look tougher sitting on the table, all casual-like when someone arrived. I checked my watch, which had been a gift from Grams. *Shit!* It had been smashed either during the fall through the window or when the guard tackled me. The glass cover was now a mess of cracked lines.

Where was everyone? I'd been in here for what seemed like hours. I pounded on the door, and it opened immediately.

"What's up?" A policeman stared at me, not moving from his place in the hallway. Did they think I was a terrorist? Were they afraid I'd escape? Or use my 5'3", slightly plump—to quote my mother's ever-watchful phrase—wits and charm to get out?

"I'm tired and thirsty. How much longer do I have to wait in here?"

He tried to stare me down, but I'd learned from the master: my mother. I knew how to deal with this crap. I didn't give an inch and matched him glare for glare. I tried to appear calm and hoped casually reaching up to put my dark hair behind my ears would show him who was in control.

He didn't notice. "We've called your parents. They're on their way. You can just wait." He smiled when he said that last bit—it wasn't a friendly smile. He shut the door and once again I was alone.

I was getting worried. It had never taken my parents this long to pick me up. I went back to the table but felt my energy seeping away.

Maybe I'd finally gone one step too far? My normally sweet Dad usually shook his head whenever I explained what had happened. He'd follow with his version of a lecture: "You've got to think about the consequences." He'd recently started to add, "You're too old for these antics, Maggie May." Occasionally, I really meant to consider the consequences, but I found that often things seemed to take off on their own.

I bet my eye wasn't the only one twitching in my family.

My parents, Renee and Alan MacKenzie, were probably in bed reading when they got the phone call from the police station. They would then have contacted our family lawyer, Gerry. This was not the first late-night call Gerry had received concerning me. I'd once heard him tell my parents that although he really liked me and my "go-for-it spirit," after each one of my scrapes he was always glad he didn't have children.

I started to lean against the wall and stopped. A closer look showed rust-coloured smears over the grey cement that sent me back to the table where I finally let myself think about Tony. I couldn't push down the bubble of tight anger rising from my stomach. *Where was he? Had he seen what happened to me? Maybe he followed the police car to the station?* His parked motorcycle had been around the corner from the store, and it wouldn't have taken him long to hop on and come after me.

I loved riding on that motorcycle, my arms wrapped around Tony's waist, the world rushing by as the wind whipped over my face and made my eyes water. Those moments were as close to perfection as anything I'd ever experienced.

Wondering about Tony's whereabouts and actions took up another 10 minutes, but I was getting even more restless.

Damn, I should have told the cop I needed the bathroom. That would have gotten me out of this smelly room for a bit.

Trying to ignore my aching wrists and throbbing knees, I looked around at the scratched and scarred walls that were also smeared with stuff whose origins I didn't want to consider. I shook my head in disgust. *They need an interior decorator. The place looks like a bomb shelter,* not that I knew what the inside of a bomb shelter looked like. *They should paint the walls a soft yellow, or maybe have an accent wall of teal—*

My thoughts were interrupted by the door swinging open and my parents rushing in. The grumpy policeman and good old lawyer Gerry were followed by my mother and Dad. There was no sign of the security guard who had initially arrested me. He was probably calling his mother and proudly telling her about his big catch.

Gerry cleared his throat. Though he was our family lawyer and old enough to be my grandfather, the two of us were buddies. He was a good guy and had helped get me out of scrapes before.

I rarely used any other word to describe my adventures because whenever I tried to explain my most recent "scrape," the word drove my mother crazy. That just showed I'd never be a good Buddhist—I enjoyed driving her crazy. My mother might appear calm and in control, but whenever I threatened what she considered our family's well-earned place in society, her lips would tighten, and she would get this scowl between her eyebrows that had once taken two Botox injections to smooth out.

My mother didn't even pretend to be polite for Gerry or the policeman's sake. The two of us made eye contact and scowled at each other, neither one of us willing to look away. She didn't even stop staring at me when she straightened her Stella McCartney jacket. I wondered if she wore Stella's designs because she had a fan crush on Stella's father, Paul McCartney.

Even I was smart enough to know now was not the time to ask.

I could also see that my mother had reached Stage #3 of being pissed off. On the trip here, she had moved from #1) talking in a rational, overly calm voice through #2) threatened consequences, and was on the far edge of #3) clenched jaw and big time consequences coming. She was breathing in long, deep breaths—not a good sign—and clutching Dad's hand so tightly I was sure his skin would still have fingernail grooves visible tomorrow morning.

Dad was shaking his head. Other than a quick glance when he came through the door, he hadn't looked at me. He stood there, his hand growing progressively whiter from my mother's death grip, his usual professional appearance looking flustered. He and Gerry exchanged a glance.

I could see this scrape was going to require more negotiating than usual.

In the past, Dad would calm my mother down and then he and Gerry worked something out with whoever or whatever the problem was. Even though my mother would walk around counting to ten and breathing deeply for a few days, everything would eventually go back to normal: my curfew would be dropped, my allowance re-instated, and my credit cards returned.

But here, now, Dad wasn't making eye contact.

I'm in deep shit. Tony, where are you?

2

"OUCH"

No one said anything. I'm not very good with silence, which might be why I was always battling with my mother.

Silence was her enemy too. She usually felt the need to fill up quiet spaces with blah, blah, blah. It was one of the few ways we were alike.

I was the cause of this meeting, so I was willing to be friendly and make the first move. "Hello Dad, Gerry, Mother."

Neither of my parents responded. Gerry pulled out one of the chairs and sat down. "Who was the other person in this break-in, the one who ran away?" he asked.

I didn't like his implied criticism of Tony and a little "ouch" slid into my heart. I'd think about that later. "This was my idea. There was no one else." No way was I mentioning Tony.

Gerry looked over at my parents. Dad shrugged. It looked like Gerry would run the show. He handed me his favourite slim silver pen, a gift from a famous hockey player he'd helped out of some sort of scandal a few years ago. *See, Mom? I'm not the only one he has to help*. "Sign this paper," he said.

I tried being contrite. "I'm sorry, it was a stupid joke, I know—"

"Not interested!" My mother's voice shook with anger. "This is the last straw!"

I hesitated for a moment. There was no need to give in right away. Then I sighed loudly and signed the paper, scrawling "Maggie MacKenzie" over the dotted line. I handed the page back to Gerry without bothering to read it. I'd have to go along with whatever it said, for a few days at least.

The policeman had remained silent during this family exchange. Gerry stood up and handed the signed paper to the cop, and they shook hands. "I appreciate how you handled this, Brian."

"Glad to help, Mr. Phillips. You did good work on our behalf last year. We all appreciated it."

I didn't know what he was talking about and didn't care. I just wanted to go home, take a shower, eat a bag of chips, and watch *The Mindy Project* reruns.

Gerry opened the door, holding it for my mother and Dad while he watched me to see what I would do. No way was I giving him or that stupid policeman the satisfaction of looking apologetic, so I straightened my shoulders and gave the policeman a regal nod. That should show everyone that Margaret Emily MacKenzie came from tough family stock. I smiled at Gerry when I passed him and followed my parents down the busy hallway. I knew I was in for a long talking-to tonight, but I'd manoeuvred myself out of similar prickly situations in the past.

Dad held the station's front door open for me. I stepped out into the night and quickly looked around, but there was no cute guy on a motorcycle anywhere. The "ouch" in my heart got bigger. Tony had deserted me. *Coward!*

"Maggie, hurry up!"

I walked toward my parent's car which was parked illegally in a police car spot and remembered that line about some animals being more equal than others in *Animal Farm*. Again, I knew enough to keep my mouth shut. Tonight, tomorrow, and maybe this whole week would be intense.

I was surprised my parents didn't stop me from climbing the stairs to my room when we got home. I kept waiting for them to call me into my mother's office—she did a lot of her charity work from home—but my parents and Gerry walked down the hallway and disappeared into the library.

After my shower, I ate not one but two bags of chips. That would show them. I called Tony's cell phone several times, but it always went to his voicemail. I didn't leave a message. He'd see my phone number and know I'd called. I couldn't concentrate on any television show and found Instagram and Snapchat a bore.

I finally gave up waiting and called Janie instead, who was quickly giving out breathless "oohs" and "wows" as I expanded on my night's adventures. I was sure Tony had told Janie what he had planned for this evening. He may have sworn me to secrecy, but he told everything to his younger sister.

I casually asked, "Is Tony home?"

There was a moment of silence. I could imagine Janie running her hand through her long hair and licking her upper lip, which she did when she was getting ready to lie. I suddenly felt sick. *Those two bags of chips hadn't been such a good idea.*

I heard the doorbell ring and before Janie responded, I quickly said, "Sorry, someone's here, gotta' go." My stomach was a tight drum. *Was I going to lose both brother and sister over this prank?* I filed that thought away to consider later and went to the end of the upstairs hall where I could look down into the foyer.

My mother came out of the library and answered the door. That was unusual, but when I saw that the person on the front step was Camille, I banged my head silently against the wall. Camille's dyed red hair shone in the outside front porch light. Of course, Camille would have been called. *Shit! Shit! Shit!*

Camille entered and hugged my mother, her bracelet-covered

wrists jingling as they walked to the library. Camille was my mother's younger sister, though how Grams could have given birth to two such different women and why such different women could like each other was beyond my understanding. "Imagine someone cool, like Lady Gaga, having an older sister like Cruella de Ville," was how I'd described it to Janie.

I adored Camille. She'd told me when I was four or five to "Stop calling me Aunt Camille because the word 'aunt' is a kinship name that puts people in boxes and focuses on family hierarchy…." She had said more, but it was way over my head, so I had just nodded and never called her "Aunt Camille" again.

Sure, she was a bit flaky, but she was funny and loved me, even if she didn't always agree with some of the things I did. I knew this because she'd told me one afternoon when we were exploring a farmer's market. She was the only person among our family and friends, other than Gerry and Grams, that I looked forward to seeing. I never complained when my mother insisted we make a stop at Camille's store to replenish the guest bathrooms with lavender soap flakes or rosewater bath oil.

When I was younger, I'd spent hours with Camille in Magdalene's Hearth. At first, I had my own small stepladder to climb up beside her when she served customers. I used to think there'd been a mix-up somewhere, and I'd ended up with the wrong sister as a mother. I'd always felt I could—and should—have been Camille's daughter. We even looked similar, with our topaz-coloured eyes that I considered my only beauty mark.

But Camille had become less important since Tony started paying me attention. And since I let myself be talked into doing something brainless.

It began when Tony teased me, saying he bet I didn't have the guts to break into a stupid store like Magdalene's Hearth. I heard the words, "Oh yeah?" come out of my mouth, and regretted them immediately, but it was too late to take them back. I was the one who'd told him the store wasn't open because it was undergoing renovations.

I hadn't told him I knew the owner. I suddenly had a horrible thought. *What if he'd known all along—from Janie maybe—and was testing to see how far I'd go?* His scorn for the New Age things that Camille sold was obvious in the sarcastic way he said, "bitch-chuly oil." I hadn't even defended Camille when he added, "Besides, wasn't Mary Magdalene a whore? What idiot names their store after a hooker?"

Even being as crazy about him as I was, I could see he wasn't always a nice guy. I didn't tell him Camille thought of Mary Magdalene as important in the Goddess Movement. I didn't get the Goddess stuff, but I could have, should have, said something to defend her. Instead, I just grinned.

Dealing with boys can be a real pain.

The house was quiet. I hate waiting so I called Jake. He's my bad-boy cousin, whose father, Earl, is as much of a pain as my mother. Earl and Renee, two perfectly matched siblings, both big fish in a big pond, and aware of it and ensuring others knew it too.

"Yo, cousin. What d'you do now?" Just hearing his voice made me feel better. Jake hadn't had an easy life. His mother had died two years ago and his father, Uncle Earl, well, calling him a World Dominating Asshole is not enough to explain his belligerent way of operating in the world, both personally and professionally. I couldn't imagine three more different siblings: Camille, my mother, and Uncle Earl. It's like Grams had somehow hatched three unique aliens, unrelated in interests, skills, or attitudes.

"Yo, yourself. I heard you've ditched one too many classes, and have to go to summer school," I said.

He sighed. "Could be, but I think Earl's organizing something with my aunt Teddy, mom's sister. I could be sent into the wilds, some desert hellhole where she works as a meteorite hunter." [**Spark Rebecca, Teen Rebel Series*]

I thought that actually sounded kind of cool, but from the way Jake had described her in the past, I knew Teddy was a recluse and odd. She'd rather live away from society than in it. She was just another weirdo in our peculiar family mix.

"There are snakes," he said gleefully, knowing how I felt about them.

We talked for a bit longer, sent each other a virtual high five, and promised to let the other know when we found out what was going to happen to us. I felt better when I hung up.

But the house was still too quiet. I snuck down the stairs and leaned against the closed library door trying to hear what they were saying. The wooden door was too thick. I silently opened it a crack, hoping to at least hear, and maybe see, what was going on.

The four adults in the library weren't talking, just looking at each other. My mother suddenly broke into tears. Dad and Camille rushed to her, patting her on the back, handing her tissues, and muttering appeasing words.

"This is it," she said, blowing her nose with the elegance she showed in everything she did. "I'm finished trying to encourage, support, and guide her. She needs to know what real life is like. Maybe, maybe she needs to be sent away—" She looked like she was going to start crying again.

Dad led her to the sofa. "Gerry, suggestions?" he asked.

Gerry turned to Camille. "What do you think? You're the one directly impacted."

"I've been to the store," Camille said, making a dismissive wave of her hand. "A window was jimmied but nothing broken or stolen that I could see. It's Maggie I'm worried about. This was not just another game." She sat beside my mother and took her hand.

"Do you want to press charges?" Gerry asked her.

"No!"

"There has to be a consequence!" My mother stood up and

began walking around the room. "She needs to learn a lesson. That she would pick on your store, that's beyond...."

"I've got an idea," I heard Camille say.

"I'm glad someone does," Dad replied. His calm voice was at odds with his restless hands, which were picking up and putting down any piece of knickknack within range. He paced toward the door, leaving me no option but to dash up to my room and miss out on the rest of the conversation.

At 10 o'clock Dad called up from the bottom step, "Maggie May, please come into the library." Just as my mother's favourite singer was Paul McCartney, Rod Stewart ruled my father's iPod collection and his nickname for me came from his favourite Rod Stewart song. Usually by this time of night they were sitting in the TV room, Mom drinking Jasmine Green tea and Dad a cup of decaf coffee watching the news. I pulled on my oversized Vancouver Canucks hockey jersey and slowly, dramatically, my head held high, sauntered down the stairs.

Here I come, ready or not.

3

THE RELUCTANT PILGRIM

My mother was on the phone and didn't turn around when I entered the room.

At first, I thought it was a punishment, but when I saw her cup her hand to the phone mouthpiece, I realized she didn't want to be overheard. Gerry sat in one of the reading chairs I loved to curl up in on rainy days. Dad was straightening books that were already straight on the shelves.

I was most aware of Camille. I wanted to turn and run back upstairs. Instead, I crossed my arms, sticking my hands inside the opposite jersey sleeve so no one could see they were trembling. My toes almost went into muscle spasms I was holding myself so tightly.

I knew I needed to—wanted to—apologize. My hands came out of my sleeves and hung limply at my side. Staring down intently at the rug, I pretended to be fascinated by the delicate red-flowered pattern.

Camille resolved the awkward situation by coming over and taking hold of my dangling hands, said, "Maggie."

I slowly raised my head and found myself staring into eyes

filled with disappointment and anger. It was impossible to look away. "Camille, I did a stupid thing, I'm sorry, there's this cute guy and he dared me—"

"I'm sure you thought there was a good reason, but sorry will not cut it this time. We all want to help you learn how to make better choices in your life, and I think we've done that." She dropped my cold hands and sat back down on the sofa.

For the first time in my life, she wasn't smiling at me.

I'd really screwed up this time.

I tried again, aware I was babbling. "See this guy we weren't going to do anything just he said he had never tried something like that before and thought it would be a blast we weren't going to do anything or take anything it was like a prank…"

No one said anything, though they were all watching me.

Dad had moved on to fidgeting with that expensive china bowl on the fireplace mantle, the one they'd brought back from their last trip to Hong Kong. I knew my mother would kill him if it broke. Didn't he realize he was in dangerous territory? I looked over at her again, wondering who was on the phone.

My mother turned and I could hear the end of her conversation. "You can talk to her yourself tomorrow. Now is not a good time. Good night." She put down the phone, crossed her arms, and, with anger and sarcasm battling for prominence, stared at me. "Who was this 'guy'?"

I clamped my lips together. Two could play the pursed lips game.

Silence ruled the library.

Gerry moved to a small computer desk in the corner and removed a stack of papers from the printer tray, saying to no one in particular, "They're ready for signing."

"Maggie May," Dad began for the third time that night. He was trying to soften what was coming. I felt myself grow even tenser if that was possible. "Maggie, after talking to Camille, who has agreed not to press charges by the way, your mother and I and Camille have come up with two choices for you."

I suddenly suspected who my mother had been talking to on the phone. "You called Grams?" I asked accusingly. There were three people I loved in this world. Two of them were in this room: Dad and Camille. The third was Margaret Anne Hamilton, my tiny, elegant grandmother who always smelled of Nivea cream, something she had continued to use even after she married my wealthy grandfather and could have afforded the most expensive skin care line in the world.

Grams was the other person I would run to when I needed a break from my mother. From the time I was six years old, I would often find Grams' chauffeur waiting outside my elementary, then high school gate. I would know Grams had received a call of despair over the latest thing I'd done or said. She was always willing to step in and give me and my mother space for a day or two. Janie had told me I was lucky I hadn't been sent away to a boarding school. She was probably right.

"We've been able to get this taken care of with the police," my mother said, ignoring my question. "Camille is being incredibly supportive and has one proposal for you. Your father and I have another. You need to choose one of them before you leave this room tonight because whichever choice you make, it begins immediately."

I laughed.

"Not a smart thing to do, Maggie," Camille said.

"I'm sorry, I shouldn't have laughed, but are you sending me to Nepal? Or wherever your latest do-good project is, Mother?"

"Be quiet!" She was suddenly in front of me, her frustration radiating so hotly that I unconsciously took a step back. "Considering the choices you are making," she paused to count to at least five, "we are offering you an experience that will hopefully help you grow up! This is the last time your father and Gerry will ever fix whatever ridiculous thing you do, and why you would pick Camille's store—" Camille started to interrupt but my mother held up her hand in that abrupt way that could make even Camille go quiet. "Your aunt…."

Camille reached up and gently touched her sister's arm, trying to calm her. "Breathe, Renee."

To everyone's surprise, my mother took a deep breath before she continued. "You know your father and I own a clothing factory in southern India, in Kerala. It provides lunch for the women who work there and has an on-site daycare. You will leave in one month's time. I'd send you tomorrow, but you need to get vaccinations for things like hepatitis A and B, typhoid, diphtheria, and to get a prescription for malaria pills. You will work in the daycare and help with meal preparation for five weeks. I haven't had time to find out if you also need to get shots for other things, like yellow fever or Japanese encephalitis. At least your polio and tetanus shots are up to date—"

Even though I was right there in that room, part of me was already running out the door, up the stairs, and diving under my bed covers. "Hold it! Japanese encepha...what? Are you nuts? Dad, is she crazy? The summer holidays are just starting. There are all kinds of things planned. Janie invited me to go with her to Hawaii—"

My mother ignored my interruption. "When you are in India you will stay with our company director's family. After five weeks, you can come home."

I was in shock. Not that I minded going to India, but I wanted to go as a cool backpacker, not an indentured servant. "Share my room with cockroaches? And I don't like curry!" I paused, suddenly apprehensive. "What's the second idea?"

Now it was Camille's turn. "You know the hiking holiday I went on last year?"

I nodded. Sure, but I hadn't really listened when she and my mother had talked about it, just enough to get the basics. "It was a really old trail, in Spain or Italy."

"It was the 1,000-year-old Santiago de Compostela pilgrimage trail. I started in France, hiked over a mountain and into Spain."

I nodded again. I looked over at the photograph of my aunt on my mother's desk. It showed her climbing up a rocky path, her backpack looking ridiculously small for the two-month hiking trip she had planned. There was a vague memory of some other pictures Camille had shown me, one of her sitting on a bunk bed in a room with 24 bunk beds in the background, and another where she was raising a glass of wine and resting her bare feet on a stone wall.

I remembered how unhappy she'd looked in both pictures. It turned out no one, aside from my mother, had known things were not going well between Camille and her boyfriend, Ryan. Dad and I learned later Camille was hiking to give herself time to decide whether to stay with him or leave the relationship.

"Then Ryan told you to come home after ten days, and you did!"

"Margaret Emily MacKenzie!" I couldn't think of the last time I'd heard my father use my full name.

"Sorry, I'm sorry, Camille," I said. "I'm confused here." But my spiteful words hung in the air.

Now it was my mother's turn to put her hand on Camille's arm. Camille's face had gone white, but she stayed focused on me. "He did, and yes, I did. We tried for another month to make it work. I don't regret stopping my hike, but I've always wanted to go back, and now I've got the chance. On one level, all of this is serendipitous. Your mother has offered to take over running the renovation crew for my store. She's been a real help so far and has gone shopping with me to pick out new shelving units and material designs." Her face colour was returning to its usual healthy glow.

"You also said it was the hardest thing you'd ever done,

climbing up mountains and sliding down wet stony paths and sharing rooms with people who snore. Is this fun hike supposed to be my other choice?"

Inside, I felt a glimmer of hope. *A month or more in Europe? Without my parents? Things were looking up.*

Then I got realistic. "What's the catch?" I asked suspiciously.

Camille once again took hold of my hands. "You know my friend Andy?"

"Of course, I know Andy!" He was often over at Camille's apartment when I dropped by, and there was a lot of "Andy said," and "Andy read about..." in Camille's conversations. "The one who wears bow ties?" I asked innocently.

"No, that's Barry, my accountant," Camille said, smiling for the first time. "I've told you this already, but Andy is a counsellor who works with youth at risk—"

I jerked her hands away. "You want me to go to therapy? We already tried that. It wasn't a success."

My mother and I looked at each other, both of us remembering the disastrous sessions we'd gone through together with Dr Tully. We might be the only mother-daughter therapy patients asked to leave by the therapist. He referred us to someone else, but our battles in front of a stranger had been exhausting for both of us. I assumed Dr Tully's referral slip was still stuck in the back of my mother's bottom desk drawer.

"No! You'll walk the Camino, the Santiago de Compostela trail, with Andy and three teens from one of his groups. He'd asked me to go before, but I'd said no, because of the renovations. He wanted a woman to go along with him, because, well, he's got this special grant to—"

"You want me to hike for a month with a shrink who has serial killers along for the trip?" I folded my arms across my chest.

Dad snorted. My mother gave him one of her looks, and he wiped an invisible dust speck from the mantle.

"They have given Andy a special grant to test a new method of rehabilitating...of working with youth who are having problems," Camille said. "Rather than send them to a youth detention centre, he will take them on the Camino hike from the border of France to the West Coast of Spain. He's leaving in a week. I talked to him tonight, and he's willing to add you, us, to his group. There are three girls, 16- and 17-years-old. Yes, they've done some things they probably wish they hadn't, but I can guarantee you, not one of them is a serial killer. You've got to admit you've got issues of your own you need to deal with."

That stung. I hadn't expected to hear something so direct from Camille. She was supposed to be on my side. The four adults were watching me, waiting.

"In fact, you might be the token break and enter expert." Camille's attempt at a joke fell plunk on the carpet, which was where I was staring.

"So, my choices are," and I ticked them off one by one on my fingers, speaking to the carpet and ignoring the humans in the room, "illness, poverty, and slave labour work in India or marching for a month in Europe with a group of criminals."

"Five weeks actually, and you need to tell us," my mother looked at her diamond-studded watch, "in the next five minutes. We're done dealing with this. It's late."

It hurt to hear my mother refer to me as "this"—not a person but a demonstrative adjective. I turned around and headed toward the door. "I'll take the Camino thing."

Five weeks in Spain? With five other people? I could suck that up and come home with a few weeks of summer left. If only Tony would return my calls. That might help my sore heart feel better.

I was one step from the hallway when Gerry called me back: "Wait!"

I stopped. *Damn, I'd almost gotten away.*

"You need to sign these." He pointed to the papers on the

coffee table. He never shouted and always spoke in a deep, clear way that I thought of as his radio voice. I'd asked him about it once. He'd been shocked, running his manicured hands through his perfectly cut white hair. "Talk on the radio? God no!" It was as though I'd suggested he had a job stapling boxes, which was something Camille had done to make money during the summer after she had graduated from high school.

Walking over to the desk, I looked down at the papers. There were five pages with yellow sticky arrows pointing to signature lines. Gerry handed me his lucky pen again.

My mother joined Dad at the fireplace, and they began whispering intensely to each other. Those five pages, filled with lawyerly text, lay on the coffee table almost like a line in the sand between me and the others.

"You've made your choice. Sign the damn things!" My mother quickly crossed the room and stabbed the top page, her pink nail leaving a dent in the paper. "This will give you access to an emergency account with $1,500 in it."

I started sputtering. *That was only $300 a week, less than the cost of a haircut and highlights at my favourite salon.*

My mother angrily tapped the second and third pages, using her long nail to point to specific paragraphs. "This gives Gerry permission to cash in a portion of your company stock. You will use that money to buy your return plane ticket and any clothes and gear that Camille decides you need."

A flame inside me went from flickering to blazing. Not that I knew what to do with that family stock, but still. It had been a gift from Grams a few months ago, on my 16th birthday. She'd said all women should have their own little nest egg and the stocks would give me financial security, aside from whatever my parents or eventual husband or my work would give me. Grams was old-fashioned in some ways, and pretty cool in others.

"You have no right to decide what I will do with my stock! Grams gave the stock to me, to use when and how I wanted to!"

"Cashing in some of your stocks will make it more of your experience. This trip is for your good."

"*My* experience? *My* trip?" I could match my mother's scorn any day. Dad sighed. He'd been in the middle of these battles for a long time.

"You have made it very clear by your marks and spotty attendance that you couldn't care less about school. We've all agreed you need to get an understanding of life beyond what you know here in Vancouver. The rest of the paperwork is for things like extended medical travel insurance."

"We will pay for that." It was only the second time my father had spoken. Mom and Gerry looked at him. Gerry looked at my mother.

"We'll pay for the additional medical travel insurance," she agreed.

"And for all of Camille's expenses," Dad added.

Camille started to say something, but Dad shook his head. "No arguments, Camille. You're making it possible for Maggie to step into a new world. It's a gift from us."

My mother kissed his cheek and this time when she held his hand, it didn't turn white.

"At least Maggie's passport is up to date," Gerry said, speaking as though I wasn't there. "I renewed it last year when she went to Ireland on Spring Break."

"Your grandmother thinks this is a good idea, by the way," Dad said. "She was the one who suggested you pay for this trip yourself and use your stock money to do it. It was your mother who insisted you have access to additional emergency funds."

"What did Grams say?"

Gerry shoved the pen into my hand, and I automatically began to sign where he pointed, my mind imagining what Grams must be thinking. Grams loved her youngest daughter. It finally sunk in that I had picked the worse way to prove I was worthy of riding on Tony's bike. My hand was shaking by the time I signed the last page. I'd screwed up big time.

But these choices? None of this was fair and if they thought I would turn into an obedient daughter, forget it!

I needed to call Grams tonight no matter how late it was because I wouldn't be able to sleep, anyway. I'd inherited more than my grandmother's name. For all her kindness to people, Grams could keep a grudge if she thought someone had consciously hurt someone else. I wanted to make sure I wasn't on the grudge list. Or if I was, that I didn't stay on it long.

Dealing with adults could be a real pain.

"I've got to get home too," Camille said, standing up. She gave me a goodbye hug. I kept my arms by my side, but Camille didn't seem bothered by my rigid stance. "We can get together and talk about what you'll need to buy for clothes and gear. This has been a long day, for all of us. Remember," she said as she kissed me on the cheek and gently put her finger under my chin, like she used to do when I was a child. It forced me to make eye contact with her. "I love you. There will be fun on this trip. And some time to think about what you want to do with your life."

I heard my mother whisper, "Thank you," just before Camille left the room.

"Time for me to call it a day too," Gerry said. He put the signed papers into his briefcase and followed Camille out of the room. He did not offer me a hug or a handshake. The sound of the front door closing behind him was barely audible in the carpeted library. I tried a dignified exit, not bothering to say anything to my parents.

As soon as I got back to my room, I grabbed my cell phone, plopped on my bed, and stared up at the yellow plastic stars I'd glued on the ceiling when I was eight. Usually, looking at them helped calm me down. I needed to work out what to say to Grams. If I could quiet my brain, I could come up with something to begin the conversation. I closed my eyes and tried to think.

Suddenly it was morning, the sun was glowing through the slit in my window curtains, and someone was tapping lightly on my door.

"Come in," I called out, still groggy with sleep. Grams peeked in, her expensive bobbed haircut looking soft and flattering around her face. I jumped off the bed, ran into her arms, and burst into tears.

"I know, Maggie, I know." Grams sat on the bed and "tutted" and patted and soon I was cried out and feeling better. "Your parents have gone out. Let's go for breakfast."

"Mick's Place?"

"Mick's Place. When I have a day like yours was yesterday, there is nothing more healing than greasy food and bottomless cups of tea."

I nodded, looking at my grandmother a moment longer than necessary. *I'd never thought Grams might have bad days.*

Thirty minutes later we were sitting in a window booth in Mick's Place where the free-range turkey bacon was crisp, the yolk of the organic eggs a sun-bright yellow, and the tea came in a real teapot that was constantly being refilled with hot water. Ok, so my grandmother's version of greasy wasn't quite the same as most peoples, but I didn't mind. We'd been coming here since my kindergarten days. That's when Grams had decided I was old enough to start drinking tea. I was pretty sure "Mick" was not a real person because the owner had changed twice over the past 10 years, but the restaurant name remained the same.

As I mopped up the last of my egg with a piece of sourdough toast, Grams poured more steaming Darjeeling tea into her china cup. Only then did she ask questions.

My version of the story didn't take long. I told her about Tony and how cute and smart he was. Grams ignored that, though her opinion of him was evident by the way her body straightened in the chair. She listened, nodded, and said things like, "Hmmm!" and "Really?" and "I see." I explained how all the girls liked Tony and his father owned a giant software company that did something with medical research, and he and his sister were going to spend the summer—alone!—in their family house on Maui before Tony returned to McGill University in the fall and I'd been invited to join them for two weeks in Hawaii but he'd said he wanted to first see if I was a "wild spirit."

No way was I going to tell my grandmother the whole story.

Of how Tony and I had been swimming in his family's colossal infinity pool after everyone else had gone inside. The air and water around the two of us had felt charged with electricity. When Tony swam behind me and said in that low, sexy voice of his, "I'm always attracted to girls with a wild spirit. Do you have a wild spirit, Maggie?" Well, I would have jumped off the roof into the pool if he'd asked. In this morning light, and seen through Grams' eyes, I understood how lame his challenge sounded.

Grams surprised me by chuckling. "Honey, if he doesn't see you are a wild spirit, he's blind."

The two of us sat in silence for a few minutes.

"Grams, I don't want you to be mad at me."

"I was, last night." Grams looked at me and shook her head. "No, I wasn't mad. I was sad, at the waste of you, your intelligence and humour and kindness."

That surprised me. I was the least kind person I knew.

My grandmother daintily took a bite of her whole wheat toast then said, "I see how much your parents care—now, do NOT snort like your father, it's not ladylike—but it is just that you and your mother seem to speak a different language. I have always hoped things would change but...."

There seemed nothing further to say, so we spent the next hour daydreaming about Europe. We'd been there before but always to major cities like Rome, Venice, and Paris. My memory of Camille's stories about the Camino was that the trail meandered through a lot of little towns, some of them so small you couldn't find them on a map.

Suddenly, a person wearing a hoodie dashed by the café window on a longboard. A gloved hand reached out and grabbed an elderly woman's purse as she stepped onto the sidewalk. The longboarder did an expert twist and now faced me. She was grinning, her blond hair falling loose around her face. She turned her board and disappeared down the nearby alley. The robbed woman was screaming. A construction worker had set off in pursuit, but he soon returned, panting and empty-handed. One waiter had quickly phoned the police. It was clear by the excited chatter from the bystanders and the robbed woman no one expected the purse to be found.

We left the restaurant, pausing to watch a policeman get out of his patrol vehicle. Grams patted my back as we walked to her car. "You'll do fine. You have MacKenzie and Hamilton blood in you."

I hoped Grams was right. Looking at Europe through my grandmother's eyes had left me feeling excited about the trip for the first time. We walked past the policeman and heard him attempt to offer the robbed woman some hope. "You never know, we may catch the kid. They usually do this kind of thing over and over. The odds are against them."

Witnessing a purse snatching reminded me of my Camino travelling companions. Suddenly the turkey bacon wasn't sitting so well. My stomach gurgled as we drove away.

Even with Grams beside me, life can suck big time some days.

4

SWEATY SOCKS

She didn't drive me home but dropped me off, protesting, in front of Magdalene's Hearth.

Grams had insisted I visit Camille and continue to make amends. Watching Grams' car drive away left me wishing I was five years old again when adults took care of any trouble I had. Turning to face the storefront, I saw the "Closed for Renovations" sign I'd designed for Camille. It only made my stupid choice to break in even stupider.

What had I been thinking?

That was easy to answer: *Tony.*

Camille was staring at a photograph in her hand when I opened the front door. I noted my attempted B&E job hadn't caused a ripple of pause in the renovation work. I couldn't avoid looking at Camille any longer, and for a moment we stared at each other. She didn't reach out to offer me a hug, something she always did.

This would be a messy visit.

I looked down and saw what Camille had been staring at when I came in. It was a photograph taken on her Camino hiking trip in

France. Her back was to the camera, and a pair of sweaty or wet socks dangled from a strap on the backpack.

"The socks dried in minutes in the hot breeze that day. It was sweltering." Although she didn't sound aunt-friendly, at least she would talk to me.

I looked at the photograph more closely. Camille had both of her walking sticks in one hand and was resting her right palm against the stone wall of a small chapel. The dirt path in front of her stretched into the distance under a canopy of leafy tree branches.

"Let me guess. That little church was dedicated to Mary Magdalene?"

Camille nodded. "The shade from those plane trees, it was so welcome. I was thinking about walking along a trail like that, with you and the others."

"Was Andy in this little daydream?" Shrugging, Camille shoved the photograph into her skirt pocket. "Because, you know, you've always told me daydreaming is good for the soul."

"Not today. This time it makes me want to eat dark chocolate that's filled with orange cream or coating a white brick of marshmallow. Drown my sorrows." She paused and made a decision, giving me a partial smile. "Shall we head to Purdy's Chocolates?" She was trying to be friendly, but I saw again it would take time for her to forgive me completely.

"It's a five-week trip, with shared accommodation," I persisted, refusing to drop the matter of Andy. I was stepping into dangerous territory.

"Andy and I are friends. This hike is the kind of thing friends can do together."

"But—"

"Camille?"

Camille spun around. Sean, her contractor, held a selection of grey-coloured countertop strips in his outstretched hand. This freckled, broad-shouldered man had always been friendly to me. The laughing crew working around us attested to his ability to make things happen quickly, efficiently, and stress-free on his job sites.

"I see we're having a visit from the burglar." Sean was watching me. "Jason told me about it this morning."

That jerk of a guard had been telling the world.

"Do you have a question for me, Sean?" Camille asked.

So, my B&E was not open for discussion. I felt a wave of relief.

"Which do you prefer for the countertop? Pewter comes in Seattle Mist, London Fog, Raccoon Hollow—"

Camille laughed, and Sean smiled back at her. "Raccoon Hollow?" She looked again at the samples in his hands. "They all look the same to me. What do you think?"

Sean showed another strip. "You'll like this one for the name, 'Revere Pewter'."

"Revere? You're right! What about—"

Her voice was a soft sound in the background as I waited impatiently for their discussion to end so we could leave.

For the first time in my life, I don't enjoy being here.

The next four days were a blur of shopping and buying lightweight gear and quick-drying clothes. Our trips were fun, not that I wanted to appear overly enthusiastic. In one hiking gear store, the two of us spent an hour trying on different backpacks. Camille had cut up her previous pack, as part of the "cleansing" she had done after ending her relationship with Ryan. The clerk had adjusted each pack's ties, making some parts looser and other parts tighter after stuffing two, two-kilogram bags of sugar inside. He made us walk around the store for five minutes wearing the packs then he readjusted all the straps until he pronounced himself satisfied. Camille was adamant neither of our filled backpacks would weigh over six kilograms, about 13 pounds, when we were on the trail.

That was such a ridiculous idea I didn't bother taking her seriously. I'd already picked out a day bag from my closet to bring along.

Janie tried to be a BFF. She might not be very smart, but she was caring and generous and sincerely wanted to make me feel better. After repeated invitations to do something with her, I finally said yes. I knew she was feeling guilty since she was the sister of an asshole.

She picked me up in her new car—a gift from her stepfather for getting above a C- in English. She chatted as she zipped in and out of traffic, telling me that #1) apparently that silly brother of hers had scooted over to Hawaii earlier than planned, and #2) the Silly Willy had lost his phone, but he would get a new one as soon as that new version of that thing came on the market and, #3) she was sure he would call me first thing when he got organized.

Janie didn't realize inviting me to go clothes shopping for the Hawaii trip that I could no longer go on was not the best way to cheer me up. She was clueless about things like that. Shopping always made her happy; therefore, it must be the same for everyone else.

I drew the line at her offer to host a farewell party for me. I told her I was still under curfew—which I wasn't, I was 16, jeez—but I couldn't bear the idea of smiling, smiling, smiling all night in a roomful of people who were probably snickering behind my back.

I'd learned a lot about my friends. Tony was a popular guy. He must have considered me a threat to his future law career. His version of the evening had quickly resulted in a distinct lack of "come and hang out" invitations. I'd never told the police or my parents he'd been with me, but it seemed Tony had spread the word I wasn't to be trusted. I guess I was lucky Janie had kept me as her friend, even if her brother was a cowardly jerk traitor.

Having an open calendar meant I had lots of time to read up on the Camino, or Santiago de Compostela, trail. When I typed

"Camino" in Amazon.com I had a choice of 40,000 links to cups, hiking gear, maps, clothes, and almost 500 books. "A lot of wannabe writers have walked the Camino," I told Camille during a trip-planning phone call.

I could imagine Camille nodding at her end of the phone, and so I wasn't surprised when she appeared the next day with two Camino travel books she thought would be helpful. She said they'd give me an idea of what was ahead. I read Jane Christmas' *What the Psychic Told the Pilgrim* in two nights. It was good but made the hike sound really tough, like the worse day in phys-ed class times one hundred tough. Camille had also picked up John Brierley's slim book of daily Camino trail maps and said it was all we needed.

"Besides," she added, "his book doesn't weigh much." That had become her standard guide when considering what to bring: "How much does it weigh?" Camille would stand in a store with two versions of the same product in each hand—a flashlight, a camping towel, a sports bra—and decide which was lighter, immediately rejecting the heavier item.

Soon I felt like an expert on the Camino. I gave Grams a short version of the history of the Santiago de Compostela trail when she and I went for a walk along the Stanley Park seawall. "So, this guy, Apostle James the Greater, was murdered in 44 AD His friends stole his body and transported it in a stone boat to Spain and buried him in a secret spot. 'Santiago' means Saint James. His bones were later 'discovered,'"—I made air quotation marks with my fingers to show what I thought of that story—"by a farmer in 813 in what came to be called,"—more air quotation marks—"'of the star,' or 'Compostela' in Spanish. For over 1,000 years, people, pilgrims, have been walking there from all over Europe, to pray for stuff."

"While trying to avoid bandits, starvation, bad weather, wet feet, and the plague." Grams surprised me by already knowing lots about the Camino.

"Is it like a poor person's holiday?" Janie had asked innocently when I explained about the hostels we'd be sleeping in and how we had to carry our food and gear.

What if Janie was right? Travelling with juvenile delinquents AND poor people? Could it get any worse?

"I wish I had gone when I was younger," Gram said wistfully. She nodded when I told her there were lots of pilgrimage routes beginning in different parts of Europe, but they all ended up in the city of Santiago, in northwestern Spain.

"Camille and I and the freaks are hiking 800 kilometres on the Camino, and if I hear Camille say, 'It's just a lot of days of one foot in front of the other,' one more time I will smack her!"

Grams laughed. She pulled a map out of her purse, already folded to allow easy viewing of the marked Camino trail. She followed the route with her finger, beginning in St-Jean-Pied-de-Port in France at the base of the Pyrenees and going right across Spain to the ancient city of Santiago. "It's only 85 kilometres from the Atlantic Ocean," she said. "This map is going on my dining room wall so each morning I can look at it when I'm drinking my tea."

One website I checked out said the Camino route was "varied scenically." I wasn't sure what that meant but guessed it involved a lot of climbing up and down mountains. We would stay in *albergues*, or pilgrim's hostels, which I imagined as #1) filled with nuns on their knees scrubbing floors, or #2) convents, more scrubbing nuns, or 3) monasteries, monks kneeling in prayer for hours while nuns scrubbed *their* floors. Many of the dorm rooms were filled with bunk beds for anywhere from 20 to 50 people.

Janie and I had shuddered in unison at the thought of sharing a sleeping room with strangers. I added "EARPLUGS" to my "to buy" list.

Because we were joining Andy's group after they already had their travel plans organized, Camille and I would fly to Paris and join Andy and his mutants at the pilgrim's hostel in St-Jean-Pied-de-Port. We would all begin the hike together from there.

"You've got to stop calling them 'freaks' and 'mutants,'" Camille said as she dragged me through another store that sold hiking gear.

"Barbarians? Weirdos?" I suggested.

"You'll see them differently when you meet them in St. Jean. I'm sorry it's not going to work out for us all to get together before we leave Vancouver, but they are all...unavailable."

I bet "unavailable" meant "under house arrest." I picked up, and quickly discarded the ugliest pair of hiking shorts I'd ever seen. "What about Andy-o?"

My aunt handed me a quick-drying, long-sleeved shirt. "We're friends."

"So you keep saying. Why only friends?"

Camille sighed. "Beats me."

"But friends with benefits, right? You obviously like him, a lot!" Now it was my turn to sigh. "Men are complicated, aren't they?"

Why was she laughing? I didn't think it was funny.

5

CAMINO CONDENSING

Two days before we left for Europe, I got the call I'd been dreading.

"Maggie, I want you to bring all your gear to my place and we'll organize it together, to make sure you've got everything you need. You keep saying, 'Later.' Well, 'later' has arrived." Camille had on her business voice, not the warm aunt one I usually heard. She said she wasn't angry anymore, and repeatedly dismissed my attempts to apologize, but her coolness was feeling like another punishment, along with this stupid trip.

I came over that afternoon, but I wasn't feeling very enthusiastic. At least I could park my car right in front of Magdalene's Hearth. I had to walk around several workmen taking a smoke break on the front sidewalk. None of them offered to help carry my bulging suitcase and day bag up the stairs. They whistled at me, and when one said something to his buddies, they all laughed.

"You should know smoking will kill you!" I snarled.

They laughed again, but none of them moved. They watched me struggle, step by step, up the stairs along the side of the building to Camille's second-story apartment. The bulging smaller day bag I'd slung over my shoulder banged against my back. They must know what I'd done. If the guard had told Sean, he probably took great joy in bragging to the other men too.

When Camille opened her apartment door, her eyes took in the day bag then quickly dropped to the large American Flyer suitcase I'd propped against the doorframe. "Take them into the bedroom. We'll lay everything out there."

I dragged the suitcase into the back room, getting grumpier with each step, and aware Camille hadn't offered to help either. The bags landed on the floor with a bang.

"Lay everything out in related piles, clothes with clothes, toiletries, and…your other stuff." Camille paused as I emptied the shoulder bag, pulling out books and my father's large camera. "I'll get us a cold drink," she muttered as she left the room, "this might take a while."

She came back just as I dumped the last of the items from the large suitcase into haphazard piles on the hand-quilted bedspread. She held out a glass of mineral water flavoured with slices of orange and a sprig of mint. "I think you'll find this refreshing. Especially after the hard work you had getting here and climbing the stairs."

I accepted the drink gratefully, wondering if there might be sarcasm lurking in Camille's comment. Opening the door of her bedroom closet, she pulled out the brand new, bright red, 38-litre backpack I'd tried on at the sports store. "I've been keeping this for you. Look!" She flipped the pack around, displaying the strip of nylon netting on the back. "It's ventilated, remember? This layer of netting will let air flow between your back and the pack. You'll keep cooler on hot days."

"Yeah, right. And this?" I held up my shoulder bag.

Camille shook her head and held up the red pack. "Only this, and you'll thank me when we're hiking."

"You've got to be kidding," I said, taking the backpack gingerly from her hand, holding it as though it was covered in snake venom. "This is the size of my beach bag!"

"Even that size can feel heavy when you climb steep hills, or after walking for six or eight hours. I want you to have some fun on this trip."

I stared at my aunt. "Fun?" *Who was she kidding?*

Camille laughed for the first time in days, patted me on the arm, and pointed to her packed blue backpack, which still had a bit of space at the top. She turned her attention to the overflowing piles on her bed. "Show me the 20 non-negotiable items."

"Everything is non-negotiable!" I heard the beginning of panic in my voice as I looked down at the things I'd brought and put into piles as directed. The bed cover was barely visible. "All these things are non-negotiable!"

"Let's start together then," Camille said, taking another moment to survey the piles. She picked up my thick, fluffy, white Turkish bathrobe. "How about this? It's bulky and heavy and will be too hot."

I paused and then shrugged. "Ok."

"And this thong? This make-up case? Imagine you are on a desert island and you could only take 20 items. What would they be?"

"All of it! We're not going to be on a desert island! We're going to a European country that has castles, a king and a queen, and where the word 'siesta' comes from."

"I have complete confidence in you!" she said. The bathrobe was the beginning of a new floor pile. She added Dad's camera and the three pocketbooks without even asking. "What about these?" Camille held up my favourite pair of cowboy boots. "I promise you won't need these for hiking."

I reminded myself it would be better to appear co-operative. *If I let some stuff go without a fuss, then I could dig my heels in for the rest, ha, no pun intended. I just need to be subtle.* I shrugged again and took the boots out of Camille's hands, plopping them on top of the bathrobe.

"You're doing great. Keep going." Camille sat down in the nearby reading chair.

I stared at the pile on the bed. "Only for five weeks? Then all is back to normal?"

"That is up to you, Maggie."

Twenty minutes later, I'd made two piles on the floor that were each larger than the bed pile. I felt very proud. The rejects consisted of things like economy-sized toiletries, a hair dryer, t-shirts, three bras, and four super-cute summer dresses.

Contemplating my version of minimum gear, Camille shook her head. "Ok, it's my turn." She stared at the items then began tossing and occasionally replacing things. In the end, what she would allow me to bring looked ridiculously small.

We spent the next half hour organizing my backpack. She kept saying things like, "Putting shirts in one large Ziplock bag and socks and underwear in another will ensure they don't get wet when we hike on rainy days. It will also make them easier to find." She held up a little plastic rectangle. "Look!" Camille unfolded it, pulling out a waterproof nylon cover that would fit over the pack to keep it dry. "Now let's go answer the big question!"

We went into the bathroom. First Camille weighed me wearing the backpack and then weighed me again without the pack. This simple math exercise showed us my pack weighed 6.2 kg or about 13 ½ pounds. "Not bad!" She held up a hand to high five me.

I ignored it. *How old did she think I was, ten?*

I didn't feel like celebrating. The pack felt clumsy on my back and I wasn't sure I could get up if I fell. Camille had wanted me to wear it around the house. She'd even suggested we go on local trial walks wearing all our gear, but just as I'd drawn the line with Janie over the goodbye party, I'd been adamant this would not happen.

"I'm going to have to cart the thing for five damn weeks. No need to start early!"

As I stood in Camille's bathroom, my sore shoulders made me wonder if I'd made the right decision. The one good thing was that my hiking boots felt worn in and comfortable. In fact, I'd never worn such comfortable footwear, not that I'd admit that to anyone. Maybe if I'd worn my backpack for a few minutes now and then—*No! That wasn't going to happen. We were leaving in two days and it was too late now.*

Camille filled up one of the water bottles and clipped it to the side of the pack. It added another 34 ounces, a little over two pounds. Who would have thought water would weigh so much? "I have one more thing!" She said as she ran into the bedroom, quickly re-appearing with two light, adjustable, aluminium hiking poles. "My gifts to you."

Looking in the full-length bathroom mirror, I thought I looked like an ad for an outdoor store. That was not a compliment. I focused on stopping the nervous tremors that were making my hands shake. Everything was so new and clean I practically sparkled.

Thank god I was travelling with strangers.

If Janie or Tony, or anyone else I knew saw me they'd be whipping out their phones and posting pictures on Instagram.

"Oh, yippee. I can't wait for this trip to begin."

And to be over.

6

STICK YOUR BUEN CAMINO

Four hours before our plane left for Europe, my stomach was feeling wonky. I just wanted to get going.

Grams slipped a 50 Euro bill into my hand, and my father did the same thing moments later. I figured I'd take whatever I could get. The money from the stocks Gerry had sold for me had shrunk by the time I'd paid for my ticket, clothes, gear, boots, and backpack. My mother had set up the emergency bank account I could access while travelling. She allowed me to add $1,000 to it and put the rest of the stock money into a savings account. My memory of previous European trips was that everything cost much more than it did in North America. I still remembered my mother going on about the $8 cup of coffee she'd had the last time she was in Paris.

Even on this day when my supposed adventure was beginning, my mother and I were our usual confrontational selves. We had bickered after my announcement I wouldn't be contacting them during the trip.

"Alan, there are days when I don't know how you stand it," I heard Camille say to Dad as she watched mom and me from the hallway.

Dad shrugged, grabbed Camille's backpack, and headed out to the car. "I go for long drives," he said over his shoulder.

But in a flip, it all changed. My mother suddenly had tears in her eyes. "Be safe, darling," she whispered into my ear as she hugged me tightly. "I love you."

It had been years since I'd heard my mother say that. Now I was getting scared. She'd made it seem as if one of us would die before we saw each other again. I pulled myself out of her arms and leaned close to her ear. "I'm with Camille and Andy and three crazy delinquents travelling in isolated parts of a country where I don't speak the language. I've got hardly any money. What could be unsafe?"

Evan as I whispered the words, I heard how mean-spirited they were, but my only other option was to start crying, and I didn't want that. I might never stop.

She stepped back, looking as though I had slapped her, and turned away.

I knew that look on my mother's face would haunt me for the next month-and-a-half.

"You look grand! I'm so proud of you!" Grams said, coming into the front hall. She looked me up and down and wistfully added, "If I were younger, I'd go with you!" She suddenly snapped her fingers. "I know what's missing!" She removed the long, Denis Colomb cashmere-cotton scarf from her neck and wrapped it around mine saying, "It looks very French, and the colour suits you, sweetie." She gave me a second hug, but she was so tiny her arms couldn't reach around me with my backpack on.

I had to get out of there. "Love you." I kissed Grams before quickly striding out to the car and tossing my backpack into the trunk beside Camille's.

After getting into the back seat, I intently looked out the side window all the way to the Vancouver International Airport, ignoring Dad's attempts at conversation. The closer we got to the airport, the quieter he got. He kept looking in the rear-view mirror at me sitting silently in the back seat.

As he started to move into the lane leading to the short-term airport parking lot, I spoke for the first time. "Dad, could you drop us off? I can't say 'Goodbye' again."

He sighed. "Sure," and moved back into the departure lane.

Camille touched him gently on the shoulder. "I'll send regular emails."

He nodded, not taking his eyes off the busy road.

My goodbye consisted of a kiss on my father's cheek when I stuck my head through the open driver's window. I quickly entered the airport not bothering to wait for Camille.

No tears! No tears! No tears! This became my mantra for the next few hours, said over and over in my head. I tossed in a few, *"God, I'm such a horrible daughter,"* for good measure when I thought of my mother's face.

Things got worse from there.

The flight to Paris was late departing. I'd seen all the onboard movies. The food was overcooked. And the guy sitting beside me drooled when he slept. I was fed up with the world when we finally landed ten hours later at the Charles de Gaulle Airport on the outskirts of Paris.

The next few hours blurred together. I don't think it's necessary for everyone to speak another language and was willing to abdicate any responsibility for travel arrangements to Camille. We may have come from a country with two official languages—English and French—but knowing French wasn't a big deal on the West Coast. Camille didn't speak French either, though she was game to try. Luckily, as soon as *"Pardon moi?"* came out of her mouth, the train ticket seller, the waitress in the cafe, and the newspaper store clerk all switched to English, asking "Yes, may I help you?"

It turned out getting to St. Jean to meet up with the others would take as long as our flight from Vancouver to Paris. It would involve a five-hour TGV—fast train—ride from Paris to Bordeaux, followed by a wait in Bordeaux before we could meet up with a small regional train to St-Jean-Pied-de-Port. We'd be arriving at 21:47, ten hours later.

"Europe uses the 24-hour clock," Camille said, oozing enthusiasm.

I loathed her.

"More travel? I'm already pissed off and exhausted!"

Camille patted me on the back. I hated her even more. It was not a great way to start a five-week trip. Not long after leaving Paris, our train screeched to a halt, and we had to wait while the police removed a suspicious package from the railway tracks. Soldiers carrying machine guns were visible outside our window. Gun-toting soldiers? Possible bomb threats? This wasn't the Paris I remembered from previous trips.

It was during our wait in Bordeaux that we saw other people with backpacks on for the first time: men and women 20- to 25-year-olds or 50- to 60-year-olds with French, German, Spanish, English, and Japanese spoken around us.

"Are they all going to St. Jean?" I asked.

Camille nodded. She was munching on her third *pain au chocolat* since we'd arrived in France and her mouth was full of flaky pastry. She looked happy. Behind her, I could see a thin woman who looked like my mother wearing a floppy, faded blue hat. I looked accusingly at Camille. The woman's headgear was like the beach hat Camille had made me leave behind. The big difference was this blue one had a tie dangling from it, to keep it on in the wind.

Behind the woman hiker was an ultra-cute, tall, dark-haired

guy leaning against a light pole. His eyes were closed, and he looked ill. He had a long, brightly-coloured, tie-dyed scarf wrapped around his neck.

I resented him taking up the pole space. I resented the crumbs sprinkled down Camille's jacket. I resented the sandpaper behind my eyes. Jet lag had always been an issue for me, and all I wanted was to lean against something and rest too.

Camille licked her lips, enjoying the pastry to the last buttery-tasting flake. "I love this place! Don't worry. We'll meet up with Andy tomorrow. Why don't you check out the other hikers? That will help pass the time."

I glared at the exhausted-looking guy leaning against the pole and couldn't care less when we met up with Andy again.

"I meant people-watch with a smile," Camille added.

Breathing loudly through clenched teeth, I took my eyes off the exhausted or ill guy and made myself check out the other backpackers. Some of them were my mirror image and dressed in shiny new clothes. Other hikers had stained and well-used backpacks. Many people wore bandanas or had a scarf casually draped around their neck. I had taken off Grams' scarf even before we arrived at the Vancouver airport. It had seemed too good to wear on a trip like this, but I couldn't refuse it. Instead, I'd shoved it into the one tiny corner of space I found in my pack.

I looked down at my feet and rubbed the toes of my hiking boots along the train station platform. They still looked new. My mother and Camille had insisted I wear them in so I wouldn't get blisters once I started hiking. I'd worn them to dinner every night, stomping into the dining room and gleefully watching my mother's lips tighten, though she said nothing.

Many people had a white scallop shell, the symbol of the Camino, dangling from their backpacks, belts, or hats. I poked Camille in the ribs, nodding toward a couple who looked about my parent's age. They had silly walking sticks in their hands. "The only people I've ever seen use walking sticks were old people or actors in 1970 European movies where they had to climb mountains."

"You'll be climbing mountains, the Pyrenees, tomorrow," Camille reminded me.

I felt like I was stuttering and stumbling with exhaustion. Her reminder about what lay ahead made me feel even more irritated. I was happy to see Camille was finally looking bedraggled, her hair hanging limp and her eyes red-rimmed.

"Only about an hour and a half to go until we reach St-Jean-Pied-de-Port," Camille promised. "Do you want a coffee?"

"I never drink coffee, you know that, and NOT in that!" I pointed to the small cup in her hand. "Plastic cups? Don't the French know about plastic pollution?"

"Well, I needed a pick me up," Camille replied and sipped on her *cafe noisette,* an espresso coffee with a dash of cream in it. She offered me a taste.

"What the heck, when in Rome..." I said. The coffee tasted good —strong, hot, and refreshing. I wished Tony was here to see how European I looked.

Or maybe not.

It was too dark to see the Pyrenees Mountains when our train finally pulled into St. Jean, but neither of us cared by then. One night before we left Vancouver, I'd looked the mountains up on Google Images. Sitting at my desk, in my bedroom, in my city house, it was obvious the Pyrenees were high, scary, and going to be hard work to climb.

Camille got re-energized when we stepped onto the St. Jean platform. "The town is nearby. First stop in the morning, the *Bureau de L'Accueil Pelegrins,* where we can get our pilgrim's passport," she told me, checking out an address in her small notebook. "Because we can't get into a hostel until we've got our *credential—*"

"I know, our pilgrim's passport."

I just wanted to lie down. It turned out Camille had booked us a room in a hotel for the first night, knowing we'd be arriving too late to go to the pilgrim's office. I'd never seen a bed and bathroom look as inviting as they did in that old hotel near the train station. I didn't care the room was the size of my closet back home. I threw my backpack on the floor, took off my boots—they were easier to wear on the plane than to fit in my backpack—and crawled into bed.

It seemed like I had only minutes of glorious sleep before Camille was shaking me awake. "If you want a shower, you'd better make it a short one."

I appeared thirty-five minutes later, showered, packed, and with my hair brushed and Camille admitted my preparation speed impressed her.

As we walked across a stone bridge over the River Nive into the old walled town, I kept shifting my backpack. It might only weigh 6.2 kg, but between jet lag and no experience carrying it, my shoulders were already aching. After hours in a plane combined with two train trips yesterday and an uncomfortable, saggy bed last night, my back was sore too.

"Now to find *rue de la Citadelle*," Camille said, which turned out to be easy because of the many signs directing us to the *Bureau de L'Accueil Pelegrins*.

"Or we could just follow them," I said, pointing to the scattered line of backpackers all heading in the same direction.

The old town was a series of narrow, cobbled streets that meandered through tall, pink, sandstone homes. Looking around, I could feel excitement bubbling—*ok, way, way down but bubbling never-the-less*—in this exotic new place. People smiled at us in the street. An old woman, wearing a patterned apron and thick black stockings, paused in sweeping her front step and said, "*Buen Camino!*"

"Buen Camino," Camille replied. She turned to me, whispering, "This is so great! We're in Europe!"

Her enthusiasm was infectious, and I didn't pull away when she slipped her arm in mine as we climbed the steep street. We both faltered when we saw the long line-up leading to the Pilgrim's Office. Backpacks were stacked against the outside wall, left by those already inside. Camille looked at me, shrugged, and got in line behind a cyclist.

Considering the number of people in front of us, it didn't take long to move forward. "Take off your pack, Maggie," Camille said after sticking her head inside the office doorway "There's hardly any room inside. We won't be able to move wearing these."

"What if someone steals them?"

Camille was already leaning her bag against the wall and stretching her back. "I'm willing to take the chance."

I shoved my backpack against Camille's and followed her through the wooden doors. Inside, a row of volunteers each sat behind a desk that had a line-up of people waiting their turn. Finally, a smiling woman with dyed black hair motioned for us to sit in the two empty chairs in front of her.

"Do you speak English?" Camille asked. She had confessed to me on the way up the last steep stretch of the cobbled street she wasn't feeling confident about her French.

"Of course," the volunteer said. "You are from?" She took our passports, filled out a form, and then gave Camille our passports and two credential booklets after first stamping them with the St-Jean-Pied-de-Port Camino logo.

"Look," Camille exclaimed loudly, "it's our first Camino stamp!"

I slunk down in embarrassment.

Next, the volunteer handed Camille a sheet listing the albergues or hostels along the route in Spain, and an English language page with advice about how to get over the Pyrenees as safely as possible. Camille had to lean in to hear the woman over the noise of the room. I felt the beginnings of a headache from the excited, loud people talking in a variety of languages all around us.

"Good luck tomorrow as you begin the Camino," the woman said.

"We are meeting friends at—." Camille said the name of the hostel so quickly my tired brain couldn't absorb it. "Is that far?"

The woman shook her head and told us to turn left outside the door. We'd see the hostel on the left side of the street. As she handed us two shells to attach to our backpacks—the Camino symbol to show the world we were pilgrims—an impatient Australian couple not-so-gently nudged our chairs, wanting to get registered. We left the office, picked up our packs, and went in search of the hostel where we were to meet Andy and the others. We passed several hikers with huge grins on their faces. Holding the credential booklet in my hand, I shook my head in disgust.

It was like the whole town was filled with "Don't worry, be happy" people.

"If everyone is smiling like this, how bad can the trail be?" Camille said.

I pointed to the mountains visible in the distance. "That bad," I said.

Everyone could take their "Buen Camino" and shove it in their espresso coffee.

7

ST-JEAN-PIED-DE-PORT SECRETS

Our welcome from Andy's group of lawbreakers wasn't quite what I'd expected.

Andy must have been waiting for us because he opened the door with a big smile before we'd even knocked. He looked at Camille first, his shirt untucked and his hair more bedhead than designer cut. He was wearing ridiculous shorts. They left his skinny legs showing blazing white between the edge of the shorts and the top of his ankle hiking socks. Camille didn't seem to notice his complete lack of any fashion sense and instead started to glow.

After what I thought was a hug that lasted much too long, Andy pulled away and turned to me with a cheerful, "Hi there, Maggie!"

Great. Just great. I stared back and forth between the two of them. I was about to embark on a dangerous trip with two love-birds and three convicts. I didn't bother to reply, just stomped my way around him and into the hostel.

"Our group is at the end of the table, near the door leading into the dorm," he said.

If I thought I was tired, the 20 people slumped at the long, red plastic cloth-covered tables looked even more exhausted. They were all bleary-eyed as they sipped—or stared down at—bowls of coffee or hot chocolate. Baskets filled with pieces of fresh baguette and jars of homemade jam were on the table in front of them.

Camille looked at the baguette basket and immediately asked the volunteer running the hostel if we could share in the breakfast. Camille slung her backpack off and leaned it against the wall. I slowly did the same thing.

"Je vais payer, bien sûr," Camille said to the apron-clad woman. Once the financial business of the breakfast was completed, Camille called out a friendly, "Hi," to everyone in the room and slipped into an empty space at the end of the bench. I tried to saunter after her, purposely not making eye contact. I promptly tripped over a corner of a rug and did an embarrassing twist and plop onto the bench.

I wished I was anywhere but here. A timid-looking Chinese girl offered me a shy smile. A tattooed teen who I guessed was another member of our group, was sitting on the other side of the long table. She looked way older than 17. She leaned her chair back against the wall, moving a toothpick with her tongue while she watched us. Her presence was unnerving. I saw people pretending she wasn't there and did the same.

I turned my body so I could avoid making eye contact with the scary teen. The Chinese girl kept twirling her long black hair around her fingers. She gave me another tentative smile and then she winked. "Bethany," she mouthed, pointing to herself.

For the first time, I thought there was a chance I might survive this trip. Having another girl to talk to made me feel better about all the days and weeks ahead.

Andy went to the doorway of the dorm which looked into a room filled with rows of bunk beds. "Jules, come on, let's go," he said, but his voice was friendly, not angry or impatient.

As Andy sat down, the tardy Jules sauntered through the doorway, her backpack slung over her shoulder. She offered everyone a big grin and an apologetic shrug. "Sorry, Andy," she said, "I got distracted."

Andy and Bethany laughed, suggesting that getting distracted was something Jules did regularly. I tried not to stare, feeling my body go even more rigid if that was possible. The person sitting beside Bethany got up, and Jules slipped into the space.

I stole glances in her direction. She was the longboarder who'd stolen the woman's purse outside Mick's Place. Did she recognize me? And like the tattooed teen, she could have passed for older than 17.

I felt like the new kid on the first day of school and I'd just met the two bullies who would make my life hell.

A bowl was plunked down in front of me. Bethany spoke so quietly I had to lean forward to hear her. "That's Gaby," she said, motioning toward the tattooed teen.

"Maggie and Camille."

"Oh, we all know Camille."

They knew Camille? Had she been attending the youth offender meetings with Andy? Or worse yet, had they come to her store on a juvie version of a field trip?

"Names are unimportant," a red-haired, early-20's guy said, his strong German accent making the words hard to understand. "Ve are now all pilgrims."

"I'm no damn pilgrim," Gaby muttered under her breath, her arms crossed. Her black muscle shirt had the name of a sports gym on it, and she looked like she worked out every day. She also had a slash on the side of her head, almost but not quite hidden by her hair. There was a puckered burn mark on her left arm. Her wrinkled clothes made me wonder if she'd slept in them, as I had mine.

Jules, on the other hand, had her blond hair in a flattering high ponytail and was tall, lean, and long-legged. She had a half-smile on her face, as though she had a private joke to share. I was quickly aware whenever she made eye contact with me, she left me feeling I was in on the joke too. It was an unsettling exchange. She grinned as she lifted her bowl of *café au lait* and took a long sip. She obviously recognized me too but didn't appear worried about my presence in the group.

Jules leaned toward Bethany and said something that made her blush and laugh softly. She was pretty when she didn't look scared.

"I am no damn pilgrim!" Gaby said it louder this time.

"No one expects you to be, Gaby," Andy said calmly. "These days, many people do this hike for secular reasons."

"What does secular mean?" Bethany asked timidly. Her heavy use of black mascara around her eyes, which seemed to shout "Look at me!", seemed at odds with her shy, nervous behaviour.

"It means non-religious," Camille said, smiling at her.

"You are such a silly little pagan," Jules laughed.

"I am not a pagan!" Bethany looked like she was about to cry.

I revised my image of the person I assumed was the youngest member of our group. It took courage to answer back to the leader of the pack. Jules put her hand out and patted Bethany's knee. Bethany pulled her leg away.

"No offence meant," Jules said, "but you've talked about your mother being into that stuff because she worships different gods, right? Isn't it all the same thing?"

"No, it's not! She's a Taoist. She, we believe everything is interconnected. And stop talking about my mom!"

"Back off. Leave her alone!" Gaby suddenly looked even bigger and more threatening. The volunteer had stopped washing dishes and had her hands on her hips, aware of the tension at our end of the table.

I looked at Gaby with surprise. It was hard to tell if she and Bethany were friends or was this an excuse to challenge Jules?

"Gaby, leave it be." Andy's voice was calm. He was standing up, and there was no doubt he was in charge. "You have one chance, and one chance only, to make this trip work. What's it going to be?"

The whole room had gone still. You didn't need to speak English to know there was drama happening. Everyone was riveted, waiting to see what Gaby would do. I could guess what her second option was. If she screwed this up, she'd be sent back to Canada, and probably jail.

"I was just asking," Bethany said.

The image of Janie's sweet, cowardly Cocker Spaniel who flipped over on her back and exposed her stomach to every other dog and human that came along popped into my mind.

Don't sit back. Don't show her you're scared. Don't break eye contact!

But who was I to give advice, even telepathically?

"Cool it, both of you," Andy said.

Jules was no longer slouching in her seat. It was obvious Gaby was the outsider, but one with physical strength that gave her a different but equal power position with Jules. She looked at Jules and shook her head dismissively, then leaned back again, the bench thumping on the floor under her sudden shift in weight. The look Gaby gave Jules was malice-filled. I pulled my sweater tighter as an excuse to wrap my arms protectively around my body.

India wouldn't have been this bad, versus five weeks walking with someone who might explode at any time? It'll be a long time before I forgive Tony for his stupid B&E idea.

Bethany gave Andy a weak smile of thanks, but he didn't see it. He continued to look at Gaby, whose face was flushed with resentment as she stared back. It was Gaby who broke off eye contact first and slowly sat back.

Everyone in the room let out a breath of relief. I looked at Andy. Yes, he was standing, but he didn't seem threatened or appear embarrassed or afraid. He looked like normal Andy. His clothes were rumpled, his hair in need of a good haircut, and his hands relaxed at his side. Without raising his voice, he'd controlled and calmed what could have become a dangerous situation.

I looked at him again. *Maybe I've misjudged him.* I realized I felt safer going on this trip with him nearby. Camille had also been sitting on the edge of the bench and only now did she sit back.

I finished my second piece of baguette and got up and wandered around the room. I subtly turned my attention to Andy and Camille, listening in on their conversation while I pretended to check out the French-language Camino guidebooks on the shelf.

"Are you doing ok? Still feeling up to this?"

"Why?" Camille asked him, sounding worried. "Are you having second thoughts about us coming along?"

"No! I was, you know, checking in, just in case...." Now he was the one sounding nervous. The big smile Camille gave him made her answer obvious. Andy still looked unsure.

I shook my head. *He was clueless.*

In too short a time, with Camille and an animated Andy leading the way, our group was soon stumbling down the cobbled street to the Porte d'Espagne and across the bridge leading out of town. I looked around with a flicker of interest. We were walking across the same stone bridge we'd gone over this morning. I liked the ancient pink and grey stone houses that lined the river with their balconies dangling over the water. All the window flower boxes overflowed with red geraniums.

Nearing the old gate that lead us to the Camino path outside the town, I caught up with Camille. "That Gaby will kill us before this trip is over!" I whispered.

Camille's hands gripped her hiking poles, but her voice was calm. "No, I have complete faith in Andy. We'll be fine. "

"Fine and dead," I said. "That'll teach my mother!"

"We're on our way! Ignore those overcast skies! This route follows in the footsteps of Napoleon!" Andy was a happy group leader who, it turned out, had a never-ending supply of historical tidbits to share.

"Look! That bakery we just passed still lists the 1789 price of wheat!"

"Who cares?" Jules said.

Andy wasn't fazed in the least. Bethany and I raised our eyebrows and shook our heads. Saying nothing, we both slowed down and started walking side-by-side. Maybe no one would know we were travelling with the others, especially the overly enthusiastic one with the goofy shorts and skinny legs.

I'd refused to use my walking poles and had strapped them tightly to my pack. No one else in our group had any, though many hikers passing us were swinging their poles in a rhythm to match the sound of their boots on the pavement. Some hikers had a single, long wooden stick.

At first, it was easy hiking along the flat paved road, but when the way began to climb, Andy called us off to the side. I was glad to have a chance to catch my breath. "It's time to do some business. I need to collect your cell phones." He held up his hand, ignoring the groans. "You know the rule." He made a point of looking at each of us teens. "There will be no calling, emailing, or texting on this trip, until we reach Santiago."

I couldn't believe what I was hearing. Not that I'd planned to call my parents, but my whole life was on my phone. I glanced over at Camille, who shrugged apologetically.

"Your parents and guardians have my cell number and Camille's, so we are reachable if there's an emergency. Put your cell phones in here," he said, holding out a flannel bag.

Wait, what? Who had a guardian instead of a parent?

I looked around, then got nudged by Jules as she sighed loudly before handing over her cell phone.

"This sucks! I wasn't told about this! No phone? I hadn't been without my phone since I was six!"

"Sorry, Maggie," Andy said, "but it wouldn't be fair to the others if you could use your cell phone and they couldn't use theirs."

I reluctantly unzipped the small side pocket of my backpack and added my phone with the others. Andy handed the now bulging bag to Camille, who put it inside the top flap pocket of his backpack.

"Thanks, everyone. Now, a further piece of business," Andy said. "As most of you know," he gave me a smile to include me in the news, "I received a Puer Foundation grant for $18,000 to test this 'novel,'" he made air quotation marks, "rehabilitation work with teens. If you take away the cost of our plane, bus, and train tickets, travel insurance, hiking gear and boots for the four of us—Maggie and Camille have taken care of their gear and travel expenses, and will follow our Camino budget—that leaves us about $35 each per day, for accommodation and food. I've got some additional discretionary funds too."

"I still say $35 a day isn't enough," Jules said, apparently rehashing an old argument.

"That also includes the $10 per day that you'll get to spend on drinks and snacks," Andy said, acknowledging Jules' comment with a nod. "We're all in this together, and I want you to be part of the financial planning. Taking the three of you," smiling, he looked over at me, "the four of you, is a beta or test project. Let's show the Foundation we can make this work." He cleared his throat. "Ok, let's talk about the pink elephant in the room."

"Pink what? What does that mean?" Bethany looked puzzled.

"It's something everybody knows, but no one talks about," Jules said impatiently.

"Everyone is here because of something they've done that could have resulted in, well, you know. Right now," Andy said, "your reasons for being here are private. It's up to each of you to decide what you want others to know. I hope trust develops between all of us, so sharing our stories will happen organically at some point. Respect your boundaries and the boundaries of your travelling companions. Are we all in agreement?"

None of us made eye contact, but we all nodded. There was no way I was telling anybody anything.

At least I'd have Bethany for company. Maybe we could distract ourselves talking about music and movies and stuff.

The paved road disappeared, and we started walking on a dirt switchback path through green meadows. The fields beside the upward climbing trail were filled with sheep. Bethany suddenly stopped and stuck out her arm, almost slapping me in the face. I thought she was going to be the first to demand we turn back. But no, she was pointing at a ewe standing off by itself from the rest of the flock. It suddenly lay down and stuck its head in the air, as though sniffing for something. Then it got up and grazed for a moment, then lay down again.

"Is she sick?" Bethany's concern was obvious.

"She's in labour," Gaby said.

"Says you," Jules muttered.

Bethany quickly turned to Andy. "Can we hang around?"

Jules and I didn't wait for an answer. In seconds we'd removed our backpacks and sprawled out on the side of the path, staring up at the cloudy sky. Bethany and the two adults were the only ones initially interested in the panting ewe. Soon even I started to catch some of Bethany's enthusiasm. Gaby had remained standing, like a soldier on duty, and hadn't removed her pack, but she too hadn't taken her eyes off the ewe. Jules continued to ignore everyone and lay with her eyes closed, happy to have a break.

After ten minutes, with no sign the birth was close, Andy roused us and off we went. That's when Jules discovered you must always check the ground before you set your backpack down. She went through her emergency toilet paper supply, wiping sheep dung off the side of her bag. Bethany kept turning around, but the path continued to climb. It wasn't long before the field with the bleating ewe was no longer visible.

"You like sheep, Gaby?" I'd slowed down to wait for her on the single-lane path. I had to reach out, or I would be nervous around her for five weeks. The longer I left it, the scarier she got.

She shrugged. "Spent time on a farm. Goats are better."

It was the first nugget of information I'd heard. She had a soft spot for animals? Maybe there was a heart under those tattoos and scowls. Bethany had apparently seen it too. She also slowed down and positioned herself in front of Gaby on the trail.

Jules was the next one to provide an excuse to halt. I almost stumbled over her when she plopped down on the path, crossed her arms, and said to no one in particular, "That's it. I'm done. Send me to jail instead." She looked so furious and silly at the same time that Bethany's giggles quickly proved contagious. This only made Jules angrier. "This is stupid! And there are 27 kilometres of this shit today?"

The laughter trickled off. *She couldn't be right,* a thought I imagined echoing in Bethany and Gaby's heads.

There was a tremor in Bethany's voice when she asked, "Twenty-seven kilometres?"

Turning to Andy, I asked the dreaded question. "How far have we come?"

"About five kilometres," he said, shrugging, "maybe."

Bethany didn't say anything, but everyone could hear her sniffle as tears flowed.

"It's ok," Camille quickly spoke up. "Andy and I have planned a surprise."

We four teens stared hopefully at the two adults. Had they hired a taxi to drive us across the border into Spain? Or second best, was a car going to come by to take our backpacks, so we wouldn't have to carry them?

"There's an albergue, a hostel, only five more kilometres. We've booked beds for tonight!"

Bethany's sniffles got louder.

"We thought we'd take two days to hike over the Pyrenees," Camille said, her voice faltering. "Since we'd probably all be tired from travelling."

I looked at Jules, at Gaby, and at weeping Bethany. "You promise? Only five more kilometres to go?"

Camille and Andy nodded. Andy reached out a hand and helped Jules stand up. When he picked up Jules' backpack, he staggered. Jules almost fell over when she went to sling her bag clumsily onto her back. She stomped up the path, swearing and muttering things we were probably better not hearing.

Andy slowed his walking pace, cleared his throat, and looked back at the rest of us. "Have any of you thought about what you'll say to people when they ask why we're travelling together?"

"Another *pink elephant*, Andy," Jules called out sarcastically.

Our heavy silence was answer enough. We'd all been thinking about that. "I'm going to say it's a history class project," I said.

Andy nodded. "Good one. Other ideas?"

There was silence again. Andy kept walking, putting one foot in front of the other with a casual ease that made it look like he wasn't aware of the backpack digging into his shoulders. Maybe he wasn't.

"You want us to keep the real reason secret?" Jules asked. "Worried people won't let us share their hostel? Or think we will rob them?"

Gaby nodded in agreement.

Staring at the green valley visible far below, we could see the Lego-looking farmhouses and nearby white dots that were more sheep or goats. Andy looked unsure for the first time. "I don't want people to get the wrong idea. This is a chance for all of you to start fresh. No baggage, no hard-luck stories. You're all smart and capable. Why should you get labelled before anyone knows you?"

Now it was Bethany's turn. "We could say we're a youth group."

"Like from church," Jules said. Sarcasm seemed to be her standard response today. The rest of us laughed.

Andy didn't immediately agree, but he didn't dismiss it either. "Any other ideas?"

"For once in my life, I don't want, I don't want to have to apologize! To anyone!" Bethany's words came out choppy, as though she was gasping for breath. "I want to look like I have a choice in being here. Let's go with Maggie's idea. Though," she paused, "maybe we could be an Outward Bound kind of group? I've always wanted to go to Outward Bound, to go zip-lining and camping," she said, her voice filled with longing.

After another quiet moment, we all began to nod.

"Problem solved," Andy said. "We're a group doing an extra-curricular activity."

"What's our school name?" Gaby asked. Hearing her say something after such a long stretch of silence caught us by surprise.

"How about 'The School for Wayward Youth' or 'Come Alive through Hiking'," Jules said. She'd slowed down and was now listening to our discussion.

Before I realized I was saying the words out loud, I said, "Andy's Mutants?"

The others looked at me and then suddenly everyone was laughing again.

"Andy's Mutants, I like that! But what about Andy's Jejunity?" Jules said. Before Bethany could ask, Jules said patiently. "It means 'the beginning stages of a being.'"

If Jules had hoped to fool Andy, she wasn't going to succeed. "I'll give you points for creativity, Jules," Andy responded, "but it also means juvenile and deficient. Let's pick something more positive."

Jules shrugged. She'd tried.

"Grace College." Camille looked self-conscious with everyone staring at her. "I was reading this autobiography on Ernest Hemingway because he loved Spain and lived in some of the places we will walk through. His definition of guts was 'grace under pressure.' I think you're all gutsy, courageous...." Her voice trailed off, and she looked embarrassed.

Jules saved the day. "It's nice you think we're courageous," she said, grinning, "but it's corny."

"I like it!" Her arrogance was getting to me. Sure, Jules was confident and obviously smart, but she was also a thief, a whiner, and being an asshole at the moment.

"Who was our college named after?" Camille wondered, getting into the spirit of making up our history. "Was Grace a scientist? A musical genius? Velcro inventor?"

"No, that was—" Andy's comment was drowned out by the rest of us groaning.

"How about an eccentric inventor who left all her money to our school," Bethany suggested, "on the condition we do challenging things with the funds?" Bethany was again showing she wasn't as quiet or dull as I'd thought.

Everyone's suggestions got sillier, but they helped pass the time. We were finally acting like a group that was getting along. Well, except for Gaby, who always walked at the back, keeping a distance between herself and us. Her dislike of Jules, who was back to muttering complaints, was obvious to everyone.

My feet hurt, one toe in particular, and I joined Jules in complaints but said them silently. We were all still checking each other out, figuring who was where in the teen pecking order.

We continued to climb up the switchback dirt path. It was beautiful, and the gloomy skies couldn't dim the multitude of green colours evident in trees, shrubs, and meadows. Puffing from the unusual physical activity, I wondered if it might be easier if I tried out my hiking poles. Maybe tomorrow I'd try them. It couldn't get any harder than this.

Could it?

8

SNORING PYRENEES

The mountain views were stunning, like a poster on a travel agency wall.

Andy said this part of the climb was sometimes an issue if there was fog. People had died when they'd wandered off the trail and fallen down the mountain.

"That's what happened to Emilio Estevez in that Camino movie, *The Way*."

Andy nodded at Bethany's comment. There was good visibility, but Andy's story added an element of danger to what we were doing that made everyone feel extra-adventurous. Even Gaby had a hint of a smile at Bethany's excitement when she realized an eagle was flying parallel with her. "Look!" she exclaimed, her joy infectious. She was almost childlike whenever she found something she thought was wonderful. Her first instinct, now that she was becoming more relaxed with us, was to share it.

After an hour, then two, I was nearing the end of my energy. The trail went on forever. I wasn't the only one panting like that ewe we'd passed. My legs hurt. My feet were throbbing. My shoulders ached from the pack. "When are we going to get there?" I asked, hearing the whine in my voice but not caring.

We finally turned a corner in what had become a meandering tarmac road and saw Refuge Orisson ahead of us, a grey, two-story stone building with a wooden roof tucked into the green hill behind it. I felt a wave of intense relief and by the looks on the faces of the other teens, they felt the same.

"I thought this place would NEVER appear," Bethany said, throwing her backpack onto the pavement and letting it slam against the building.

Across from us a fenced wooden balcony filled with long tables and chairs jutted out over the mountainside. It provided amazing views of the road ahead, the valley below, and the surrounding mountain peaks. Two middle-aged women, one plump and standing, the other thin and sitting, called out, "*Buen Camino*!"

Inside the refuge, the large front room had a small bar on one side and long tables already set for dinner on the other. Two enthusiastic French-Canadian women, who were volunteering as *hospitaleras,* or hosts, for a week, welcomed us.

After we'd signed in and had our *credentials* stamped, Andy explained that my grandmother had offered to pay for everyone for the first night. This privately run refuge cost 36 Euros, about $54 CN, per person, but it included dinner and breakfast.

"No way was that in our travel budget!" he said.

"It's good you made reservations," the shorter of the two *hospitaleras* said. "We're booked for the night."

The news of who was paying was a surprise to me. I stumbled over a step when we went around the back and up the outside stairs to reach our rooms on the second floor. I felt a sudden homesickness for Grams.

Not for anyone else though.

It turned out five of us could share one room. Another hiker had already thrown their night things on one bottom bunk of the three bunk beds set closely together. Someone would have to sleep in the adjacent room. At least there was a long, horizontal window that let light into the sparkling clean space. Gaby stood in the doorway watching us as we removed our backpacks, stretched our sore back muscles, and began the process of claiming a bed. Each bunk had a blanket and pillow, but Camille had been right, there weren't any sheets.

"I'm going to the next room," Gaby said and left without waiting for a response. Andy paused, shrugged, and that was that.

I watched Camille rest her pack against one of the bunk beds. Andy was right behind her. I dashed ahead and leaned my backpack on the bed next to Camille's. Andy barely paused before choosing a bunk near the window. I felt a twinge of guilt, but only a twinge. It was bad enough they would be in such close quarters for five weeks. There was no way Andy could claim all of Camille's attention. I sat down on my lower bunk and promptly banged my head. There wasn't much space between the upper and lower bed frames.

"Shit!" I gave my head a rub and untied my hiking boots, letting out a sigh of pleasure as I began to rub my feet. "I can see this is going to be one of the best parts of the day. A place to sleep, boots off, shower calling. Ouch." Twisting my leg around and resting my ankle on my other knee I stared at my bare heel. There was definitely the red beginnings of a blister. "Geez! And I think there's another one beside it."

Camille was already pulling out her first aid kit. She crouched down, gently took my foot and went to work cleaning the blister area with an antiseptic wipe, then covered it with a piece of padded, stretchy, clear plastic blister bandage. "The best protection is Compeed. It's better than a Band-Aid, but I found it never stays in place, so I'm going to put a strip of first aid tape on too." She took out a roll of white medical adhesive tape, cut off two strips and gently pressed them along the bottom and top of the Compeed patch. When it was all done, she held my foot up for the rest of the group to admire.

"That Compeed will protect your blister, and it should go away on its own. Can you shower without getting it wet tonight?" Camille asked.

I stood up and hobbled the short distance to my backpack. "If it helps these suckers go away faster, you bet."

Bethany was inspecting her feet. "No blisters, but the bottoms of my feet ache."

"Your feet will toughen up," Andy said.

"Or not," Jules muttered. She was rubbing her feet too. "My mom's a nurse. She used to always put her feet up against the wall when she came home from a shift, said it was good to let the blood flow down."

In seconds we were all lying on our back on our bunk bed with our feet extended up against the wall.

"I'm feeling pretty silly doing this," I said.

"I'm glad to be lying down," Bethany said. She was speaking so quietly it was hard to hear her. "What if I can't do this? My feet are so sore."

"Your feet will toughen up, or so Andy claims," Jules said, having overheard Bethany's comment, but she sounded like she was trying to convince herself too.

Bethany's answering sigh was so loud I bet Gaby could hear it in the next room. I knew what Bethany meant. I was exhausted, and we'd only gone nine kilometres. At least my legs, after this short period of rest, were no longer feeling wobbly, but the soles of my feet ached like a sledgehammer had pounded them.

"We've all got city feet. They'll toughen up," Camille repeated.

To get the shower to work, I had to shove a token into a small box inside the stall. I washed quickly, worried about getting the Compeed patch wet. Or that the hot water or my coin amount would run out before I was finished, but I made it.

Next came the washing of that day's underwear, socks, and t-shirt. When I went outside to hang them on the clothesline behind the refuge, there was very little space left. All the clothes pegs had been claimed. Shaking my head at the inefficient way some people had used the pegs, I looked around then quickly re-pegged a few of the items. This freed up six clothes pegs for my use. The wind was blowing so hard I doubted it would take long for things to dry.

On my way back into the building, I ran my hands through my hair. The versatile Dr Bonner soap that Camille had bought me to use three ways—for washing my clothes, hair, and body—was ok but my hair didn't feel clean.

Ugh. Greasy hair. One more thing to get used to.

Dinner that night was much better than any of us had expected. The *hospitaleras* set out bottles of red wine, jugs of water, and baskets of bread at regular intervals along the table.

The wine caused a minor pause in our group as we sat down. Andy looked at our teenage faces staring at him, all of us aware we were two and three years away from legal drinking age in Canada. He turned to Camille, and they had one of their telepathic conversations.

"This is Europe," he said, "and the drinking age isn't an issue here. I know you will find ways to drink regardless of what I say, so how about this? You can drink a small glass of wine at special dinners, like this first night together. It's usually provided with pilgrim's meals, but this is a mutual respect issue. Otherwise, it's water, iced tea, or pop. Deal?"

Bethany and Jules immediately filled their small water glasses with the tart, local wine. When Janie and I got together with our friends we usually drank beer or shots, but in France I planned to enjoy whatever was offered. I promptly filled my glass to the rim.

"I don't drink," Gaby said, her voice sounding loud even in the noisy room.

Jules snorted and shook her head, mouthing the word "Loser!"

"It's all about choice, Gaby," Andy said. He passed her the water jug.

One of the volunteers plunked several large bowls of vegetable soup down on the table for everyone to serve themselves, followed by more bowls filled with a thick meat stew. Dessert was a flan tart with a buttery crust and a warm cream custard filling. We were all so hungry everything tasted delicious.

The glitch came after dinner when we found out we hikers were the entertainment. One of the *hospitaleras* was obviously a wannabe game show host and was so animated she was exhausting. Bethany made eye contact with me and stuck her finger into her mouth pretending to gag.

This trip might be ok, I thought, and grinned back at her.

Everyone had to stand up and say their name and where they were from, something Andy described as "quite a jovial affair" several hours later when we were settling into our bunk beds. I slid into my silk liner, like a thin sleeping bag. It took a moment to get my feet comfortable, but the silky material felt cool against my tired skin. Andy had fallen asleep almost immediately, and his deep breathing could be heard coming from the nearby bunk.

Andy's use of the words "jovial affair" had struck Bethany and me as particularly funny and in our exhausted state the two of us started to giggle and couldn't stop. I could already see that Andy would regret his use of the word "jovial." I bet Jules would use it in every conversation with Andy for the next few days.

"I liked the short German woman, the one who called out '*Buen Camino'* when we arrived," I whispered. "Her name's Marina and her friend, who's a lawyer, is Elka."

"They're lesbians," Bethany said sleepily.

"So?" I said, sitting up, ready to battle. I'd seen the teasing my friend Sasha had endured from some kids at school. "You aren't homophobic, are you?" But Bethany had already fallen asleep.

It was a struggle to get up the next morning. Bethany and I had stiff legs and sore shoulders, even after only walking four hours yesterday. None of us had slept well. Our room was quiet, but there was a man next door whose rumbling snores were so loud they travelled through the walls into the other rooms.

"I can handle snoring," Andy said as he spread jam on a piece of baguette and sipped the hot cup of *cafe au lait* Bethany had poured for him. She was having hot chocolate while Camille was enjoying her usual morning cup of Rooibos red tea. There was a small zip-lock bag of tea packets beside my aunt's cup, brought along in case she couldn't find her favourite tea.

"My father snores," I said, "but that starting and stopping, the snuffling followed by silence long enough to tease you into thinking he'd stopped and then, BAM, sssnnufffllle, snort. My earplugs were useless."

The Englishman I had been talking about appeared, his cheeks already flushed red, as though he'd walked up a hill before breakfast.

"He will have a heart attack before he reaches that place in Spain we're going to," Bethany whispered to Camille.

"Good morning," Camille said to the Englishman, but even she looked worried. He nodded and sat down beside her, piling his plate with three people's bread portions.

After packing up and filling our water bottles from the tap outside the refuge, we set out again, a straggling line of tired hikers making our way slowly along the winding tarmac road. The best part of the day was the weather. The sun was rising, and shadows filled the valleys below. It was going to be a good day to walk.

"My mother would call this a 'sun-drenched' day," Camille said.

I had a sudden memory of Grams standing on a hot beach on a family holiday to Mexico three years ago. She'd been facing the water, her arms stretched out, her head tilted back, with her feet in the warm water. She'd closed her eyes and started to sing, "These Are a Few of my Favourite Things." Her happiness had been so infectious I'd joined her, only a little embarrassed initially. She made so many of our times together fun.

I touched Grams blue scarf, which I'd wrapped around my neck in the French way this morning. I was aware my stiff muscles were quickly becoming limber. Soon my hiking poles were swinging in a steady rhythm. I took a deep breath, feeling joy for the first time in weeks, maybe months. The poles felt right in my hands and gave me the power to pull myself forward. I'd discovered I also liked the clicking noise they made on the tarmac.

Who cares what anyone thinks? I'll never see these people when the hike was finished.

I had made my way to Jules' side, wondering if she might say something about the purse robbery. She hadn't mentioned it so far. But Jules was in a grumpy mood this morning and other than a grunt acknowledging my presence, she stayed silent. Looking at her scowling face, I decided to let her be the one to bring it up.

Besides, it was a secret that gave me some power if she ever turned on me.

Over the next few hours, we continued to climb. We walked across grassy meadows and along dirt paths and even had to make our way through a herd of grazing horses. The horses looked up, but the only ones who moved were several colts that bounced away and hid behind their mothers.

Bethany was beside herself with joy, chatting happily to Camille who smiled at her enthusiasm and let her go on and on. I could see Bethany was either going to be an enjoyable travel companion or a real pain, depending on the mood of whoever had to listen to her.

Gaby was behind us again today, though Andy slowed down several times to let her catch up. Gaby's response was to slow down even more, making sure the same distance remained between her and the rest of our group. Andy got the hint but continued to look back regularly to make sure Gaby was still visible.

After walking for two hours, Andy insisted we stop and rest, have a drink of water, and take off our socks and boots to air our feet. Jules threw down her pack and kicked it. "This is shit!" she yelled at Andy. "I hate this! I want to go home! Now!" Her dramatic declaration caught all of us by surprise. It had been obvious she was sulking, but not even attentive Camille had realized how unhappy she was. "My shoulders hurt. My feet hurt. I'm hungry. I missed a Whitecaps soccer game last night! I! Hate! This!"

She kicked at a clump of green that unfortunately covered a rock. Hopping around on one foot she yelled at the sky and the meadows and Andy and cursed everything green and said France was crap and Spain would be worse and if her mother knew what this was like, she wouldn't have made her go this damn trip!

Andy did his composed Andy thing and let Jules rant until she was too tired to keep going. He waited until she finally plopped down where she was, again not looking to see if there were sheep turds or nettles. He calmly brought over his water bottle and a granola bar. Jules grabbed them out of his hands without bothering to say, "Thanks," gulped down the water, and ripped open the bar, eating it in three bites. Bethany held out her granola bar, and Jules grabbed that one too, gobbling it down, saying, "I miss my protein shakes. Organic raspberries and a banana and Greek yoghurt, all frosty with ice. And I HATE THIS PACK!"

She looked like she wanted to kick someone. Bethany and I took a step backwards.

"I have a suggestion, Jules," Camille said, sitting down beside her. "What if we sort and repack your bag tonight when we're in Roncesvalles? I bet there are things you'll find are unnecessary now that you've started your trip. We can lighten your load."

Jules sat huddled over, looking unsure for the first time, her head bowed, and the empty granola bar wrappers clenched in her hands. She was embarrassed now that her anger had been yelled out. Camille put her hand on Jules' arm. The teen started to pull away, but then the tension left her body.

I felt jealous and proud. Camille was going to become everyone's aunt on this trip.

"Do we have to wait?" Jules asked in a quiet voice. "My pack is so damn heavy!"

Camille looked over at Andy, and he immediately picked up Jules' backpack and set it down beside her. Their ability to read each other's mind was not a good sign to me. Things must be getting very serious.

Smiling her thanks to Andy, Camille asked, "Do you have a spare garbage bag?" He nodded and went to get it.

Camille unzipped the top flap of her backpack and pulled out her raincoat, spreading it on the ground beside Jules. Then she waited. Jules hesitated—the rest of us were not helping the situation by staring at her—before slowly unloading her pack.

What came out was a surprise to all of us.

Jules had a bizarre mixture of bulky, heavy, and ridiculous items. She didn't have many clothes, but the pile quickly began to include three heavy bracelets, an expensive folding leather travel alarm clock, three paperbacks and one hardback novel, a thick Spanish-English dictionary, and a smaller one of relevant phrases. There was even a long, thin, wand-like thing.

Bethany picked it up and turned it around in her hand. "What's this?"

"A UV disinfectant light-scanner. You move it over phones, bus and toilet seats, and it gets rid of bacteria and germs," Jules said defensively.

There was a snort from Gaby. Even Andy had trouble keeping a serious face.

"It's from my mother!"

Jules had also gone overboard on hiking paraphernalia,

bringing along three large tubes of sunscreen, two designer sunglasses in cases, a pair of insulated gloves, and a battery-powered, hand-held fan. Camille looked at the mixture of necessary and absurd in the pile.

"Maggie," she called out, "could you open the small, side zipper pocket of my pack and get the empty bag you'll find there?" I did as she asked. This was the bag Camille had planned to use for food shopping. Nodding her thanks to me, Camille laid the bag on the ground beside the garbage bag Andy had given her.

"My food bag is for expendables that will be left at the next hostel or thrown out; you can sort that part when we get there. This larger green bag will be things we'll mail home from Roncesvalles, ok?"

Jules wasn't keen, but she'd asked for help. She looked more miserable than ever. Camille and Jules did a quick and ruthless separation of items. The unnecessary things, like the bracelets, a large headlamp (she already had a small flashlight) and UV-Tech water purifier along with the second pair of hiking boots were set on the designated "mail home" pile, while the heavy dictionary and a silver gadget that Jules sheepishly said worked as a mosquito repellent went into the "give away" collection.

The two bags filled up very quickly, but it was when Jules reached into the bottom of her backpack and pulled out a large make-up kit that there was a collective "Ooooh!" It looked like she'd assumed she was heading into some remote jungle. The full-to-bursting bag's zipper could barely close. Camille spread out Jules' travel towel so she could dump the kit contents onto it. The towel was like mine, small and good for quick drying, but it was not big enough to hold everything and stuff spilt onto the grass. There were doubles and even triples of things: two shampoos, three brushes, a hair dryer with a European adapter on the plug, a battery-powered toothbrush with a second adapter, and a large bottle of Calamine.

"For insect bites," Jules said.

"What is it about you and bugs?" Bethany asked innocently.

In a very short time, everything had been sorted. The new "to keep" pile was one-quarter of the original size. When it was all over, Jules looked at the left-over clothes and gear on the ground and the two nearby bulging bags of unnecessary items and shook her head in embarrassment. "What an ass! Why did I…." She didn't bother to finish her sentence.

"Now you repack, Jules," Andy said. "Then you'll know where everything is."

It didn't take Jules long to put everything back in, and this time when she clicked shut the clasps, there was so much extra space she had to tighten the straps.

"Excellent! Care to lift up the two garbage bags?" Andy was grinning, but his words sounded like a challenge.

Jules picked up one bag in each hand. "Wow! These are stupidly heavy!"

"Now put on your backpack."

Jules set down the bags and slung her backpack on, a look of delight appearing on her face. "Wow!" she said again.

"I think what Jules' has done here is a good idea," Andy said, looking at the rest of us. "Let's all empty our bags tonight. After this day and a half of walking, we have a better idea of what we're willing to take with us. Sound good?"

His suggestion wasn't high on Bethany or Gaby's fun list, but neither said no.

"I'll take one bag, Jules, but you must carry the other one."

Jules wasn't happy at having to stick the smaller bag back into her pack but knowing it was only for a few more hours helped. It didn't stop her from letting out a groan when she once again settled her backpack onto her tired shoulders. With some shoving, Andy managed to fit the heavier bag in his backpack. The clasps barely fit to click shut.

The rest of the day's hike took too long, or so some of us thought. Although no one commented on it anymore, we were aware of how beautiful everything was around us. We trudged over the Pyrenees in sunshine and wind, making our way across the invisible border of France and entering Spain by walking through more herds of horses and along country roads. A group of white specks—sheep or goats—were visible grazing in a valley below. The air was filled with the sounds of their tinkling bells.

At one high point, as the road turned a corner, I looked back and could see the winding path we'd walked stretching out behind us. A few other hikers were visible.

A smiling Bethany appeared at my side. "I love being in front, with slowpokes behind. My muscles are sore. I'm tired. But I still feel pretty good. Not bad, huh?"

I knew what she meant. It was exhausting and great at the same time.

Andy had arranged for the Refuge Orisson to make each of us *poulet crudités,* chicken sandwiches on half a baguette. We had a picnic lunch sitting on rocks, looking out at a world visible in all directions. No one talked, all of us content with silence. It was one of the most delicious sandwiches I'd ever tasted. Camille pulled out an extra-large dark chocolate bar and passed it around. We must have been hungry. There weren't even crumbs left for the waiting birds when we finished.

"We'll have to start making our own dinners and lunches," Andy said as he swung his pack onto his back. "But until we get into the groove of things, we'll treat ourselves occasionally."

"What a jovial idea," Jules said.

The explosion of laughter that followed was completely out of proportion to what she'd said, but we couldn't stop. We were a happy, chatty group, well, not Gaby of course, for the rest of the day. The only hitch came when we somehow missed the red and white lines that had been marked on stones and trees all along the route so far. This meant we missed the supposedly easy trail heading into the valley. We ended up slipping and sliding our way down the mountain on a steep and rocky path.

After walking two kilometres through a shady forest, we finally came out at the back of a church. The sight of the blue-roofed Roncesvalles Abbey, our hostel for the night, was a huge relief.

"This small town only has 100 full-time residents," Andy said, sharing another of his info tidbits. It looked like it was full of exhausted pilgrims and hikers on this afternoon. He said some people were making this trip for religious reasons. They were offering prayers along the way to ask for healing for themselves or someone they loved, or to give thanks. Many of the hikers, though, were there with other intentions: a walking holiday, it was a cheap way to see Europe, they liked the outdoors, they had finished school, or quit a job, or been through a divorce, or were trying to figure out what to do next in their life.

Or not going to jail, I thought, as I headed toward the towering building where we would spend our first night in Spain.

Once inside the huge hostel, which had originally been a monastery, we spied a table filled with items: cosmetics, sandals, a ground sheet, several pairs of sunglasses, hats, socks, underwear, one hiking boot, and even a small tent.

Andy looked over at Jules. "I'd say this is the perfect place to dump the extra bag. This table looks like it's lost and found and left-behind stuff." With almost ceremonial seriousness, he handed Jules the heavy bag he'd been carrying for her and she added her no-longer-needed items to the giveaway pile.

"Good idea," Jules said. She set down her backpack and pulled out the sack of things she had planned to mail home. "I don't need any of this stuff. Let someone else carry them." She upended the bag and the extra pair of boots along with other items tumbled out. Bethany began to clap, and the rest of us joined in. It was hard to tell if Jules' flushed face was from appreciation or embarrassment.

We made our way to the long desk and the Dutch *hospitalero* faced six grinning Canadians. He registered us quickly, stamping our *credentials*—the booklets that proved we were pilgrims—and assigned each of us a specific bunk bed number.

While we waited for Andy to get his credential back, I saw Jules casually wander over to the Lost and Found box. She reached in and pulled out what appeared to be a pair of expensive sunglasses. She slipped them into her jacket pocket and only then noticed me watching. The look she gave me wasn't friendly. I turned away. It wasn't my business, so long as she didn't try stealing from me or Camille.

Another volunteer, this one an impatient Dutch woman, pointed to the long shelves in a small separate room near the entrance. The room had rows of dusty hiking boots and running shoes. *"Botas, alli!"*

"What if someone steals them?" Jules demanded of the woman.

She shook her head and said, "We are all pilgrims. Your boots will not be stolen."

I looked at Jules. Like my mother, she was a master of the withering stare which she now focused on the *hospitalera*. It flustered the older woman, but she remained adamant: "Rules are rules here!"

As we climbed the stairs, Jules was still complaining about leaving her expensive hiking boots behind on the boot rack. I didn't say anything but was glad I'd brought earplugs. Maybe I'd use them during the day to block out her whining.

What a hypocrite!

When we reached the top of the stairs, we discovered that our allotted cubicles each held two sets of IKEA-like wooden bunk beds. Andy, Camille, and Gaby were down the hall from Jules and Bethany.

I would have to share space with the same red-haired German guy we'd met in St. Jean, the one who'd told us names no longer mattered now that we were pilgrims. He was sitting cross-legged on his top bunk meditating. Two friendly women in their early 20's welcomed me with grins and a cheery "Hey!" as they continued folding dry clothes I assumed they had brought in from the clothesline. They'd already scored the bottom bunks, so I leaned my pack against the bed frame and began digging through it, quickly throwing my silk sheet, towel, cosmetic bag, and clean clothes onto the available top bunk.

"Where are you from?" the spiky-haired woman asked. She finished stuffing most of her clean clothes back into her pack and flopped down onto her bed with a sigh of relief. "I'm Annie, and that's Liz."

"Maggie. Vancouver, Canada."

Liz, her blond hair freshly washed, was now sitting on her bed, groaning as she rubbed her sore feet. "South Dakota?" she said. "*Dances with Wolves*? *The Revenant*? Mount Rushmore?" she added helpfully.

I was too tired to talk. I nodded and grabbed my shower items. I stopped at the entrance to our little sleeping pod and motioned toward the meditating guy on the bed above Annie. Annie looked over at her friend, and the two of them giggled, shaking their heads and rolling their eyes. "Don't worry about him," Annie whispered. "He's been like that for an hour." She stuck out her leg and mimed giving the bottom of his bunk a shove with her foot, but she didn't do it. "Enlightened being," she joked.

Liz let out a half giggle, half cough, quickly clamping her hand over her mouth. That only made the two of them laugh more. When they had calmed down, Liz began to recite in a singsong whisper. "'I don't eat meat? I will walk 40 kilometres a day on a walking meditation? Spain is stupid? This place is not well run?'"

"He's a barrel of laughs," her friend said.

"Where is the shower?" I asked.

Annie pointed at the far end of the hall. "It's busy. Good luck!"

I gave Jules and Bethany a weary smile when I passed their cubicle. They were still unpacking and didn't look happy about sharing such a small space. Next door to them, Andy was lying on the lower bunk with a sleeping Gaby in the bunk above. I didn't see Camille and guessed she was already in the washroom.

One room I passed was empty, except for a bright tie-dyed scarf dangling off the side of a top bunk. I'd last seen it around the neck of the cute guy at the Bordeaux train station.

The women's washroom was buzzing. There were women in various stages of undress as they washed underwear in a sink, brushed their teeth, or waited to get into a shower stall. I saw two women laughing so hard in the shower lineup they had to hold on to each other to stand up. A stall door opened, and Camille stepped out wearing a bra and panties and clutching the rest of her clothes. One women stopped in mid-laugh and slipped by Camille. She slammed the shower door in her eagerness to get inside.

I made my way to the lineup, thinking unkind thoughts about the other women in the room. I hated the noise. I hated the laughter, and the talk going on in Spanish, French, English, Italian, Japanese, and wow, was that Danish, or Dutch? I hated the long strands of hair left behind in the nearest washbasin.

"Looks like some people didn't learn to clean up after themselves," I said loudly to Camille, who was brushing her wet hair. Several women looked over. I didn't care. If I was going to share bathrooms with 10 to 50 women at a time, they could at least be considerate. I expect the dark storm cloud over my head was visible to everyone.

"Is this your first day?" an elderly English woman asked.

"We started yesterday. Stayed at Orisson last night," I replied curtly.

Now it was the English woman's turn to pat me on the back. I clenched my teeth. *I am not a dog!*

"You'll get used to it, dear," the older woman said kindly. I hated kind people. "This is my second time walking the Camino. It does get easier, I promise."

She had hiked this before? And come back? Was she nuts?

"Why?" I blurted out. "Why would anyone in their right mind do this more than once?"

Other women had paused and were listening to our conversation.

"You must find that out for yourself, but for me, I walked it the first time furious. Now I'm walking it in gratitude."

I still didn't get it. I would be grateful not to have to walk it at all.

The woman patted me on the arm again. "We can talk about this in a week or so if we meet at another albergue."

Looking at the older woman, I gave her a tight-lipped smile and turned away. My group was young and healthy and would easily get days ahead of her on the trail. There was no way that old woman would keep up.

Youth will win this one, lady. Daydream all you like.

The glitch came after dinner when we found out we hikers were the entertainment. One of the *hospitaleras* was obviously a wannabe game show host and was so animated she was exhausting. Bethany made eye contact with me and stuck her finger into her mouth pretending to gag.

This trip might be ok, I thought, and grinned back at her.

Everyone had to stand up and say their name and where they were from, something Andy described as "quite a jovial affair" several hours later when we were settling into our bunk beds. I slid into my silk liner, like a thin sleeping bag. It took a moment to get my feet comfortable, but the silky material felt cool against my tired skin. Andy had fallen asleep almost immediately, and his deep breathing could be heard coming from the nearby bunk.

Andy's use of the words "jovial affair" had struck Bethany and me as particularly funny and in our exhausted state the two of us started to giggle and couldn't stop. I could already see that Andy was going to regret his use of the word "jovial." I bet Jules would go out of her way to use it in every conversation with Andy for the next few days.

"I liked the short German woman, the one who called out *'Buen Camino'* when we arrived," I whispered. "Her name's Marina and her friend, who's a lawyer, is Elka."

"They're lesbians," Bethany said sleepily.

"So?" I said, sitting up, ready to do battle. I'd seen the teasing my friend Sasha had endured from some of the kids at school. "You aren't homophobic, are you?" But Bethany had already fallen asleep.

It was a struggle to get up the next morning. Bethany and I had stiff legs and sore shoulders, even after only walking four hours yesterday. On top of that none of us had slept well. Our room was quiet, but there was a man next door whose rumbling snores were so loud they travelled through the walls into the other rooms.

"I can handle snoring," Andy said as he spread jam on a piece of baguette and sipped the hot cup of *cafe au lait* Bethany had poured for him. She was having hot chocolate while Camille was enjoying her usual morning cup of Rooibos red tea. There was a small zip-lock bag of tea packets beside my aunt's cup, brought along in case she couldn't find her favourite tea.

"My father snores," I said, "but that starting and stopping, the snuffling followed by silence long enough to tease you into thinking he'd stopped and then, BAM, sssnnuffflllle, snort. My earplugs were useless."

The Englishman I had been talking about appeared, his cheeks already flushed red, as though he'd walked up a hill before breakfast.

"He's going to have a heart attack before he reaches that place in Spain we're going to," Bethany whispered to Camille.

"Good morning," Camille said to the Englishman, but even she looked worried. He nodded and sat down beside her, piling his plate with three people's bread portions.

After packing up and filling our water bottles from the tap outside the refuge, we set out again, a straggling line of tired hikers making our way slowly along the winding tarmac road. The best part of the day was the weather. The sun was rising, and the valleys below were still filled with shadows. It was going to be a good day to walk.

"My mother would call this a 'sun-drenched' day," Camille said.

I had a sudden memory of Grams standing on a hot beach on a family holiday to Mexico three years ago. She'd been facing the water, her arms stretched out, her head tilted back, with her feet in the warm water. She'd closed her eyes and started to sing, "These Are a Few of my Favourite Things." Her happiness had been so infectious I'd joined her, only a little embarrassed initially. She made so many of our times together fun.

I touched Grams blue scarf, which I'd wrapped around my neck in the French way this morning. I was aware my stiff muscles were quickly becoming limber. Soon my hiking poles were swinging in a steady rhythm. I took a deep breath, feeling joy for the first time in weeks, maybe months. The poles felt right in my hands and gave me the power to pull myself forward. I'd discovered I also liked the clicking noise they made on the tarmac.

Who cares what anyone thinks? I'll never see these people when the hike was finished.

I had made my way to Jules' side, wondering if she might say something about the purse robbery. She hadn't mentioned it so far. But Jules was in a grumpy mood this morning and other than a grunt acknowledging my presence, she stayed silent. Looking at her scowling face, I decided to let her be the one to bring it up.

Besides, it was a secret that gave me some power if she ever turned on me.

Over the next few hours, we continued to climb. We walked across grassy meadows and along dirt paths and even had to make our way through a herd of grazing horses. The horses looked up, but the only ones who moved were several colts that bounced away and hid behind their mothers.

Bethany was beside herself with joy, chatting happily to Camille who smiled at her enthusiasm and let her go on and on. I could see Bethany was either going to be an enjoyable travel companion or a real pain, depending on the mood of whoever had to listen to her.

Gaby was behind us again today, though Andy slowed down several times to let her catch up. Gaby's response was to slow down even more, making sure the same distance remained between her and the rest of our group. Andy got the hint but continued to look back regularly to make sure Gaby was still visible.

After walking for two hours, Andy insisted we stop and rest, have a drink of water, and take off our socks and boots to air our feet. Jules threw down her pack and kicked it. "This is shit!" she yelled at Andy. "I hate this! I want to go home! Now!" Her dramatic declaration caught all of us by surprise. It had been obvious she was sulking, but not even attentive Camille had realized how unhappy she was. "My shoulders hurt. My feet hurt. I'm hungry. I missed a Whitecaps soccer game last night! I! Hate! This!"

She kicked at a clump of green that unfortunately covered a rock. Hopping around on one foot she yelled at the sky and the meadows and Andy and cursed everything green and said France was crap and Spain would be worse and if her mother knew what this was like, she wouldn't have made her go this damn trip!

Andy did his composed Andy thing and let Jules rant until she was too tired to keep going. He waited until she finally plopped down where she was, again not looking to see if there were sheep turds or nettles. He calmly brought over his water bottle and a granola bar. Jules grabbed them out of his hands without bothering to say, "Thanks," gulped down the water, and ripped open the bar, eating it in three bites. Bethany held out her granola bar, and Jules grabbed that one too, gobbling it down, saying, "I miss my protein shakes. Organic raspberries and a banana and Greek yoghurt, all frosty with ice. And I HATE THIS PACK!"

She looked like she wanted to kick someone. Bethany and I took a step backwards.

"I have a suggestion, Jules," Camille said, sitting down beside her. "What if we sort and repack your bag tonight when we're in Roncesvalles? I bet there are things you'll find are unnecessary now that you've started your trip. We can lighten your load."

Jules sat huddled over, looking unsure for the first time, her head bowed, and the empty granola bar wrappers clenched in her hands. Now that her anger had been yelled out, she was embarrassed. Camille put her hand on Jules' arm. The teen started to pull away, but then the tension left her body.

I felt jealous and proud. Camille was going to become everyone's aunt on this trip.

"Do we have to wait?" Jules asked in a quiet voice. "My pack is so damn heavy!"

Camille looked over at Andy, and he immediately picked up Jules' backpack and set it down beside her. Their ability to read each other's mind was not a good sign to me. Things must be getting very serious.

Smiling her thanks to Andy, Camille asked, "Do you have a spare garbage bag?" He nodded and went to get it.

Camille unzipped the top flap of her backpack and pulled out her raincoat, spreading it on the ground beside Jules. Then she waited. Jules hesitated—the rest of us were not helping the situation by staring at her—before slowly unloading her pack.

What came out was a surprise to all of us.

Jules had a bizarre mixture of bulky, heavy, and ridiculous items. She didn't have many clothes, but the pile quickly began to include three heavy bracelets, an expensive folding leather travel alarm clock, three paperbacks and one hardback novel, a thick Spanish-English dictionary, and a smaller one of relevant phrases. There was even a long, thin, wand-like thing.

Bethany picked it up and turned it around in her hand. "What's this?"

"A UV disinfectant light-scanner. You move it over phones, bus and toilet seats, and it gets rid of bacteria and germs," Jules said defensively.

There was a snort from Gaby. Even Andy had trouble keeping a serious face.

"It's from my mother!"

Jules had also gone overboard on hiking paraphernalia, bringing along three large tubes of sunscreen, two designer sunglasses in cases, a pair of insulated gloves, and a battery-powered, hand-held fan. Camille looked at the mixture of necessary and absurd in the pile.

"Maggie," she called out, "could you open the small, side zipper pocket of my pack and get the empty bag you'll find there?" I did as she asked. This was the bag Camille had planned to use for food shopping at the end of the day. Nodding her thanks to me, Camille laid the bag on the ground beside the garbage bag Andy had given her.

"My food bag is for expendables that will be left at the next hostel or thrown out; you can sort that part when we get there. This larger green bag will be things we'll mail home from Roncesvalles, ok?"

Jules wasn't keen, but she'd asked for help. She looked more miserable than ever. Camille and Jules did a quick and ruthless separation of items. The unnecessary things, like the bracelets, a large headlamp (she already had a small flashlight) and UV-Tech water purifier along with the second pair of hiking boots were set on the designated "mail home" pile while the heavy dictionary and a silver gadget that Jules sheepishly said worked as a mosquito repellent were put into the "give away" collection.

The two bags filled up very quickly, but it was when Jules reached into the bottom of her backpack and pulled out a large make-up kit that there was a collective "Ooooh!" It looked like she'd assumed she was heading into some remote jungle. The full-to-bursting bag's zipper could barely close. Camille spread out Jules' travel towel so she could dump the kit contents onto it. The towel was like mine, small and good for quick drying, but it was not big enough to hold everything and stuff spilt onto the grass. There were doubles and even triples of things: two shampoos, three brushes, a hair dryer with a European adapter on the plug, a battery-powered toothbrush with a second adapter, and a large bottle of Calamine.

"For insect bites," Jules said.

"What is it about you and bugs?" Bethany asked innocently.

In a very short time, everything had been sorted. The new "to keep" pile was one-quarter of the original size. When it was all over, Jules looked at the left-over clothes and gear on the ground and the two nearby bulging bags of unnecessary items and shook her head in embarrassment. "What an ass! Why did I…." She didn't bother to finish her sentence.

"Now you repack, Jules," Andy said. "Then you'll know where everything is."

It didn't take Jules long to put everything back in, and this time when she clicked shut the clasps, there was so much extra space she had to tighten the straps.

"Excellent! Care to lift up the two garbage bags?" Andy was grinning, but his words sounded like a challenge.

Jules picked up one bag in each hand. "Wow! These are stupidly heavy!"

"Now put on your backpack."

Jules set down the bags and slung her backpack on, a look of delight appearing on her face. "Wow!" she said again.

"I think what Jules' has done here is a good idea," Andy said, looking at the rest of us. "Let's all empty our bags tonight. After this day and a half of walking, we have a better idea of what we're willing to take with us. Sound good?"

His suggestion wasn't high on Bethany or Gaby's fun list, but neither said no.

"I'll take one of the bags, Jules, but you'll have to carry the other for now."

Jules wasn't happy at having to stick the smaller bag back into her pack but knowing it was only for a few more hours helped. It didn't stop her from letting out a groan when she once again settled her backpack onto her tired shoulders. With some shoving, Andy managed to fit the heavier bag in his backpack. The clasps barely fit to click shut.

The rest of the day's hike took too long, or so some of us thought. Although no one commented on it anymore, we were aware of how beautiful everything was around us. We trudged over the Pyrenees in sunshine and wind, making our way across the invisible border of France and entering Spain by walking through more herds of horses and along country roads. A group of white specks—sheep or goats—were visible grazing in a valley below. The air was filled with the sounds of their tinkling bells.

At one high point, as the road turned a corner, I looked back and could see the winding path we'd walked stretching out behind us. A few other hikers were visible.

A smiling Bethany appeared at my side. "I love being in front, with slowpokes behind. My muscles are sore. I'm tired. But I still feel pretty good. Not bad, huh?"

I knew what she meant. It was exhausting and great at the same time.

Andy had arranged for the Refuge Orisson to make each of us *poulet crudités,* chicken sandwiches on half a baguette. We had a picnic lunch sitting on rocks, looking out at a world that was visible in all directions. No one talked, all of us content with silence. It was one of the most delicious sandwiches I'd ever tasted. Camille pulled out an extra-large dark chocolate bar and passed it around. We must have been hungry. There weren't even crumbs left for the waiting birds when we finished.

"We'll have to start making our own dinners and lunches," Andy said as he swung his pack onto his back. "But until we get into the groove of things, we'll treat ourselves occasionally."

"What a jovial idea," Jules said.

The explosion of laughter that followed was completely out of proportion to what she'd said, but we couldn't stop. We were a happy, chatty group, well, not Gaby of course, for the rest of the day. The only hitch came when we somehow missed the red and white lines that had been marked on stones and trees all along the route so far. This meant we missed the supposedly easy trail heading into the valley. We ended up slipping and sliding our way down the mountain on a steep and rocky path.

After walking two kilometres through a shady forest, we finally came out at the back of a church. The sight of the blue-roofed Roncesvalles Abbey, our hostel for the night, was a huge relief.

"This small town only has 100 full-time residents," Andy said, sharing another of his info tidbits. It looked like it was full of exhausted pilgrims and hikers on this particular afternoon. He said some people were making this trip for religious reasons. They were offering prayers along the way to ask for healing for themselves or someone they loved, or to give thanks. Many of the hikers, though, were there with other intentions: a walking holiday, it was a cheap way to see Europe, they liked the outdoors, they had finished school, or quit a job, or been through a divorce, or were trying to figure out what to do next in their life.

Or not going to jail, I thought, as I headed toward the towering building where we would be spending our first night in Spain.

Once inside the huge hostel, which had originally been a monastery, we spied a table filled with items: cosmetics, sandals, a ground sheet, several pairs of sunglasses, hats, socks, underwear, one hiking boot, and even a small tent.

Andy looked over at Jules. "I'd say this is the perfect place to dump the extra bag. This table looks like it's lost and found and left-behind stuff." With almost ceremonial seriousness, he handed Jules the heavy bag he'd been carrying for her and she added her no-longer-needed items to the giveaway pile.

"Good idea," Jules said. She set down her backpack and pulled out the sack of things she had planned to mail home. "I don't need any of this stuff. Let someone else carry them." She upended the bag and the extra pair of boots along with other items tumbled out. Bethany began to clap, and the rest of us joined in. It was hard to tell if Jules' flushed face was from appreciation or embarrassment.

We made our way to the long desk and the Dutch *hospitalero* faced six grinning Canadians. He registered us quickly, stamping our *credentials*—the booklets that proved we were pilgrims—and assigned each of us a specific bunk bed number.

While we waited for Andy to get his credential back, I saw Jules casually wander over to the Lost and Found box. She reached in and pulled out what appeared to be a pair of expensive sunglasses. She slipped them into her jacket pocket and only then noticed me watching. The look she gave me wasn't friendly. I turned away. It wasn't my business, so long as she didn't try stealing from me or Camille.

Another volunteer, this one an impatient Dutch woman, pointed to the long shelves in a small separate room near the entrance. The room had rows of dusty hiking boots and running shoes. "*Botas, allí!*"

"What if someone steals them?" Jules demanded of the woman.

She shook her head and said, "We are all pilgrims. Your boots will not be stolen."

I looked at Jules. Like my mother, she was a master of the withering stare, which she now focused on the *hospitalera*. It managed to fluster the older woman, but she remained adamant: "Rules are rules here!"

As we climbed the stairs, Jules was still complaining about leaving her expensive hiking boots behind on the boot rack. I didn't say anything but was glad I'd brought earplugs. Maybe I'd use them during the day to block out her whining.

What a hypocrite!

When we reached the top of the stairs, we discovered that our allotted cubicles each held two sets of IKEA-like wooden bunk beds. Andy, Camille, and Gaby were down the hall from Jules and Bethany.

I was going to have to share space with the same red-haired German guy we'd met in St. Jean, the one who'd told us names no longer mattered now that we were pilgrims. He was sitting cross-legged on his top bunk meditating. Two friendly women in their early 20's welcomed me with grins and a cheery "Hey!" as they continued folding dry clothes I assumed they had brought in from the clothesline. They'd already scored the bottom bunks, so I leaned my pack against the bed frame and began digging through it, quickly throwing my silk sheet, towel, cosmetic bag, and clean clothes onto the available top bunk.

"Where are you from?" the spiky-haired woman asked. She finished stuffing most of her clean clothes back into her pack and flopped down onto her bed with a sigh of relief. "I'm Annie, and that's Liz."

"Maggie. Vancouver, Canada."

Liz, her blond hair freshly washed, was now sitting on her bed, groaning as she rubbed her sore feet. "South Dakota?" she said. "*Dances with Wolves*? *The Revenant*? Mount Rushmore?" she added helpfully.

I was too tired to talk. I nodded and grabbed my shower items. I stopped at the entrance to our little sleeping pod and motioned toward the meditating guy on the bed above Annie. Annie looked over at her friend, and the two of them giggled, shaking their heads and rolling their eyes. "Don't worry about him," Annie whispered. "He's been like that for an hour." She stuck out her leg and mimed giving the bottom of his bunk a shove with her foot, but she didn't do it. "Enlightened being," she joked.

Liz let out a half giggle, half cough, quickly clamping her hand over her mouth. That only made the two of them laugh more. When they had calmed down, Liz began to recite in a singsong whisper. "'I don't eat meat? I will walk 40 kilometres a day on a walking meditation? Spain is stupid? This place is not well run?'"

"He's a barrel of laughs," her friend said.

"Where is the shower?" I asked.

Annie pointed at the far end of the hall. "It's busy. Good luck!"

I gave Jules and Bethany a weary smile when I passed their cubicle. They were still unpacking and didn't look happy about sharing such a small space. Next door to them, Andy was lying on the lower bunk with a sleeping Gaby in the bunk above. I didn't see Camille and guessed she was already in the washroom.

One of the rooms I passed was empty, except for a bright, tie-dyed scarf dangling off the side of a top bunk. I'd last seen it around the neck of the cute guy at the Bordeaux train station.

The women's washroom was buzzing. There were women in various stages of undress as they washed underwear in a sink, brushed their teeth, or waited to get into a shower stall. I saw two women laughing so hard in the shower lineup they had to hold on to each other to stand up. A stall door opened, and Camille stepped out wearing a bra and panties and clutching the rest of her clothes. One of the women stopped in mid-laugh and slipped by Camille. She slammed the shower door in her eagerness to get inside.

I made my way to the lineup, thinking unkind thoughts about the other women in the room. I hated the noise. I hated the laughter, and the talk going on in Spanish, French, English, Italian, Japanese, and wow, was that Danish, or Dutch? I hated the long strands of hair left behind in the nearest washbasin.

"Looks like some people didn't learn to clean up after themselves," I said loudly to Camille, who was brushing her wet hair. Several women looked over. I didn't care. If I was going to share bathrooms with 10 to 50 women at a time, they could at least be considerate. I expect the dark storm cloud over my head was visible to everyone.

"Is this your first day?" an elderly English woman asked.

"We started yesterday. Stayed at Orisson last night," I replied curtly.

Now it was the English woman's turn to pat me on the back. I clenched my teeth. *I am not a dog!*

"You'll get used to it, dear," the older woman said kindly. I hated kind people. "This is my second time walking the Camino. It does get easier, I promise."

She had hiked this before? And come back? Was she nuts?

"Why?" I blurted out. "Why would anyone in their right mind do this more than once?"

Other women had paused and were listening to our conversation.

"You'll have to find that out for yourself, but for me, I walked it the first time very angry. Now I'm walking it in gratitude."

I still didn't get it. I would be grateful not to have to walk it at all.

The woman patted me on the arm again. "We can talk about this in a week or so if we meet at another albergue."

Looking at the older woman, I gave her a tight-lipped smile and turned away. My group was young and healthy and would easily get days ahead of her on the trail. There was no way that old woman would keep up.

Youth will win this one, lady. Daydream all you like.

9

PAMPLONA ROMANCE

The shower room line shuffled forward.

When I finally got in the tiny stall, I didn't care about the water-covered floor. The shower was as close to heaven as I could imagine. *I'm NEVER taking a shower for granted again!* The hot water pounded on my sore shoulders, helping me forget about the lineup of women waiting their turn on the other side of my stall door.

When I returned to my sleeping cubicle, my roommates had gone, including the meditating weirdo. I was too tired to think about washing clothes and decided the left side pocket of my pack would be where I stuffed my "to wash" things. I felt proud of myself—I was getting organized.

Gaby appeared in the doorway without warning. "Dinner," she said, walking away without waiting for any response. The rest of our group was already outside. Everyone but Gaby had obviously had a shower. Camille looked like she could pose for the cover of a New Age fashion magazine, her clothes fashionably hippie-chic.

Andy, looking his normal rumpled and kind self, beamed at everyone. "Hungry?"

I hated it when people asked obvious questions.

"Starving," Jules said.

Gaby grunted, which could have meant anything.

"Remember, we'll soon have to start cooking our own meals. You've all done a great job walking what the guidebooks call the 'hardest part of the Camino' and going through a 'baptism by fire.'"

I noticed he chose not to mention Jules' meltdown. Gaby looked over at Jules but didn't say anything. Jules' jaw tightened, but she kept her eyes on Andy, looking so attentively at him that he might have been giving a winning election speech.

Camille slipped her arm through Gaby's. To our surprise, Gaby let my aunt's arm stay there. "Let's go eat then!" Camille said and the two of them headed toward the La Posada restaurant.

It turned out we were eating a nine euro *plato del peregrino*. It was the first of what Andy said was a standard pilgrim's dinner: pasta starter, fish or pork with fries, and small, plastic, store-bought tubs of chocolate pudding for dessert. Each large round wooden table held several bottles of red wine. A Korean family made up of an attentive 30-year-old-son, a silent mother who didn't speak English, and a talkative father were already at our assigned table. Camille sat in one of two, side-by-side empty chairs, but as Andy was preparing to take the other, I slipped in ahead of him. He looked at me but didn't comment, just walked around the table and sat beside Gaby.

A Polish couple, Katarzyna and Kodek, arrived late and promptly found two chairs and joined us, forcing all of us to move our chairs closer together. They were so chatty and friendly it was hard for anyone to stay annoyed long. They said they wanted to become documentary filmmakers.

"Call me Kata," the mid-20's woman said, running her hands through her short, still wet hair. "It will be easier to remember."

It quickly became clear that Kata and 30-year-old Kodek were skilled interviewers and even before a waiter removed the empty spaghetti plates everyone had shared a mini-version of their life story.

Or at least the version they choose to tell.

I looked around the crowded room and wondered who else was telling a not-so-true version of their life?

The Korean man was elated his family had climbed 1,450 metres above sea level.

"We've all done it," Jules said impatiently.

Andy's Mutants made eye contact. We raised our glasses of water—no wine tonight—and offered a silent toast to each other. Even Gaby took part. We'd accomplished a lot in two days.

Although the lights didn't officially go out until 10 pm, everyone was in bed by nine o'clock. I agreed with Jules and Gaby and refused to go to the evening Pilgrim's Mass. Jules made it clear she didn't have any interest in anything religious.

"I like rituals," Bethany said defensively. "Besides, one of us has to go and get blessed on this trip."

When I returned to my cubicle from brushing my teeth, the meditator was already asleep, rolled up in his sleeping bag with his back to the rest of the world. I climbed up into my bed and slid into my silk liner, letting out a sigh of pleasure.

Annie and Liz came in, still chatty but trying to keep their voices down so they didn't disturb the sleeping lump.

"Are you going to Pamplona for the running of the bulls?" I whispered and didn't see why my question made them laugh. It was a legitimate possibility. Pamplona was only 44 kilometres away—if we managed 22 kms each day—and the Festival of San Fermin, which included bulls running through the streets chasing people, was due to start in three days.

"I grew up on a farm and have spent my life being chased by cows and bulls. It's not something I want to waste my time on. Been there, done that!" Annie said.

The soundproofing here was no better than Orisson. Each

cubicle was open to the common hallway, and I could hear Gaby's soft snores and the quiet talk between Andy and Camille. Camille's response laughter to something Andy said and her quiet "good night" sounded too intimate.

I was starting to like Andy, but was he really the best match for free-spirited Camille? Plus, she was two years older than he was. Not cool!

I was almost asleep when the lights went out, part of the enforced curfew. I added it to my list of Camino annoyances. I hated rules and curfews; this was just like home.

That was the last thought I had until I woke up to find the lights back on and people in the hallway and other cubicles talking quietly as they dressed or rustled through their backpacks. The meditator had already left, his blanket neatly folded at the end of his bed. Liz and Annie were also missing, though they'd left their clothes and hiking gear scattered around the small cubicle, including on the floor. I stretched then quickly got dressed, not worrying about people passing by in the hallway. The thought of coming face to face with a perky Andy was not something I looked forward to. I let out an involuntary "Ouch" when I swung on my backpack.

Andy was suddenly standing in the open cubicle doorway. "Morning!" he said, practically singing the word.

Just like I thought, perky. I scowled at him.

"Do you need to sort your pack? I've helped Gaby and Bethany with theirs."

"Camille beat you to it before we left Canada," I said. "Thanks," I added, grudgingly. He looked at me for a moment, almost as though he was going to say something, but instead he gave me a nod and headed toward the stairs.

I slowly made my way down to the front entrance, one grimacing step at a time, but picked up speed when I saw my group milling around the boot shelves. Camille was the only one who said, "Good morning." The others nodded, looking as tired as I felt.

Jules motioned with her head toward the Lost and Found table located in the hallway. "We've dumped some extra if you've got anything you want to toss out, or share." I shook my head. The large table was overflowing this morning with hardcover and paperback books, different-sized plastic and aluminium water bottles, and a hodgepodge of new and worn hiking gear. It looked like Jules wasn't the only hiker who'd lightened a backpack.

"Look what I found!" Andy was attaching a single, tightly rolled, blue thermal sleeping pad—it looked like a well-worn yoga mat—to the top of his bag. "We can sit on this when we stop for our lunches!" he said gleefully.

"No more worries about sheep shit, eh, Jules?" Bethany's innocent question helped to lighten our sour morning moods.

"Or thistles!" Jules was referring to the sticky, thorny menace I'd had to help Bethany pick off her pants after she had tripped on the trail yesterday and fallen into a patch of purple thistles. But Jules was smiling when she said it, and there was definite goodwill in the air now.

Andy leaned his pack against the wall and started to lace up his boots. "We can pick up breakfast along the way. It's only three kilometres to Auritz."

"Hemingway used to fish there," Camille said. Everyone was too tired and sore to care what Hemingway had done.

The day passed quickly. Twenty-two-and-a-half kilometres later, we arrived in Zuburi, after having climbed rocky paths in sun so hot it almost scorched our heads right through our hats. It was late afternoon before we finally walked on the arched stone "Bridge of Rabies" over the Rio Arga, arriving in a dusty town empty of people and cars. Even the panting dog we passed barely lifted its head. It only thumped its tail twice and then lay still.

"I'm soaking my feet in that river," Andy said after we'd found our hostel and chosen our bunk beds. "Anyone want to join me?"

"I'd go, except it means I'd have to walk," Jules said. "Let me die here." She had stretched out on her bunk without changing her dusty shorts and t-shirt. Her arm lay over her closed eyes. "Ignore me. Just bring back food, if any of you have the energy to eat."

The imagined feeling of icy cold water flowing over sore feet was enough to give the rest of us a burst of energy. Happy, noisy children were splashing around in the water when we arrived at the base of the bridge, but it was easy to ignore the childish screams once we'd limped into the water. The rocks along the shoreline dug into my aching soles but the cool, soothing water made up for any additional discomfort.

"Why's it called the Bridge of Rabies?" Bethany asked. She was sitting on a rock, her legs stretched out in the water, busy searching for flat stones to use as skippers. When Gaby realized what Bethany was doing, she joined her, and the two of them started a silent stone-skipping contest.

The water was flowing fast under the bridge, which made it hard to keep the stones skipping but they didn't seem to care. Their feet were in refreshing water in the shade of an overhanging tree, we'd finished walking for the day, and the pilgrim's dinner was being served in 30 minutes in the bar next door to the hostel.

Camille shrugged. "Can't answer that. Left my guidebook in my pack."

Andy knew, of course. "The villagers believed the pillar in the middle of the bridge had special powers and could cure rabies, so farmers would make their animals walk across the bridge three times as an insurance policy."

I stared vacantly at the bridge, daydreaming, wondering what Janie was doing in Hawaii. *Probably sitting in water too, but there would be soft white sand under her butt.* Wiggling my toes and sighing in pleasure, I suddenly realized I didn't care what Janie and Tony were doing. I was the one having adventures. I turned to Bethany and saw her focused on the playing children.

"Remind you of a childhood holiday?" I asked, giving Bethany a playful splash. She didn't take her eyes off two children pushing a wobbly log that held a third child. The log tipped. A loud splash, followed quickly by louder laughter, came as the third child stood up, sputtering and wiping water from his eyes.

"Fat chance," Bethany said. She got up and gingerly made her way across the shoreline stones to her sandals under the tree. "I'm heading back to the hostel. See you at the bar for dinner."

I mentally kicked myself. *I should have guessed Bethany's childhood didn't contain any memories of happy days by the river.*

Small town after small town made up most of our fourth day of walking: Larrasoana to Zuriain and then through Villava. Much of the Camino trail followed the meandering Rio Arga. We hiked along a range of beech, oak, and Scots pine-covered hills. Farmland began to appear and finally, a sign that read: "Pamplona 4.8 km."

Back home that sign would have thrilled us. It was a distance that could be covered in only minutes of driving, but walking 4.8 kilometres? If we continued our standard four kilometres per hour that meant we had another hour and fifteen minutes to go.

"I'm never, ever taking a car ride for granted again!" I said pausing to shift my pack on my sore shoulders.

We arrived in Pamplona by crossing another medieval stone bridge, though this one was for foot passengers only. The hostel Andy had chosen was on the outskirts of the city and turned out to be totally disorganized. We had to wait one-and-a-half hours for two helpful but clueless German *hospitaleras* to register us.

Sitting in a chair along one wall in the small front room, I picked up the guest book and read the entries. Our waiting experience was not unique. People had left nasty comments. I couldn't read them all—many were in Spanish, French, and what I guessed was Swedish, or Dutch—and frustrated pilgrims had added exclamation marks.

After the tenth moan from Jules, Andy lost his patience. "Yes, they're taking a long time," he whispered loudly, "but the *hospitaleras* are volunteers. Remember that!"

"Volunteers because they're so slow they can't get any other work," Jules said.

"I thought one of the requirements to become a *hospitalero* was you must have hiked the Camino first," I said siding with Jules. "Don't they remember how tiring it is?"

Finally, we were ushered into the office where the two smiling women, one standing by a map of the city and the other sitting behind a huge, scarred wooden desk, offered us tea, water, or juice. The women then proceeded to go back and forth taking turns giving very long and detailed explanations about the hostel rules and where to find restaurants and laundromats in Pamplona. Camille and Andy used their basic high school German and Spanish to translate for us.

The woman sitting behind the desk requested everyone's passport and slowly began to write our information into the large brown ledger in front of her. I wanted to leap across the desk and take over the writing.

"This is like a bad Will Ferrell comedy skit," Jules said, loud enough for the women to hear, but she smiled when she said it. They didn't understand English and smiled back. Gaby was the only one who looked calm. By now, even Andy's smile was forced. Jules passed the time by wandering around the room checking out the maps and photographs on the wall and the religious statues on the shelves.

Bunks were assigned to Gaby, Jules, and Andy in the same

room on the ground floor, while Camille, Bethany, and I were sent upstairs into a cramped room with six bunk beds.

Two of the bunk beds had already been claimed by Italian women: one plump and smiley, the other skinny with unwashed hair. One of them had smelly feet. I quickly opened the window, hoping fresh air would help dissipate the odour by the time we were ready for bed. The two Italians kept on talking to each other but gave us friendly smiles of welcome. The dark-haired woman removed the clothes she had spread out on my bunk bed. She also scooped up a pile of jewellery—several bracelets and two religious necklaces, one with a silver cross, the other a purple stone with an embedded metal face sketch of Saint Mary—and casually shoved them into the top flap of her backpack. The stone necklace slipped off the bed and fell onto the floor.

Bethany picked it up, passing it to its owner. "This is beautiful, *bello*, no, I mean *bella*," she said.

The woman nodded happily in agreement, explaining "*Da mia madre*."

"It was a gift from her mother," Camille explained.

I watched Bethany watch the woman tuck away her jewellery in a zipper side flap on her pack and hoped I wouldn't have to worry about Bethany stealing things too.

Ah, pleasure time: the shower. Though the shower facilities had varied in comfort and cleanliness in the few albergues we'd stayed in, a shower was still a physical and emotional rejuvenator. I'd discovered that shower stalls in Spain rarely had hooks or shelves. This made it a struggle to keep my cosmetic bag and clothes dry.

When our group met in the back garden 40 minutes later, we were all shiny clean and hungry. I was again wearing Grams' scarf. If it was good enough for the trail, it was good enough for a restaurant.

Once we arrived in the central part of the city we explored the exterior of the large bullring. Before long we were forced to make our way around streets already blocked off by wooden fences in preparation for the bull run taking place in two days. Gaby paused at one of the festival posters plastered on many of the houses and store walls. Jules joined her. The two of them stared at the picture of men running through uneven stone streets with big black bulls charging them. They looked at each other. It was one of the few times I'd seen them consider something together. Jules grinned.

Camille shook her head. "Crazy if you ask me."

Gaby was again staring at the poster. "Might be a buzz, you know, knowing they were so close behind you," she said, putting more words together in one sentence than we'd heard her say in days.

"I agree with Jules and Gaby," Andy said. "Though maybe crazy is a strong word. Will 'nuts' do?" He grinned. "You can both come back another time when I'm not responsible for you." He gave Gaby a friendly pat on the back. Gaby didn't respond, but she continued to pause at similar posters as we made our way through the streets.

Bethany was disgusted. "What's the attraction? Why do it?"

She looked at Gaby when she asked, but Jules answered. "I'm with Gaby on this one. I bet it's an amazing adrenalin rush. That sense of excitement and fear. I bet there's a big jolt of fear! That makes the rush greater!"

"Have you noticed there are never women in those race pictures?" I said.

"Camille, you probably know something about this. What does Hemingway say?" Jules asked.

I was never sure when Jules was being sarcastic. She was a master at sounding sincere.

"I think it's more about tradition," Camille responded. "Men run with the bulls to show love for their wives and girlfriends."

Jules turned to Bethany and said with ghoulish relish, "They kill the bulls, you know, once they've run to the bullring and taken part in a bullfight." Bethany took a step back into the street, horrified.

Shrugging, Jules said, "It's not like you raised them from calves." She looked thoughtful. "Are young bulls called calves or is that only for young cows?"

Someone standing behind her answered. "Before they're weaned, they're called bull calves. When they're a year old, they're yearling bulls." We turned to see who was speaking. It was the guy who owned the tie-dyed scarf, the one I'd last seen leaning tiredly against a railway pole. He smiled at us, but when he made eye contact with me, a bolt of lightning went through my body. I hoped no one noticed.

Jules shrugged again. "Who cares?"

Bethany stepped further away, putting distance between her and Jules, pretending to look at the long row of artifacts in front of the stores along the street. It was tourist junk, in my opinion, all of it relating to the festival. Along with a variety of bull statues in all sizes, there was wood, metal, *papier-mâché,* and silk handmade pennants, red and white flags, along with glass ashtrays, necklaces, cards, and pens covered in paintings, photographs, and sketches of bulls.

"Look," Camille said, "white t-shirts and red scarves, what the bull runners wear." She was standing near Bethany, both of them staring into a shop window.

The guy hadn't moved on. He was tanned and wearing his small pack as though it was weightless. He wasn't wearing his silly scarf this time, and I wondered if he'd stuffed it into his backpack, which, come to think of it, was another odd thing. Why hadn't he left his bag in his hostel? Maybe he hadn't signed in anywhere yet. He saw me staring and gave me a nod.

"Hi," he said. "I saw you at the train station in Bordeaux, didn't I?"

I felt myself blush, but not for the reason he might be thinking.

I'd suddenly remembered the unkind thoughts I'd had when I first saw him. I was glad we didn't live in a world where people could read minds, well, not counting Camille and Andy.

"Where are you staying?" The others had moved on, distracted by Bethany's exclamation at the sight of a bull's horn for sale, its tip painted a vibrant red.

The guy pointed vaguely toward the ancient city walls. "In a park over there. I don't usually stay in albergues. Most of them are too expensive. Only if it's by donation or if I can do work in exchange."

I was paying eight Euros to stay in our hostel on the outskirts of town. Eight Euros was too much? That was like 12 Canadian dollars. *He must be very poor.*

He guessed what I was thinking because he grinned, and another bolt of heat flashed down to my toes and back up.

At that moment, on a street in Pamplona, Spain, all my wishes to see Tony again and ride on his motorcycle vanished.

"It's because I like to eat."

Oh no, was he going to ask for money?

"I like to eat five-star food," he said, grinning again. "I sleep outside and eat *pan* and *queso*, you know, bread and cheese, for a few days, which means occasionally I can afford a special lunch. Lunches are always cheaper than dinners in amazing restaurants. See?"

He pulled out a folded, laminated map, displaying a list of cities along the Camino route. Each city had an accompanying list of restaurant names. "Unfortunately, there aren't any Michelin star restaurants along this part of the Camino in Spain, but these," he stabbed the paper with his finger, "these all have great ratings. Now if I was hiking the Camino in France, this would be a different story."

He sighed wistfully, but then he grinned again, and I experienced yet another rush of heat. "There is Casa Marcelo in Santiago. I'll get to eat in a Michelin starred restaurant at the end of my trip! Do you like to cook?"

I debated lying but then thought better of it. I shook my head. "I grew up with a housekeeper who was also a great baker. I did a lot of watching in the kitchen and eating raw butter and brown sugar cinnamon bun dough. I have recently perfected my grilled tomato and cheese sandwich skills though!"

He laughed, and that was it—we bonded over my inability to cook when cooking was his passion. He said he was waiting to hear if he'd been accepted into The Culinary Institute of America in New York City. I didn't know you could get a bachelor's degree in cooking. This one apparently also included wine seminars in California.

"The CIA," I joked. He grinned and nodded.

Why had I ever thought he looked glum?

I zoned out a bit, watching his mouth and his animated hands move. He was passionate when he talked about food. I let myself daydream about having a boyfriend who could cook and saw myself sitting on a stool watching him at the stove while I ate from a plate of hand-made chocolate and cream-filled pastries.

Bethany had come back and was listening intently. "That must be expensive," she said. I stared at her. Bethany was getting bolder with each day on the trail. She gave him a big smile. And waited.

"Bethany," I hissed. Bethany ignored me, and kept smiling, her head slightly tilted while she continued to wait for him to say something. She looked pretty now that she'd stopped piling on the gothic makeup. I'd never noticed how Bethany's shorts, even if they were second-hand and well-worn, showed off her figure. Her long dark hair shone in the late afternoon sunlight. Her skin, lightly tanned from four days of walking six to eight hours outside, glowed.

I slumped against the stone wall. What hope would I have

competing with glamorous, exotic Bethany when she looked like that?

"Guess we better go," I said, worried Bethany had tossed any thoughts of anyone else out of his male brain.

"I'm waiting to hear if I get one of their scholarships," he said.

"You can call yourself a CIA graduate when you're finished, right?" Bethany laughed little tinkles of enjoyment. *Shit!* It was probably an old joke everyone at that school had to put up with, but he gave her one of those smiles that were like lightning bolts for me.

"Bethany. I'm with her." She jerked her head in my direction and held out her hand. He shook hands, and she held on longer than I thought was necessary.

"Ben," he responded.

I wanted to scream. *I hadn't even asked him*!

Bethany finally pulled out of the handshake and slipped her arm through mine. "Andy says it's time to go. See you on the trail, Ben."

She began to steer me toward our group. Both of us were surprised when Ben called out, "Wait. I don't know your name!"

"It's Maggie!" I yelled back, hoping he could still hear me on this busy street.

"Bye, Maggie." He waved and headed into a nearby cafe.

"Well, *Maggie*, I'd say you've found a hunk. Good for you!" Bethany grinned.

I felt like a spider in a web. If we met up with Ben again, I would now have to worry about Bethany as competition.

She looked at me with wide, innocent eyes. "Come on. The others are waiting." She strode ahead, unaware of the men who stared at her as she passed by.

How had I missed Bethany turning her innocence on and off?

I'd never noticed before how she swung her hips when she walked. *She has a hooker's walk,* I thought glumly. *No, that wasn't fair.*

I slowed down and tried putting one hip forward then another, but when I saw myself reflected in a store window, I snorted, and straightened my back. I looked like I had a bruised tailbone.

If Ben and I did meet again, I wasn't going to be anybody but myself.

Trying to be cool hadn't worked out all that well with Tony.

10

HUGGING HEMINGWAY

Following the curve of the street, I saw Camille waving to me from church steps.

The others were sitting nearby eating hot, sugar-sprinkled *churros,* a Spanish doughnut. We'd already passed several street vendors selling them. As I got closer, Camille tore off a piece of hers and held it out to me. I accepted it gladly, feeling in need of something sweet to get rid of the sour taste of envy in my mouth.

Andy stood up, licking the last of the sugar from his lips. "The next stop is for Camille." Camille looked surprised. He took her hand and pulled her along with him down one busy street after another, the rest of us following.

We found ourselves face to face with a line of instrument-playing, conga-dancing, drunk, but very happy people, most of them wearing a white t-shirt with a red bandana around their throat.

Jules resisted a drunken man's attempts to pull her into the conga line. He reached out for the next woman standing on the street and yanked her toward him, shoving her in front and grabbing her waist. The long, snake-like line grew by one more. He held his hand up to his head in the international symbol for a phone, miming "call me" to Jules. Jules laughed. Some things don't need translation. The conga line danced its way down the street, keeping the noisy, off-key band company.

It was hard work making our way through the packed streets and getting wherever it was Andy wanted to go.

When we passed a group of drummers, I heard myself say, "I'd like to try that." *Where had that thought come from?* I looked back repeatedly until the drummers were no longer visible. Andy led us to a plaza in front of an ornate six-story building, its white awning covered with the words "Cafe Iruna."

"Oh Andy," Camille said awe in her voice. She ran toward the cafe entrance. The rest of us looked at each other wondering what was up. Shrugging, we followed Camille, who led us down steps into a darkened room where we saw a life-sized bronze statue of a man leaning against the bar railing, one arm casually resting on the countertop.

"Hemingway. Ok, I get it," Jules said. She'd told us yesterday she'd had to read Hemingway's *The Old Man and the Sea* for her English Lit class and thought the old man should have jumped overboard and put himself and anyone who had to read the book out of their misery.

Camille handed her iPhone to Bethany, who was standing closest to her. "Take a picture please." She turned and pretended to be talking to the statue. I felt embarrassed for her, but if it made my favourite aunt happy, so be it. Bethany took the picture and then Camille insisted the rest of us crowd around the statue for a group photo. She found a tourist willing to be the photographer.

Once the picture taking was finished, Camille reached into her fanny pack where she kept things she didn't want to worry about losing, like money and our passports, and pulled out a pocketbook. "See?" We peered at the title, *The Sun Also Rises*, with the author's name, Ernest Hemingway, in bigger letters above it. "It's about a group of American and British people who came here for the San Fermin festival, for the running of the bulls and to watch bullfights."

"Murderers," muttered Bethany, stepping away as though the statue had leprosy.

"Yeah, and they spent all their time having sex, talking about having sex, and drinking abin..." Jules paused.

"Absinthe," Andy said.

"Absinthe. And then—"

"No spoilers, Jules!" I said. Camille smiled at me. I knew she had read the book before, but it was the principle of the thing.

Camille sighed in pleasure and gave the Hemingway statue a hug. "There's something so great about reading a book when you're in the actual place. Thank you, Andy!" Now it was his turn to get a hug. The rest of us pretended to be interested in the paintings on the walls. She giggled at something he whispered in her ear, and I felt myself cringe for a second time, hoping Jules wouldn't say, "Get a room."

Gaby only spoke when it was necessary. It was one of those times. "Dinner," she said and turned to go outside again.

"Let me give you a treat now," Camille said, leading us to a long table in the main room of the restaurant. The room's gilded ceiling and walls made a nice contrast to the square black and white tiles covering the floor. She ordered a variety of *pinchos,* which turned out to be small, open-faced sandwiches, the chunks of bread covered with tuna, cod, grilled pork or lamb, and decorated with slivers of marinated red peppers, or *pimientos rellenos,* sweet red peppers stuffed with fish paste, everything held together with a toothpick.

"See," she said pulling a toothpick out of her mouth after eating two shrimp, "*pinchos* is Spanish for skewer. Skewered food. It's

Pamplona's version of tapas." We were so hungry no one cared what they called the food. It tasted delicious and looked like an exotic picnic.

My favourite quickly became a long line of alternating olives, anchovies, hard-boiled egg, and grilled red pepper pieces that had been stabbed by a toothpick to hold them together. There was also a delicious potato pancake stuck on top of a piece of bread. I wasn't sure if these snack foods would fill Gaby up though. Andy must have had the same thought because he also ordered three plates of *patatas fritas* or French fries.

"Treat number two coming up," he said when the waiter set down not only the plates of fries but also an oval bowl filled with green olives and slivers of anchovies mixed in with pickled hot green peppers. "*Guindillas*," he told us and grabbed one, munching on it and looking like it was food for the gods. Jules and Gaby joined him. Camille, Bethany and I watched, shaking our heads.

"Pickled hot green peppers? I'm thankful we're not sharing a room with you three tonight," I said. They were in a room with an older German man. Bethany let out a giggle, and soon we were all laughing.

It felt good to know we'd walked all that distance today. We knew where we were going to sleep. Our stomachs were full, and our tired feet and legs were feeling less painful. The people sitting at the next table wore hiking clothes too, and they grinned in camaraderie. It was enough we were part of the same club—not tourists but hikers.

On our way back to the albergue, Gaby was again in the rear. I paused, willing to wait for her. She was a mystery, and I was getting more and more curious about her but, as usual, when someone waited, she just slowed down.

I decided it was a lost cause and caught up to Camille who was chatting happily to Andy. I not-so-subtlety pushed my way in-between them, and they pulled apart to make room for me, not that it stopped Camille from talking.

When we reached the front door of the hostel, Andy stepped aside to let me go first. No sooner had I entered the building that Andy and Camille were holding hands and walking up the stairs behind me, still chatting. I felt discouraged. Maybe I'd have to up the ante, get more aggressive with my tactics. Camille couldn't be serious about the guy. He was ok, but he was too nerdy for her.

It wasn't until I was near the top step and looked back that I noticed Bethany was standing at the bottom of the stairs talking to Gaby who was leaning down listening to her. There was a smile on both their faces. Gaby said something in response to Bethany's comment. They were actually having a conversation.

When Bethany came into the hostel bedroom, I was already in my night shorts and t-shirt and had gathered my gear ready to make my final bathroom visit. I gave her a grin and raised my eyebrows. She shrugged and began to search for something in her bag.

The first thing I noticed when I returned from brushing my teeth was that the feet or boot smell was as noticeable as before. I opened the window to air out the room. The dark-haired Italian woman smiled at me, climbed down from her top bunk, closed the window, and got back up into her bed. She mimed shivering, worried she'd be cold in the night.

I waited until the woman began snoring gently before slipping out of my silk liner and, inch by silent inch, opened the window as far as it would go.

"It could be worse," Bethany whispered, laughing. "We could be with the pickled hot pepper eaters!"

"Shh!" the other Italian woman said. We tried, we really did, but it took a few bursts of stifled laughter before we could stop. We were all equipped with earplugs for snoring, but no one had warned us we might need nose plugs too.

This had been a good day. *If Ben turned up tomorrow, that would mean two perfect days in a row.* I fell asleep listening to frogs croakily courting in the pond below our window.

Croak away. It just goes to show friendship and romance can come at you in a lot of different ways.

11

MOUNT OF FORGIVENESS

As always, morning came too soon.

The others were more grumpy than usual. Someone had come into their room at 5:30 a.m. singing *"Gelukkige verjaardag,"* over and over, which apparently means "Happy birthday" in Dutch. It turned out the singer's friend wasn't in that room and after hasty apologies, the man had quickly left. By then, everyone was awake.

The only thing that saved the morning was listening to Andy trying to reproduce what the Dutchman had said. He then challenged us to find a word that rhymed with *"Gelukkige verjaardag"* and that took up the first 30 minutes of our hike.

The Camino route out of Pamplona was easy to follow. The round silver plates set into the sidewalk combined with the yellow arrows on trees and sides of houses to make leaving the city stress-free.

As we waited for the red light to change at one crosswalk, two stooped, elderly nuns wearing what Jules sarcastically whispered to me as "their hanging-out-with-the-people clothes"—ankle-length grey skirts and light blue sweaters over blue blouses—

stopped and with loving smiles, asked us where we were from. The youngest one, who looked about 80, spoke some English. The light turned green, but before we could leave, the nuns insisted on giving us a blessing for a safe journey.

"That was creepy," Jules said, walking as fast as she could. I turned back, and the two elderly women were still watching, smiling and waving. I waved back. They were odd, maybe, but not creepy. In fact, it was sweet.

I felt like Grams had appeared right on my path, slightly altered in look and language but present, nonetheless. I decided I would get her scarf out of my bag during our next break; that would make it seem like she was walking with me.

We soon came to Cizur Menor, a small village suburb of Pamplona. As we passed the open door of a café, I looked in and saw two plates on the bar filled with triangles of *tortilla de patatas* that were becoming my favourite breakfast. I called out to Andy and pointed inside. He nodded and sat down in an outside café chair. Camille and Gaby joined him, but the others came with me to buy their breakfast. Bethany couldn't decide between having the *tortilla* on its own or getting the sandwich version.

"Go for the one with the most filling," Jules said, her mouth full. "Crispy outside bread with potato and egg filling in the middle. It doesn't get much better than this!"

In-between bites, I sipped my *cafe con leche,* a steaming cup of coffee with milk which was quickly becoming my drink of choice. I'd come a long way from hating coffee at the train station. I stood at the bar and watched Camille and Andy confer over their guidebooks.

"Delicious," Bethany said, using her spoon to scoop the last foamy milk from the bottom of her coffee cup. She looked up and saw what I was starting at. "I think Andy would've been a bit too perky to stand if he'd been the only adult we had along with us."

"Camille's saved us from being the ones who have to talk about maps and historical stuff all day. I'm glad she's here," Jules said.

"She's too nice to him," I muttered.

"Jealous much?" Jules said. She poured salt onto her *tortilla de patatas*. "God, I miss ketchup!"

Blushing, I said, "No, I'm not! He's just so damn..." I couldn't even think of a word that fit his over-the-top enthusiasm. "He's so earnest. Zesty."

The other two started to laugh. "Zesty?"

I didn't think it was funny. Didn't they see how he poured his enthusiasm over everything? "You don't think he's that perky all the time, do you?" They both nodded.

"Have you ever seen him mad, or impatient?" Jules asked.

I didn't have to answer because the man in question called out to us to come and see the map he was holding. He always wanted us to know where we were going each day, so if we ever got lost or separated we'd at least know where we were supposed to end up. "You can eat and look," he said. We continued to eat our tortillas as we crowded around Andy. His finger traced the route we'd be walking. "The beginning will be tough. It's uphill, but at the top we'll see two cool things."

"How far?" Bethany asked, voicing the daily question.

Andy closed his guidebook and put it back into the top slot of his pack. "Twenty-four kilometres." We moaned, though truthfully, if he'd said two kilometres we would have whined just as much. It was the principle of the thing.

The climb up to *Alto del Perdón* felt as tough a hike as going over the Pyrenees. We walked through boxwood and gorse, which we only knew because Andy knew it and insisted on telling us. The sun was already hot on our heads, and there was no wind to offer fresh air.

I'd been proud of myself for how my body was holding up, and thankful my blisters were healing and not giving me much discomfort, but here, on day five, it was finally sinking in how hard my body was working. Even the amazing scenery of Pamplona visible in the distance behind brown fields wasn't enough to distract me from my gasping lungs and aching legs.

An hour and a half later, things looked brighter when we met a thin, friendly, mid-20's Hungarian man who offered us cookies before inviting himself to join our group.

It didn't take long for the brightness to dim. Camille got angrier and angrier as the man encouraged us to follow the "only" right religious path, which would ensure we didn't end up "burning in hell, or even worse, having babies out of wedlock and turning to drugs because if you don't have faith, you'll fall under the devil's spell!"

Bethany moved closer to Gaby.

Finally, when we were almost at the top, I could see that Andy's polite ignoring of the man had reached its end, but it was Gaby who stepped forward and gave the guy a little push. The man got the hint. He made a sign of the cross in the air and quickly left us.

"If there is one thing I can't stand it's a sanctimonious, judgmental jerk who thinks he knows the answers to everything!"

"And to do it with a smile on his face, while handing out cookies!" Camille said.

Jules gave her a big grin. "Amen, sister!"

"That man has some serious Yin Yang issues," Bethany added.

Only then did Andy let us rest, taking advantage of a bench and a few trees that offered a bit of shade. It had worried him that the fanatic would have us as a captive audience if we stopped for a break. "But before eating, you all need to take off your boots and socks and air your feet." Andy was convinced it was because he insisted we let our feet "have a breather" every two or three hours that everyone's feet were healthy, except for a small blister or two.

We all dug into our individual snack rations and ate granola bars and handfuls of nuts in silence, alternating food bites with gulps of water, and happily accepting our share of another big chocolate bar that Camille passed around.

When we reached the top, we collapsed onto the ground, at first not giving any thought to the view. Bethany and I leaned back against each other, our backpacks providing support. There wasn't a piece of shade in sight, just a long line of rusted, flat metal statues of pilgrim's silhouettes striding energetically along the hilltop: one was on a horse, another pulled a donkey loaded with gear, while others were walking. A row of tall, bright white, modern windmills was visible along the nearby ridge top.

Jules pointed at the rusting silhouettes of pilgrims and the distant windmills. "Let me guess," she said, looking at Andy. "They're 'cool'?"

"Well done, everyone! You've climbed over 1,000 feet!" Andy passed out oranges he'd been carrying in his pack. The sweet, juicy fruit was delicious. The view on the other side showed us where we were going next. Rested and refreshed, the trail ahead could be admired. It was beautiful; a flat plain made up of a patchwork of fields and villages that seemed to go on forever into the distance.

I was quickly learning that when you go up on the Camino, it just means you'll soon have to go in the opposite direction.

The hike down into the valley on the other side was as hard as the ascent, and even more dangerous. The dirt path, which wound between dwarf oaks, forced us to make dorky-looking dance moves as we tried to keep our balance on the loose stones. The descent resulted in me falling in love with my hiking poles; they made the trip down manageable.

After one particularly tricky, stone-slippery spot, I passed my second pole to Bethany who was shaking in exhaustion. She gave a weak smile of thanks. It was soon obvious the pole helped her stay upright and feel more in control on the downward slope. She made it to the bottom with no mishaps, though she broke into tears when she realized there were still seven kilometres to go before Puente La Reina where we were staying tonight.

Thankfully, the rest of the day was all gentle downhill walking and "easy-peasy," another Andy phrase Jules filed away for future use. We passed through the small villages of Uterga and Muruzabal, and it wasn't until we reached Obanos that we could stop at a bar to buy a cold drink and use the washroom. The owner was unfriendly and acted as if we were a bother instead of good for business.

"Jerk," I muttered after the owner again nodded, acknowledging Jules' waving hand but continued talking to his friends at the other end of the bar. "Things have to be easier walking across this flat plain, right?" I said aware of how desperate I sounded. I felt wilted, that was the word. My hair hung limply along the side of my face, and I didn't know if I could get up from the chair.

"Only two kilometres to go," Bethany said, reading from Camille's guidebook.

Jules had ordered a Coke when we first entered the bar, and somehow, in the exchange, she'd irritated the owner. When her drink finally arrived, the owner plunked it down roughly, spilling the soda. Jules grabbed the lukewarm can and gulped the drink down. Not long afterwards, she disappeared into the bathroom and came out as we were getting ready to leave. She had a smirk on her face, visible to Bethany, Gaby, and me but not to Andy, Camille, or the owner.

It wasn't good news when Jules smiled like that. Andy and Camille strode ahead, leaving the three of us to crowd close to Jules on the trail.

"Ok, what did you do?" I asked.

With that same complacent grin, Jules shrugged. "Who said I did anything?"

I snorted.

"She wants to tell us," Gaby said. "We just have to wait."

Jules responded by giving Gaby a friendly poke in the arm. "What would you do with an asshole like that?"

Silence. Gaby didn't answer immediately, then said, "You plugged the toilet."

I reached out my palm, ready to high five Gaby, but she ignored my hand.

"No, but that would have worked too." Jules refused to say what she had done, which was more effective because we could never get it completely out of our mind, wondering throughout the day what her revenge had been.

We entered Puente La Reina along a path that paralleled a busy road and quickly got sick of cars zooming by. The passing vehicle tires spit stones at us and the air stank of exhaust. Trucks were the worst and for the last 30 minutes, I'd been sending out curses involving flat tires in rainstorms.

We learned a new Spanish term, *calle mayor*, or Main Street. "What a joke," Jules said, looking at Puente La Reina's narrow, dark road.

"You've got to remember it's 800 years old," Andy explained. "Think of who was using this road eight centuries ago!"

Jules shook her head and gave her standard refrain: "I don't care." By that time of the day, we three teens agreed with her.

That night in Puente La Reina, we had to deal with another hostel issue. The mattresses on our bunk beds had cotton sheets on them, but they weren't clean. I made the grossest discovery: rust-coloured drops of dried blood stained the mattress cover on my bunk. No one else was around, so Jules helped me switch mattresses with a bed at the other end of the room. It wasn't quite the Camino camaraderie way, but someone else hadn't thought it a big issue to leave the stains there.

We learned too late that the hostel kitchen was closed for repairs, and so once again, we had to go out for dinner.

On our walk to find an open restaurant, Andy reminded us that things like the bloodstained mattress cover came with staying in an albergue that only cost nine Euros a night. To make matters worse, our *Menu de Peregrino* that evening was terrible: our meals took a long time to arrive and came on small plates with skimpy, overcooked portions.

"Where's all this supposedly wonderful Spanish food?" I complained as I looked down at my uninviting plate. "All our Pilgrim meals consist of dry pork and cold French fries. Boring! I can't believe I'm saying this, but I'm missing vegetables!"

Sitting at the table almost too tired to walk back to the hostel, I wondered what my parents were doing. I'd only thought of them occasionally, like when I saw a young girl run toward her father and jump into his arms in Uterga.

We'd kept to Andy's anti-technology rules. No one—at least as far as I knew—had tried to phone home or check emails, which was amazing, considering we were all used to second-by-second access to social media sites. We were usually so exhausted by the time supper ended, we were happy to stretch out on our bunks and read or talk.

Maybe there was no one any of them wanted to hear from. Or maybe, like me, they were afraid of finding out who hadn't tried to contact them.

Andy reminded us he'd been emailing our parents and guardians regularly and would do so again tonight. "Was there anything special you want me to share, or ask?"

I still wanted to know who had a "guardian." That secret was still a secret, so far. "You can tell my parents everything is fine and that thankfully for us poor mortals you know lots of things, so they don't have to worry. Blah, blah, blah. They'll get the idea," I said and turned to Bethany. I spent the rest of the dinner trying to put my parents out of my mind.

Walking back to the hostel, we strolled along cobbled streets and around medieval stone houses and shops. After only a few days, we were already getting blasé about the historical buildings we passed and the stone and brick roads beneath our feet.

Jules was scathing about the churches and chapels present on both the trail and in the towns. "They all look alike. Hasn't anyone on this continent heard of architectural diversity? And they're always empty!"

"Yes, but the doors are unlocked. That says something," Andy countered.

As I was setting out my silk liner on my upper bunk, I felt a hand on my shoulder.

"We need to talk," Camille said.

With a tight stomach, I turned around. "Why?"

"Maggie, what's with your attitude around Andy?"

"What attitude?"

Camille didn't say anything, just sat and waited.

God, I hate silence. "Well, he's so darn...happy all the time."

Camille still said nothing.

"And so...enthusiastic. He's like a puppy dog, always bouncing around, friendly with everybody. It gets a bit much, you know, all that puppy bouncing."

"And?"

Now it was my turn to be silent. I picked at a loose thread on the mattress sheet.

"And?" Camille said again.

"Look at you!" I pointed to Camille's rainbow coloured outfit. Everything she wore, from her pants to her socks and shirt, were in different colours, though they still matched in that gypsy-style way that Camille could pull off. "You're like a bright red Northern Cardinal songbird. Andy's a, a, a knobby-kneed heron. He's not good enough for you!"

Camille's reaction was not what I expected. She started to laugh. "A knobby-kneed heron?" She shook her head. "Honey, Andy is funny, honest, kind, and confident about his place in the world. I couldn't ask for a better, well, I don't know what we are. But look," she paused, thinking about what she wanted to say. "Are you worried my relationship with Andy will somehow make me love you less? You're 16. Soon you'll have lots of people pulling you in different directions. I'll always be here, Andy or no Andy. Trust me."

We shared a long hug. "And please," Camille said into my ear, "stop pushing your way in-between us."

"Ok," I said, aware of how grumpy I sounded, "but he better not hurt you like Ryan did! You haven't got the best track record with men!"

Camille was laughing again. "You don't need to worry. I'm fine. Are you?"

"Oh, yeah…." I couldn't think of a zinger comment before she got up and headed toward the bathroom.

We fell asleep that night so tired we didn't care about dirty sheets, aching feet, or even thinking about the next long day of walking ahead of us. I was the first one to complain the next morning because the tiny Swedish woman in the bunk below me had turned out to be a snorer. Or maybe it was the large Spanish man across the aisle.

"I couldn't tell who it was, but I hate them both!"

"Good thing snoring doesn't come in accents, right?" Jules said. "Come on! Let's start the day, to quote our leader, zesty!"

I gave her a jab in the arm, but I was smiling when I picked up my backpack. We left the hostel before the sun was up. It was going to be another scorcher, and Andy wanted us to cover 22 kilometres by noon so we wouldn't have to walk in the hottest part of the day.

The morning laugh-until-you-think-you're-going-to-pee moments came when Jules and I tried to outdo each other giving examples of what a snore would sound like if it came with a German, Swedish, British, Spanish, Italian, and Korean accent. The others joined in until Andy declared it a tie. He promised to buy us all a drink at the next cafe as a group prize for participation.

"You'd think we were five-years-old and needed stickers," Jules said, but she was looking forward to a cold drink as much as the rest of us. We hiked across more stone bridges, through dry wheat fields, stepped over sleeping dogs, and trudged through a tunnel under the highway which at least provided a break from the blazing sun. We moved from the shade of one olive tree to the next, trying to avoid the large prickly purple thistle bushes.

The village of Lorca looked inviting in the distance as it spiralled down from the top of a small hill. My tired and bored brain was making a bullet point list of things I'd seen. Hour after hour of putting one foot in front of the other left lots of time for obsessive brain chatter, something the Dalai Lama described as the Buddhist concept of "monkey mind."

I wasn't keeping a journal and began to wonder if I should. Would I remember the day-to-day smells, sights, and sounds? Or the people we were meeting? Grams would have so many questions. What if I couldn't remember specifics?

Bethany had a thin school exercise book she pulled out every night and sometimes during the day, bending over it while she wrote in letters so tiny it was impossible to read anything on her pages. Her secrecy was beginning to bug Jules, especially after she'd tried reading over Bethany's shoulder several times, which only resulted in the book being slapped shut.

Jules kept her secrets tucked away but didn't like anyone else hiding theirs.

After leaving Lorca behind, a flat-topped mountain range with white, sheer cliffs appeared far in the distance.

"I hope we don't have to hike that!" I said.

Andy kept quiet. Bethany's chin began to quiver.

"Another cute little chapel," Jules said, sarcasm dripping from each vowel. I thought the sand-coloured building in front of us, with its many stained-glass windows and a bell at the top of the false front, was beautiful. These chapels always provided a pew to sit in for a few moments of restful, cooling darkness. Unlike Jules, I'd become fond of chapels and churches along the Camino. Camille and I were often the last to leave these quiet, shady rest spots.

Andy continued to insist we take regular breaks, stopping for a drink and snack every two hours, and taking off our boots and socks. We were all drinking more water than we'd ever drunk before in our lives. We'd quickly learned to refill our water bottles at village troughs whenever possible. By now we knew to look for the "*agua potable*" sign, which meant the water was drinkable, versus "*agua no potable*." We'd also learned that most Spanish graveyards had taps with drinkable water.

"Bizarre! It's not like these guys need it," Jules said, pointing to the ornate tombs and enclosed individual gravesites.

In every bar we passed the TV screen showed video clips about the Pamplona bull run of the day. The run began at 8 a.m. for the seven days of the San Fermin Festival, and the funniest and most violent visuals from that morning's run were broadcast over and over, all day long. Fifteen deaths had occurred since record keeping began in 1924 but no one had been killed this year.

"Not yet, anyway!" Jules said gleefully.

I was bored with drinking water and decided to buy a coffee in the next town, but the next village we walked through was so small it didn't have a café or bar. All we could find was a coffee machine stuck out in the blazing sun against the wall of a little store whose shelves were mainly empty. Unfortunately, I lost money in the machine when I didn't see the small sign—in Spanish, of course—taped to the side that said the machine didn't give change.

We were almost across the medieval stone bridge at the entrance to the Villatuerta when Bethany and I had to jump out of the way of two cyclists who zoomed up behind us and only called out a warning at the very last minute.

"Get a bell, assholes!" Bethany yelled at them. They didn't bother to respond and were quickly out of sight. It wasn't easy to move hastily out of the way when your feet hurt and you were loaded down with a backpack.

Even so, Bethany's wrath was unexpected. She was usually so kind, but everyone was getting punchy and tired, and impatient with anyone who didn't give us space and respect. "I might stick out this hiking pole and shove it between their spokes! Maggie, I promise I'll buy poles in the next town with stores."

"We're the ones doing all the hard work," I grumbled, agreeing with her punishment idea for the next inconsiderate cyclist. "Doing the Camino on a bike is like, cheating!"

"I was a cash-only bike courier. Once I turn 19, I can work for a licensed company," Gaby said. "It's fun."

"Haven't you guys been replaced by email?" Jules asked. Gaby didn't reply.

"At least your feet don't hurt!" I said.

"Only your butt!" Bethany laughed, punching Gaby who gave her a rare smile, and they walked on together in companionable silence.

Another little chapel was suddenly visible. It had white stone picnic tables scattered under the surrounding stumpy trees. Camille read from her guidebook, "This is called the Hermitage of San Miguel de Villatuerta, 10th century."

Andy held up his notebook. "My notes say the 11th century."

Camille and Andy leaned toward each other as they compared guidebooks, their heads almost touching, both passionate about history and Spain. I rolled my eyes at Jules and shook my head, but I watched them with a smile on my face. I had to admit these two adults were good travelling companions.

I felt a rush of pride that Camille was my aunt. Today she was wearing bright orchid pink prAna pants. *Who else could wear those pants and get away with it?* The pants didn't hide the dirt or dust, but Camille loved colour and wasn't afraid to wear clothes that expressed her carefree spirit.

Just before Estella, we came upon a memorial for a Canadian pilgrim who'd been killed in 2002. She'd been struck by a car. It wasn't the first memorial we'd seen, but this one, because she'd been Canadian, caused us to stop and stare in silence. Looking at the stone statue, I wondered if my mother was sleeping or at a meeting.

I don't care. It's not like she'd be wondering where I was or how I was doing.

"I'm going to put stones on all the Camino markers and crosses we come to," Bethany announced, pointing to the pile of rocks previous hikers and pilgrims had made at the base of the memorial. "I read that with each stone, you can leave behind a problem, or say a prayer, though Taoists don't pray, we meditate. So that's what I will be doing, meditating." She looked at us with a hint of defensiveness in her voice, waiting—expecting—someone to make fun of her.

No one did. I joined her, the two of us searching for interesting stones we could add to the next marker.

Camille had been quietly putting rocks on the top of markers and at the base of wooden and metal crosses ever since we left St-Jean-Pied-de-Port. She'd told me she was leaving stones and saying a prayer for a friend who was going through a difficult time.

I'd wondered if she meant my mother.

"And maybe I'll wish for things for me," Bethany added, bending down to check out another dusty rock. "I'm allowed to wish for things," she muttered.

Are we? I wondered. *Just how much could we ask of the world, before someone came to collect the debt?* I shook my head, trying to clear away the gloomy thoughts while I kicked up dust on the dirt path that stretched into the horizon.

It turned out looking for the perfect stone to put on the next cross or Camino marker gave Bethany and me something to do during hours of boring walking. "I can only admire the scenery for so long, and without music things start to churn around in my head," I said to Camille as we trudged behind the others. "But I don't always want to talk, at least not like Bethany. I seem to put my energy into obsessing." Camille smiled and kept walking. *Why was she smiling?* I felt grumpy for the next hour.

I didn't share that I'd also held long conversations with that jerk, Tony, telling him what I thought about his cowardly behaviour in abandoning me, when it had been his idea to rob Camille's store in the first place. I also thought of all the things I could have said, or not said, to my mother. Then I started to think of the things my mother had said to me.

It was not a fun or restful brain process.

Bethany hummed to herself when she walked or talked to whoever was closest. Gaby continued to be the quiet one. Jules had that familiar smirk on her face, and the rest of us assumed she was in plotting mode. Someone would get payback for something they'd done or said at some point. Camille and Andy chatted with each other or took turns walking beside each of us teens so they could "check in" and "make sure everything was all right" and to remind us they were there if anyone needed to talk.

Jürgen, a 21-year-old guy from Austria, had claimed the bunk bed on the other side of me last night. Everyone on the Camino seemed to share their most personal stories very quickly—or at least whatever version they wanted to put out to the world. I'd learned Jürgen had finished his mandatory military service and would start university in the fall.

Who knew there were still places in the world with compulsory time in the military, even if only for half a year?

He'd seemed fragile, tall and thin with wiry red hair, and was skittish at loud noises. I didn't know if this was because of something that had happened to him during the last six months or if he'd always been that way. He confided his story when we were hanging our laundry up in the hostel's small backyard, telling me he'd almost had a breakdown in the fourth month of his service.

I didn't want to hear that personal a story, but there was something about long hours on the trail, the intimate, close-quarter hostels, and the relaxing, shared meals with other pilgrims and hikers that somehow set up a safe space for people to talk. Knowing they would never see a person again, or knowing they are in a limbo of sorts while they walked, each one far from home, away from family and friends, and not in a normal work, school, or life routine, somehow that gave everyone permission to let it all spill out.

Andy's Mutants—as we now called ourselves—were the exception. I'd never heard Gaby, Bethany, or Jules tell anyone why they were walking. We all repeated the school course credit story when people asked why we were travelling together.

Who would crack first? Bethany? Jules? Gaby? It would not be me!

I figured our personal histories were strictly on a "need to know" basis.

I still hadn't asked or been told what mess the others had gotten into that made them lucky candidates for this hike. I'd made up stories during long walking hours that Gaby came from an alcoholic family and Jules was one of those bored rich kids I'd been around all my life who did stupid things to make the time pass quicker. Bethany looked like she shopped at Walmart; she was probably a charity case.

We might keep secrets from each other, but the four of us now stuck together. We'd become a pack, though I wasn't sure who the Alpha leader was because we hadn't yet found ourselves in a place where anyone needed to claim that role. When we first met in St.

Jean, I'd assumed it was Jules, but she'd whined too much on this trip for any of us to take her seriously as a leader anymore. Gaby? I didn't know if she would step forward. She'd protect Bethany, but I wasn't sure she'd do the same for the rest of us.

Thankfully, after passing orchards and a factory, we could finally see the next town, Estella. We were only on the trail for six hours, which meant we were still walking at the steady rate of four kilometres per hour. It seemed amazing how far we travelled each day, but we'd met people who were walking 35 to 40 kilometres each day. Jules called them "the stupids."

One of Estella's stone bridges was invitingly cool to rest against, and without anyone suggesting it, we stopped during our walk up and over the bridge's arched middle section, pausing to look into the fast-flowing river below. Mallard ducks were paddling contentedly in the clear water, the bottom of the rock-covered stream visible below them.

"I bet their little webbed feet don't hurt," Bethany said.

"I can't wait to take off my boots and stick my feet up in the air," I said. All of us had continued with Jules' initial suggestion and always tried to get a bunk bed near a wall so we could lie down and raise our feet up for 20 minutes at the end of the day. If only one of us got the wall bed, the rest of Andy's Mutants shared it. It probably made a funny picture to see three or four of us on one bed, our butts against the wall and our feet up in the air. Often one or more of us took a nap in that position.

The local municipal albergue in Estella was huge: three floors high with a fully equipped kitchen on the ground floor.

"Be extra careful of your things," the anxious-looking *hospitalera* said as she registered us. "I've been getting emails from other albergues. They say someone has been stealing things in St. Jean and Pamplona."

"So much for this being a pilgrimage," Jules snickered. "There are robbers everywhere." She looked at me and winked. I felt my stomach tighten. Was she trying to include me in her longboard theft, or did she know about my reason for being here? I clenched my teeth, willing my face not to blush. Then Jules looked at Gaby and grinned. Maybe her comment wasn't personal. Maybe it was only Jules, wanting to poke and see what happened.

Gaby ignored her, passing the woman her credential booklet to be stamped. Two seconds later, the woman started apologizing, not having realized she'd held the stamp upside down. "Don't worry. It's fine," Gaby said. The woman looked relieved and took an extra-long time to register the rest of us, double-checking to ensure she had stamped our booklets correctly.

After showering and hand-washing underwear, socks, and t-shirts and hanging them up to dry in the enclosed back courtyard, we all felt better, but not everyone was keen to explore the city. Our feet still hurt. Andy wanted us to use the albergue kitchens, so we could save money, but it meant we needed to take time at the end of our long days to buy food for dinner and breakfast. Pasta, spaghetti sauce, onions, cheese, yoghurt, apples, bread, and jam were our staples.

Unfortunately, every store and restaurant was shut. This Spanish tradition of closing businesses between 2 and 5 o'clock and closing restaurants between 4 and 8 pm was a real pain for our Canadian stomachs and Camino hostel hours.

We finally found two bars located side by side with tables and chairs squished together on the sidewalk. Andy again ordered several plates of French fries to go along with our cold drinks.

"It will tide you over," he said.

Poor guy, he'd stepped into it again. I watched Jules mouth, "Tide you over." She was already working those three words in future conversations.

There were two noisy groups in the next bar. The first consisted of loud, drunken men between 30- and 40-years-old who were trying to impress the nearby table of equally drunk, mid-20's women. Bethany looked both fascinated and horrified and kept stealing glances at the yelling groups. Jules and I looked at each other and raised our eyebrows before ignoring our rowdy neighbours.

I looked over at very calm and big Gaby and relaxed. We had our own gladiator. Gaby had taken the chair beside Bethany, so she was between her and the drunks.

No one on the street could miss hearing the drunken conversations. The men were yelling at each other, saying in English how they were going to take the 45-minute bus ride into Pamplona tomorrow and bragging about how fast they would run when they charged ahead of the bulls.

"Except for old Georgie," one guy said. "Not with his history of falling over his feet!" Poor old Georgie got a lot of thumping on the back but took it with goodwill.

"It's cheaper to stay here than in Pamplona during the San Fermin Festival," Andy told us, leaning forward so we could hear him over the shouting men and the wild shrieks of female laughter. I almost missed his next comment, about people choosing to stay in Estella, because I'd been floored by the sudden awareness that the 47 kilometres we'd walked during the last two days those drunks would drive in under an hour.

"Jeez, we will never get to Santiago at this rate!" I blurted out.

As we walked back to the municipal albergue, Andy cleared his throat. "We've been walking for a week now and if anyone wants to use my phone to call home, they can." He looked at his watch. "It's 7 o'clock so it'll be 10 am in Vancouver." We met his offer with silence. I snuck a look at the others, wondering if it was Bethany or Gaby who had guardians. Both seemed to have a big secret. Well, so did I, but that was different.

Jules was the only one who said she'd like to talk to her mother. Bethany was slower to respond, but she eventually muttered, "Sure, but a short one."

Gaby shook his head.

"Maggie?" Hearing my name made me realize they were all looking at me.

"You've let them know how things are." I hoped I looked as nonchalant as I was trying to feel. I might talk to them next week, if I had something I wanted to say.

Or that they wanted to hear.

12

I SHOT THE SHERIFF

After the phone call back to Canada, Jules became silent and stretched out on her upper bunk bed staring at the ceiling.

I saw Andy casually lean against the end of Jules' bunk. Whatever Andy said was apparently the right thing because soon Jules was laughing, then she and Andy left to make sure we knew the correct route to follow out of town tomorrow morning. Leaving when it was still dark, as we had been doing for the last three days, meant we all had to look for yellow arrows on trees, walls, and roadways so we didn't get lost.

Camille was sitting quietly on her bunk bed writing in her journal.

Bethany, on the other hand, had become a babbling maniac, pacing up and around the long room until Camille stood up and put her hand on Bethany's shoulder during one of her frantic passes.

"I've got aromatherapy oil that I can rub on your wrists, Bethany. It's calming."

Bethany looked startled, then embarrassed, "Sorry."

"Was everything ok at home?" Camille asked.

That's all it took. Bethany started to cry. "It's just, my brother, he makes me crazy." She grabbed hold of the metal end of the bunk bed and clenched the pole so tightly her fingers went white. "My mom's sick and he, he said," Bethany looked like she was going to start wailing. She let go of the pole and clenched her hands before dropping onto Camille's lower bunk and putting her head in her hands, not wanting anyone to see her tears. We could barely hear her. "He said it's better I'm here and not there because I'd only upset her." The face she turned to Camille was pain-filled. "Not my mom! I'd never want to upset my mom."

Camille pulled Bethany into her arms. I didn't know what to do, so I sat down on the other side of my weeping friend and rested my hand on her back. Together Camille and I supported Bethany's shaking body, the silence only broken by Bethany's sobs.

The other people in the room had gone quiet, looking over at the three of us before returning to their packing or unpacking. Tears were common on the Camino, and it was obvious Bethany had friends. No one felt the need to step forward and offer help.

With a hiccup of breath, Bethany finally pulled herself out of Camille's hug. Without looking at us, Bethany reached and touched each of us on the leg. "Thank you," she whispered. "It's just, if I do everything right on this hike, I can move back in with my mom. And if I mess up again. . . ." Then still without making eye contact, she climbed up into her bunk above Camille's and pulled the silk sheet over her head.

"Should we...?" I started to ask, then stopped.

"She'll be fine. Tears are a cleanser," Camille whispered. "You were a good friend right now. We've all had an exhausting day. I'm going to brush my teeth and go to bed."

She picked up her small bathroom bag and left me sitting on

her bunk, prepared to wait as long as needed for Bethany's head to come out from under the cover.

"Bethany?" I asked tentatively when she finally climbed down the ladder and started to put together her night things. I was shocked at how young she looked. No one would believe she was 16.

"Don't worry, I'm fine. I feel better than I have in years!" She stretched. "My family, well, things are the same as they've always been, but you know what? I realized that's my last call home." She smiled. "I'm going to make this hike all about me and all of you, and I'm going to have adventures and enjoy every minute!"

Bethany picked up her nightclothes from her bunk and started to head toward the bathroom, then came back to me. "But you should at least talk to your grandmother, Maggie. I like the stories you've told me about her." She laughed self-consciously. "I let myself daydream yesterday when you were telling me about the time the two of you visited Mexico. It must be amazing to have a grandmother like that. Don't miss out on talking to her any chance you get!" She left me staring after her.

Now it was my turn to feel tears coming. I quickly flopped down on top of my silk sheet and lay there for a long time, listening to the snores and farts and rustling sounds as people settled down, or sorted out their packs, or moved in their sleep. My legs ached, and I shifted my body to find a more comfortable position. I knew I was lucky. Grams, my father, and Camille loved me. *Tomorrow, I'll look for the perfect postcards to mail home.*

The next morning, I was startled awake by Bob Marley singing from somewhere on the ground floor. "I Shot the Sheriff" was so loud I'm sure everyone in the 100 bunks could hear it regardless of their floor or dorm.

The kitchen was a mass of people. Plates, cutlery, and pots to boil water for coffee and tea were in short supply. One woman was sitting sideways at the end of a bench, taking up two spaces. She'd also spread her blister repair kit on the table and was cutting, scraping, and taping her feet while chatting in Spanish to the woman beside her.

She was the same woman who'd taken a call on her cell phone last night, even though many people in the nearby bunks were already asleep. She hadn't bothered to lower her voice or leave the dorm room. I'd heard Jules swear. Other people turned their backs to the talker, and one man adjusted his earplugs before pulling his sleeping bag over his head. For five minutes, the woman chatted to her *te amo*.

Suddenly I'd had enough. I got out of my silk sheet, stomped over to her top bunk, and hissed, "Get out if you want to talk to your boyfriend! Some of us are trying to sleep!"

The woman looked shocked by my anger and only then looked around, as though aware of the other people in the room for the first time. She shrugged, nodded, and lowered her voice slightly, but she didn't leave or end her phone call. It appeared her morning awareness of others was no more active than her evening sensitivity.

"I've lost my appetite," Jules said in disgust, seeing the woman trim a blackened toenail. She turned around and left the kitchen without bothering to fix her bread and jam breakfast. "I'll buy a *tortilla* at the first open bar we find. Jeez, my mother wouldn't be happy if she saw what that woman was doing. It's unsanitary!" Her righteous indignation would have been funny if it wasn't so true.

The first open bar had a rack of postcards showing men running from bulls through the streets of Pamplona. I bought three, all with international stamps already on them, and scribbled a funny message for Grams and my cousin Jake on two and a shorter note on the third card to my parents. That final look on my mother's face still bothered me. Maybe this would be a step toward showing I was sorry. I didn't know Janie's Maui address so I couldn't reach out to her.

There was one bright star in Jules' morning. About three kilometres out of Estella we came to Bodegas Irache, a bodega or winery with a wine and water fountain for pilgrims. Even though we'd been among the first to leave the albergue, there were already people milling about the free wine tap sticking out of the side of the winery. One guy wearing jeans had a bulging backpack that looked much too heavy for his thin body.

"Who wears jeans on the Camino? They chafe and take forever to dry," I said.

"Look at the weight he's carrying. I bet he started in Pamplona!" Jules added.

Gaby shook her head in disgust. "Tourists!" she muttered.

The skinny guy was laughing with his friends as he emptied his water bottle, getting ready to fill it with wine.

"He's going to drink it all!" Jules said and ran to the tap.

"Wait," Camille called out. Jules skidded to a stop, looking disappointed.

Andy started to repeat his standard Camino refrain, told to us on the first day as we neared Orisson: "It's all about being respectful, *et castitate*." The last bit was the Latin translation and although meaningless to us, and not the right language to be using in Spain, it seemed like such an Andy thing to know and say.

"Who speaks a dead language like that these days?" Jules had said as we sat at an outdoor table at Orisson, enjoying a cold iced tea and staring down at the green valley below and the mountain ranges all around us.

"Yeah, I know more Klingon than Latin. It's the 21st century!" I'd replied, making the others laugh.

"You know Klingon?" Gaby asked.

I was sure I heard judgement in her voice, so I turned away and asked Bethany about the tattoo I'd seen peeking out from under her sleeve. *I should learn to keep my mouth shut,* I told myself as

Bethany pulled back her shirt at the wrist, exposing the tattoo. *Speaking Klingon isn't something everyone's proud of.*

"It's the Yin and Yang symbol," she said. The circular tattoo looked like two teardrops, one black, one white, swirling around each other. There was a white dot in the middle of the black teardrop and a black dot in the middle of the white teardrop. "The dark one is Yin, representing the feminine, the moon, shadows, and water, while the white one is Yang, male, light, and fire. Taoists believe life is a balance between the two," she explained.

"And the dots in the middle?" I asked.

"There is always lightness even in the dark, and darkness even in the light." She smiled, but it quickly disappeared. "My mother was horrified when she first saw it and told me tattoos were for gangsters, but she decided if I had to get one, at least I'd picked something that would remind me that our lives hold both light and darkness."

"Your mother and Camille would like each other," I said. "Camille's into Goddess worship and it's got some similar beliefs."

Bethany pulled down her sleeve and covered up her wrist. "I don't know about that."

"Sorry," I'd muttered, "I just meant…" but I don't think she'd heard me.

Camille now stood in front of the wine fountain. "We can do something now to mark this as a special hike," she said setting down her pack. She untied the Camino shell that usually dangled from the top flap of her pack, rinsed it under the waterspout, and only then did she move to the other tap to partially fill it with wine.

"What would you like to receive from this walk? Think of this as a Camino moment of gratitude," she said. She offered the shell first to Jules, who barely paused before she slurped the wine up, not even pretending to give her words any consideration. Camille then refilled it and handed it to Bethany, who was almost reverential when she held the shell before drinking.

Gaby moved to the other side of the iron gates, shaking her head unnecessarily though Camille had made no motion to offer her the shell.

What do I want to receive from this 800 km hike? Do I want Tony, or Ben, in my life? Do I want my mother to back off and give me space? Or that Grams would never die? I think I'm done with Tony, and it was respect, not space, I wanted from Mom, but yes to Grams living forever.

None of the wishes were exactly right. My turn came, and I took a sip then another from Camille's shell, still not clear on what I wanted to ask for. I'd sort that part out later. Camille served Andy and finally herself before stepping aside for the next person waiting impatiently in line.

Some of the day's trail was on a partially tree-lined path, which meant there were occasional rest spots from the scorching sun, but they were never enough. We all scurried from shady spot to shady spot.

As we passed through Azqueta, the hills in the distance finally appeared closer. At one point, we walked through what looked like a ten-foot high drainpipe, but it was actually a tunnel under the highway. At Villamayor de Monjardin we stopped to eat a snack and enjoy yet another *cafe con leche.*

An American man, so thin and muscular he looked like a marathon runner, had his left leg stretched out on a chair resting his Achilles tendon on a bag of ice. He nodded at us, aware of our curiosity. "Tendonitis," he said, shaking his head in frustration, "but I can't stop now. I only started in Pamplona."

"If any of you suffer from tendonitis," Andy said, sounding fierce though he spoke so quietly only we could hear him, "we're stopping immediately! You can damage your Achilles heel forever if you don't rest when it's inflamed! That guy is making a big mistake!"

The trail from Villamayor to Los Arcos was a long gravel path that went off into the distance. We could see far ahead of us, even though we were walking through an area of gently rolling hills. It was a 12-kilometre stretch of the Camino without a single village in it. More bikes zoomed by, but these riders called out early enough for walkers to step off the path. In the distance, a tall haystack came into view. The closer we got, the taller the stack appeared until finally we were walking by it, stunned by its size.

"That sucker is eleven rows high!" Jules exclaimed.

Passing by the last tower of bales, we could hear raised voices and saw a man and woman, both in their early 20's, huddled together. The woman was crying with great wracking sobs, barely able to get words out, while the man squatted in front of her holding her hands and trying to calm her down. Andy paused, but it looked like the boyfriend was managing all right and our leader quickly caught up with the rest of us.

When we finally walked into Los Arcos, it came sooner than we expected. We'd already hiked 24 kilometres, but none of us felt ready to stop. It was too early in the day. Andy held a group meeting and we all agree we were feeling fine, yes, a bit tired but nothing a lunch break with chocolate pieces for dessert wouldn't fix.

We sat in the Los Arcos village square eating our baguette sandwiches and considering our options. I wiggled my bare toes, letting the sun soak into my skin. I knew my nose was pink, though I'd been slathering on sunscreen. I pointed to Bethany's ankles then looked at my own and held them up. We were all developing a Camino hiker's tan—white feet meeting tanned legs in a straight line at ankle sock height.

Andy had a Plan B in mind. "Only five kilometres from here is a jazzy little place I've read about—"

"Jazzy? Do people really say 'jazzy'?" Jules interrupted with a laugh. "And will it be a jovial affair?"

Andy grinned. "It's called Sansol. It says here in my notes," he held up his book toward Camille who bowed, conceding his notes were fine, "there is a private albergue with a swimming pool." Cries of excitement and groans of pleasure greeted his comment.

"A swimming pool?"

"Please, please, please, Andy!"

"Let's go there!"

"It's decided then," he said. "Eat up, my hearties." His pirate accent earned him more groans, but we finished our lunch in record time. A swimming pool was calling our names.

We continued to walk through beautiful rolling wheat fields that Camille said made her feel like she was in the middle of a Van Gogh painting.

"This sun will fry my brains," Jules said, adjusting her baseball cap to ensure it covered the sunburned tips of her ears. She had slathered so much sunscreen on that her ears it looked like she'd covered them in vanilla icing.

"I can see for miles!" Bethany exclaimed.

"What a weird, but oddly nice, person," Jules said to me. I'd kept expecting her to eat Bethany alive with nasty comments, but she seemed as touched by Bethany's innocence as the rest of us. Sometimes, though, after one of Bethany's comments about living in harmony with the Tao or the need to stand in your bare feet on the ground to absorb healing energy, Jules stared at her as though she was from another galaxy.

We turned a corner and there was the small village where we hoped to spend the night. We were all dragging our feet by then. The last two kilometres had felt more like ten. Bethany and I both let out a whimper of pain when we looked up and realized that to reach the hostel with the swimming pool we had to climb up a paved hill road. “I hate the word ‘up’!” I said. “There’d better be beds for us!”

Camille had told us on the first day no one could reserve ahead in Spanish albergues, though apparently you could do this in France. Thankfully, the albergue had room. We quickly took off our boots, dumped our backpacks in the two small rooms allotted us, and dug out our bathing suits. We arrived in the small courtyard, clutching our small hiking towels and staring at what looked like a large bathtub sunk into the floor of the patio.

“It’s wishful thinking to call this a swimming pool!” Jules said, standing on the edge in her bikini. The rest of us nodded in sad agreement. I noticed that Gaby’s puckered scar on her arm stood out on her sunburned skin.

There were already two, mid-30’s, Irish couples using the pool.

“Hot tub? Luxury! Why in my day we were lucky to have buckets!” Andy said.

I cringed. It sounded like he and Camille were about to recite one of the many Monty Python comedy skits they both knew by heart. We’d had to put up with listening to those not-always-funny sketches before.

“Buckets? We were glad to have water from a cup!” Camille responded.

“A cup?” said one man, his Irish accent adding a lovely lilt to his words. “We were lucky if we had dew drops in our hands!”

The speaker climbed out of the mini-pool, followed by his friends, giving up the refreshing space to the six of us. “I’m Fergus and this is my girlfriend, Brigit, and our friends, Meara and Neil.” Neil, who was sitting on the side of the pool letting his sore feet soak in the water, gave us a wave.

“Wow, you’re like a walking advertisement for Ireland with those names,” Bethany said. She was wearing a skimpy bikini and with her exotic Asian face could have posed for a fashion magazine. I looked down at my two-piece Victoria's Secret bathing suit and felt frumpish.

"Got to watch the sun, Bethany," I said, "you'll get a bad burn." I had a smile on my face, but even I could tell my words didn't come out friendly. She looked at me, surprised. I sighed. "Sorry," I mumbled. "You look great." Her friendly grin only made me feel even more embarrassed by my jealousy. I was what I was: tall like my father and a bit overweight and would never look like I needed protecting. *As if I wanted that.*

Andy played host and introduced us to Fergus and his friends. In a short while, everyone was laughing so hard at the Irish couples' stories that I wondered if I'd have a sore stomach tomorrow to go along with my sore feet.

It was a glorious afternoon. Yes, the pool was small. Yes, our feet hurt, but we'd walked 29 kilometres. The simple dinner that came with the albergue fee was delicious, though the landlord could have been serving another meal of dry pork, overcooked fries, and packaged chocolate pudding and we would have called it a feast. Andy and Fergus had pushed four tables together, turning the meal and evening into a party.

The Irish couples were in a celebration mood, but unlike the drunken men and women we'd seen in Estella, these four included us in their jokes and storytelling. This was their second year of walking the Camino in a two-week stretch and they'd be flying back to Dublin soon. Fergus had proposed to Brigit that afternoon, and she'd replied with a passionate "Yes!" We all fell asleep with a smile on our face that night.

Those smiles disappeared before anyone had a chance to eat our meagre granola bar breakfast. We staggered into the hallway, startled awake by Andy's loud curses. He looked dishevelled and furious.

I'd never seen him mad before. Worried, yes. Insistent, yes. Perky, yes. But never angry. He was pacing in front of the almost empty boot shelf. Like all the albergues we'd stayed in, no one could bring boots into the dorm rooms and the hallway shelves held our dusty, dirty footwear. I quickly gathered that our Irish friends had already left. Camille sat on the steps leading up to the rooms on the next floor, looking remarkably calm.

Andy, on the other hand, was red in the face with his hands clenched at his side. "My boots are gone! Someone stole my boots!"

So much for Camino miracles. Poor Andy. This Camino moment sucked.

13

BOOTS AND BEDBUGS

As Andy paced and cursed, Camille explained the owner of this private albergue didn't live on site.

He wasn't answering the emergency phone number posted on the front door. It was also Sunday and nothing in this Spanish village of 150 people was open.

"I'd call a taxi if there was such a thing and get out about five kilometres down the road and wait and watch every pair of boots that went by!" That wasn't a realistic possibility and Andy knew it, he just needed to let off steam.

"What else have you got for your feet, Andy?" Jules' question was a valid one. All of us had an extra pair of sandals or running shoes.

"My flip-flops. That's all I've got." At that point, thinking Andy had had enough time to pace and rave, Camille stood up and took charge.

"Let's check for extra boots. Anyone?" It turned out no one's shoes could become a spare pair for Andy. Jules' feet were one size too small, Gaby's bigger, and Camille, Bethany, and I couldn't provide any footwear close to Andy's size 12 feet.

"Just how big are your feet, Gaby?" Bethany asked.

There was a loud crashing sound as the front door was flung open. Feet pounded up the stairs and a red-faced Fergus appeared. He immediately began to apologize. "I'm sorry. So sorry! It must have been the drink last night. Or not wanting to disturb you when we left this morning, so we didn't turn on the hall light to see what we were doing." He held up his right foot. "I took someone's boots." He crouched down and pointed to a barely visible, very similar pair shoved far back under the bottom shelf. "Those are mine."

Fergus sat on the same step Camille had occupied and started to unlace the boots he was wearing. "I can't believe I did that. Oh, the others. I'll never hear the end of it. In fact, Neil has probably already uploaded a photo on Instagram of me running back here. Andy, are they yours? Here man." Fergus was embarrassed but Andy was so relieved there was no way he could stay angry. He held out his hand and the two men exchanged a forceful handshake. Fergus looked relieved. "I feel like I owe you a gargle!" At our startled looks, he grinned. "A beer, a gargle is a beer."

"There's no need. Thanks for coming back. How far down the road did you get?"

Fergus looked shamefaced. "About two kilometres. I kept thinking my feet didn't feel quite right, but you know, I'd had a bit too much to drink last night and I thought maybe I was feeling the kilometres we'd walked the last few days. It was Brigit who asked me why I was limping. When I told her my feet hurt, she looked at my boots and called me a knobhead because we could both see they weren't mine. The others are waiting on the road."

Andy laughed. Fergus quickly put his own boots on. "I'm off then. Best of luck." He left as speedily as he had arrived.

Now it was Andy's turn to look sheepish. "Sorry, I went immediately to the worst-case scenario. I should know better. This is the Camino. The Camino provides. I could use a *café con leche*!"

Camille didn't think there was a café open, but we were so glad to see Andy back to his usual cheery self that if he wanted strong coffee with hot frothed milk, we would help him find it.

Unfortunately, nothing was open until we'd walked for two hours to Viana which, with its population of 3,500, was a bustling city after tiny Sansol. We paused in front of the Iglesia de Santa Maria, the church where Cesare Borgia had once been buried outside the front door because the resident Bishop didn't like his family.

"His sister, Lucrezia Borgia, was a suspected poisoner," Jules said cheerfully, looking down at the nameplate inserted in the ground at the entrance to the church. "If any of you think your family is screwed up, the Borgias had real personality baggage!"

Bethany looked at Jules with new interest. "Do you have a screwed-up family?"

"Do I! Yours?"

"Don't get me started on my family. You should—"

A shout attracted our attention. We saw Fergus and his friends sitting at an outdoor café opposite the entrance to the church. Meara had been the first to spot Andy and had immediately waved wildly to attract his attention. They pulled up extra chairs to their table while Fergus retold the stolen boots story and the others added to the growing tale. Who knows what it would sound like by the time they got home to Dublin?

Fergus stood up, and after finding out what everyone wanted to drink, disappeared into the bar. By the time we said goodbye, we were all satiated with *potato tortillas,* sweet pastries, iced tea, and more laughter.

After Viana, the flat, sometimes tarmac, sometimes gravel track stretched out in another long vista. We were in vineyard country now and spent much of the day walking through or beside vines heavy with grapes that were not ready to harvest. That didn't stop Jules and Bethany from picking fruit before spitting them out.

There was no fear of missing the trail because someone had recently spray-painted bright yellow arrows on the road. We continued passing tall piles of stones precariously placed on top of Camino markers, and Jules was getting impatient with Bethany's continual stopping to set down a stone and do a short meditation. The next time Andy called a rest stop, Jules told Bethany it would great if she meditated less. "Can't you add a stone say, every ten kilometres?"

"I didn't realize I was holding you back," Bethany stammered. "You don't have to wait for me. I always catch up."

"That's not the point," Jules said. "We have to stick together, right, Camille? Andy?" Andy and Camille didn't hear her question. They had sat down under a Charlie Brown-like Christmas tree with spindly branches that barely offered any shade and were busy discussing the trail ahead. Jules turned to Gaby. "What about you? You never talk! Have you got an opinion about this?"

"I'm fine with whatever Bethany wants to do," Gaby said, lying stretched out on the ground with her eyes closed.

Jules shook her head. "You're boring, you know that?" She turned back to Bethany. "And you, you're always doing the right thing. Don't you ever want to scream at someone? Or kick something?"

Bethany looked closer to crying than screaming. Gaby stood up, looming over us. Jules shook her head in frustration, muttered "Little Miss Perfect," picked up her pack, and walked further down the path until she found a shady tree to lean against.

Little Miss Perfect. That was an expression I'd heard Grams use to describe one of her Bridge-playing partners. It hadn't been a compliment. Apparently in Bridge the good players had cut-throat directness.

"I won't do it as often, ok?" Bethany said. She took a drink from her water bottle and a bite of her granola bar. "But I'm not stopping! I will keep putting stones on crosses and markers and meditating!"

Later, the gravel path began a steep decline and for the first time, Gaby strode ahead and silently offered help to any of us who needed it. Camille, Bethany, and I were happy to clutch onto her strong hand as we picked our way down a tricky, single lane, rocky trail. "This is a damn goat path!" I muttered after stopping myself from sliding for the third time.

We passed olive trees whose leaves glistened when they moved gently in the wind. It became a day of steep winding gravel trails alternating with long, dry stretches, and then scary moments walking along the highway as we got closer to the next city. We'd learned to watch for church steeples, which were usually the first sign of a town up ahead. Logrono was no different. Many of the houses we passed had beautiful gardens filled with luscious bushes covered in red, yellow, blue, and gold flowers. Flowerpots filled with red geraniums were everywhere. I guess in this perpetually sunny, hot country, it's easy to have a beautiful garden.

A middle-aged woman, wearing the standard sleeveless and flower-patterned apron that many older European women seemed to wear, was waiting patiently behind a cloth-covered table under the shade of a large umbrella. Her stand was right on the Camino trail into Logrono. Andy and Camille exchanged a happy grin. Apparently, an elderly woman named Felisa had stood in this very spot for years, stamping *peregrinos*—pilgrims—*credentials* and selling drinks and Camino postcards and bookmarks.

"When she died—" Andy began another story as we took a short break sitting on the benches provided by Felisa's family.

"She was 93 years old," Camille added.

"—at 93 years old, her niece, also named Felisa, took over."

Camille looked thoughtful and pulled out her guidebook, flipping quickly to a page and holding it out to Andy. "Mine says this Felisa is her daughter." She stood, planning on asking the woman what her relationship to the original Felisa was when a group of five excited Japanese hikers appeared and surrounded the table, hiding the older woman from view. Shrugging, Camille pulled on her backpack and started to do up the waist strap. "Time to go. Logrono calls."

Hiking in the country meant walking for hours in dry, dusty valleys and staying in small, silent villages at night.

As we approached one of the few large cities on the Camino, I found the busy streets and tall apartment and office buildings too big and loud. It always took a while to get used to people walking by without a glance, occupied with their own business, or to know the lounging teenagers in a café were laughing at us. Adjustment time was required to adapt to sidewalks crowded with people we were forced to walk around. Our silent pilgrim's world was suddenly filled with the smell of pizza and the sound of pounding construction work sites. My senses always felt bombarded.

We entered Logrono after passing a graveyard, then rambled across a long stone bridge over the Ebro River. We had a pleasant surprise when we found out the huge municipal albergue, with space for 88 people, was not too far away but, like many of the Camino hostels, it wouldn't open until 3:30 pm. We joined the already long line of patient hikers standing or squatting against the outside wall. A pilgrim told us this albergue had a kitchen along with internet access and a phone.

Sitting among the laughing, chatty hikers, I rubbed my aching legs. Unexpectedly, I craved hearing my parents' voices. I'd been doing fine, not missing them at all. What had triggered this homesickness?

Forget it. Let Andy and Camille call them. It was their fault I'd been branded a juvenile delinquent, a young offender, a hooligan.

After all, Bethany's brother felt her mother was better off without her. What if mine felt that way too?

I wasn't oblivious to my role in the way things had turned out, but my mother was still to blame for me missing a trip to Hawaii.

After we claimed our bunkbeds, did our laundry, and ha a shower, I happily wandered the streets on my own. Bethany and Gaby had invited me to join them as they set off to explore the city, but I felt desperate for time alone. I guess my hesitation wasn't very subtle.

Bethany had given me a sweet smile and said, "No problem. Maybe we'll run in to each other. It's not that big a city, right?" Only someone originally from Toronto, with a population of 2.6 million, would consider a 150,000-person city "not that big."

Logrono turned out to be a city filled with parks and gardens and lots of cool artwork and life-sized statues. Artists were respected here. The city was an interesting mixture of old and new and I liked how the ancient churches and cobbled streets blended with modern magazine stores and outdoor cafes.

I headed for the main square, the Plaza del Mercado, which in most European cities was near, beside or in front of the largest church or cathedral. The plaza fronted the tall twin Baroque towers of Santa Marie de la Redonda Cathedral. I knew they were Baroque because Andy had told us, along with the fascinating fact —*Not!*—there was a famous relic inside. Or maybe that was another Logrono church.

I just wanted to sit and people-watch and think. I had enough time to do that every day, footstep after footstep, but it was a different experience to daydream when you're surrounded by strangers and white noise made up of voices, children crying, cell phones ringing, and horns honking. I decided I loved city sounds. It was hard to believe that only two hours ago I'd been lamenting leaving the quiet countryside.

I found an uncomfortable bench near a shady tree and stretched out my tired legs, letting my eyes and mind wander for an hour. I thought about Tony and Ben, questioned why such unflattering baggy pants seemed to be fashionable in Spain, and wondered what Grams was doing. *Probably playing Bridge, no wait, I was going the wrong way.* Vancouver was nine hours behind, not ahead of Spain, which would make it breakfast time.

What will I do when all this fun ends? I didn't have a clue.

I set out to do more exploring and when I got tired, I sat down on some church steps, until the smell of urine got too unpleasant and I decided to return to the albergue. My feet were tired and sore, but I was wearing my comfortable Keen sandals and felt light without a backpack. I'd happily noticed yesterday how easy it had become to swing my pack up and onto my shoulders in the morning, and I often forgot about it during the day. Unless we were climbing a hill. I hoped I looked as healthy as I felt.

I'd lost weight too, or maybe my muscles had tightened up. *My mother will be pleased.*

I started to walk across a bridge and saw a group of older women hikers coming toward me from the other side. Several of them were talking at the same time and I could easily hear their loud voices over the passing cars and trucks. I stopped, amazed.

The woman now passing by and laughing so hard she was almost doubling over was the same elderly woman I'd met in the bathroom at Roncesvalles, the one walking the Camino for the second time in gratitude. She radiated happiness and vitality, and the fact she was here, at the same time and in the same town as me and my group, meant she was hiking just as fast and far as we were each day.

But there are hundreds of kilometres go to, lady. Let's see if you reach Santiago.

I arrived back at the albergue just before 6:30, the time Andy had suggested we meet up for dinner. This was Spain, after all. Most Spaniards don't even start thinking about dinner until 10 o'clock. It's a different story for pilgrims and hikers though. Rising early meant we went to bed early too.

Bethany was standing beside our assigned bunk beds holding a wooden walking stick reverently in her hands. She showed her prize to me, a huge smile on her face. "It's a Camino gift!" She ran her hand along the side of the pole, pausing to outline an etched scallop shell with her finger. "I met a Spanish teacher who was ending his Camino walk here, so he gave me his stick!"

The previous owner was obviously artistic, or someone he knew was. The handle was smooth and unmarked but the length of the pole was covered in hand-carved images of Camino arrows, scallop shells, the Tao cross, and an outline of a hiking boot. I was impressed and envious. My light-weight aluminium, store-bought poles suddenly seemed very plain, but I was happy for Bethany and gave her a hug.

Bethany leaned over and pulled my pole from under her bed. "Thank you! There were places I couldn't have gone up or down without this."

I hung the pole from the end of my bed, adding it to its twin.

Bethany leaned down and showed me her second big find. "Look, a *PEOPLE Magazine*! I met an American girl who didn't want it anymore." She hugged the magazine to her chest. "Gossip, Hollywood, fashion!" She reverently tucked the magazine under her pillow for reading later. "And guess who's here?"

"Hopefully not the religious fanatic from the hill outside Pamplona!" I answered.

Bethany shook her head. "Guess again."

I started to name people we'd met, but each one just got another head shake. "Guy with tendonitis? Jerk bar owner? Korean hospitalero? Italian woman with smelly feet?"

Bethany held up her hand. "Wait, I did meet her. She's in the other room. Gave me a big hug, like we were long, lost friends. I think she said to say, 'hello.'"

"That's the Camino way," I said. "Ok, let's see." I tried to think of other people we'd met over the past week. My stomach suddenly did a flip-flop. "Not—"

Bethany grinned. "I told him you'd be back at 6:30. He's having dinner with us."

Jules came into the dorm room. "Who's having dinner with us?"

"Ben," Bethany and I said at the same time.

"Jinx!" Bethany said, but I wasn't paying attention. I looked down at my stained prAna pants and dusty feet in my comfortable but unflattering, clunky-looking Keen sandals which showed off my abrupt ankle tan line. My nose was bright red and peeling. I looked at Bethany and my despair must have shown.

"Ben? Who's Ben?"

Bethany took control, ignoring Jules. She put her hands on her hips and surveyed me with a critical eye. "You will look good tonight! Come on. I've got the perfect shirt you can wear, to match your Grandmother's scarf too. The colour shows off your eyes. I'm going to make you look French cool."

I refused her offer of makeup. If Ben and I were going to meet up on this trip, he might as well get used to seeing me as I was day-to-day.

He was already sitting at our group table in the albergue kitchen when Bethany and I arrived. He stood up and gave me a hug. I was suddenly breathless. *Everyone hugged on the Camino, right?* Ben turned back to Gaby. The two of them were in the middle of an intense discussion about science fiction TV shows. Gaby liked science fiction? I was a sci-fi super-fan. How did I not know that about her? It turned out Gaby had even gone to a Comic-Con in San Diego.

"Let me guess." Ben looked thoughtfully at Gaby, at her size and serious expression. "You'd rather watch *Battlestar Galactica* reruns than a new episode of something on Space or the Syfy channel."

I sat down beside Gaby. It was as close to Ben as I could get.

"I'm a *Firefly* fan," I said.

Gaby looked at me with interest for the first time. "You like *Firefly*?" She gave me the first grin she'd ever directed my way.

And that's how we became friends, because of a space western. I guess that had been interest from Gaby when she'd asked if I spoke Klingon, not judgement. It's tough reading people sometimes.

It was a typical laughter-filled albergue meal with a variety of languages spoken all around us. One of our few group chores was to take turns working with Andy buying supplies and preparing our dinners. The menus were repetitious, with cheap and filling pasta meals, but we were always so hungry no one complained.

Tonight, it had been Jules' turn to be sous chef and help Andy. Dinner was spaghetti covered in three cans of tomatoes mixed with three cans each of tuna and peas. It was not a combination I'd eaten before this trip, but it had quickly become a favourite with all of us.

As usual after dinner, Jules caught us up on our finances. Andy had picked her to be the official finance person including being responsible for handing out each week's spending money to Bethany and Gaby. Camille gave me mine.

The first time Andy had given his three teens their weekly drink and food treat of $10 per day allowances, Jules had looked at the cash in her hand and begun sputtering. "This is it? You've got to be kidding. There's no way this is enough for seven days!"

"Thank the Canadian to European exchange rate," Andy said.

Jules complained so loudly for the next 30 minutes that Andy had finally stopped and announced that Jules was now in charge of handling their group's budget. The unexpected result was that Jules had become interested in exchange rates and always asked everyone she met from another country how their money compared to the Euro, or the American dollar.

"I need to take economic courses," she'd started to say. "This is a bank scam I want to learn more about."

A Spanish couple in their 30's entered the kitchen, each carrying an armload of *pan de barras*, a Spanish version of a baguette, which they shared with everyone in the room. They were on their honeymoon and buying bread to give away at albergue meals was a way of celebrating their good fortune at finding each other. They were also deeply religious and saw the breaking of bread together and with Camino friends as a sacred act.

Ben and I continued to talk around Gaby, leaning forward to share Camino stories and trying to outdo each other with a game of "I met the weirdest pilgrim." Ben was constantly being recognized by people coming into the kitchen. His back was slapped, or he'd get a hug and greetings that varied from, "Hey, man, I haven't seen you since…" to "*Bonjour, mon ami*," and "*Bueno verte*!" I was both jealous and proud of this guy I was attracted to. There was a question I needed to ask though. "I thought you were sleeping outside, to save money for fancy meals?"

Ben became quiet, shrugged, and said, "Some money came through for me. I've got enough now to eat in restaurants and sleep in albergues." His emotionless voice left me wondering what the story was behind this windfall. He didn't seem willing to say any more and I didn't press it. There was time. Or so I hoped.

"How far are you walking tomorrow?" I asked him.

This was one of four questions that pilgrims and walkers asked each other daily, along with: "Where did you start from? How far did you walk today? How far are you going on the Camino?"

"How far are *you* going tomorrow," he asked, instead of answering my question.

"It's a place that starts with N…Naja something."

"Najera?"

Andy had overheard our conversation and while reaching for another piece of bread to mop up the last of the spaghetti sauce, he nodded. "That's the place."

"Me too," Ben said. We looked at each other. "Nice scarf," he added.

The next morning, Ben was waiting for us in the kitchen, a large cup of Nescafe instant coffee in front of him.

I shuddered. "How can you, of all people, Mr. Wannabe Chef, drink that stuff?"

He gave me a morning smile that sent an electric flash down into my toes.

This was a definite complication. He'd go home. I'd go home. That would be it.

I liked mornings. At the start of each day I still had energy and my feet didn't hurt. This morning was no exception. The dark world of empty cobbled streets, haloed street lamps, and star- and moon-filled sky felt tinged with magic. We walked by parks where sprinklers wasted water on sun-burned, spindly grass. A calico cat, covered in scabs and its ribs showing, slunk by us and disappeared into the building shadows.

Passing through Alta Grajera, a lone, darkened farmhouse was visible in the middle of an empty field.

"This looks like the perfect location for a horror film," Jules said.

This would be one of our longest days so far, 31 kilometres. I was feeling pressure to appear strong and capable. I didn't want Ben to see me as a complainer, but I was worried. I'd discovered that 15 to 18 kilometres were easy to walk. After 20 kilometres, I was bagged. By 25, I was deep into grouchy and complaining mode. I crossed my fingers and sent out a plea to St. Jacques, the Dalai Lama, and Grams that I could make it through the day with only a bit of pain.

We stopped for a *café con leche* in Navarette, 13 kilometres from Logrono. Somewhere along the Camino we'd all become coffee drinkers. It felt very European. It was also one of the cheapest drinks and gave us an often-needed energy boost.

Ben and I started talking about our favourite films. It was amazing how many movies we'd seen in common. The only disagreement we had involved horror films, which I couldn't watch but which he loved. He and Jules started to act out scenes from different horror movies, leaving the rest of us gasping for breath we were laughing so hard.

The minute they ran out of movies to parody, Bethany took things in a new direction and started humming movie and TV series theme songs, insisting we all guess what they were. Even Gaby threw out occasional suggestions, and I was sure I heard her laugh aloud when Camille and Andy started imitating an over-dramatic rendition of Captain Kirk's famous words from the original *Star Trek*: "Space. The final frontier. These are the voyages of the Starship Enterprise." It turned out we all knew the words and walked down the trail saying them three times in a row. Jules started humming *The Simpsons*' theme music, and we all joined in.

By noon, we'd walked on gravel and tarmac paths through, across, and beside more vineyards than I'd ever seen in my life, the vines heavy with sour grapes.

"When are these grapes going to be eatable, or do I mean edible?" Bethany said, spitting out yet another sour fruit.

We passed little stone windowless huts, each with a tiny door barely tall enough to let anyone enter. They were scattered in the fields and along the roads. I thought they looked like something out of the *Grimm's Fairy Tales* book that Grams used to read to me. Andy said they stored grain and provided shelter for farmers and their livestock, "Though you're right," he said, peering inside one, "it would be a great troll house."

Najera turned out to be a small city tucked along a riverbank. It had been a long day and for the last two hours none of us had any extra energy to talk. Ben had kept up without any trouble, but he too looked exhausted. There was a flash of panic when we found out the albergue Andy had decided on last night was no longer operating. This was not the first time we'd found his two-year-old guidebook was out of date.

The next piece of bad news was that the municipal albergue was full, but the friendly *hospitalero* looked at the seven of us and said he had a friend who might help.

"Sit. Wait," he said, before disappearing down the road.

I needed to go to the bathroom. Bethany came with me into the municipal albergue and both of us couldn't get out fast enough. It was standing room only, in both the kitchen and the large, open sleeping area that was packed so tightly with bunk beds that people had to turn sideways to walk between the three rows of end-to-end bunks. Everything about the place, regardless of all the smiling, welcoming fellow walkers, felt claustrophobic, and not very clean.

"Maggie!" I was engulfed in a hug first from Liz, then Annie, my roommates in the Roncesvalles albergue. That seemed so long ago. They were enthusiastic about everything and kept talking over each other as they asked me questions about where I'd come from and how far was I walking each day? They were joining several Australian men for dinner and invited me and Bethany to come along, but I shook my head.

"It's great to see you, but we're still trying to figure out where we're going to sleep tonight."

Annie motioned toward the long rows of squished bunk beds. "I don't think you're missing anything by not staying here. Good luck! See you again, I hope."

"It's like we have good friends all along the Camino," Bethany said as we headed back to our waiting group.

Three French men and two Korean women had joined Andy and the others, as well as the newlywed Spanish couple who'd been giving out bread in Logrono. The Korean women were obviously mother and daughter. They'd recently stayed in an albergue with bedbugs and the daughter had an inflamed line of red bites from her forehead to her neck.

At the beginning of our trip, Camille had been adamant that

everyone spray the inside and outside of their backpacks with anti-bedbug spray. She insisted we do this once a week. She also insisted that no one put their backpacks on any bunk bed. Ever! It was the one non-negotiable rule she had given us.

"Bedbugs were a big issue in France when I first hiked the Camino," she'd told us the first night in Orisson. "No way will I let any of you go through what I saw other people experience." Her intensity was the same as Andy's had been when he later insisted none of us would suffer from tendonitis like the man we'd met resting his foot on a bag of ice.

The *hospitalero* came back and was now chatting with Andy. Andy could talk to anyone about anything. He was leaving a string of new friends behind him and his little journal was filling up with the contact email addresses and phone numbers they had given him. The Spanish *hospitalero* grinned and pointed toward town, away from the river we'd followed to get here. "No problem!" he said excitedly and began to lead us, like the Pied Piper of Hamlin, through winding streets until we came to a modern-looking apartment building. "My friend has bought a floor and made it into a hostel. He has just opened it. You are lucky!"

He shrugged apologetically, using a key that needed wiggling in the lock to open the front door. He explained there was only this one entrance key, and he had to give it back to his friend. One of us would always have to be in the rooms to answer the front door buzzer and let the others in.

"That's a problem that could require the United Nations," Ben whispered to me.

Once inside, we climbed the stairs to the second floor and stood in the doorway of the first of three sparsely furnished but shining-clean bedrooms.

None of us could believe what we saw. Every room held four bunk beds. We'd been told the cost was seven Euros, about $10 CN, and yet, even for that small sum, the owner had made up each bunk with clean sheets and also left a fresh towel folded neatly at the foot of each bed. Luxury beyond belief. There were also three very clean bathrooms on the same floor and each one had a bathtub. Albergues usually only ever have showers.

The second glitch, after the lack of a key, was that the new hostel didn't have a kitchen. This fact didn't bother Andy. "You've all earned a break after our long hike today. Ben, can you join us? I have discretionary funds and I'd say dinner out tonight is a darn good way to spend that money."

The newlyweds and the Frenchmen decided to come to the same restaurant. The Korean women didn't want dinner and the daughter, who spoke a little English, said she would let us in when we got back. "No late?" she asked. She had no need to worry. Hiking just over 30 kilometres had exhausted all of us.

It was fun to watch Camille as we walked through the town in search of a restaurant that could take such a large group so early in the evening. She had her iPhone out and was holding it up while we walked, searching for unsecured WiFi, or *WeeFee* as they called it in Spain. She wanted to check emails and send out "All is ok" messages. A lot of bars and cafes along the Camino had signs in their windows claiming they had WiFi, but she'd quickly learned that wasn't necessarily true.

"*Problema,*" the barmaid or owner would say, shrugging, not looking like they cared very much. Camille couldn't find any unsecured sites this evening. We'd seen her do this before and always had to stop and wait if she suddenly squatted on the sidewalk to take advantage of the available unlocked internet. She would quickly download emails and check the next day's weather.

The combination of our exhaustion and the noisy restaurant meant no-one had the energy to talk much. The *menu del dia,* the "menu of the day," was over-cooked and tasteless. Somehow Ben and I ended up at opposite ends of the long table. My feet ached so much I just wanted to get back to the albergue to take 600 mg of

Ibuprofen and stretch my legs out. I wasn't the only one at a low point. We were all in bed by 8:30.

"Wild life we're leading," Bethany said sleepily from the bunk above me. "You should have taken a bed near Ben in the other room. Then you could have talked more."

I didn't tell her I'd tried to arrange that, but the *hospitalero* had assigned beds and it seemed too obvious to say, "No!" when he started separating the men and women. The one exception he made was for the newlywed couple. He let them have an upper and lower bunk in the same room.

What a shitty day! I fell asleep thinking maybe things weren't meant to be between me and Ben.

Our long hike yesterday had left us tired today. We were quiet as we walked out of Najera in the dark, passing drunken teenage boys held up by their girlfriends. We had to climb a steep hill to get out of town, which irritated me. "I hate hills! I especially hate hills early in the morning!" I said to Bethany, who nodded in sympathy.

"To 'go over the hill' is slang for escape from prison," Gaby said from behind us. Her comment made me feel much better. Hills and prisons were connected; that made sense. I'd had an experience of both, if the interrogation room at the police station after my B&E could be considered a prison.

"I'm feeling over the hill today, you know, tired," Bethany said.

She seemed oblivious to the fact I wasn't in the mood for verbal games. I growled and focused on gingerly setting my sore feet down on the trail over and over again. I found it helped to pass the time by listing all the people in my life I'd love to throw off a hill. I finally started to feel better, leaving an invisible trail of bodies scattered on the trail behind me.

In fact, it felt so good I threw certain people off twice. *That would show them.*

14

GRAÑÓN GRATITUDE

We passed Azofra 90 minutes later and walked by vineyard after vineyard.

Stone crosses along the path kept Bethany busy. She hadn't stopped setting down stones but now her meditation moments were more like short prayers. I didn't think she should change her Taoist ritual just because of Jules' grumblings, but she had shrugged. "Compromise, Maggie," she said.

Little brown lizards darted out from under stones and scurried across the dirt path, sometimes running over our boots. The long, gravel road stretched out forever in front of us, with little shade and very few water fountains, drinkable or otherwise.

Ben was silent all morning. I began to worry I might have said something he took the wrong way last night. I felt sick. *It must be the heat.* When I asked about his tie-dyed scarf, which he was wearing today, he just shrugged.

"It's been in the family," was all he would say. He re-wrapped the scarf around his neck and picked up his walking pace, joining Jules and Gaby.

Camille slowed down to let me catch up with her. She was chatty, but I wasn't, and soon she also walked in silence.

We rested in Santo Domingo de la Calzada. It had excited Andy when we reached the town, explaining it was a famous stop on the Camino for two reasons. "First of all, it had this huge cathedral, built in 1232, which 'celebrates Saint Dominic, a monk who made roads and bridges to improve the safety and ease of pilgrims walking to the city of Santiago,'" he read from his guidebook.

"Another church?" Jules moaned.

There was also a famous Camino story involving a hanging and a rooster. "During the 14th century," Andy told us, "an 18-year-old German pilgrim passing through the village was falsely accused of theft and hung as a thief. His parents pleaded for his life before the local magistrate who told them there was as much chance of their son being released as the roasted rooster and hen in front of him coming to life. Both birds promptly squawked, jumped off his dinner table, and began to sing."

"How do roosters and hens sing?" Bethany asked.

Andy smiled at her but didn't stop telling his story. "The youth was cut down from the gallows and revived. To this day, a rooster and two hens are on display in cages." He wanted us all to see this, but when he went into the church and discovered there was an entrance fee, he was furious. It was only 3.5 Euros, $5 CN, but he said it wasn't the amount that mattered. "How many ways do they think they can make money off pilgrims and hikers on this thousand-year-old pilgrimage route?" he fumed.

It was surprising to find what made Andy mad. He was usually so calm about everything. "It's the principle of the thing," he said, standing outside the church entrance.

"I'd say the principle of the thing is that they keep hens in a cage in a church," Bethany said with disgust.

"They change the birds every three weeks," Camille read from her book. She showed us a photograph of the birds, barely visible behind heavy, ornate black iron bars.

"Good! But there's still no way I would give them any money!"

"You get mad at the weirdest things, Bethany," Jules said shaking her head, "and then take crap when you should get mad."

Bethany blushed and got busy retying her boot laces. Gaby looked at Jules in a way that made me nervous, but Jules just shrugged and turned away from both of them.

We ate a picnic lunch of shared baguettes, slices of sausage—none for Bethany—along with tomatoes, slivers of onion, and chunks of cheese, all while leaning against a stone wall and people-watching in the town plaza. Ben contributed a cantaloupe. He cut it up, and we slurped it back. No one worried about the juices dripping down their chin.

"I'm going to check this albergue out," Ben said suddenly, wiping his Swiss Army knife on the paper bag the cantaloupe had come in. "It's a Cistercian Monastery run by nuns. I hear it's a cool place."

No one said anything, but Bethany looked at me before quickly turning away when it was obvious I was as surprised by his announcement as everyone else.

When it was time to leave, Ben shook hands with everyone, including me. *He shook hands with me?* I wanted to weep. Camille gave him a goodbye hug. "Next time we meet, I'll buy a cake," she said.

"An interesting thing about the Santa Domingo de Calzada bridge," Andy said as we crossed over the Rio Oja on our way out of town, "is that it has—"

"Fifteen arches," I said, interrupting him. I'd counted each one, anything to take my mind off Ben.

Boys could be a real pain, on any continent.

The day turned overcast, which provided a break from the

burning sun. I hadn't used my nylon backpack rain cover yet; maybe I'd finally get to try it out. Rain would suit my mood.

Two hours and eight kilometres later, we passed another cemetery and entered the tiny village of Grañón.

How was this happening? We were walking like we'd been doing this forever.

The wind had picked up, making us glad to see the Grañón church steeple. Church steeples usually meant a village which meant a bar or café, which meant we could get a cold drink, refill our water bottles, and use the toilet. We'd hiked 30 kilometres again.

"Enough already with these long days, Andy," I told him. He nodded, as tired as the rest of us.

The sound of our boots and walking sticks echoed between the cement and stone buildings as we made our way toward the church, whose second floor was also the albergue.

We turned a corner and saw Kata and Kodek, the Polish couple we'd met so long ago in Roncesvalles, walking ahead of us. Andy called out their names, and it was like a family reunion. Kata and Kodek kissed everyone, once on each cheek. I wasn't sure if that was a Polish custom or if they had gotten into the Spanish spirit of things. I'd finally learned to kiss the right cheek first after messing it up every time on the first few days of our hike.

We walked up to the Grañón church together, passing through the trimmed, waist-high hedges that surrounded the church courtyard and entrance. Many people were sitting on the stone benches or stretched out on the grass. There was even an exhausted-looking German Shepherd dog wearing a dusty, red neck bandana.

"Who would bring their dog along on this trip? What about their poor paws?" Bethany said.

A man wearing a camouflage outfit and a similar red bandana around his neck came out of the building carrying a bowl of water. He squatted down in front of the dog, setting the bowl beside it.

The dog's tail thwacked the ground a few times, but it made no move to drink. Bethany immediately strode over to the animal's owner.

"Isn't it too hot and hard for a dog to walk on this rough Camino trail, with stones and burning hot tarmac on the soles of its feet?" she demanded.

The man stood up. He towered over her but didn't look like he'd taken offence at her comment. He nodded and spoke with a French accent. "You're right. But Bella and I only walk 10, rarely 15 kilometres a day. I have a small tent for her to sleep in. Most places won't let her come inside. You have a dog?"

Bethany sighed and shook her head. "Some day. Can I pet her?"

"Of course. She loves attention." On cue, Bella began thumping her tail against the grass. She rolled over on her side, exposing her belly when it was obvious Bethany was a potential tummy scratcher.

"Bethany," Camille called. "We've got to register."

"See you later," Bethany said, speaking to the dog. She gave the owner a quick smile too and followed us indoors.

We climbed a twisting stone stairway and on the second floor could see by the number of boots stacked along the wall that there were more people here than the hostel was supposed to hold.

"Shit," I said loudly. "I can't, just can't, walk anymore."

A stunningly beautiful Spanish woman, her long curly black hair framing a model-perfect face, came to greet them. "*Bienvenido*! Welcome!" Maria turned out to be one of three *hospitaleros* volunteering for two weeks. With our group of nine, there were now 60 people staying at the church albergue, even if the actual space was set up for 26.

"Father Luis never turns anyone away," Marie said, shrugging resignedly. We would have to sleep in the winter chapel though since there was no room left in the sleeping loft above the kitchen and dining area.

Sleep with or without mattresses? I wondered. There were so many people around it was hard to ask questions and not sound ungrateful. I figured I could make do with a floor to sleep on and a roof over my head. Or maybe there were pews?

Once our *credentials* were stamped, Maria explained the albergue rules: Mass was at 7, dinner at 8, meditation at 9, sleep at 10; mats were inside the winter chapel; there were separate showers for men and women; and wake-up time was not to be too early because it was important to be restful for yourself and others while walking the Camino. Breakfast was part of the deal too, which was a nice surprise since this was not something Spanish albergues usually provided. The fee was *donativo*, by donation.

"You only pay what you feel is right, when you leave." She pointed to an open wooden box that had something written in Spanish on it. "It means, 'Give what you can, take what you need,'" she said.

"You've got to be kidding," Jules said, shaking her head. "Do people actually pay or do more of them take?"

Shrugging again, Maria said, "Father Luis believes people will respect this sacred place and only take money if they seriously need it." She smiled, but her lips were tight, and all signs of sweetness were gone. "I love Father Luis, but I think maybe, some people take more than they need. They will find out God sees everything!"

It seems Maria wasn't as empathetic as Father Luis.

I looked at Jules. Andy was watching her too.

Maybe I wasn't the only one thinking there might be a connection behind the string of robberies taking place along the Camino and my light-fingered travelling companion. Albergues had reported more items stolen since Pamplona. I wondered if I would even know if things were missing from my bag. Probably not. I'd assume I left them behind in the last albergue. Jules had designer clothes, sunglasses, and equipment, but how would I know what was hers or if anything new had been added?

My suspicions were based both on my memory of her long-board purse grab and the way she often watched people, staring at something they were wearing or had set out on their bunk. Just yesterday morning, I'd noticed she was checking out the gear being sorted by the older man in the bunk beside hers. I'd thought she looked predator-like, on the hunt—but for what?

Jules wasn't an easy person to know. She had a nervous energy that sometimes resulted in her babbling non-stop for hours. Then, later in the same day, she'd be silent and morose. I wondered if she was bipolar or manic-depressive, not that I knew the difference. I'd become more attentive of my personal items after seeing how Jules watched others unpack and repack their bags.

The small, separate winter chapel was already crowded. Each member of our group grabbed one of the brown sleeping mats from the remaining pile in the chapel entranceway and claimed space together.

I loved this end of the day ritual: laying out my silk bed sheet, having a shower, and putting on clean clothes.

I quickly ran back into the main building and up the winding stairs to the women's shower where I bumped into the woman coming out of the shower stall wearing a clean t-shirt and pair of shorts. It was Irish Meara. Another squeal, hug, and it felt like old friends surrounded me. Meara and the other Irish hikers had arrived an hour earlier, in time to be allotted mats on the floor of the now packed loft.

"The shower's brutal," she said, her Irish accent adding an exotic sound to what I quickly saw was unpleasantly true information. The energy of this albergue community might be wonderful, but the shower was small, old, and the bathroom floor covered in water that had leaked out of the shower stall. Unlike most Camino showers, this one at least had a bench where I could leave my hairbrush and clothes.

Later, I was debating whether to stretch out on the sparse grass outside or on my sleeping mat when I saw Camille heading back up to the kitchen area. "Come on, let's go help. We can chop and chat," she called out.

The next few hours were a revelation. Maybe I was being flooded by good Camino energy. Or maybe it was running into people like Kata, Kodek, Meara, Neil, Fergus, and Brigit, and feeling how glad they were to see me and the others in my group.

Dinner was to be green salad, a potato and beef stew, a fruit-filled Sangria to drink, with a fruit salad for dessert. The kitchen was ridiculously small considering the number of people we had to prepare food for, but Maria and two other volunteers, plus one elderly German man who'd already walked the Camino three times, divided up vegetables, fruit, pots, and knives. I found myself surrounded by animated conversations in three different languages. Five minutes later, a Hungarian man appeared with his guitar, pulled up a chair, and began to play and sing for us.

"If he doesn't work as a musician and singer he should," Camille said. His much younger, red-haired wife sat nearby, her eyes closed, her body swaying in time to his songs. I was happier and more content than I'd ever been in my life. Riding on the back of Tony's motorcycle didn't compare with this feeling of camaraderie.

Eating the dinner was as much fun as preparing it had been. Other pilgrims had trickled in and were assigned duties: setting up tables, covering them with plastic table clothes, laying out cutlery, and filling jugs with Sangria. It quickly became obvious there were not enough chairs and benches so wooden boxes were upturned and anything that could be sat on was brought to the tables.

Father Luis, a short, bearded, and energetic priest wearing a long black robe tied at the waist with a white, knotted rope, appeared partway through the dining room set-up, quickly introduced himself, and began to help. He had been occupied earlier talking to a pilgrim who was struggling with a personal crisis.

Camille and Bethany were the only ones who went to 7 o'clock Mass. I wasn't sure if we would get in trouble for not going, but guilt-tripping was obviously not something that happened on Father Luis' watch. Dinner was served promptly at 8 pm, though getting everyone on a seat required people to sit shoulder to shoulder. One stick-thin and muscular cycling couple offered to share a chair, which suddenly fixed all the seating problems. After Father Luis said a prayer, the food was distributed with remarkable ease, large bowls of stew and salad passed down one long table and up the next.

I looked over and saw Gaby talking earnestly with Irish Fergus. It seemed Gaby did have social graces. She was just choosing not to use them with us, apparently. Jules and Bethany were in an animated discussion with Polish Kata, unable to believe the stories she was telling them about both the hardships and the positive experiences of growing up in a communist system in Poland. Brigit, Meara, and Camille were all leaning toward each other, their heads almost touching as they tried to carry on a private conversation.

A plump, dark-haired woman in her late 30s sat down next to me. It turned out Diona was a Romanian judge. It didn't sound like her work was very easy, but I'd never met a woman judge before, let alone one wearing black capris and a too-tight t-shirt with a picture of Paul McCartney on it.

The t-shirt made me think of my mother. *How would she have coped with this place*? Shaking off thoughts of home, I asked Diona what kind of cases she heard in court. Before she answered, she refilled my glass with Sangria. I had discovered I loved Sangria. I loved Grañón and all 65 people in this room: pilgrims, hikers, volunteers, and one sweet but possibly gullible priest. I leaned across to the older German man who had been helping to prepare dinner and caught the attention of the laughing woman sitting beside him. She was the same elderly British woman I'd met in the shower room at Roncesvalles and seen again walking across the bridge in Logrono.

"I get it," I told them both.

The German man leaned toward me, cupping his right ear. "*Bitte?*"

"I get it," I repeated. "I see why you have walked the Camino more than once."

He heard me this time. "*Ya, is sehr gut*. Many friends, much heart."

"Much heart, that's just what I say," the British woman said, nodding.

I knew what they both meant. This dinner felt the way I'd always wanted my family meals to be like, but they never were.

How different could things have been if my mother and I were not always so prickly around each other?

Afterwards, everyone helped clean up. People washed dishes, put away the chairs and boxes, and reset the tables for breakfast. Then it was 9 pm and time for "meditation." Who knew people meditated in a Catholic church? Along with most of the people in that church, I wasn't ready for this feeling of fellowship to end. All six of my group and many other pilgrims followed Father Luis upstairs to a candle-lit chapel.

There were enough ornate, high-backed, wooden seats for everyone. Father Luis set a restful tone. In the glow of the white candles, seeing Fergus grinning from across the room, and with Diona's shoulder touching mine, I never wanted tonight to end. After a short prayer and a song, Father Luis said this was the chance for people to share why they were walking the Camino. I felt my stomach tighten for the first time since I'd come through the church doors five hours earlier. I glanced over at Andy, but he was watching Bethany, who had shrunk back into her chair.

"No one is required to speak. You can say, 'pass,'" Father Luis said, and several people let out an audible sigh of relief. The pilgrims who wanted to share their Camino reasons spoke very personally. No one joked about taking a cheap holiday or needing to lose weight. One man pulled out a simple gold chain he wore around his neck, showing everyone the wedding ring dangling from it, and described the grief he felt for his recently deceased wife. A woman said she hated her job and needed to decide what to do about a promotion she had been offered. The man sitting next to Marie was walking to give thanks for his successful healing from cancer.

Not one person said they were there instead of going to jail.

When it was my turn, my head was ready to say, "Pass," but my mouth opened and "My mother and I fight all the time. I want it to stop," came out.

Camille looked as shocked as I felt. Did I really want it to stop? Sometimes it was fun winding Mom up, but I also had to admit it was exhausting. I hadn't been able to forget that hurt look on her face the morning Camille and I left for the airport.

Feeling embarrassed and nauseated, I waited in the semi-darkness for the next person to fill the silence.

"I hurt someone." Gaby's voice was loud in the small room. "I don't want to do that again."

Without thinking, I reached for her hand, and she entwined her fingers in mine. We stayed like that for the rest of the sharing.

Jules hoped the Camino would help her figure out what to do with her life.

Bethany was one of the few who shook her head and said nothing.

Camille said she was walking with her niece and loving their time together. I began to cry in the darkness. Gaby's fingers squeezed my hand.

When it was Andy's turn, he paused for so long I'd started to worry he would get emotional. Which, considering my tears, wasn't fair. "I'm looking for new ways to help people," he finally said.

Father Luis nodded. He had faith the Camino would provide everyone with what they needed.

Later, snuggled in my silk insert, wearing all my extra clothes because there were no cover blankets left and the chapel was unheated, I fell asleep wondering what Ben's reason would have been.

The next morning, we got lost.

Somewhere after Grañón we took a wrong turn, but two men coming from the opposite direction stopped to ask if we were looking for the Camino trial. We hadn't seen any yellow arrows on trees or stones for a while. The men looked at Andy's map and pointed to where we were. It turned out we had to do a two kilometre backtrack, which translated into 30 extra minutes of hiking in our day.

We spent much of the day walking beside a busy highway, our senses pounded by roaring trucks, and bombarded by the gusts of wind and the smell of gasoline. There were wheat fields on our left, but they just made me feel even more hemmed in.

A farmer driving a tracker waved at Bethany, and she waved back. "See?" she said, "there are friendly people everywhere in the world. Who would have guessed that?"

At that moment, a black, exhaust-spewing truck from Bulgaria roared past, spraying all of us with loose gravel from the edge of the road.

"And then there is everyone else," I said, my flagging goodwill disappearing completely as I rubbed a spot where a rock had ricocheted off my leg. I could feel my anger building, which gave me extra energy to stomp my way along the path for the next few kilometres.

In Belorado we saw white storks for the first time, the black tips on the huge bird's wings visible even when they were standing still on their large, five-foot-wide twig nests on the top of electric poles.

"Watch where you're kicking your soccer ball!" I yelled at some kids when their ball slammed into my knee.

"Football, Maggie, not soccer!" Jules immediately dumped her pack and joined in, displaying fancy footwork and even scoring a goal in the street net. "Played on my regional team," she said radiating happiness, the kids around her applauding, "Striker."

"Like Filippo Inzaghi," Bethany said.

"You know who Filippo Inzaghi is?" Jules asked in surprise.

"Right mid-field," Bethany replied, "and famous for my right foot kick. I've been on a soccer team since I was six."

Jules nodded, and they exchanged a high five. Bethany had definitely moved up in Jules' estimation.

That night we stayed in Villambistia in the municipal albergue, which consisted of seven bunk beds squished into one room on the second floor of the small, box-like village bar. We met more friendly people, including an American family and another Irish woman named Sinead whose father was walking with her for one week before she continued on her own. I still wasn't sociable. I'd felt bitchy all day and would have preferred a bottom bunk, so I could pretend I was in a cave and separate from the world.

It's like Grañón was the top of my Camino experience and today was the bottom.

It didn't help that two of the people staying in the albergue were the couple we'd seen fighting behind the haystack several days earlier. It turned out they weren't a couple. She (Swedish, smoker, helpless) had latched on to him (British, smoker, whipping boy desperate to get away). He just hadn't figured a way out yet.

We learned all this the next day from Jules, who'd chatted with the chain-smoking Brit while they watched the day's bull racing highlights on the bar television.

"The poor sucker sounds desperate but says he can't ditch her. I told him to put peddle to the metal and get the hell out of there."

"Want to bet he's still with her when we reach Santiago?" Gaby spoke up.

Jules shook her head. "Not a bet I'd take because you're probably right."

"Rescuers are the worse victims," Gaby said. That was the last we heard from her for the rest of the day.

But it left me wondering, *Is Gaby a rescuer or a victim?*

15

BURGOS BRIDGE

The next day was a killer.

We hiked up one long hill and down another, the wide paths reminding me of old British Columbia forest roads I'd explored with my parents. The most exciting part of our day was walking beside a field filled with cattle, but the cows weren't interested in trudging humans.

The animals made Bethany nervous. "You've got to remember, I'm from the city," she said, her voice shaky. She moved closer to Gaby, not leaving her side until after Juan de Ortega when we came to a wooden cross that directed us toward an area of pine and oak trees. She walked the rest of the day chatting with Jules about soccer.

We finally arrived in Atapuerca after 20 tedious minutes of a history lesson from Andy. "The 800,000-year-old remains of *Homo erectus* were found here!" Of course, Jules snickered. Andy ignored her. "This is the common ancestor for humans and Neanderthals. It's like, like finding the first human European! Did you know...," we met his pause with a collective groan, "that *Homo erectus* predates *Homo sapiens?*"

Camille was flicking through her guidebook. "Ah ha!" She pointed to one page in particular. "My book says one million years!"

Before Andy could respond, I stepped between them. "It's only a 200,000-year difference. Million smillion. Cool it, you two!" It made them laugh and took our minds off our aching feet and the approaching heavy grey clouds. By now my feet were throbbing, and I was accompanying each painful step with a curse directed at Tony for getting me into this. I tried to concentrate on first lifting my now heavy boots, plunking them down and lifting them up again, each step taking me closer to the end of our day's hike. I'd already discovered it was hard to stomp in anger when the soles of your feet were as painful as a toothache.

The first albergue we came to didn't have any empty beds. The second was close to the church and had space. It was also the most rustic of any we'd stayed in. The small kitchen area described in Andy's guidebook was closed, but we only found that out when Andy pointed at the bare counter. The wiry *hospitalero* shrugged.

"Because so much peoples, so much messes," he said, shaking his head angrily. The man had been welcoming up to this point, dismissing the buckets placed strategically on the floor with a casual flip of his hand. "Maybe rain, so maybe rain inside too." He was the only one who laughed.

Large Polish men wearing black shirts and pants had already claimed three of the bunk beds. I passed the youngest man who was sitting on the edge of his bunk reading. He looked up and offered us a cheery "*Witam*!"

"What did he say?" Bethany whispered to me. "Vitamin?"

"*Witam*!" I said. "It probably means 'howdy' in Polish." The young man had returned to his reading, his head again bent over the book on his lap.

"Pellegrino's menu. I take you. Later." The *hospitalero* disappeared out the front door as quickly as he had stepped inside.

"Pasta and tomato sauce for the next two nights," Andy warned. We'd been doing a good job of sticking to our budget, but unexpected restaurant meals like this always meant we had to eat cheap, homemade dinners for a day or two afterwards until we were back on financial track.

One of the Polish men looked at his watch, called out to the other two, and the three of them left after giving everyone a grave nod.

"Maybe they each have a date," Jules said grinning. It wasn't until Andy and Camille came back from exploring the nearby small church that the rest of us found out the men were Polish priests. The church attendees had been Andy, Camille, and a sullen village woman in charge of the church front door key. The three Polish priests had officiated at a short church service.

"It was nice," Camille said, "very peaceful."

"Peaceful because it was empty and in Polish and neither of us knew what was being said," Andy added.

"You napped," Camille told him, laughing.

At dinner that night, we learned that one priest spoke passable English. He made it his job to entertain the long communal table of pilgrims and hikers, only pausing occasionally to check in about a joke detail with his travelling companions. All the jokes were about priests, and not all were funny, but his enjoyment in entertaining all of us was so infectious that it made everyone feel like laughing, regardless.

A scowling Spanish woman from the other albergue sat at the end of the long restaurant table glowering at everyone and complaining in a loud voice to the restaurant owner about having to eat with people who didn't speak Spanish. I could understand her frustration. Her lack of English and Polish meant she was being left out of the conversation, but she didn't try to join in, just glared at us throughout the meal.

It was raining when we ran back to the albergue, and it didn't take long for all of us to brush our teeth and burrow inside our silk liners or sleeping bags. The light coming from the single dangling light bulb was so weak it barely provided enough brightness for us to miss the buckets that were filling up with water.

All night long we heard the constant plunking of dripping water. I think one priest must have gotten up and emptied the buckets because they were only half-full when we woke up the next morning.

At least the rain had stopped, and the ground didn't look too muddy.

My feet were still sore, but what could I do about it? I felt very brave when I was pulling on my boots. I'd noticed Gaby grimacing occasionally, especially when we had to walk on stony paths, the uneven rocks jutting into the soles of everyone's feet, but she never said a word of complaint. If it had been anyone else, I'd have asked how she or he was doing, but Gaby didn't invite friendly reaching out. I wondered if "curiosity" might be a dangerous word in her world?

Maybe I should see if Bethany knew how she was doing?

The walk out of Atapuerca took us along another rough stone path that made my feet ache more. At the top of a hill, we passed a tall wooden cross just before walking beside a barbed wire fence separating us from a military area. Next came a spiral-shaped labyrinth with a stone-lined path winding around into a centre circle and then winding out again.

Bethany immediately took off her pack and began to walk slowly toward the centre on the labyrinth path. Jules swore, then plunked down her backpack and stretched out her long legs.

Gaby sat down too, using the unexpected break to pull off her boots and socks. I was standing close to her, staring off into the distance, thinking about Ben, but when I looked down, the state of Gaby's feet shocked me. How could she keep going? Her toes looked like they belonged to an Egyptian mummy they were so wrapped up with bandages and first aid tape. Several toenails were still visible, but they had turned black and would probably fall off soon.

Ignoring my plan to check out the labyrinth, I sat beside Gaby. "Gaby, sometimes being tough and silent is ridiculous. You should talk to Camille. She's good at healing." Gaby began shaking her head. Without thinking, I took one of her hands in mine. "You don't have to do this on your own, you know. Isn't that what Andy keeps saying? Let us help you."

It was one of the first times we'd looked at each other, eye to eye. I refused to let go of her hand or break eye contact. I could feel the resistance seep out of her.

"Ok," she said sounding defeated.

I jumped up and went over to Camille, who had joined Bethany and was making her way slowly around the labyrinth. "Camille?"

She shook herself, as though waking from a trance, "Yes?"

I nodded toward Gaby, who was using a stick to draw a mountain in the dirt, refusing to see if Camille would come.

She had barely finished her drawing before Camille was kneeling in front of her. She gently picked up Gaby's right foot and began to inspect it. "Being brave again, Gaby?" she asked but said it with a smile. Gaby shrugged. "You've done a good job of bandaging these blisters. Now, how about tonight you let me do it for you? I've got salve and Compeed. How much pain are you in?"

The teen shrugged again.

"I have Ibuprofen," I said, squatting beside Gaby.

Bethany was still lost in her labyrinth walk and unaware of what was going on.

"I don't take pills," Gaby said.

"Won't or can't?" Camille asked quietly.

What? The idea Gaby might have a drug problem had never entered my mind. She obviously worked out and didn't drink. She didn't seem the druggie type.

"Won't. Too much addiction shit in my family," she said, sharing a rare piece of family history.

Camille gently set down Gaby's foot and looked at her with such caring that I leaned back, refusing to give in to the tears that felt ready to spill out. *I loved this kind woman so much. How could I have been such a bitch to her?*

Gaby was still staring at Camille's compassionate face. She shrugged for the third time, "Ok."

That single word said everything we needed to know about how much pain she was in. I jumped up, readjusted Gram's blue scarf that had slipped when I took off my backpack, and in seconds was handing Gaby two pills from my easily accessible first aid kit. She gulped them down, refusing my offer of water.

Camille stayed close to her the rest of the day, not talking, not walking beside her, but always only a few feet away.

Burgos was getting closer. Andy had promised we could stay in a hotel for one night when we got to that city of 180,000 people.

"Just think," I said. "A city, which means stores and sale signs and make-up counters." I caught Jules staring at me. "I won't buy anything. You think I want to add any weight to my backpack? Still, I can window shop. Maybe I'll buy socks."

Andy and Camille exchanged a grin. Only a few weeks ago no one could have imagined me being getting excited about a new pair of socks.

"The Camino works its magic," Camille said softly.

Our wildlife adventures of the day belonged solely to Jules. When she tried to pet a large dog tied up to a tree, the dog started barking and went into attack mode. Jules backed away so quickly she fell on her butt, thankfully landing beyond the end of the dog's chain. Later, she had to make a second hasty retreat after climbing over a fence to "make friends" with a flock of white geese who took one look at this large creature and charged.

"Making up for not being able to run with the bulls in Pamplona?" I asked.

Jules laughed and tried to trip me.

I tried to settle into a walking meditation using the repetitious crunching sounds of my boots on the stone path, then later focused on the rhythmic clicking of my hiking poles touching the tarmac—anything to take my mind off my aching feet. My legs were sore, but they were nothing compared to the soles of my feet which felt more sensitive and painful today than yesterday.

If that was possible.

After seeing Gaby's feet, I didn't think I had the right to complain, so I kept to myself, hunching my shoulders and ignoring everyone.

We were all worn out by the time we reached Villafria, having walked long, flat stretches with no shade. Andy called a break and was soon in a whispered conversation with Camille. The rest of us sat on the edge of the trail, too tired even to eat a snack. Usually chatty Bethany was silent, fidgeting as she tried to find a more comfortable way for her backpack to rest on her sore shoulders.

"We're taking the bus into the city," Andy announced, his words resulting in shocked silence before quickly being followed by a chorus of "Yahoo!" and "No way!" and "Thank God!" Both guidebooks stressed how long and unpleasant the walk into Burgos could be, one book describing it as a "hard slog" through an industrial area. For the Spanish equivalent of .85 cents, a short bus ride would cut out almost two-and-a-half hours of walking.

Not only did Andy let us get three hotel rooms, but he and Camille also decided we needed a rest day. I wondered how much the state of Gaby's feet had played in that decision, but I was glad for the break too.

Once we'd settled into our rooms—Gaby and Jules in one, Bethany and I in another, and Andy and Camille in a third—we all had a shower or, luxuries of all luxuries, a bath. We met for dinner in what Jules considered a "working man's place," not bothering to hide her shudder as Andy and Gaby rolled several not very clean, stand-up barrel-tables closer together so we could eat and drink as a group. No one else cared. This packed place specialized in tapas on small plates that only cost one Euro each.

As soon as our food and drinks arrived, which we ate standing up using the small barrels as a table, Jules began kidding Andy and Camille about sharing a room but stopped after getting kicked on both shins by Bethany on one side and me the other.

"Joking," she muttered, but she stopped her teasing and went back to eating a Burgos favourite, *morcilla de Burgos*, a spicy blood and rice sausage dish.

Andy filled up the silence by talking about El Cid, a medieval hero whose tomb was inside the Cathedral, even suggesting we all go tomorrow. We met his enthusiastic comment, "It's the second largest Cathedral in Spain and I think you'll find it pretty cool," with barely polite silence.

"Like that will happen," Jules said.

"There's a Mary Magdalene painting by Giampietrino, a student of da Vinci's, somewhere in the Cathedral. Want to come, Maggie?" The viewing prospect excited Camille.

I shook my head. "I don't want to do any more walking. Is that ok?"

"Of course, it's ok. I wanted to make sure you knew you were welcome to join us." She looked around. "Anybody?"

The others got busy concentrating on the food in front of them.

She laughed. "Ok, I get it. How about we leave the day open for everyone and meet again for dinner tomorrow night?" Relieved nods met this suggestion.

Clearing his throat to get our attention, Andy leaned forward. "We'll take a rest day tomorrow because for the next seven days we are travelling through what's called the Meseta. It's like a desert—

flat, dry, and with long distances between villages. We must make sure we always have lots of water and some food with us, but it's also supposed to be one of the most beautiful stretches—"

Jules interrupted him. "Really, Andy? I heard one guy say most people take the bus and avoid it because it's so barren and isolated."

"That's true," Andy said. "But we're tough Canadians. There's this little place 26 kilometres from Burgos called San Bol. That's where I want us to stay the first night. It only has room for 12 people, so we'll have to leave early to make sure we get beds, but it sounds cool. It's got a swimming pool!"

Snorts of disbelief greeted that statement.

"We all know your idea of a swimming pool," I said, but like the others, I had a smile on my face at a shared memory of Fergus and his friends.

"Ok, the second thing is, it's almost the end of week two. Does anybody want to call parents, siblings? Friends?"

The table went silent again. Gaby spoke first, surprising all of us with her voice but not her answer. "I don't need to speak to anyone." She took a drink of her mineral water.

"Not me," Jules said. "I talked to my Mom last week. That'll do for a while."

Bethany nodded. "I'm with Gaby. I've decided," and she looked defiantly around at all of us, "I've decided this trip is for me. If you could let my mother know I'm ok, Andy, that's good enough for me."

Bethany's declaration made me think about my situation. Did I want to talk to my father? My mother? There was only one person I'd like to call. "Can I talk to my grandmother?" I asked.

"Sure," Andy said. "I've got my phone here. You can call her after we eat. We're nine hours ahead so it's 8 pm our time and that'll make it 11 am for her."

I felt a wave of happiness flood through me and ate my food quickly, impatiently wishing the others would eat faster.

Andy must have gotten fed up seeing me fidgeting because he reached into his pocket and handed me his cell phone. "I've programmed in everyone's home contact numbers. Margaret's number is in there too."

"I know it!" I said but gave him a smile of thanks and dashed out of the restaurant. I leaned against the outside stone walls while waiting for Grams to answer.

"Hello?"

Hearing my grandmother's voice, I broke into tears.

"Sweetie! Are you ok? What's wrong?"

Trying to calm myself, I gave a shaky laugh. "I'm fine. It's just so good to hear your voice. How are you?"

"It's Maggie! She's calling from Spain!" I felt a rush of love, hearing her voice. "Sorry, sweetie, it's my turn to host the Bridge Club. I'll go into the kitchen."

The next five minutes consisted of overlapping sentences, both of us talking over the other in our excitement at trying to catch-up on two weeks' worth of news. Grams told me the latest gossip about one of the Bridge club members who was dating a man in his late 60s. "He's ten years younger!" my grandmother whispered.

She started tossing out so many questions at once that I had to interrupt. "I have so much to tell you, Grams," I said, "and yes, there have been adventures, but I don't know if I can make you, or anyone who hasn't walked the Camino, understand. This hike is," I paused, "it's the hardest physical thing I've ever done. There are too many hours when all you do is think and think, until putting one sore foot in front of the other sore foot becomes like, like a reflex, because there's nothing else to do, and there's nothing around to distract you, just fields, and trees if you're lucky. Camille is amazing though. Andy and the others, yeah, I like them. We laugh and sing, and it's been pretty good so far. My feet hurt all the time, but everybody's feet ache, so I suck it up."

The relief in my grandmother's voice showed how worried she'd been. "Have you talked to your parents yet? I've heard from your mother after Camille's phone calls."

At the sound of my quick intake of breath, Grams paused. "Oh, maybe I shouldn't have told you?"

Why was I surprised? Of course Camille had been calling my parents regularly. They were paying for part of the trip. "It's ok. I hadn't thought about it, that's all. I sent you a postcard a few days ago, but I don't know when you'll get it."

"Honey, hearing your voice is the best gift I could have gotten today." Grams paused. "I'd like to tell your parents I heard from you. Is that all right?"

"Sure, no problem," I said and felt my stomach tighten. "And I will phone them," I added, "just, you know, it's been busy and stuff."

There was silence on the other end before Grams let out a sigh. "Your mother's been worried, not that anything's happened to you, but you are her daughter and she loves you."

"Yeah, right," I said, and then felt childish. Now it was my turn to be silent.

"Hold your horses, Caroline! Sorry, honey, I have impatient Bridge partners!" I could hear a murmur in the background followed by laughter.

"I have to go anyway, Grams. Say hi to Caroline and the others." I'd attended a lot of Bridge games when I was younger, playing in a corner of the room with my dolls or, as I got older, reading the new book Grams always bought me as "thanks" for coming with her. There were also plates of cakes, cookies, and tiny sandwiches to sweeten the invitation.

"All right, Maggie. Now you call anytime, day or night. I love you."

"I'm wearing your scarf, Grams."

"Good, and every time you put it on, you imagine me wrapping my arms around you and giving you a big hug. I'm so proud of you. Goodbye, sweetie."

With "goodbye" echoing in my ears, I turned off the cell phone and bumped into Gaby as she came out of the restaurant at the same time. The others followed.

"All ok?" Camille asked.

"Sure, Grams sounded fine." My response was abrupt. I'd just never thought about the content of those phone calls Andy and Camille were making. I suddenly felt exposed.

Just how much—and what—had Camille told my parents?

16

DONKEY TRUST

I spent the rest of the evening chatting with Bethany and Jules.

Gaby ignored us and lay on her bed with her eyes closed. She and Bethany seemed to have argued about something and were no longer BFFs. Camille and Andy had gone on from the restaurant to check on the route we follow when we left town. This had become a regular evening outing for them. We teens assumed it was more so they could have time alone rather than because they were concerned about the next day's path.

It was a luxury to have a 24-hour rest day. Staying in hotel rooms meant we could sleep in and leave our backpacks behind when we set out to find food and explore the city. Most albergues had a rule you had to be out of the building by 8 am and take all your gear with you.

Burgos was a beautiful city: tree-lined streets, a series of canals and rivers, and with another stunning gothic Cathedral topped with spiky, lacy-looking spires stretching up into the sky.

Looking at the ornate Cathedral exterior, I couldn't resist

taking a quick peek inside, but it worried me I'd run into Camille and have to talk to her, so I kept my visit short. The nave area was as beautiful as the outside, filled with multi-coloured stained glass windows and lavish artwork. I even saw El Cid's tomb set in the transept's floor area of the church.

I'd told Bethany my reason for exploring the city was to find a *farmacia*, a Spanish pharmacy, and get something to help my sore feet, but there was also the possibility I might run into Ben. I'd looked for him at each albergue and at cafes when we stopped for a break, and I'd been asking people on the trail if they knew him or had seen him recently. People immediately smiled at the mention of his name. "Ben? The guy with the coloured scarf? Wants to be a chef? Isn't he great? He should be at—" and the answers always changed as they named a village or town one, two, or three days ahead.

One woman shook her head. "I heard he'd left the Camino. It was a family thing."

My heart sank. I nodded and said, "Oh, too bad," but I didn't stop asking.

Flashing green neon crosses, the standard Spanish symbol of a *farmacia*, were common in the city and I found one close to the hotel. No one spoke English, but all I had to do was mime walking with my hiking poles and point to my feet, and all three women in white coats standing behind the counter said, "*Ah, peregrina*!"

I was quickly offered an array of creams, salves, and ten kinds of bandages, including Compeed. I bought a variety of foot care products and was happy to discover that Ibuprofen was the same in Spanish as it was in English.

On the way back to the hotel, I stopped to get a *tortilla de patatas* and three chocolate bars. I paused at the front door of an internet cafe and then stepped in, thinking I would do a quick check to see if Janie, or Tony, had sent an email. *So what if it was against the rules?* But I quickly stepped outside, having seen Jules hunched over a computer keyboard at the very back of the poorly lit room.

This would have been the perfect time to talk to her about the robbery, but I decided I was no longer interested. I'd had my private time in the Cathedral. She was welcome to hers. I returned to the hotel planning on spending the rest of the day reading, napping, and resting my aching feet. Bethany had gone window-shopping, and the room was mine for several hours. Time alone was more of a luxury than even access to a bathtub.

We were all quiet when we met for dinner that night. The extra day in Burgos had initially been welcomed, but although no one talked about it, we were restless and ready to get back on the trail.

Getting out of Burgos in the dark proved easy thanks to Andy and Camille having checked out the route. As the sun rose and the day got hotter and hotter, we walked near a highway and then on a high plain, passing fields of what Andy told us were wheat, barley, and oats.

It was after we passed through the village of Rabé de las Calzadas that a familiar photograph seen on numerous Santiago de Compostela book covers, posters, blogs, and Google images became real: a sandy path that stretched ahead as far as we could see, a tan-coloured ribbon in a treeless land.

An hour into our walk, we caught up with a slow-moving man and woman. The woman was talking to the man in Spanish and held a hiking pole in one hand and clasped the man's elbow in the other. They offered us the standard, "*Buen Camino*!" but were soon far behind us on the trail.

"He's blind!" Bethany's voice was hushed. "Imagine walking this in the dark?"

"That woman with him—maybe his wife or sister—was describing everything," Camille said. Her comment left the rest of us thoughtful for the next kilometre, each of us imagining what it would be like not to see the world around us.

"We should try it," Bethany said suddenly.

"Try what?" Jules asked.

"We each take turns, being blind and then becoming the guide."

"I think that's a great idea," Camille said.

Not everyone was as keen, but who could say no to Bethany when she was in one of her happy moods?

"Jeez, I had to do a trust game before at—" Jules went silent. She shrugged. "Let's get this over with!" For all her initial muttering, she quickly forgot her reluctance and took over organizing us into rock-paper-scissors teams to find out who would be a guide first. Andy and Camille gave each team a scarf or bandana to use as a blindfold.

I was partnered with Gaby. Although I was apprehensive when I had to be the first one "blind," it turned out to be an enjoyable experience. I ended up leaning into Gaby's hand on my elbow, trusting her to guide me safely over rocks. She'd quietly say, "There's a stone ahead," or "There's a little dip in the path," then continue with her softly spoken description of what she was seeing. She seemed positively chatty compared to her usual silent way in the world.

"You can feel the wind on your face. It reminds me of a sailing trip I did with this guy out of Coal Harbour." Her casual mention of one of the downtown exclusive Vancouver boating dock areas made me wonder again what else she'd done in her life. "We were in a hurry. It was a beautiful day, and the sky was this riveting blue. But about 45 minutes out of Vancouver, that blue got darker, like a storm, brooding. That's what this sky looks like. Oh, and the wheat field is swaying."

We heard Bethany yelling. She and Jules were partners, and it seemed to have turned into a battle as soon as she started leading Jules on the road.

"You deliberately let me stub my toe!" Jules yelled.

"You are such a controlling jerk. Let me lead!"

Gaby and I turned around. I was reaching up to rip off the bandana covering my eyes when Gaby turned me back on the road again.

"Andy stepped in. He took Jules with him, and Camille is now Bethany's partner."

"I wonder what's going on with the two of them?"

"I'd say you might get a new uncle when you get home," Gaby responded.

"That's not what I meant..." I let my comment die out. Gaby knew who I was referring to. How did I feel about Andy having a more permanent place in Camille's—and therefore my—life?

Ten minutes later Gaby and I switched roles. It took longer for Gaby to relax than I had taken with her, but soon she was letting me lead her while I described what I saw.

"We've got company up ahead," I said. A nasally "hee-haw, hee-haw" filled the air. A lone donkey in the nearby field had shoved his head as far over the fence as he could. "Each time he calls his top lip pulls back. His mouth is all teeth."

"There's an apple in there, can you get it for me?" Gaby motioned toward the top pocket in her pack. I got the apple and put it in Gaby's hand, then directed her arm toward the donkey's mouth. The donkey bit into the apple and lifted it off Gaby's hand, though Gaby said afterwards all she felt was a swipe of wet lips. We stood there, one of us watching, the other listening, as the donkey devoured the apple in one bite.

The others were getting further ahead, so I gently took hold of Gaby's arm and started to lead her on the trail again. I was aware of my hand resting on part of the long, puckered scar that ran from her elbow to her wrist and I shifted my fingers, thinking she might not like to be touched there. She seemed to sense my concern, and for the first time on our trip put her hand on mine.

"It's ok. My Dad did that. He got mad when he drank." We walked in silence. I thought about what she had said, forgetting I was supposed to be describing the world around us. It was only when she stumbled that I gave myself a little shake and looked more closely at the path ahead.

"There's a slight dip—"

"I hurt my father."

Our voices had overlapped. I looked at Gaby, but she was facing forward, her eyes still covered by Andy's bandana. "He went after my mom one too many times. I hit him and didn't stop."

"And here you are."

She sighed. "Here I am."

It seemed like the right time. With a slight break in my voice, I said: "I, I broke into Camille's store. All because I wanted to impress a guy, my best friend's older brother."

"Camille's store? But she's here with you!"

Shrugging, and then remembering she couldn't see me, I said, "Yeah, she's the one who suggested this."

Now it was Gaby's turn to put her hand on my arm. "Lucky you. She's amazing."

I nodded, feeling tears near the surface again. Camille was amazing. She could have reacted in so many ways.

Gaby put her hand under my elbow and gave it a little squeeze.

The trust exercise ended at the next break. After passing out oranges from a bag Andy pulled from his pack, he asked how the experience had been for everyone. There was an awkward silence. Although no one looked at Bethany and Jules, we were curious to know what had caused the fight. Bethany crossed her arms and stared down the road, shifting her body so her back was toward Jules, who scowled and sneered at the same time.

"It was fun," I said, uncomfortable with the silence. "Gaby was great. I felt," I paused while I searched for the right word, "safe."

Gaby looked down and used her boot to scrape at a small pile of dirt on the path, but she was smiling.

Bethany remained tight-lipped. "It was a stupid thing to do. I hated it!" She grabbed her pack, swung it onto her shoulders, and began trudging down the path..

Later in the afternoon, Camille slipped in beside me, catching me by surprise. "Are you mad at me?" she asked.

I debated echoing Bethany's silent treatment, but the question made me angry enough that I wanted Camille to know exactly what I thought of her. "Grams told me you've been phoning Mom regularly!"

"Yes, I have been. They're worried about you." Camille paused, watching me knock aside a branch in the path with my hiking pole, causing the dry piece of wood to sail through the air and smack against a tree trunk. "I'm sorry. I assumed you knew. We're with this group, but we're also separate, here under different expectations." She paused again. "What do you think we should do?"

I turned on Camille and had trouble catching my breath I was so furious. "You're like, like a snitch! Reporting to the warden! About me! I thought we were friends, but I get it now! You will pass on anything I do and say. I'm not telling you anything anymore. You made a choice. Well, so have I!"

Camille pulled me off the path and with a gentle push plunked me down onto the rough grass along the edge of the trail. She sat down too. My jaw ached I was clenching it so hard. The others continued walking passed us, aware something was going on, but also seeing it was better if they kept going.

"Look, I'm sorry. I never intended to do anything behind your back. I'd have happily told you what I said each time I called and what they wanted to know, but you made it very clear in the final goodbye at your house you wanted distance from your parents. Or at least from your mother. That hurt her very much, but she's respected your wishes and so have I."

Camille hadn't told me about the calls because she thought that was what I wanted?

I felt an explosion of accusations rising and forced myself to take a breath and calm down. Unfortunately, Camille's assumption made sense. I clenched my teeth again, hating to admit anything. "Just don't talk about me behind my back!"

"I won't. In fact, you're welcome to be in the room when I phone, but I'm going to keep calling every few days. I made that promise to my sister and I plan to keep it. You know, don't you, that if you had been phoning them, I wouldn't need to be the one keeping them in the loop?"

Shaking my head, I could only choke out, "I can't, not yet."

Camille stood and held out her hand. We stared at each other and then I allowed her to pull me up. At the same moment we went into each other's arm for a comforting, forgiving hug.

Why wasn't it this easy with my mother?

"I don't like it when we're not talking," Camille said. "Come on. Let's catch up."

I was quiet for the next hour, thinking about the things I could say and didn't want to say and that I wished my mother would say.

Dealing with adults can be a real pain.

Soon we came to a fork in the trail where three different Camino markers with yellow arrows all pointed to the right. Andy called another rest stop. We took off our boots and socks and ate our rustic Spanish bread and cheese lunch.

Bethany was finally feeling better and made an expansive motion with her arms at the brown, flat world around her. "Listen!" she said. We all went silent. "Can you hear that? I thought the desert was quiet."

"Cicadas," Andy said, "like crickets, but with bigger hind legs."

"I can hear birds too," I added.

"And the wind," Bethany said, raising her face to the sun and closing her eyes. I knew what she meant. My face felt warm and the skin tight from the sunburn that never turned into a tan, but also never got redder. My skin had never spent this much time outdoors.

I sat down and looked up at the sky. I felt tired, healthy, and happy. I hugged my knees, closed my eyes, and felt a wave of gratitude, almost like a prayer, wash over me.

"Maggie."

I opened my eyes and Bethany was standing in front of me. She showed me a garland of wildflowers she had woven together. I didn't feel it when she set it gently on my head. "Your crown, oh queen," she said laughing, "for being such a good friend." She touched my shoulder and went back to the others. I felt like crying. At least I had been a good friend to someone.

Camille stretched out her arm and ran her hand along the nearby grass stubble. "'Mid the silver rustling of wheat,'" she quoted. Seeing the puzzled faces around her, she explained, "Ezra Pound? 'The Alchemist'?"

"Wheat rustlers?" Jules asked.

For the rest of the day, we took turns calling out, "Camille, Camille! I hear wheat rustlers!" She would laugh and bow and accept our kidding with her usual good grace.

As we walked through Hornillos del Camino, there was an audible sigh of relief when Andy told us we only had five kilometres to go before we reached San Bol.

Hornillos was depressing. It was filled with abandoned, closed buildings, many of them showing "*Para Venta*" signs, which Andy didn't need to translate for us as "For Sale." There were no flowers in any windowsills, something we'd grown used to seeing in most of the towns we passed through. An elderly couple, bent over from years of hard work, sat on a bench in the sun and silently watched us go by.

"Creepy," Jules said. No one disagreed.

It only took us an hour to walk to San Bol. Our hiking speed was increasing. Gaby was always at the back of our straggling line, but I wasn't sure if that was because of her sore feet or her dislike of being part of a group. I'd seen Camille check in with her during their last break. Gaby continued to take off her boots but never her socks, so I hadn't been able to see if her feet were any better. Andy kept Gaby company during the last few kilometres as we walked down into the small valley of San Bol.

When Andy and Gaby finally arrived at the albergue, they found us sitting on the covered porch, backpacks and boots discarded. An Italian man who looked model handsome and his Camino-found blond German girlfriend offered their words of welcome: "*Benvenuto*!" and "*Guten tag*!"

"Good news, Andy," Camille called out. "There's space for all six of us!"

"How much further would we have had to walk, if there wasn't?" I asked, wiggling my toes and enjoying the feeling of the sun on my tired feet.

Camille tossed her guidebook to me. "Look it up." She was always trying to get us to be curious about where we were and where we were going, but so far only Jules had shown any interest in looking at the maps.

Bethany and I finally felt refreshed enough to stick our heads inside the basic stone building where we would be sleeping. It was dark, the only light coming from a few windows. The cool tile floors felt so good on our bare feet as we carried our packs into the small back room where we each claimed a bunk bed.

We spent the rest of the afternoon going back and forth to dip our weary feet in the freezing spring water that flowed through a pipe into a small "pool" that was too cold and too small to swim in.

Gaby and Andy went to sleep in the grass in the middle of the grove of trees that surrounded the albergue.

"An oasis, that's what this place is," Camille said to me as we sat at the porch table listening to Alessandro, the Italian man, play the guitar he had found leaning against the dining room wall. The *hospitaleros* arrived, a middle-aged, married couple from Romania who stamped our *credentials,* collected eleven Euros from each of us—five Euros for the bunk bed plus six Euros for the communal dinner, with wine included for the adults—and quickly and efficiently began to make the chicken paella main course.

As he played a sad tune, Alessandra nodded toward the spring-fed pool. "It is healing water. Will make your feet and heart better if they are not good."

I looked at Camille who was smiling and watching a sleeping Andy. Gaby sat up and stretched. She remained sitting and staring off into the nearby empty field. Camille got up and in minutes had convinced Gaby to soak her feet in the pool. The two of them sat on the edge of the pool. I saw Camille's face register shock when Gaby took off her sandals and socks and slowly eased her painful feet into the icy cold water. Camille started out softly speaking to Gaby, but soon she got louder in her frustration.

"You can't go on like that!" Camille's voice was audible on the porch, and everyone looked in her direction. Gaby didn't say anything, just shook her head and crossed her arms. Andy was now awake and watching them.

Camille stood up abruptly and left Gaby, going over to sit by Andy. They were quickly having an intense, whispered conversation. Neither of them looked over at Gaby, but everyone knew she was the object of their discussion.

We ate our communal dinner in the small, beehive-shaped dining room with its domed ceiling. Gaby was silent, but what was different about that? Alessandro, who sat beside her, tried to make conversation, but soon gave up and flirted with Camille, who laughed a lot but didn't seem to take anything he said seriously. Andy kept looking over in their direction and as soon as we finished dinner, he asked Camille if she wanted to go for a walk. She nodded, and they disappeared down the road.

The *hospitaleros* stayed long enough to clean up the dinner dishes before jumping into their little white Dacia car and driving toward a town on the other side of the hill.

When Camille and Andy returned, Camille went to the fridge and pulled out a circular, plain sponge cake and set it on the table. "Maggie, would you get Bethany? And the others?"

Everyone staying in the albergue was soon standing around, unsure what was going on. Andy had stuck in five used, partially melted candles that he'd found on a shelf. He lit them, and then the two of them turned to Bethany and began to sing: "Happy birthday to you, happy birthday to you, happy birthday, dear Bethany—"

Alessandro joined in the song, singing in Italian, "*Buon compleanno*," and Ingrid added to the international flavour with her German version, "*Alles gute zum geburtstag*," and the song ended in an off-key cacophony of languages and laughter.

Bethany was weeping. Camille hugged her close.

"Blow the candles out, or the cake's going to be covered in wax!" Jules said. They seem to have made up during the day, and any tension between them had disappeared hours ago. Gulping down tears, Bethany leaned down, closed her eyes, and blew. It took her two tries, but everyone clapped and cheered.

Andy handed Bethany a knife, and as she started to cut into the cake Jules suddenly said, "Don't forget, you can't let the knife touch the plate on the first cut." Bethany started to cut into the cake again when Jules added, "And make a wish!"

"Because," I chimed in, "we all know there isn't a difference between a wish, a prayer, and meditating, right?" Bethany shook her head at us and finally cut a piece without being interrupted.

Later, when we were all sitting outside on the porch watching the darkened sky, Ingrid pulled her phone out of her pocket and began to walk slowly around the front yard. "*Scheisse*!" She swore in such a multitude of languages that Jules and Alessandro applauded in admiration. "Vat?" she asked. She hadn't stopped moving around the yard though she was now waving her phone high up in the air. "Is no goddamn reception!" Alessandro tried to calm her down.

"Yikes, when she needs to talk to someone, she really needs to talk to someone!" Jules continued to watch the exchange between the now fighting couple. Alessandro's attempts to appease Ingrid had apparently backfired. They both stomped off in different directions.

Even though Alessandro wanted everyone to stay up late and sing on the porch, by 9 o'clock I wasn't the only one yawning.

"No *hospitaleros* or monks or nuns, so no curfew!" Alessandro repeated several times, but he couldn't convince anyone. Ingrid had gone to bed an hour ago and was lying in her bunk with her back to the others. I tiptoed passed her brooding body and settled into my upper bunk. I stretched out, giving a small sigh of appreciation for this silk sheet, this bed, and this place. Alessandro came into the sleeping area, looked over at Ingrid and moved his sleeping bag to one of the two empty bunks on the other side of the room.

"I've never had a birthday cake," Bethany whispered in the dark from her bunk below me. I put my hand down over the edge and Bethany reached up.

We held hands in silence, my mind full of memories of all the parties my mother had organized. The one family rule that caused annual mother and daughter fights had been that I could only have as many friends as my age. There had been one fight of mythic proportions when I turned ten but had 15 girls I wanted to invite to a birthday sleepover. My mother refused to change her mind. On the flip side, she never forgot my birthday or my favourite Neapolitan ice cream cake.

I must say something about that to her one day.

I could smell coffee when I woke up. Ingrid and Alessandro's beds were empty, but during the night someone else had come in and was buried in a sleeping bag in what had originally been Alessandro's bunk. Everyone was getting up as quietly as we could so as not to wake the late arrival, but the body in the sleeping bag stirred, stretched, and poked out his head.

No! It can't be!

17

MESETA SPAGHETTI

Some mornings were too good to be true.

"Ben!" I couldn't stop myself from standing beside his bunk and staring down at him with what I realized too late was probably a stupid grin. His slow smile gave me that familiar electric buzz.

"Hey, dude," Jules called out. "Good to see you. And now we get more cake!"

Camille laughed and continued packing the last of her gear into her pack. "You're right, I promised. We'll have to get a second cake." There was nothing left from last night's birthday treat.

The morning was a blur. After breakfast, we started on another 27-kilometre day aiming for Itera de la Vega.

He's here! He's here! The words rang in my head.

Bethany came over and gave me a big hug, whispering, "You go, girl!"

It was a glorious, magnificent day. The weather was perfect and the land around us wild and beautiful. I couldn't stop smiling. Ben made his way through the group, catching up on everyone's news and leaving them laughing before moving on to the next person, his multi-coloured scarf rippling in the breeze.

Bethany muttered to herself as she plodded along. She had a bothersome blister that wouldn't go away, though no new ones had appeared. I fell into step beside her. "This Meseta thing is boring," she moaned. "No wonder people take buses to avoid the dust and heat!" Before I could respond, Ben joined us. Bethany stopped and bent down. "You two go ahead, I need to fix my shoelace," she said, giving me a wink.

I felt a rush of appreciation for Bethany's tact, then panicked. What could I say?

"How are your feet?" Ben asked.

"No blisters."

He stood on one leg like a stork, fondly patting his left boot. "These babies are holding up. My feet hurt like hell by the end of the day but, and I must keep saying this gratefully, no blisters either."

"Unlike poor Bethany," I said, "and Gaby. She's having feet problems, though Gaby is like Clint Eastwood in those Italian western movies my Dad likes."

"Stoic?"

"Exactly!"

That was the end of our conversation. Even usually gregarious Ben was silent.

"*Buen Camino*!"

Two women on the path had been gaining on us. They turned out to be lawyer Marina and her girlfriend Elka that we had first met at Orisson on day one. We'd seen them at different times, but usually only exchanged a wave. It turned out Ben had walked with them on his travels, and the three of them hugged like old friends.

It was always a surprise to meet up with someone days after you'd met them, having missed each other on the trail, or not staying at the same albergue the next night, or maybe you had gone one town farther or stopped one town sooner for the night. Our two groups exchanged the standard "How far?" and "How are your feet?" questions and answers. Marina was an avid amateur historian, and it turned out they were taking rest days whenever they came into a city so they could visit the historical sites.

Ben joined Marina and Elka, who were faster walkers than we were, but he said he'd wait on the path after an hour until we caught up. I watched the three of them quickly disappear over the next ridge and fell into step with Bethany again. I mentally slapped myself for being tongue-tied earlier.

No blisters? What a stupid thing to say, you twit!

At least there was dinner to look forward to tonight and that would be my chance to find out where he had been. It seemed beyond coincidence Ben should have turned up at San Bol.

"It's a Camino thing," Bethany said to me, as though she could read my mind. "Miracles happen on this pilgrimage."

Maybe it was the openness, the sense of space and freedom all around on this flat, dry Meseta desert walk, but whatever the cause I felt light and joyful in a way I'd never experienced before. Knowing I'd see Ben's smiling face again that evening filled me with so much happiness I thought I'd burst.

Camille and Andy looked happy too. They often walked holding hands, and their affection for each other was so visible no one teased them anymore. "They don't get mushy," Jules had said last night with approval. "That would be too much—we'd have to talk to them." She didn't see why Bethany and I found that funny.

Hontanas came upon us unexpectedly. It was in a deep valley hidden from sight until we started walking down into it. Camille couldn't find a bakery, but in the small food store, she bought all the individually wrapped Magdalenas on the counter. She considered these little sponge cakes both a good luck sign and as helping her fulfill her promise to Ben. She had enough for everyone to eat two as we walked out of the village, passing a field of bright yellow sunflowers that stretched as far as we could see.

"*Helianthus annuus*," Jules said. Looking embarrassed, she added, "My mom's a gardener and sunflowers are her favourite flower." She did one of her silly routines and scrunched down, sticking her head up behind a tall yellow flower surrounded by other swaying bright yellow flowers. She demanded Camille take a picture, which my aunt did, promising to email the photo to her mother the next time we stopped somewhere with WiFi. Camille then insisted we all do the same. I wasn't keen, but she calmly waited for me to walk the short distance into the field and then face the camera. I gave in, scowling.

We met up with Ben 45 minutes later. He was waiting in front of the stone archway of Arco de San Antón, which had once been a thriving 12th-century monastery and hospital for pilgrims and lepers. The resident *hospitalero* ran a small information stand inside the hospital ruins and offered to stamp our *credentials*. We took a short break, eating bananas and drinking lots of water.

"I wonder what it was like to work here," Bethany said, running her hand along the scarred stone. "All those pilgrims, some even ill with leprosy. The air would've been filled with the smell of rotting flesh. Faces would be missing noses, stubs instead…."

"Stop!"

"Please, enough already!"

"Ok," Bethany said to me and Jules, "but you two don't have any imagination!"

We could soon see Castrojeriz, a village jumbled together at the base of a hill and looked down upon by the abandoned ruins of a castle, but it was the next hill that made my day. As we approached it, we could see a long dirt path inching up the side of the escarpment to what Andy called "Alto Mostelares," a high plateau we'd have to cross to get to the next valley.

Ben came up behind me and whispered in my ear, "Let's beat

the time Andy's book says it takes to get to the top. Want to?" Without waiting for an answer, Ben called out, "Can someone remind me how long it takes to hike up this hill?"

Andy didn't bother to check his guidebook. He only had to look at something once for it to be etched into his brain. "Thirty minutes," he said.

"Watch us!" Ben took my hand, and we started walking faster and faster. I ignored my sore feet and concentrated on his face, his laughter, and his hand in mine. Our conversation flowed back and forth as we ran.

When we reached the top, we were both breathing hard from the steep climb. Ben looked at his watch. "Thirteen minutes, Maggie! Less than half the time the book said. We're incredible!" He grabbed me around the waist, and although he couldn't quite swing me around because of the weight of my backpack, we did a little shuffle dance of celebration. My heart was pounding. It wasn't just from the strenuous climb.

Ben started walking again, and I immediately followed him, although I wished we could have sat on one of the wooden benches in the covered rest stop. In a short time, we neared the end of the plateau and stopped to stare down at the tarmac road leading into the valley. "Want to run?" he asked.

Knowing I would regret it later, I dashed ahead. I could feel my feet getting hot but, oh, it was like flying, freedom at its best. We arrived at the bottom of the hill breathing hard and plopped down on our packs to wait for the others.

Suddenly feeling shy again, we looked around, pretending interest in the flat fields on either side, both of us avoiding eye contact.

"So, any adventures since we last saw you?" I finally asked. I could see Andy and the others making their way down the hill and knew I only had a short time alone with Ben.

He shrugged. "Met a Swiss guy who'd retired on a Friday and

on Monday set out from his front door. He's been walking for four months. I had to deal with family stuff."

He slipped that last line in so quickly I wasn't sure what to say. I had questions, but Ben's focus on his stick told me now wasn't the time to ask. "I'm sorry," I said, "and I hope that doesn't mean you'll have to give up on the Camino and go home early?"

"No, I've dealt with it."

We sat in charged silence for the ten minutes it took the rest of the group to reach us. Jules immediately slapped Ben on the back.

"Wow! You're badass! I could use you on my soccer team!"

"Don't forget Maggie. She was beside me the whole way down."

In record time we passed the 26 kilometres mark and arrived in Itera de la Vega.

"Let's keep going," Jules suggested. Her suggestion was a surprise, not that she ever complained about how far we were going each day, but she was usually one of the first to grab a bunk and take a nap after our day's long walk.

Camille and Andy had a silent communication moment, looking at each other and somehow exchanging information. I bet they were thinking of Gaby and her feet.

"Let's check in with each other after a 20-minute break." Andy said. We all nodded, happy for a chance to eat, drink, and take off our socks and boots.

Jules looked across at Gaby, who was wearing hiking sandals, with socks. "I have to tell you, Gaby, I know it might be comfortable, but it looks uncool to wear socks in your sandals with your shorts. People will think your name is Ethel or Auntie Em."

There was a moment of charged silence as Bethany and I waited to see how Gaby would react.

Her only response was to shrug. "Yeah, you're probably right, but, you know, my feet are gross."

It was a huge admission from her. Jules put her arm around

Gaby's shoulders and said, "I get that. Nothing worse than ugly feet to scare away guys!"

Gaby didn't push Jules away, and she grinned, actually grinned.

After ten minutes, Andy casually got up and moved over beside Gaby. He leaned in and quietly asked Gaby something. Gaby shook her head. Everyone heard her answer: "Let's keep going."

Still looking unsure, Andy pulled out his guidebook and looked at us. "Are you all ok with going on?" He waited, but no one said anything. "There's no shame in admitting you've had it. The next albergue is two hours away."

"Shit!" Jules spoke louder than she'd intended. Everyone looked at her. "I don't mean I want to stay here. I said that because two more hours of walking will not be fun. My feet are sore, and they'll be sorer, but two hours means two hours closer to the end, right? Andy, please give me something to look forward to!"

"I have just the thing. Listen to this. The Boadilla del Camino albergue, Maison de Campagne, has 'delightful peaceful gardens and a swim—'." Before he could finish the word, we pelted him with socks and plastic water bottles. Laughing, he held up his book. "Honest, it says so right here."

We made the extra eight kilometres in less than two hours, walking down a gentle incline and passing brick and wooden pigeon lofts set on stilts. We were all exhausted by the time we arrived at Boadilla del Camino. Our first impressions of the tiny village were not encouraging: deserted streets, none of the windows had flower boxes, and there were no children playing in the village square in front of the church.

That quickly changed when we walked through the albergue courtyard entrance and stopped in stunned silence. We were facing an enclosed oasis: lush gardens and a lawn with potted bushes, overflowing stone flower boxes, large metal sculptures of pilgrims, and in front of us was a regular-sized swimming pool. We'd arrived later than usual, but luckily, there were available beds for all of us, including Ben. No sooner had we finished registering and getting our *credentials* stamped than a party of six cyclists arrived.

"No beds? No problem," their leader said. The mixed age and gender group began setting up their tents, taking over a large portion of the albergue lawn. No one seemed to mind. An oasis is an oasis, and after a long day on the pilgrim trail, everyone deserved a rest spot, though Jules thought the older men and women could have been more private about changing out of their biking shorts.

"Too many saggy bits," she said shuddering.

Bethany's toned and bikini-clad body attracted attention, as it always did. She was using the last hour of sunshine to sunbathe on the lawn. She had the same ankle tan line that all Camino walkers had, where our socks ended and our legs began. She'd told me she was going to get rid of that visual line. I felt proud of my ankle tan line. It announced to everyone we met I was walking day after day on the Camino.

I'd got a bunk beside Ben, but he'd gone quiet and distant from me again.

Maybe I didn't need to take it personally? Yeah, right. Of course I took it personally.

He'd been surrounded by five, mid-20's French hikers the minute we walked into the courtyard, and I overheard him telling Gaby and Jules that he'd walked with this group of engineering buddies for two days in-between Logrono and Burgos. He spent the rest of the evening hanging out with the Frenchmen who were loud, intent on partying, and trying hard to catch Bethany's attention. I imagined Ben was being pestered for information about her. Gaby and Jules sat beside Bethany, one on each side, in definite big sister mode.

It was my turn to help Andy with dinner. At 7:30 the two of us called the rest of our group to the table we'd claimed in a corner of the outside courtyard. We were all exhausted, hungry, and proud of ourselves having walked an impressive 34 kilometres, our longest day yet. Camille described the pasta, with its sauce of canned tomatoes, tuna, and lentils, along with cheese, baguettes, and slabs of sweet Spanish onion, followed by a selection of not so fresh-looking fruit for dessert, as "ambrosia, and so good it was fit for Greek gods."

"You've been hanging out with Andy too much," I said shaking my head. "Especially if you saw where we had to do our food shopping." I described the dingy store we had found that afternoon. "It was the front room of the guy's house, very dark, not very clean, and haunted-house creepy, but it's the only shop in this village. Andy told me only 150 people live here, so I guess we were lucky to find anything."

Gaby reached out and grabbed a bruised apple, taking a big bite out of it. Jules had paused when I was describing the dirty store, but her hunger had won out, and she had eaten everything on her plate.

I pretended to be asleep when Ben and Jules finally came to bed. I heard Jules whisper something and Ben try to suppress a laugh.

Ok, that was it. I'm done with men. I put my arm over my head and tried to block out their quiet voices.

I woke up in the middle of the night when Jules got up to go to the bathroom. She didn't bother to take her flashlight, and on her way back she tripped over a pack that was leaning haphazardly against the end of a nearby bunk bed. She stuffed everything back in that had fallen out, while muttering unkind comments to sleeping pack owner. When she slipped back into her bunk, she was breathing heavily.

"You ok?" I asked sleepily.

"Banged my damn sore foot against that asshole's bag," Jules whispered.

"I don't want this to end," Bethany said talking in her sleep. She snuggled down deeper into her silk sheet with a sigh of contentment.

It took me a while to fall back to sleep. *Did I want this trip to end? It looked like Ben was out of my life. As was Tony. Camille would be busy with Andy. Grams would die someday, and I would be alone.*

With those gloomy thoughts, I fell asleep at 5:45.

At 6 o'clock, the room lights came on, and people began to prepare for another Camino day. It was still dark when we left, and we had to use flashlights and headlamps to find the yellow Camino arrow markers. We'd been so tired last night that Camille and Andy hadn't done their usual exploration routine to ensure they knew the way out of the village.

As dawn light gave us more visibility, we saw the terrain was changing. By now, we were in our walking pace and passed several slower pilgrims who all wished us a "*Buen Camino*." One side of the path had vegetable plots and poplar trees, and after two kilometres the trail began following the Canal de Castilla. Flatter farmland surrounded us, but at least the larger town of Frómista was only six more kilometres. Andy said we could have our breakfast of *café con leche* and *tortilla de patatas* there. No one wanted to talk. We concentrated on walking, knowing this was another 27 kilometres day.

Bethany was the first to break the silence. "Listen!" she said stating the obvious. Darting birds had accompanied us for the last two kilometres filling the air with their singing. "I never grow tired of that." She looked healthier than she had only two weeks earlier. Her tanned face glowed. She was tiny and slim, but she had no trouble swinging her backpack on in the morning and after each rest break.

I walked beside Ben and Jules. I hadn't planned it, but suddenly we were three in a row on the trail. They gave me a welcoming smile but continued a soccer debate that had started at breakfast. I know nothing about soccer, so I ignored them both and told myself I was doing a walking meditation.

That didn't last long. Each step I took was accompanied by an imaginary kick to Jules' butt to get her to move on. Or maybe I could trip her. The three of us caught up with Andy and Camille, and thankfully, Camille had a question for Jules, who sped up and joined her.

I was ready, having decided I wasn't going to let yesterday's cold shoulder routine impact my time with Ben today. I'd come up with several potential topics: weather, food, music, and movies. There was also that no-fail Camino conversation starter: "How are your feet?"

We approached a lock at the end of the canal and watched a boat prepare to be lowered. "I always thought it would be fun to rent a houseboat and go down a canal, though I was thinking more of England," I said.

"Doesn't everybody who lives in Vancouver own a boat?"

"Some do. We don't. My mother doesn't like the ocean."

Silence.

"What's your favourite band?" I asked. That turned out to be the best question in my roster of possibilities. Ben was almost as passionate about music as he was about food and liked everyone from Bruno Mars, Drake, and the Beatles, to film composer Johann Johannsson. Bethany had been listening. "I like Katy Perry," she said, then blushed and walked faster, catching up to Camille.

Ben gave me one of those intense looks that resulted in an electric jolt. "And you?"

"I'm kind of all over the place too, but I like a French-Canadian singer, Owen Pallett. He plays a lot of instruments and uses the loop pedal, like Andrew Bird, you know, recording himself playing and then singing with the recorded instruments playing in the background. It's like, when I listen to him I close my eyes and I ache, and music is the air, and I am the music—" I stopped in embarrassment.

That was way more than I'd planned to say.

"I get it," Ben said, nodding. "I feel something like that when I'm alone in the kitchen, and I'm cooking, and the room is filled with the smells of whatever I'm making, and there's the sound of the sizzling frying pan, and I'm tasting spices and herbs and chopping vegetables, and it's all blending together." He paused. "It's when I'm happiest."

He waited for me to go first across the single-person wire-mesh bridge over the canal. We were now walking on the opposite side of the waterway, though the view hadn't changed. It was still flat, brown, and boring, but the silence gave me a window of opportunity to ask something personal. "Brothers? Sisters?"

It was as if a block of ice had suddenly dropped between us. "Sister." He paused. "She taught deaf children."

I wasn't ready to stop my digging. "You said you had family stuff you had to deal with? Did it involve your sister?"

He didn't answer my question directly. "She was so great." The "was" rang loudly in the air. I waited. When he finally answered, he spoke so quietly I wasn't sure at first if I'd heard correctly. "She died two years ago. Hit by a car, and the driver wasn't even drunk, just distracted when he tried to avoid a dog running across the street."

"I'm so sorry, Ben." I started to reach out and then pulled my hand away.

"She left me some money," he continued, "but I just got it. I needed to get away, or I would have killed the guy." He kicked a stone and sent it flying into the canal. "I'd started stalking him, after he got out of jail. Jail, shit. Twenty months is all he got. Jail is a joke!"

He went silent. I knew I should say something, but I was still thinking about what he'd said. *Jail wasn't a joke to me.*

He sighed. "She wouldn't have wanted that, so here I am. This week, it's been hard, knowing that two years ago she was alive."

"What was her name?"

Ben looked at me with appreciation. "Thank you. I haven't been able to talk to anyone about her and not being able to say her name...I didn't realize I'd miss that. Leia. It was Leia." He surprised me by laughing. "My parents were—are—huge *Star Wars* fans. My Dad is always saying, 'You had to be there to understand the impact of that movie.'"

"Don't tell me you're named after—"

"Yup, Ben Obi-Wan Kenobi. It gets weirder. My parents do cosplay, dress up in an embarrassing way for Comic Cons. I went to my first *Star Wars* convention in Los Angeles when I was seven. I was a storm trooper. Leia was Princess Leia." We were both laughing when we caught up with the others.

We stopped for a short rest and food break in Frómista, which Andy told us had been a very important town in the Middle Ages. "So what?" someone mumbled

Rather than leaving feeling refreshed, the rest stop made us aware of how exhausted we were after the last few days. The only energy came from Bethany. She yelled, "Shut up!" when Jules told us we had 20 kilometres to go before reaching our albergue for the night.

Once out of the town we were quickly on the *senda,* a wide, easy-walking, white gravel path that ran beside the highway. It also meant we were again bombarded by the noise and diesel fumes of the large trucks that roared past.

"I love this path!" I said several times. "No hills! Have I told you how I hate going up?" My burst of enthusiasm lasted until I had to go to the bathroom and realized that a lack of trees also meant there were no sheltered areas to go pee. Camille, Jules, and Bethany solved the problem by forming a protective semi-circle around me as I squatted, providing at least a small pocket of privacy while the others waited patiently ahead.

We stopped to get our pictures taken by a road sign that said, "Santiago 464 KM." We spied Carrión de Los Condes in the distance and our spirits rose, but the city never seemed to get closer. We were walking in a vast expanse of nothing: no trees, no houses, no animals, and only the occasional pilgrim and hiker visible on the trail behind us.

We finally reached Carrión de Los Condes at 1:30. After our tiring day yesterday, there was no talk of going any further. Tomorrow was another long walk, including an 18 kilometre stretch with no place to get water or provisions.

Andy insisted we use the afternoon to rest. A group of laughing, happy nuns ran our albergue. The dinner was a communal affair, all of us sitting at a long table overloaded with dishes contributed by everyone staying there: a selection of pastas, a bean soup, an omelette, a big bowl of boiled potatoes, five baguettes, several salads, and even a jar of pickles. It was an eclectic meal that included conversations in six different languages: Spanish, French, English, German, Korean, and Italian.

The next morning, we again left in darkness, wanting to arrive at our albergue destination before the damn afternoon heat sucked us dry.

"How many streetlights do you think we've walked under?" Bethany asked Gaby. Gaby just shrugged. She'd been silent for two days, and I'd seen Camille and Andy watching her, monitoring her pace and how she was holding her body. Camille had been checking everyone's feet each evening and taking care of any hotspots or blisters. Bethany was always at Gaby's side during this nightly ritual, and I was sure she wanted to reach out and take Gaby's hand in support, but Gaby was not someone who invited physical touch.

"Oh joy, another 25 kilometres day," I said as we walked

through scrub woods. "The first thing I'm doing when I get home is kiss my driver's license!"

Jules pointed out the single hiking boot dangling from a branch of a tree. We all had the same thought, though Bethany said it aloud: "Where is the other one? Maybe someone just had enough." It was as good a possibility as any. We had already passed several pairs of boots left on stone markers.

"How sad, to have come this far and not finish," she added.

We could see large white windmills turning in the distance again, a movement that gave electricity to who knows how many homes.

Bethany suddenly burst into tears. She had spied a butterfly resting on a rock. "It's so perfect," she sobbed, "the most beautiful thing ever!"

We crowded around to see what the fuss was about. It wasn't a colourful butterfly, though its plain brown wings were outlined with an uneven but dazzling white line. The butterfly's wings quivered. The rest of its body didn't move; it was resting in the sun and heat and one of the most peaceful creatures I'd ever seen.

"The Greeks say that butterflies are the souls of the dead," Andy told Bethany, offering her a piece of toilet paper to use as a tissue. At the sound of Bethany blowing her nose, the butterfly rose and fluttered through them, landing on Ben's scarf.

Jules started to say something until she saw Ben's face. He was silent, not moving a muscle, while tears streamed down his face.

Andy quietly got us walking again, giving Ben private time. I waited, then moved ahead slowly, wanting to stay but afraid I'd be intruding.

Ben caught up with us ten minutes later. Everything about him radiated calm and he looked at peace. He took my hand in his and walked beside me for the rest of the day without saying anything.

Yahoo butterflies.

18

KNIGHTS TEMPLAR DANCING

The others gave us privacy, though Jules kept looking back until Bethany swatted her on the arm and said something that made Jules flinch.

Ben still hadn't spoken when we stopped for our lunch break. I sat beside him, feeling a vibration flowing back and forth between us, something loose but powerful, like a repeating line of music.

He cut a pear in half and shared it with me. "Leia loved butterflies so much she had a tattoo of one on the back of her neck," he said quietly. He looked at me and this time the electric shock went back and forth between us both. "It was like she was right there, with me, saying hello. Or goodbye."

We stayed close for the rest of the day. Camille watched us but didn't say anything. At Ledigos, only three kilometres from Terradillos de Templarios where we planned to spend the night, the trail went through fields again. We'd been walking on a straight road for four hours, with little shade and no rest points along the way.

"This is the Via Aquitana," Andy read as our weary feet picked up dust that settled on the next person. "It's a 2,000-year-old

Roman Road!" His awe barely penetrated our tiredness. This stretch was mind numbing.

"Wow." Jules could have been counting buttons for all the enthusiasm in her voice.

We passed sheep that didn't bother to lift their heads from their grazing. The shepherd, a squat, silent man so still he could have been one of the statues we'd passed along the trail, didn't take his eyes off his animals. Three German Shepherd dogs sat at his feet, panting in the heat, with their bodies tense and poised to dash off the minute the man moved his arm and whistled a command.

"This is Knights Templar country," Andy said as we neared the next village. "They were soldier monks who ensured pilgrims along this stretch of the Camino were safe from bandits. They built pilgrim hospitals and hostels." He did a little dance in the dusty trail, embarrassing us even though we all laughed. "And what is our happy dance news?"

"We get to go out for dinner?" Bethany asked tentatively.

"We'll never have to eat that bland chocolate pudding ever again?" Jules said.

"Something even better!" Andy tried to do a leap in the air, but it was a clumsy air stumble because of the weight from his backpack. "This is the half-way point! We're *officially* half-way to Santiago!"

Bethany burst into tears for the second time that day. "*Only* half-way? We've still got, what, 400 kilometres to go?" Gaby patted her on the back while Camille tried to find a Kleenex.

We had a choice of two places to stay in this hamlet of 75 residents and Andy picked "Hostel Jacques de Molay," named after the last Grand Master of the Templars. It had a small, enclosed courtyard and although there were no pilgrim kitchen facilities, the pilgrim's meal turned out to be delicious and provided by a family who made sure hikers left the long communal table with a full stomach. Andy and Camille sat beside two British men who had started walking in Burgos. Steve was getting married, and this was his "last chance at freedom," he told us, his smile showing he didn't mean it. His best man, James, kept telling us Steve had forced him to come and he'd only agreed to walk for five days.

"Thank God!" James said, "I only have two days left on this hell trip!"

Ben and I stayed close but didn't say much.

Jules rolled her eyes and shook her head when she saw Bethany looking wistfully at us, the newly declared couple. "Who would have thought grumbling Maggie would be the one to meet up with someone on the Camino?" I heard her say.

Ben surprised me by leaning over and taking my hand. "Are you ever going to tell me why you're doing this hike?"

He'd asked the question I'd been dreading, and I suddenly felt short of breath.

"I get there are secrets here, sort of a mystery group thing that you all have going on, but Maggie, I'd like to know what's up with you." He let go of my hand when he felt me pull away.

We sat in silence. My head was spinning.

What should I say? Once I told him, he'd be gone in a flash. Like Tony.

I looked toward the kitchen and began to talk, directing my words toward the whitewashed door, afraid to see the disgust I imagined showing on Ben's face. I told him everything. "My mother and I fight all the time and my best friend's brother dared me to break into Camille's store and I got caught doing a break and enter with this guy, Tony, that I liked, and my parents gave me the choice to go to India or do this hike. Camille seems to have forgiven me, but I still need to clean things up with my mother and I'll understand if you don't want to be around me anymore, if you want to head off on your own—."

"Maggie!"

I couldn't look at him.

"You're better than that," he said. "You deserve better than that stupid dare. I've seen you mad. Sad. Laughing. Kind. Arrogant. You're a constant friend to Bethany in little ways, like waiting for her when she stops to set down another stone. You're protective of Camille. And you've never laughed at my scarf."

That made me look up. He was grinning.

"Another time I'll tell you my faults. We can compare notes but listen."

My stomach tightened. *What did he want now?*

"Let me punch that guy, Tony, if I ever see him. I know it's kind of a Neanderthal male reaction, but if not a punch then how about I give him a good kick?"

I felt like laughing and crying at the same time. "Maybe you could cook him something that would give him diarrhoea?"

"Done! I'm going to be a Michelin star chef one day. There's nothing wrong with making mistakes along the way and trying out questionable recipes! We all get what we deserve." He nodded toward the others scattered around the courtyard. "You deserve us."

I'm not sure about that.

He motioned toward the others. "And the rest of your group?"

I shook my head. "Not my stories to tell."

It was another dark morning start to our walk the next day, with more flat, barren terrain visible for 360 degrees. The streetlights were still on when we reached tiny Moratinos, though dawn wasn't far off.

"It's barren, bleak," acknowledged Camille an hour later, "but I can say whoever can't stand this Meseta desert stretch hasn't been in Saskatchewan!" This triggered a good-natured debate between Jules and Camille, as Jules' aunts and uncles were all prairie farmers.

We spent most of our day walking alongside the highway again, pausing in Sahagun to refill our water bottles and amble our way through a street market, buying food and checking out the stalls. There were scallop shells etched on lampposts and into the pavement, making it easy to find our way in and out of the town. We walked under a huge archway and crossed the languid Rio Cea on a Roman-built stone bridge. Soon we were walking on one of the driest stretches of land I'd ever seen.

"*Ultreia*!" Jules yelled out to the parched land. The word roughly translated as "onward" and was a pilgrim version of "hello," though I thought it was silly. Besides, there weren't any other hikers in view, and hardly any Camino markers, but who needed them? There was only this path to follow.

"How can anything survive here?" Bethany's face looked tight with tiredness and her sunburned nose a bright, unflattering red, but when she spied two soaring eagles high above us she was again content.

We walked for hours on land similar to the African Savannah or Australian outback, the reddish soil coating our boots and legs with a fine powder.

A final incline took us to the edge of the village of Calzadilla de los Hermanillos. It was another unimpressive hamlet and only two of the 200 people who lived there were outside to watch us arrive, two stooped, elderly women sitting on a shady bench set against a brick house. They wore what many elderly European housewives seemed to wear, neck- to knee-length flowered aprons. This place also had more dogs than we'd seen in days, a motley crew of skinny and furtive brown and black animals that wandered the streets, their growls unsettling even dog-friendly Bethany.

Andy had scribbled one blogger's impression of the local albergue in the margin of his guidebook. "It says, 'Nothing wrong with it,' not exactly an overly enthusiastic endorsement." He wasn't sure if the albergue cost was five Euros or *donativo*, by donation, though he always insisted we pay at least ten Euros per person.

"We are not freeloaders!" he said, in response to Jules' question of why we had to pay so much for a free place when two or three Euros would do it. "These *hospitaleros* donate their time, their energy, and their work cooking and cleaning, and we will at least offer financial support to them in return, even if it's paying a few more Euros than you think we should!" Andy rarely got angry, but Jules had gone too far.

They both said, "Sorry," at the same time, their spoken apology sounding like one word.

Gaby and Bethany stared in shock at Andy. He and Jules had moved on to talk about currency exchange rates and it seemed they had already forgotten their disagreement. I saw Bethany and Gaby turn to each other in silence. When Gaby raised her eyebrows, Bethany gave a barely perceivable nod, and I had an "ah ha" moment. Could it be that exchange between Andy and Jules was the first time Gaby and Bethany had heard an adult apologize to anyone, let alone a teenager?

I'd done more than my share of apologizing through the years, but I had to admit my parents also said, "Sorry," if they felt they'd over-reacted or misunderstood something I'd said or done. I'd never thought of an apology as an expression of respect before; it had always seemed to be about power. That final look on my mother's face before we left for the airport flashed in front of me.

I've got unfinished business, a mess to clean up when I get home.

Walking through the open albergue door, we saw the two Italian women we'd shared a room with in Pamplona. They were sitting on the benches that lined both sides of the long, plastic cloth-covered table and once again we got a big welcome with enough double kisses on each cheek to make anyone think we were blood relatives. Behind the small kitchen area were two rows of cubicles with two bunk beds in each little box room, like those in Roncesvalles.

My group immediately aimed for beds in cubicles away from

the Italian women. "Sure, they're nice," I told Ben, "but let someone else deal with their stinky feet."

Jürgen, the Austrian hiker, was the next to arrive. He was limping and told us what was obvious. "I have a new blister."

"I love these reunions," Bethany said happily.

Camille came back into the kitchen and handed Bethany a tube of anti-itch naturopathic ointment, "This will help," she said. Bethany and I had discovered our ankles were covered in itchy, red dots, which Camille thought could be spider bites or more likely, a heat rash.

In a multi-language conversation, we decided that each person staying there would contribute three Euros and share a communal meal. Andy and Camille said they'd do the cooking. Ben was initially shy, but he couldn't hold back when they began discussing possible menus that involved yet more pasta and canned tuna. "This is my world," he said, "let me make dinner." He collected money from everyone, and he and Andy went to see what they could find at the small village store.

They were back in 20 minutes loaded down with cans of tomatoes and white beans, along with a bag of dried green lentils, four loaves of bread, potatoes, onions, garlic, and two wilted heads of lettuce. As a surprise, Ben had persuaded the store owner to sell him a spicy chorizo sausage from his own private food supplies. Andy had also bought lunch and snack items for our walk tomorrow.

Chef Ben, along with sous-chef Andy, were soon busy working around each other in the minuscule kitchen that consisted of limited kitchen gear, a tiny sink, equally tiny counter space, and two, two-burner hotplates. The rest of us sat around the long table and watched them.

A sudden rapping noise on the open door was followed by the arrival of a boisterous Spanish man who swung two backpacks off his shoulders and plopped them on the floor. The Italian women jumped up from the table and expressed their appreciation with a caricature of expansive hand movements and loud voices. They both disappeared down the hallway, taking their packs into their cubicle.

"True pilgrims carry their own bags," Jules said dismissively. It was not the first time I'd been made aware of the Camino hierarchy. Some people had their bags driven from albergue to albergue, an action many hikers looked upon as both lazy and cheating. "I could understand it if it was because of a health or age reason, but they're not that old." She looked around at the others in the room and said, with pride, "We are true pilgrims!" Even Gaby nodded.

Bethany and I cut up the bread and found some flowers to set in a chipped glass jar to decorate the table. Forty-five minutes later, we were all waiting impatiently for the cooks to serve up their feast, our mouths salivating from the kitchen smells.

With a "*Bon appetit!*" Ben set a huge pot down on the centre of the table and began to ladle out a bean chorizo stew. It turned out he carried some spices he refused to be without on the Camino and had added "bits of this and that" to the meal. Whatever the magic ingredients were, it was one of the tastiest dinners we'd eaten.

A small, wizened man appeared in the albergue doorway just as Ben was filling up our soup bowls. It took only a little coaxing to get him to sit down and join us. It turned out he was French, retired, and had recently sold his restaurant in Paris. He had two bottles of red wine and a bag of cherries in his backpack which he promptly contributed to the dinner.

"Blessings on this meal!" Camille said, raising her glass in a toast to everyone at the table and then to Jacques, the late arrival. "I'm grateful we are all together, enjoying this food and each other's friendship."

"And wine!" Jules added, nodding to Jacques.

The dinner was a feast, and definitely a step up from our usual fair. Ben also presented us with a salad after we'd licked our plates and the stew pot clean, all of us using pieces of bread to mop up the last of the sauce in the pot. His salad dressing involved a lot of garlic, which helped make up for the wilted lettuce and shrivelled sliced carrot bits. The Italian women had contributed standard packaged chocolate puddings, but now we had cherries to dunk in the pudding. The albergue didn't have a coffee or tea pot so Andy scrubbed the large stew pot, filled it with water, and threw in a handful of Camille's tea bags.

I looked around at the laughing people who had shared this meal with me and listened to the conversations being translated into different languages, which allowed everyone to be in on the jokes and stories, and felt a weight settle on me. I began to wonder, *What if?*

What if I never know this kind of friendship again? What if this is as good as it gets, and I have to leave it all behind?

Jacques complimented Ben on his cooking. When he found out Ben was waiting to hear if he'd been accepted into a prestigious cooking school, he told one restaurant story after another, some funny, some not. Most of us went to bed as soon as the dishes were washed; only Ben and Jacques talked quietly for another hour.

I was exhausted and took two Ibuprofen to help my aching legs and sore feet, but my sleep was disrupted. The howling, barking dogs roaming the streets continually jarred me awake.

Jürgen's groaning in the bunk opposite woke me at 6 o'clock. He was sitting up and scratching. Even in the poorly lit cubicle, I could see a long row of inflamed red bites covered his face and neck. Ben was in the bunk above me, but he hadn't stirred. I jumped out of bed and quickly checked myself, feeling a wave of selfish relief at not finding any bites. Even the bites or rash on my ankles was less red and itchy thanks to Camille's cream.

"Bedbugs, I think it is bedbugs," Jürgen said, unable to hide the quavering in his voice. The only person I'd seen bitten was the

Korean daughter in Najera. Bedbugs had continued to be one of the few things Camille was fanatical about, going so far as to lift mattresses and sheets in every place we stayed, always checking for tiny blood blotches or dots of feces, sure signs bedbugs were present. She'd trained us too, and last night my bed hadn't shown any tell-tale signs when I'd checked it.

The albergue *hospitalero* didn't live on site but arrived when we were making a morning pot of tea. He looked at the long row of red welts on Jürgen's face, neck, and stomach and nodded. "*Si, chinche*." He was concerned, but not surprised. "So many people, here, there," he said, shrugging philosophically.

Everyone in the albergue was awake by then, but no one else had any bites, so it was either the bunk Jürgen had slept in or he'd picked them up at his last hostel. The *hospitalero* said he would phone later to see if anyone else at Jürgen's previous albergue had reported being bitten. There was an active exchange of bedbug information up and down the Camino among the albergues, convents, monasteries, B&Bs, and hotels. Andy offered to stay and help, but ex-restauranteur Jacques and the *hospitalero* said there was no need, they'd take care of Jürgen.

Before we left, Camille made us spray our backpacks—inside and out—with the anti-bedbug spray she had packed. Our group left quickly after that, both to get on the road before the day got too hot and because we were fed up with Jules' badgering us to get moving.

"I'm glad to leave there!" she said, walking faster than her normal early morning lagging pace.

"I bet it was like that in the Middle Ages when someone had leprosy. Everyone wanted to leave them behind," I said. I kept hearing Jürgen's quavering voice.

"So?" Jules was clear where her priorities lay. "It's not my problem."

Our day consisted of more of the same flat, dry Meseta, the

route so monotonous that I felt a thrill of excitement when I spied a long row of windmills and later a railway track in the distance. We'd seen a farmer on his tractor earlier working in his cornfield, turning over dry land and leaving behind unexpectedly rich-brown soil. There were a few blobs ahead of us on the trail we assumed were other pilgrims, and a blob or two behind us, but considering the thousands of hikers on the Camino every summer, they weren't any people near us all that day.

"It's like there's no one else left alive," I said.

"You've all got to see *The Last Days*," Jules said. "It's an incredible, kick ass movie. Andy, how do you say, 'the last days' in Spanish?"

"*Los ultimos dias*."

"*Los Ultimos Dias*. It's a Spanish apocalyptic movie, about a mysterious—"

"Of course, it's mysterious," I said, rolling my eyes.

He ignored my interruption. "—a mysterious epidemic that makes everyone afraid of open spaces because as soon as they go outside, they die and so the survivors have to live underground, and I've only seen the trailer on YouTube but wow, does it look good!"

"Maybe we'll see another train," Bethany said, not listening to Jules.

"Who cares about trains?" Jules said. "I wish I could sit in front of a big screen, and smell popcorn and taste 'buttery goodness.' How about the next time we come to a city we see a movie?"

"We can see movies back home," Bethany said.

Jules snorted. Bethany blushed.

"I like trains." Gaby and I both spoke at the same time.

"Jinx," I said, but she didn't smile back or give the word any attention. I guess she thought we were too old for that game.

"How about, whoever sees or hears a train first gets to have first dibs on their bunk bed of choice tonight?" I suggested. Bethany gave me a small smile of thanks.

Today was a hike of 27 kilometres and again had very few places on the trail to buy food and drinks. Andy had granola bars, a bag of dried fruit, and a selection of *bocadillos*—those traditional Spanish baguettes filled with things like chorizo sausage or a potato omelette—and let each of us decide which one we wanted.

There was no question for me. The omelette filling was my favourite. *Bocadillos* were quite plain by North American sandwich standards and never included things like butter, mayonnaise, or lettuce, but that also made them safe to eat after being shoved in a backpack for several hours. We all carried two water bottles. The full bottles meant a heavier pack but were necessary on the Meseta.

We'd chosen the *Via Romana* route, the old Roman Road, when we left Calzade del Coto yesterday because it mattered to Andy. The other option was to follow the *senda* which eventually led to a long stretch along the dreaded highway. This parallel rough road we were walking on gave us two days of relative quiet before we joined up with the highway again. It also meant we had to be much more self-sufficient.

Hoping to cheer us up, Andy read from his guidebook: "Listen. Brierley calls this the 'most perfect extant stretch of Roman Road left in Spain today.'"

"What does 'extant' mean?" Bethany asked.

"Boring, exhausting, mind-friggin'-numbing," Jules said.

"Gruelling, ghastly, arduous," I said. We gave each other a high five.

"It means 'in existence,'" Andy said, shaking his head at us. "This was the Roman Road that linked Bordeaux, France to the Spanish mines of Astorga."

"Look at me!" Jules called out, "Mine bound!" She did a dash down the road but stopped suddenly and began dancing on one foot while trying to hold her stubbed toe. It might be a straight Roman Road, but it wasn't an even surface and was made up of crushed and partially broken stones and rocks of all sizes. It was exhausting to walk on and was always potentially dangerous ankle-twisting territory.

"I hate the Romans!" Jules said swaying as she tried to balance and rub her injured toe through her hiking boot.

Andy gave up sharing his love of history, for that day anyway. After hours of walking and seeing two fast trains in the distance, which Bethany spotted first both times, Andy pointed to a slight rise of land on the horizon. "Mansilla de las Mulas!"

"Great! How much longer?" Bethany asked.

I could immediately see Andy regretted bringing up our destination. "Well, um, about eight kilometres."

Bethany's wail was expected. "Two more hours? Kill me, kill me now!"

I wanted to wail along with her.

At least we got to walk through valleys and pass two riverbeds. Yes, they were dry riverbeds, but they hinted that water had come through here at one time. Like the others, I'd already emptied one water bottle and was three-quarters through the other. This hot and dry section of the Camino sucked the liquids right out of our bodies.

When we walked through one of the four gates into the walled city of Mansilla de las Mulas, it reminded me of just how different and exotic this adventure was. *This beats going to Hawaii,* I thought, which reminded me I needed to buy a postcard for Janie, though I wasn't sure if it would mean anything to her. *I wonder if Janie ever thought about me?*

Andy darted into a *panaderia,* a bakery, and came out with several bags of churros, the long, sweet, Spanish version of a donut that we'd become addicted to eating. "It's not popcorn, Jules, but maybe it'll do as the next best thing."

We ate our churros while searching for a place to stay. The first albergue we came to was privately run and beds cost 15 Euros a night. "Too expensive," Andy said, and kept walking. He was looking for the albergue he'd heard about that was named after a garden. This search for a bed at the end of each day always seemed unnecessarily long. After crossing a busy street, he brought us to a front gate that opened into an enclosed courtyard already filled with lounging pilgrims, many that we'd met at previous hostels. When he heard the cost was only eight Euros per person, he quickly approached the registration desk.

"Ben!" Again my—maybe—boyfriend was recognized and welcomed by other hikers. He gave them all a friendly wave but followed Andy inside to register. It turned into a relatively uneventful night. We showered, dealt with blisters—Gaby said her feet were healing but she admitted she was now minus two toenails that had turned black and fallen off—then we did our laundry, caught up on the news of people we sat beside at dinner, and went to bed early. Jules had told several people about Jürgen's misadventure. Everyone seemed to have a bedbug story they'd heard or witnessed.

Only one person had been impacted personally, and she didn't want to talk about it. "Horrible! It was horrible, and for almost a week afterwards, some places wouldn't let me stay when they saw my bites."

By 8:30, I couldn't stop yawning and went upstairs to our room with Andy and Camille. Bethany, Jules, Gaby, and Ben didn't take much convincing either. Ben leaned in and gave me a long good-night hug, which left me floating through my bedtime routine. It was so hot we all stretched out on top of our silk sheets.

"Good night." Camille fell asleep facing Andy on the bunk across from her, a smile on both their faces. I felt happy for my aunt. Andy was nicer than that previous jerk.

"I haven't gone to bed at 8:30 since I was, like, two years old!

No one back home better find out about this or they'll never let me forget it," I said, yawning again. There were no barking dogs here, my spider bites or heat rash were still red but no longer itchy, and Ben was nearby. I too fell asleep with a smile on my face.

He hugged me in public. Dealing with guys was awesome sometimes.

19

TYMPANUM, SCHMYMPANUM

After leaving Mansilla de las Mulas, we crossed a pedestrian stone bridge over the Rio Esla.

We were once again on a path that paralleled the N-601 highway, which we would apparently follow all the way into León.

"I hate highways," I grumbled, "almost as much as I hate up."

This morning involved having to walk too close to cars and trucks. The stone bridge that stretched across the Rio Pormo and led us into Villiarente was impressive to look at initially. Unfortunately, things quickly got scary. The bridge started out with a sidewalk that deteriorated into a thin strip of pavement barely wide enough for a person with a backpack.

Jules swore with each step. She gave one uncaring driver the finger after he came so close the car's side mirror bumped her. "If I had a key, I'd have reached out and scratched your car!" she yelled at the driver.

Signs for the city of León were common now. "It's got a population of 130,000!" Jules said as she ate an apple and read from Camille's guidebook. She was getting restless again. All this time in barren lands and staying in hamlets, villages, and small towns were making her crave city excitement. "I'm so desperate for some action I'd be happy to go bowling!"

"There is a Spanish version, *petanque*," Andy said. "We could always ask to join a game the next time we pass one."

"Throwing little metal balls to see who can get close to a smaller wooden ball sitting on a bed of sand? No thanks. I was joking, you know."

"My Italian grandfather used to play bocce every weekend," Gaby said. "It's similar, but not as easy as it looks."

Bethany and I stared at Gaby then quickly looked away. Another piece of family information casually dropped into the conversation. That seemed to be the only way we were learning about each other. Considering the fact we spent 24/7 together, walking side by side during the day and hanging out in the evenings, I wondered why more sharing of personal stories hadn't taken place between us. Andy and Camille were the only ones who occasionally told a family story, usually funny, at their own expense.

Everyone else we met spilled their life history with the first step you took together or during dinner or while sharing a sink in the communal bathroom. Or hanging out laundry, like with Jürgen. I'd learned more personal details from Camino strangers than I knew about most of my friends back home. I'd heard Jules say, "TMI," to Henri, one of the Frenchmen at the Boadilla del Camino oasis several days ago. Sharing "too much information" happened a lot on this hike.

"Seems to be ok here to share a lot of stuff," I said to Camille.

"Perhaps they give themselves permission," Camille said.

"Ok, permission, to say anything, everything, to anybody. I don't like it."

"I don't mind hearing their stories," Bethany said, "but when they go silent and expect you to tell yours, that's what I hate."

"What do you say?" I'd had the same experience.

"It's easy," Jules said. "I ask them another question about something they've already told me and they're off again, giving me more information. Works every time."

"Speaking of." Bethany slipped one arm through mine and forced me to slow down, putting distance between ourselves and the others. "Any more news about your Ben's background?"

I blushed, partly because of Bethany's use of the word "your" and partly in embarrassment at my lack of information. It also worried me that I'd say something that wasn't mine to share.

"I don't know much. He's inherited a bit of money, and he's using it to travel. He's still waiting to hear if he got into that cooking school."

"I know that last bit. Come on, there must be more!" Bethany wouldn't let go of my arm and continued to look at me in wide-eyed innocence.

I just shrugged. Bethany patted my arm. "I don't believe you, but when you're ready—" Bethany let her sentence hang in the air as she strode ahead to meet Gaby.

Seeing Jules pick up speed and head toward Ben worried me. What was she planning? Should I warn Ben he might get attention from someone skilled at finding out who, what, when, where, and why? Or maybe she would make a play for him? She hadn't seem interested before. Ben was at the front of the group, laughing with Camille at something Andy had said. Even with his goofy scarf wrapped around his neck, he looked healthy and confident, and sexy.

I decided I didn't need to worry. Ben could take care of himself. Jules didn't stand a chance. *I hope.*

When we finally crossed the neon blue pedestrian bridge that led into León, all of us were ready for a shower and a cold drink. The city looked huge, spreading out in all directions. I ignored the distant hazy view of mountains, not wanting to think we might be heading in that direction tomorrow. I focused on my oh-so-standard aching feet but wasn't having any success in willing, wishing —*no, ordering*—them to stop hurting.

We soon saw the spires of the León Cathedral, which Andy told us were 1,100 years old and built in early Gothic architecture style, with 125 stained glass windows, and a clock and bell tower. It was one of the three most important Cathedrals along the Camino. We'd already seen the first in Burgos, and the third awaited us in Santiago.

"The Cathedral de Santa Maria is the fourth church built on this site over the ruins of Roman baths, and its stained-glass windows—." Andy was reading with enthusiasm and, as usual, everyone but Camille had stopped listening. But we couldn't help being impressed when we stood in front of the Cathedral staring up at the sculpture-lined towers and its impressive west facade with the crescent-shaped doorway framed by rows of religious sculptures.

Even usually silent Gaby spoke up. "Jeez!"

"That's called a tympanum," Andy said.

"Andy," I said, "I get how incredible this is, but I want to feel it. I won't remember anything you tell me about facts and dates, but I will remember how I felt."

He nodded. "Got it, but if you want to know specifics…." He waved his guidebook at us good-naturedly. We stopped laughing when we got a "shh!" from an elderly, one-legged man begging outside the Cathedral entrance.

We were a more subdued group when we left 40 minutes later, having spent part of our visit resting in the pews and people-watching tourists and other pilgrims. We got a nod from anyone who wore a backpack or had a hiker's ankle tan.

"It's like we're part of a top-secret society," Bethany whispered. "I like it! Maggie, did you see all the dead people buried here? There are even kings and queens!"

"I find it all gaudy," Jules said. Then he grinned. "Get it? Gaudi?" Her joke using the name of Spain's most famous architect fell flat. "Oh, you philistines!"

Andy held out his guidebook to Jules. "Check this out. *Bolea,* it's another version of Spanish bowling." He showed Jules a photo of several men standing around nine pointy, tall pins set out in three rows of three in a sandy area. "You get half a ball and have to knock them down. It's played in the Plaza San Marcos, not far away. We could go tonight."

Jules shook her head.

We registered at the Benedictine Nuns monastery and albergue. It was clean but sparse, cost five Euros, and had a 9:30 curfew.

"As if any of us would stay up late," I said. I was looking at Gaby, who had begun limping two hours out of León. Not that she would ever say anything about being in pain. While we waited in the main room for a nun to take us to our dorm, I sat down beside Camille and motioned at Gaby.

She nodded. "I know, I've been watching her too."

Andy sat beside Camille, his attention also on Gaby, who was now sitting with her eyes closed, leaning against the wall. "I asked her how her feet were when we walked through Valdelafuente but she brushed me off," he said. "We may have to corner her once we've settled into our room."

The tiny, smiling, hunchbacked Spanish nun who led us to our room talked all the way, though it must have been obvious we couldn't understand what she was saying. Although the nuns preferred to separate men from women, the only spaces left meant we were all in one room with a row of single beds on each side. A group of middle-aged Spanish women had already claimed most of the beds along one wall and welcomed us loudly with "*Hola*!" when we entered.

"I need to find an ATM before dinner," Andy said, as we got ready to hit the showers. "I've read they are few and far between until we reach Ponferrada in about four days." He then went over to Gaby, who was lying on her bed with her eyes closed. "Gaby, I've seen you limping today. How are your blisters?"

Bethany was immediately by Gaby's side, ready to assist or defend. Without a word, Gaby sat up, swung her legs over the bed, and pulled off her socks. Her feet looked good, the smaller blisters hidden by Compeed.

"No blister problem," Gaby said. "See?" She held up first one foot then the other.

Andy wasn't giving up. "Why were you limping?"

Gaby shrugged.

"Tell him, Gaby!" Bethany said.

Gaby looked everywhere but at Andy. "It's not my blisters. It's my ankle. It hurts."

Camille joined them. She squatted down and took Gaby's leg in her hands, sliding her fingers over the teen's heel and up her Achilles tendon. "Here?" she said, gently touching one spot.

Gaby nodded, grimacing.

"Tendonitis, I think," she said. "Gaby, this is not the time to be a warrior. We can help you, but the longer you walk on this, the longer it will take to heal. It is R.I.C.E time: resting, ice, compression, and elevation. Bethany?"

"Got it." Bethany dashed off to find ice.

"You must get your leg up. I'll ignore my 'no backpack on the bed' rule for once." She put Gaby's backpack at the end of her bed, covered it with a blanket taken from the bed, and gently rested the injured leg on it. "And you have to drink lots of water. One of the possible causes of tendonitis is muscle dehydration. Jules?"

Jules immediately went to the bathroom to fill Gaby's water bottle.

Watching my aunt swing into action, I had to smile. Camille enjoyed looking after people. She was this way with customers at her store too, which was why so many of them kept coming back.

For the first time in weeks, I thought of Magdalene's Hearth and wondered how the repairs were going. Camille hadn't mentioned the store once, at least not to me.

I felt a flush of shame. *Why would she? I should have asked, or at least shown some interest.*

"I'm a terrible niece," I blurted out. Camille looked up at me in surprise. "I haven't once asked how the renovations are going."

"They're fine. Your ever-efficient mother told me in our last phone call that the work is ahead of schedule. The store will be ready to reopen when I get home."

What kind of friend and wife and mother was I going to be if I could forget something so important to someone I love?

While I waited my turn in the shower lineup, I didn't know if I wanted to cry or kick a wall, or both.

We'd all offered to be the one to bring Gaby something to eat after Camille had been adamant Gaby had to keep her leg up and walk on it as little as possible. Bethany wanted to stay with her, but Andy insisted she come to dinner. It was when we were all sitting around the restaurant table waiting for our standard pilgrim menu of French fries, pork, and boring chocolate pudding cups that Bethany understood why.

"We need to decide what we're going to do concerning Gaby and her injury," Andy said, "and it has to be unanimous, a group decision. Suggestions?"

There was no lack of ideas. One of us would stay with her. No, we'd all stay. Maybe Gaby could rest for a few days at the albergue.

"That won't work, unfortunately. You can only stay one night in each albergue," Andy gently reminded us.

"Besides," Camille said, "tendonitis can take weeks to heal."

The ideas kept coming. We could find her a hotel room. No, that would be too expensive. She could move to a different albergue each day. There was a municipal albergue plus lots of private hostels in León.

We were grasping at anything because none of us wanted to say the solution we knew was probably for the best: send Gaby home.

It turned out Gaby had been obsessing on her own back in the monastery. When we returned, we crowded around her bed, providing a shield for Bethany as she handed over three *empanadas*, Spanish meat pies with a filling of chorizo sausage covered in a garlic, onion, and tomato sauce and then wrapped in dough and fried in olive oil.

"We had to sneak it in," Bethany whispered to her. "These nuns are scary!"

Gaby barely looked at the still warm, wrapped Spanish pies in her hand. "I've been reading up on tendonitis," she said, nodding toward Camille's guidebooks on her bed. "It's going to take too long to heal. I don't want to hold you back. I should go home."

There was a loud explosion of "No way!" and "I don't want you to go!" and "There has to be another way." Our voices slid into silence.

"Not alone you won't," Ben said, speaking up for the first time. "I've been thinking about it all evening too, and I asked the waiter at our restaurant, and he knew how I could do it. If I fly with Gaby to Paris and get her to her plane, then fly back to Bilbao on the northern coast of Spain and catch the train to Ponferrada, I can meet up with you again there." He was breathless when he finished talking.

Andy stepped forward and offered his hand. Ben took it, a little embarrassed. Jules gave him a hug, followed by me, Camille, and Bethany.

Camille took Gaby's hand. "Are you ok with that?"

Gaby looked like she might not be keen, but she saw Bethany glaring and sighed. "Yeah, all right. This won't cause any problems with you, Andy, like this won't be a failure and cause a problem for your grant or I'll have to—"

Andy interrupted her. "This is not your fault. You've fulfilled your part of the bargain. I'll take it from here." He said he would make the flight arrangements to Paris tomorrow. Everything was closed now, and it was too late to finalize plans. "There are direct flights from Paris to Vancouver. And for you, Ben, I'll find an ATM and get some cash for the trip. And give you my second credit card too." Ben immediately started shaking his head, but Andy was adamant. "It's not negotiable."

"I'd like to pay for Gaby's flight. I've got this trip account." I said surprising myself as much as the others. "It's got emergency funds from my mother." Now it was Gaby's turn to shake her head, but I kept going. "It feels right, Gaby. It's the right thing to do!"

The loving, proud look on Camille's face made my offer extra worthwhile.

"Ben, we'll book the two of you on the first plane possible. Buy yourself food and drinks too." Andy also wanted to ensure a family member could meet Gaby when the plane landed in Vancouver.

"Don't worry about it," Gaby said, shaking her head. "I'll get home on my own."

That was unacceptable to all of us. Andy came up with the solution. "I have an idea. I'll see if Maggie's grandmother will meet you. She's good at looking after people. Just like her daughter, and granddaughter."

He smiled at Camille, then me, and I felt myself shrink inside, drowning in a wave of panic, and embarrassment. When had he met Grams?

"She had a suggestion for me the last time Camille and I had dinner with her," he continued. "I was to consider her an emergency contact and problem-solver if we needed one. And Maggie's parents also volunteered, but I think you'll find Margaret more fun, Gaby. Nothing personal, Maggie," he added quickly, thinking I might be offended. I wasn't. It showed he knew my parents—or at least my mother. *But what else don't I know?*

Gaby shook her head again.

Bethany stood up and glared at her, her hands on her hips. If she hadn't looked so angry, the rest of us might have grinned at her indignant stance. "So, you don't want to be in debt to anyone? What else is new! Suck it up, buddy. Take this hand that Ben and Andy and Maggie and her grandmother—" she looked at me.

"Margaret," I said.

"—Margaret are extending!"

Gaby was finding it hard to look away. "All right."

That settled the matter. Camille and Andy went to phone Grams.

It didn't take long to arrange as much as we could, and when Camille and Andy came back, none of us had moved from our places around Gaby's bed. Jules had been trying to gross Bethany out, but her jokes only left Beth shaking her head and rolling her eyes. Bethany had developed tougher skin on this trip.

"All set," Camille said. "She's looking forward to meeting you, Gaby."

Gaby looked down at her knees, suddenly looking shy. "I need to tell you something before I leave."

We all went silent. My stomach tightened. I was sure I knew what was coming. Was this the moment I'd been worried about, when everyone started to talk, and we'd all have to share our stories?

"My Dad used to beat me. He did this." Gaby held out her scarred arm and pulled back her hair, exposing the cut. "And he hit my mom too, but she wouldn't do anything. They took him away, twice, but he always came back. Three months ago, when he started beating my mom, I lost it. I hurt him." She looked around at us, her jaw tight. "I don't regret it. I'd do it again!"

"I'm like a walking episode of a TV soap," Bethany said, her free hand clutching the side of the bed. "A mother who's always sick, and an A+, super smart, *shining star* brother. He's the successful one in the family." Sarcasm covered those words. "He says, he says

I'm the reason she's sick, because she's always worried about me. He told everybody I stole from his office, but I didn't! Mom asked me to get something, and I didn't have any money and he wouldn't give me any, so I borrowed some, just borrowed it, I would have paid it back, when I got home and got it from Mom, but he wouldn't listen...." She sighed. "I can't win with him. I never do the right thing."

"He's an ass!" Gaby looked like she wanted to punch someone.

Shifting in his seat on the end of Gaby's bed, Ben reached up and unwound the scarf he always wore. He held it up. "This was my sister's. A guy busy with his phone when he was driving hit her. I thought I was going crazy and wanted to kill him. I had to get away. It's been a year, so I'm here, to clear my head. Maggie has helped."

He looked at me, and I'm sure it was obvious from the way I looked back at him that our friendship had moved up a notch into something else.

"Thanks, to all of you. You welcomed me into your, like secret society," Ben said. He grinned and then got serious again. "I think I could go home now, and even if I don't get that scholarship and can't go the school, I'll be ok." With no conscious thought by either of us, Ben's hand found mine and we linked fingers.

"Shit! Ok, before this gets too mushy," Jules said, "I steal things. I'm good at it. But not on this trip," she quickly added.

I thought of the designer sunglasses she'd taken from the Lost and Found box in Roncesvalles, but maybe she didn't consider that stealing.

"Andy made it clear to me I didn't get a second chance with him. I've been to Juvie before and let me tell you, it's a bitch." Jules paused, looking at me, her head tilted as she thought about what she wanted to say. "And Maggie, she saw me steal a purse, before we met, but never told any of you. I kept waiting, thinking she'd say something." She shook her head, still staring at me. "You never did. I don't get that. Anyway, Andy found the purse and made me give it back the same day. I guess I'm lucky because my mom is great, and the woman was just happy to get her stuff back. My last psychiatrist told me I have ADHD and get bored and maybe stealing gives my day a blast of energy."

"We're working on other ways for you to get that blast, aren't we, Jules?"

Jules nodded. "I'm working on it, Andy."

No one looked at me, but I could feel them waiting.

Camille quietly reached out and put her hand on my back. "It's ok, you don't—"

Straightening my shoulders, I looked directly at Camille. "Yes, I do." I looked around at the others, forcing myself to make eye contact with each of them. I pulled my hand out of Ben's. It was such an embarrassingly stupid story, but if it was ever going to be told, now was the time. "There was this guy, Tony, I thought I liked him, and he dared me to break into Camille's store, and I did, and I got caught, and it was this or India for five weeks working in my mother's clothing factory."

Bethany looked horrified. "You would have to work in a sweatshop?"

"No, my mother's pretty progressive about stuff like that. I was going to be in the factory daycare she set up for the women. You know, play with the kids and help serve lunch and stuff. But there were probably going to be lots of bugs. And curry." I shuddered. "I don't like curry."

Ben laughed, which was again not the response I would have expected, from anyone, let alone the guy I was in love with. "It cracks me up that because of curry and bugs you decided to walk 25 to 30 kilometres a day for over a month with a bunch of people you don't know?"

"A bunch of criminals," Jules said.

"Bunch of mutants," I corrected her, looking around at the others. Thankfully, they grinned back.

"Weirdos," Bethany added.

"Villains!" I didn't move fast enough and got smacked on the arm by Jules.

Camille put her hand on Gaby's and gave it a gentle squeeze. I put my hand on top of Camille's and quickly there was a stack of hands-on-hands. Equally quickly the stack, as though having a mind of its own, exploded up into the air with a chorus of loud "Weirdoes! Villains! Andy's mutants! Juvies unite!"

And with that the secrets were shared and none of them mattered to any of us.

Who would have thought it would be so easy to do? Why did we wait so long?

The Spanish women, who had been talking among themselves all evening as they sorted, packed, sewed, and read, looked over, curious about the explosion of sound.

But just when the world looked warm and fuzzy, a splash of cold water came pouring down. Jules offered to help Gaby make a final trip to the washroom for the night. Camille asked Andy to hand Gaby her bathroom kit.

"I've got it," Jules said, but Andy was already digging in Gaby's bag.

"It should be near the top, in that side pocket. I just keep shoving things in, but the stuff I use is at the top—" Gaby said.

Andy's arm had gone still. He'd reached into the bottom of the pack, but slowly pulled out three iPhones and held them out.

Gaby looked stunned. "Those aren't mine!"

"Gaby!"

I was not sure who said her name. Everyone was looking back and forth between the items in Andy's hands and Gaby. "They're not mine!" she repeated. Bethany hadn't moved from her spot.

Andy, slowly, sadly, shook his head. "Where did you get them?"

Gaby looked around at all of us and saw embarrassment, disappointment, sadness, concern, and anger. Bethany reached out to take Gaby's hand, probably as a show of solidarity, but it was ignored. "Take them, then. It looks like I'm leaving at just the right time. You've caught me red-handed."

Something didn't feel right to me. I stared at Jules. She had moved back slightly from the bed and was standing, arms crossed, staring at Gaby.

"Tough break," was all Jules said.

"Jules—"

Andy interrupted me. "Jules? Do you have something to say? Do you know anything about this?"

Now it was Jules' turn to shake her head, but she did so with sadness, not anger. She held her hands out, palms up, a peace offering to Andy. "It wasn't me! No way was I risking going back to juvie."

"Jules?" My question hung in the air.

She looked at me and shook her head again. "This isn't going to be fixed, Maggie. Not by parents or Andy. Not by anyone. It's all in Gaby's corner."

Gaby sighed. "It's what people like me do, right?"

Why wasn't she fighting this?

A tremor went through Bethany's body. "No, I don't believe it! Gaby, you need to tell them you didn't take these things!"

Gaby just closed her eyes, tuning all of us out.

"You need to empty your bag," Andy said.

Gaby shrugged, leaving Andy with the unpleasant task of pulling out clothes and toiletries, but there was nothing else that didn't belong to Gaby or looked out of place.

None of us slept well that night, all of us restless in our beds and aware of the others also tossing and turning.

The next morning, after Andy had made phone calls to Grams and organized flights, Jules, Bethany, and I stood around shuffling our feet, unsure of what to say or do as Gaby appeared at the monastery front doors. She avoided eye contact with any of us and limped in silence to the cab. Ben threw first his backpack then Gaby's into the taxi trunk. Bethany was crying and didn't care who saw it.

Ben pulled me aside. He took off his scarf and set it gently around my neck. "Would you wear this for me, so my sister's memory at least gets to continue walking the Camino? I'll get it back from you when we meet up in Ponferrada."

Even in one of the saddest moments I'd ever experienced, I felt my heart expand.

Who knew two opposite feelings could co-exist?

"May the Force be with you!" I pulled him close and kissed him. He kissed me back with a ferocity that helped me finally understand a line I'd only heard in movies and read in books: "He took my breath away."

After the taxi drove away, it was too abrupt an ending and left us feeling like there was unfinished business.

Andy and Camille had sat on the outside steps after everyone went to bed last night. Unfortunately, they were near the open hallway door and we had to lie in bed and listen to their discussion about what to do with the iPhones. Gaby refused to offer any explanation or defence. Who knew how long they'd been in her pack? Her silence didn't help her cause.

With obvious frustration in his voice, we'd all heard Andy tell Camille he'd leave the iPhones with the nuns and they could post something on the website used by the Camino hostels, hotels, and religious houses that took in hikers. Maybe someone would remember the things being reported lost or stolen.

We all looked as miserable as we felt. Even sitting at an outdoor cafe with *cafe con leches* in front of us, our backpacks resting against the base of the tree that gave some shade from the hot sun, didn't help our heavy spirits. We missed Ben, and Gaby. The thought of Gaby still unsettled us. We'd been together constantly for weeks now and to have one of our group gone so unexpectedly left a loud space we weren't prepared to deal with.

Andy looked at our sad faces. "We can do something completely different, you know," he said. We didn't bother to answer. He pulled out his guidebook and flipped to a specific page, an action that gave us a moment of panic thinking he was going to suggest a city tour or a museum visit.

It's not like we had a choice anyway. Being a teen under the control of adults is a real pain.

20

ASTORGA CHOCOLATE

None of us made eye contact with Andy, preferring to sit in silence, our shoulders slumped.

"We've got an industrial area to walk through getting out of León, plus we'll be walking along more busy roads. What if we take a vacation?" Now he had our attention. "The León bus station is across the river. There are buses to the next largest town, Astorga, every 30 to 60 minutes. It's about a 50-minute trip and will cut out two days of walking. We can take a rest day there because, and Jules, you'll be excited to hear this. There is a building in the main town square designed by Antoni Gaudi. Interested?"

Our emotions lightened a bit. Then I thought of a problem. "What about Ben?"

Andy looked sheepish. "I already told him this was planned. We'll keep in touch by phone and make sure he knows where we are."

In a remarkably short time, we were on a bus and heading west. We sat in our comfortable bus seats, stretched out our legs, and didn't feel an ounce of guilt when we looked out the window at the steady stream of pilgrims walking on the Camino path paralleling the highway.

I wasn't in any more of a mood to talk to Bethany than Bethany was to talk to anyone. I kept fiddling with Ben's scarf, running it through my fingers, folding the end, unfolding it, and then starting the whole process over again.

Bethany had been quiet since Gaby's taxi had disappeared around the street corner. Suddenly she turned to me and said, "You're the luckiest person!"

Lucky? Me?

"No, I'm not," I said, aware of how bitter I sounded. What did Bethany know?

"You've got a grandmother AND parents who offered to help strangers. Maggie, you are lucky! I'd be so grateful to have what you've got, and yet you never seem happy about it. Not everyone is as blessed as you!" She turned away, keeping her eyes focused on the passing highway scene. "That was my birthday wish," she said to the window.

The initial hit of irritation I'd felt seeped away and I relaxed my clenched fist.

If only things could be more like Bethany imagined them at home.

In just over an-hour-and-a-half, we were standing in the main square of Astorga taking in the incredible sight of the Gaudi-designed Bishop's Palace.

"It's like a Spanish Disneyland," Bethany said in wonder. Even in her sadness she was fascinated by the grey granite walls, towers, glass windows, and the arches over the entrance and turrets. I thought it looked more like a weird Tim Burton movie set, and it was easy to imagine ghouls living in this castle rather than princesses. Or Bishops, as originally planned. These days it was a museum devoted to religious art in honour of the Camino pilgrims who passed by every day.

After a lunch spent in silence, Camille found a cheap hotel

three streets away from the town square, but every room had a television and private bathroom.

Jules sighed in pleasure when she quickly looked in the three rooms assigned to us. She had the smallest one, but it was all hers, while Andy and Camille shared the second, and Bethany and me the third. I looked at Jules, realizing my feelings had changed. I didn't believe her and was sure she was the one who'd stolen the iPhones, but if she wouldn't confess and Gaby had all but said she did it by refusing to claim her innocence, what could I do?

Make sure my valuable gear is always near, for starters.

Andy's cell phone rang in the middle of our pilgrim's dinner that night. It had never happened before, which made all of us stare at it wondering who was getting bad news.

It turned out to be Ben calling to say he and Gaby were at the Paris airport and Gaby's flight to Vancouver was leaving in a few hours. Andy was repeating to us what Ben said as he spoke. Ben had bought a ticket for a flight that would have him in Bilbao first thing in the morning, and then he could hop on a bus to catch up to us.

"I hope Gaby can find one short, elegant, white-haired woman in that airport crowd," Andy added. "Margaret said to tell Gaby she'd be wearing a red rose in her hair. I think that was a joke?" He looked over at Camille, then me. We both shook our heads.

Knowing Grams, I could see her turning up at the airport with a flower, maybe even two, tucked behind her ear. My grandfather had always said the fact he never knew what Grams would do next is what kept him laughing in their marriage. I knew another debate had taken place about whether Gaby should go to Grams now that she was a thief, but Grams had settled that. She'd insisted Gaby was welcome. She told Camille she knew another delinquent who had a good heart, and she was willing to believe the same of Gaby. "I'll teach her bridge and that will keep her busy," she'd said.

"Ben says hi," Andy said quietly to me when we left the restaurant.

What's the opposite of an "ouch" to the heart? A whoosh? A joyful burst?

Andy had been more worried than he'd shown. His smile of relief that they had made it to the Paris Charles De Gaulle Airport safely and on time lasted long after the phone call ended.

We could sleep in the next morning and met at 10 o'clock in front of the Bishop's Palace. After all our early morning starts, sleeping in until 9 am made me feel half the day had already passed. The only touristy thing Andy insisted we do together turned out to be unexpectedly fun and just what we needed. He took us to the *Museo de Chocolate,* where we learned how chocolate bars were made. Camille and Andy insisted on buying us individual bags bulging with chocolates from the museum store.

My feet weren't the only ones hurting. When we came to the benches in the town square, we were content to sit and watch everyone else dash around while we ate our museum treats. It was such a pleasure to know we didn't have to walk anywhere except back to our hotel. I used the time to daydream about Ben. And think about that goodbye kiss.

Mid-way through the afternoon, Diona, the Romanian judge I'd sat beside at dinner in Grañón, walked into the square chatting with a tanned, fit woman in her early 20s. After we'd all exchanged hugs and double-cheek kisses, Diona introduced the woman beside her as Gretchen from Germany. Gretchen had been walking for months and recently passed the 5,000 kilometres mark. She wasn't sure when she would stop.

Yes, Santiago was her goal, but, "Maybe, just maybe, I'll turn around and walk back home," she said.

I heard Jules mutter, "Bat-shit crazy."

"Interesting scarf combination," Diona commented. Her conspiratorial grin made me wonder if she'd met Ben somewhere on the trail. I wanted to sing his name out to the whole plaza but held myself back and just shrugged. "See you tonight," she said after we'd agreed on a restaurant for dinner.

At 6:45, as we walked back into the square to wait for Diona and Gretchen, Marina and Elka, our lawyer and lawyer's aid friends, entered from the other side of the square. They joined us in what was quickly becoming an impromptu party group.

"Nice accessory," Elka said smiling, recognizing Ben's scarf. I felt embarrassed and proud and grinned back at her.

Gretchen was happy to speak German with Marina and Elka. She and Elka quickly found out they had both gone to Heidelberg University and they started to compare favourite and despised university professors and student bars and barely took part in the rest of the evening's conversations. The only awkward moment was when Diona asked where Gaby was and after a moment of silence, Andy casually said Gaby had developed tendonitis and gone home early. Our group discomfort was obvious there was more to the story, but Diona and the others let it drop. Just as people often told others their innermost secrets on the Camino, it was also a place where you could choose what you shared.

The food wasn't great, and the restaurant wasn't clean, but none of us cared. Looking around at the laughing faces of my group and our Camino friends, I once again got why the Santiago de Compostela pilgrimage had this mystical attraction for people. This was community as it should be. And tonight we needed to feel that connection.

Although the stories could have kept coming for several hours more, Andy finally insisted it was time we went to sleep. We'd planned an early start tomorrow, but he said he was willing to be flexible.

"Seven o'clock instead of 6:30?" We met his suggestion with groans rather than the appreciation he'd expected. We exchanged email addresses and said goodbye with a genuine hope we'd all meet again further along the trail.

Reality set in the next morning. It was pouring rain when we left the hotel. I imagined it was hard for others to see where each hiker began and their backpack ended. We were all lumpy creatures wearing blue and red raincoats or ponchos, our packs also invisible under protective rain covers.

"We've been lucky, haven't we?" Camille said as we sloshed our way out of town.

"Please, Camille, it's too early," Jules said looking over her shoulder so we could hear her in the downpour. She radiated irritation. Something was bugging her big time. We gave her space, and no one tried to include her in any conversation.

Andy had told us at breakfast we'd be experiencing another change in terrain. Soon we entered an area of rolling hills. We'd have a steady climb for about 22 kilometres as we made our way up to Rabanal del Camino. After that, there would be six kilometres of climbing to reach our goal, Foncebadon.

"Some people have written that Astorga to Ponferrada is the most beautiful stretch of the Camino—"

"Some people write too much," Jules said. I nodded in agreement.

"There are small villages along the way, but we still need to bring food and water. We'll be walking through oak and broom and," Andy paused dramatically, "the next day will have a surprise."

No one placed much faith in one of Andy's surprises.

"Just wait. You'll see," he said.

The wet morning continued and resulted in one soggy footstep after another. The route again ran parallel to a busy two-lane road with cars and trucks zooming by and splashing us with irritating regularity.

We'd only walked five kilometres by the time we entered the village of Castrillo de Polvazares via its slippery cobbled main street. Jules and I weren't the only grumpy ones. We felt marginally better after we'd each had two hot cups of *cafe con leche* but all it took was a second of looking out at the dreary wet day to sink our spirits again.

The rain finally stopped three hours later. By then, we were in-between damp and wet. It had been a successful first try with our rain gear, but we discovered it was exhausting work lifting wet boots caked with mud, again and again, step by step. Our plastic raincoats and ponchos also made us sweat. Our spirits finally lifted when we came upon another friendly donkey who kept sticking his neck out to be scratched and who continued to bray at us long after we were out of sight.

Once we passed Rabanal del Camino, the track was lined with heather. Camille told us if the weather had been better we'd have been able to see mountains in the distance. At one point the trail was so slippery Andy suggested we leave it and walk along the road. We passed through a herd of cattle and then another. Bethany was courageous enough to reach out and touch their velvety-brown backs. Many of the animals had horns and looked intimidating, but they were more interested in eating grass or lying down and chewing their cud than making any aggressive moves.

"Seems like a good place to practice your bull running, Jules," I said, and then could have bitten my tongue. My teasing comment reminded us of Pamplona, which reminded us of Gaby.

Another long row of white windmills was visible in the distance.

"Same old, same old," Jules said, ignoring my comment.

We finally approached Foncebadon, but it looked uninviting, eerie and abandoned with partially ruined buildings and piles of debris and garbage both on and beside the dirt road leading into the village.

"Another great location for a horror movie," Jules said, a flicker of interest flaring and then fading away in exhaustion after the 27 kilometres we'd hiked so far. The last 500-metres climb to Foncebadon never seemed to end.

Bethany went up to a wooden cross on the side of the road and leaned down, reading the sign on the stone base: "'Please don't leave stones on this cross.'"

"In four languages, no less," I said.

"You'll see why tomorrow," Andy said in his Darth Vader voice.

To our pleasant surprise, our albergue was modern, the dorm rooms painted white and less crowded with bunk beds than most of the places we'd stayed in. Andy had been warned in Astorga by a Portuguese man who'd walked the Camino before that one of the albergues in this tiny place was dirty and run by "not good people." Even though we'd learned how subjective each person's experience was at albergues—influenced by the weather, your health, the season, and even the attitudes and snoring skills of other pilgrims staying there—Andy had taken the man's advice. He'd put a line through that albergue in his guidebook and registered us in the only other place available.

Our roommate looked up from sorting his pack and introduced himself as, "Paulo, from Florianopolis, the safest city in Brazil," he said proudly.

"Jules, from Vancouver, British Columbia, the safest city in Canada," Jules said with a straight face.

Paulo told us he had made a reservation for a medieval meal at *La Taberna de Gaia* next door. "Yes, it looks like an ancient stone cottage, but the food is—" he almost moaned in pleasure. "The servers, a mother and daughter, wear medieval clothes, you use your hands to eat, and the food is so *deliciosa* as to be unbelievable! *Pao fresco*, um," he groped for the correct English words, "fresh homemade bread, water from their well, deer stew, venison, *anguia* —eel—and a cheese tart for dessert that is—" He moaned again in anticipation.

He was freaking Bethany out.

"Eel?" I said and shuddered.

"Deer?" Bethany said.

Andy shook his head. "At 25 Euros per person—that's about $39 Canadian—it's beyond our budget."

"It's listed as *numero um,* the number one, *muito bom,* the very best restaurant in Foncebadon," Paulo said.

Jules laughed, then stopped when she realized Paulo was serious. "Doesn't he know this town has a population of 13?" she said, after Paulo had left. "But I will say that this little derelict place has moved up on my 'favourite hostel' list. It doesn't have a church or a Cathedral!"

Ben would have loved eating dinner at that special restaurant. Maybe he'd already planned it but hadn't said anything when he offered to accompany Gaby?

The sky was overcast, but the rain stayed away as we set out the next morning, climbing again, this time up to 1,505 metres, the highest point of the whole Camino trail. "That's where you'll see Andy's next surprise. It's two kilometres away," Camille said.

Even with the low clouds, it was a beautiful walk along a winding dirt path through wild country covered with pink- and purple-flowered heather and yellow broom bushes.

We finally saw Andy's surprise 500 metres before we reached it: the *Cruz de Ferro,* the Iron Cross. It stretched up into the sky, an iron cross on the end of a tall oak pole sprouting out of a hill of stones. For as far up as people could reach, the pole was covered in photographs, envelopes, pieces of clothing, boots, drawings, toys, and several Khatas, the long white silk scarves that Tibetan Buddhists get blessed by a Lama. Some rocks resting against the pole were wrapped in paper I thought might have prayers written on them.

"Hey, check out the empty wineskin," Jules said, pointing halfway up the pole.

"The tradition here," Camille said, "is that you lay down the stone you've been carrying from home at the base of the cross. The stone can represent a burden, a fear, or a wish. In the medieval days, it represented sins, but I think that's too heavy for us. See all these stones that have built up around the base of the pole? They've been laid down by pilgrims for hundreds of years. That means millions of pilgrims. Even walking on the stones to reach the cross is a sacred act. I mentioned this to you the first day we met. Do any of you have something you'd like to place there?"

Bethany immediately pulled out two items from the small pocket in her backpack's waistband but kept them hidden in her hand when she started to climb the hill.

No one else moved. I took off my pack and unzipped the top pocket, pulling out four stones I'd taken from my backyard, one each for Grams, Janie, Camille (not that I told her), and one for myself. I followed Bethany and found the top of the stone pile revealed more pilgrim stuff: cigarette packs, a sock with a hole in the toe, and an empty wine bottle.

A kneeling man was praying at the base of the cross. Tourists and pilgrims walked around him as though he was invisible. Bethany was the only one who showed him any respect. I joined her, unsure if I should also wait or go ahead. Bethany took my hand, and the two of us stood patiently together.

I closed my eyes and thought of the first stone. Into it, I projected all the love and appreciation I felt for Grams. The second stone was for Janie, for being a friend when I needed one. I moved the stones around in my hand, rubbing them with my fingers. The third stone was for Camille, to ask for her forgiveness. Sure, she'd said she was no longer angry, but I was still mad at myself and felt I needed to make retribution in some way.

But what kind of apology could begin to make up for what I'd done?

I was still struggling to find an answer to that question.

I waited until the man was finished praying. He made the sign of the cross and had stood up before we started to move in front of him. He was crying. Bethany stepped forward and smiled at the pilgrim with such love and understanding he looked dazed. Suddenly he was smiling too, and wiping away his tears.

I stared at this sweet, compassionate, often goofy person who had enough space in her heart for others in need. We hadn't heard specific details about Bethany's home life, but we could all guess. There had been emotional abuse, for starters. How could Bethany have remained loving and understanding? I took off Grams' blue scarf that had travelled so many kilometres with me and draped it around Bethany's neck. She started to shake her head, but her hand was already stroking the silky material.

"The colour suits you," I said. "Grams would be happy to see you wearing it." Then I reached for Bethany's hand again and together we walked up to the cross and laid down the stones we'd brought.

I bet one of Bethany's two stones was for Gaby.

I now had one stone left, this one for myself. My mean, impatient, hurtful nature seemed too big and heavy for one little stone to carry away all my burdens. I turned and flung the fourth stone as far as I could, startling several tourists in the parking lot below.

It would be another 27 kilometre day, but there were advantages to daydreaming about Ben. It made the time pass quicker. And Ponferrada meant Ben's return.

One moment we were starting our descent and the next we were walking down into a small valley and through Marjarin. It looked like just another abandoned village until we passed a collection of flags from different countries and a home-made signpost listing the distance to major cities around the world.

"Tomas, who built this austere albergue, is famous on the Camino," Andy said.

"Austere means severe," I whispered to Bethany when I saw her mouth the word. We didn't stop but couldn't help staring at the rundown building and the labelled wooden planks pointing in different directions: "JERUSALEM 5000 Km," "SANTIAGO 222 Km," and "ROMA 2475 Km." There was no sign of Tomas, though several cats stretched out on the stone walls watched us.

"Tomas dresses like a Knight Templar. We can always stay. There are mattresses on the floor, a solar shower, wood stove heating, and an outdoor toilet," Camille said, sounding excited about the possibility.

"Funny, Camille," I said. Bethany shuddered and nodded in agreement.

Soon the Camino trail left the road and we began a steep hike up toward Acebo with its slate-covered houses.

I'd thrown that stone with intention.

I didn't deserve to lay anything down, yet.

21

PONFERRADA NOISEMAKERS

We hiked down 600 metres on a rough and steep trail littered with large, sharp rocks.

When we walked through Acebo, we came upon a monument to a German cyclist who had died of a heart attack on the Camino. The metal bike sculpture appeared to be leaping into the air out of its stone slab base.

The artwork fascinated Jules. "I wonder what my memorial will look like?"

"A foot kicking a soccer ball rising out of a piece of stone in the shape of a goal post?" Bethany suggested. She grinned. "It has to be the right foot," she added.

Jules gave her an affectionate, gentle poke. "You get my mojo!"

We walked into Riego de Ambros, bought snacks, and made our way through a chestnut forest before descending more steep trails and crossing a medieval stone bridge into Molinaseca.

"It's hard to believe that we were walking across the dusty Meseta only a few days ago," I said, looking around at all the shops and restaurants. Yellow broom and sweet-smelling lavender, which Jules told us was *Lavandula* in Latin, were everywhere.

Bethany twined lavender sprigs in her hair while I snapped off fragrant pieces and kept rubbing them under my nose. Everything I saw, smelled, tasted, and touched added to my growing sense of peacefulness and helped ease the ache I still felt at Gaby's absence. The views were amazing, and we could see mountains, valleys, and even Ponferrada long before we entered the city.

As we searched for the albergue, we were quickly exhausted by screeching car breaks, screaming children in a school playground, and the pounding of a drill in a street being dug up to replace old pipes—all city noises we'd forgotten while walking in the country. Andy told us the 12th century Templar Castle overlooking the city was initially built to shelter Camino pilgrims. None of us had the energy to consider checking it out.

"Then next time," Andy said.

Was he crazy? Next time? In another life!

The albergue was very modern and even had a small pool in the middle of the front courtyard. It looked great for soaking sore feet, but during the 16 hours we were there I never saw anyone use it. We were told to pick any free beds in a cavernous basement dorm room where most of the 50 bunks had already been claimed.

Our Italian friend with the smelly feet gave us a friendly wave from her top bunk next to the dorm door.

"Tough place to be," Jules said, turning practical. "She'll get woken up every time someone goes to the bathroom during the night. Bet you most of these guys won't think to keep the door from slamming." We'd been through that kind of nighttime thoughtlessness before and knew she was right.

There weren't enough empty beds together in any section, so we ended up being scattered throughout the room, glad just to find a bunk to sleep in.

We tried to save a bed for Ben but, nice as they were, the *hospitaleros* shook their heads and said, *"Por orden de llegada,"* which we assumed was a Spanish version of "first come, first served." There was a well-equipped kitchen inside the entranceway where we could make dinner. Camille took Bethany with her to food shop while I sat at an outside table and watched for Ben.

A late-20s Irish couple were drinking beer in the shade on the other side of the courtyard. The man sitting beside them waved to me. It was James, the "best man" that we'd met at the albergue in Terradillos, the one "forced" to hike with his soon-to-be-married buddy. Irish Chloe and Liam would not stand for me to be sitting alone. They insisted I join them.

James explained to Chloe and Liam where he and I had first met, asked me about the rest of my group, and explained he just couldn't stop after two days so here he was, heading to Santiago. Chloe and Liam were happy to have someone new to listen to their jokes and gentle digs at each other. They were both teachers enjoying their summer break and considered the Camino a tester before getting married in the fall.

"I figure if this bird can handle me bollixed on the Camino, then she can handle me in my day-to-day state," Liam said, grinning.

"Ah, you're an eejit!"

But their mutual affection was clear in the way he rubbed her bare feet resting on his lap and the attentive way she reached out and pulled the chip bag closer so he could reach it. They also insisted on buying me something to drink. I accepted an iced tea, which they thought was a scandalous drink, but Liam got up and bought one from the nearby vending machine.

Their table gradually grew to include an American teenager who was anxious about the state of her teeth since she couldn't whiten them regularly on the trail and a German who casually removed his shirt to show off his muscles and hopefully hook up with the American girl.

I saw Camille and Bethany return from their shopping and head indoors after they motioned for me to stay where I was.

Twenty minutes later I felt a tap on my shoulder. I turned, and there was Ben. I jumped up and threw my arms around him, worried I might be holding on a bit too long but not willing to let go.

"How did I miss seeing you arrive? When did you get in?" I had a hundred questions and was proud of myself for keeping it down to two. I took off his scarf and wrapped it around his neck, the gesture intimate.

"I got in about three hours ago, but I was so tired I had a nap. I'm on the second floor. It's great, only four beds."

"Lucky you! We're in a basement dorm room. I'm not expecting a quiet night. Did Camille and Andy see you?"

Ben nodded. "I think dinner is ready."

Liam's unsubtle throat-clearing made me turn around quickly. I made introductions and couldn't help but notice the American girl's interest in Ben.

Chloe grinned, giving me two thumbs up. "He's lovely!" she mouthed.

Blushing, I said, "It's been a fun afternoon. I hope we see each other again, and thanks for the iced tea."

Our group had claimed part of a table near the kitchen door. Our standard pasta and vegetables dinner—vegetarian tonight in honour of Chef Bethany—was filled with lots of crosstalk as Ben caught up on our news and we heard all about his trip with Gaby. He kept his stories casual. None of us asked how Gaby's spirits had been. Or if she had told Ben anything else. The unasked questions hung heavily in the air, making our laughter sound forced. Ben sat beside me and held my hand under the table.

He insisted on cleaning up. "In my family, if one cooks, the other cleans," he said, shooing Camille and Bethany away from the sink.

I helped. It gave us a chance to talk, though we still didn't mention Gaby. We hugged for a long time at the stairway before he went upstairs, and I went down.

The basement dorm turned out to be one of the worst nights I'd experienced on the Camino. Two hours after everyone in the dorm was asleep, the lights suddenly switched on. Four drunken men came singing into the room. People told them to be quiet, but the drunks couldn't have cared less. They opened the small back door that led to the outside stairs up to the courtyard and took turns going out for a smoke. Unfortunately, the open door allowed their talk and smoke to come back into the room.

I lay in my bed and sent out every Camino curse I could think of. I wished them blisters and sunburns, stolen bags and lost gear, and imagined the shape of the bedbug bites that went up their bodies from shins to hairline.

A woman in a nearby bunk heard me cursing and gave me a tired nod before covering her eyes with her arm and trying to block out both the light and the noise.

"Shut UP!" I finally yelled.

The men looked around to see who'd spoken. They pretended to be quiet as they got ready for bed, but one would trip, and the others would laugh. One man thought it was funny when he farted. So, he farted again. His friend, who was already in bed, pretended to snore. Loudly. All of them thought this was hilarious. By the time they settled down, it was too short a night for anyone to awaken rested.

The room lights came on at 6:30 but the four jerks didn't wake up. I looked at their sleeping lumps and thought of how to get revenge. Jules would have been proud of how my mind was working. I got out of bed and squatted down to grab one of my aluminium hiking poles shoved under my bunk.

"You're not going to hit them, are you?" the woman in the other bunk asked. She looked more hopeful than apprehensive.

I shook my head as I headed toward the sleeping men's bunks. I took my hiking pole and began slamming it against the metal bedposts, moving back and forth from bunk to bunk. The men sat up, groggy. I hoped they had hangovers. One almost fell out of the top bunk in his abrupt waking. They all looked at my calm face, then at the pole in my hands.

"Assholes!"

There was no need for translation. I pounded their metal bed frames a third and fourth time. Everyone else in the room started to clap, loudly. The men looked around, startled, but they grinned, and like last night, couldn't have cared less. One man tried to laugh, but it trickled off when someone swore at him in Spanish. I pulled out my night bag and departed for the bathroom, my head held high like the star I was.

I let the Force be with me and it felt great. Wait 'till I tell Ben.

22

ANARCHY STINKS

After leaving Ponferrada, Bethany was dancing with joy as she watched baby goats prance and butt each other in fields while nanny goats grazed on the sparse grass

The next highlight of the morning came when we saw a large stork's nest resting on the top of a tall pole beside a small church. The nest was so big it was hard to understand how it stayed balanced and didn't tip off. We stocked up on supplies in Camponaraya and spent the rest of the morning walking through vineyards or by the side of the highway.

During a flat stretch outside Cacabelos, two Dutchmen, Lars and Diedrerik, caught up with us. They'd also been in the Ponferrada basement dorm the previous night and wanted to thank me for my display of temper this morning. "*Moed* is how we say it in Dutch, it means 'courage'," Lars said.

Andy bought us hot cinnamon-sugar coated *churros* in Cacabelos because he wanted to celebrate the fact we'd walked 600 kilometres. For once Bethany looked pleased at how far we'd come. The *churros* tasted delicious. I doubt any of us would ever be content with a Tim Hortons' doughnut again.

Lars told funny stories about growing up in a Dutch family, and yes, he had IKEA furniture in his house, even though it was from Sweden, not Holland. He offered us a Dutch liquorice drop, which turned out to be salty and not at all like North American black liquorice. Diedrerik's stories were very different. He had become an anarchist when he was at university and had felt compelled to drop out of school. He horrified Bethany with his explanation of what "anarchist" had meant to him: using violence to overthrow the present government so that regimes and laws would no longer exist, and everyone could do what they wanted to.

"Wouldn't that mean the biggest, loudest, and strongest rule?" Bethany asked.

He paused. "Well, it's not that simple."

"It is if you're small," she said, "and female. Even with the laws we have now, bad things happen. Imagine what the world would be like if there weren't *any* laws!"

"But don't you see? That's what I mean! Even with laws bad things happen, so what if—"

"I think anarchy stinks," Bethany said, and she refused to talk to him.

She became friendlier when we passed a fruit stand on the side of the road and Diedrerik bought a handful of grapes, offering them to her before anyone else. She then bought an apple for him, which he accepted with a bow.

"I'm not an anarchist anymore, you know," he said, munching on his apple.

"Good!" she replied, popping a grape into her mouth, "because anarchy sucks!"

We entered Villafranca del Bierzo after an almost enjoyable 25 kilometres on country dirt paths. We had passed people working in vineyards, kids on bikes, and always had the view of the mountains on the horizon. The town reminded me of home. It wasn't the stone houses, winding roads, or large castle. It was the mountains. They made me think of skiing holidays in Whistler. Camille, Andy, and I sat in a bar and drank cold iced tea, but only after drinking several glasses of water first. There were times on the Camino when I just couldn't fill up my body's need for liquid.

We headed back to the albergue ready for a nap, something Bethany was already doing. Ben and Jules had gone off with Lars and Diedrerik to see the castle. We all had a quiet night in the recently opened hostel, though it took me a while to fall asleep. The two Dutchmen planned to hike the alternate Dragonte route before it rejoined the main Camino trail at Herrerias. Although this was the original Camino path, they had been warned it was poorly marked, very remote, and meant they'd have to walk over three mountain ranges. They had no deadline for reaching Santiago, so time didn't matter.

"We want the challenge," Lars said with a grin. He and Diedrerik said their goodbyes while drinking a cup of *cafe con leche* the next morning.

Not long after leaving the town, Andy commented on how the landscape was changing yet again. We had to climb a path that followed another highway, sometimes with no barrier between hikers and vehicles.

The town of Trabadelo, at the bottom of a valley, appeared deserted and had one of the longest *carretera principal,* main roads, we'd had to walk on the entire Camino. Jules couldn't resist looking at Andy's guidebook and what she found wasn't encouraging. She held it out to me, and I could see from the drawing we had a steep climb ahead. We both knew not to say anything to Bethany.

Many hikers walk all the way to O Cebreiro in one day, a picture postcard tourist town of stone-built oval houses with cone-shaped thatched roofs. Andy had looked at the map and decided we would only go as far as Laguna de Castilla, which he described as a "picturesque farming village."

"I hate picturesque farming villages," Jules said. I agreed with her but didn't say anything, content to nod so I didn't appear whiny in front of Ben.

But maybe it was too late.

The climb up and then down to Trabadelo was in the "oh shit" hiking elevation chart I'd devised. My range went from "awesome" (flat) to "ugh" (a steep climb that went on forever), to "oh shit" (when the trail went straight up or down, and death by heart attack was a possibility).

That hard climb made the gradual walk from Trabadelo to Herrerias easy, but the trail changed, and the path from Herrerias up to Laguna de Castilla was the worst stretch I'd experienced. My feet hurt, but they always did these days. I didn't know if I was more tired than usual or if the rock-strewn trail was as horrible as I found it. I didn't even care if Ben heard me gasping for breath.

My pace slowed, and I focused on putting one foot in front of the other. I developed a system. First of all, ignore the other hikers. Second, look up, pick a tree or a rock in front of me then look down and start counting. I would not look up until I'd counted to #1) 117, the total number of *The Mindy Project* episodes, or #2) 76, Grams' age, or #3) 165, my height in centimetres.

Each time I told myself that's when I'd check to see how close I was to my target object.

But I never lasted. It was too hot. The urge to look up and see how much further I had to go was intense, and every time I cheated and looked before I reached the end of my assigned count, the tree or rock goal still seemed far away. Stop cheating, I'd tell myself, but I didn't.

The sunken trail was several feet deeper than the pasture beside it, making the trail feel like it was a tunnel without a roof. Andy told us this deep trough was the result of millions of people walking the path over 1,000 years.

It didn't help that we had to avoid stepping in piles of cow dung. The dung presence was explained when eight cows with sharp horns came slowly plodding toward us down a particularly deep, sunken section. The animals paused now and then to scratch at an exposed rock or to eat small tufts of grass growing out of cracks in the dirt wall. The only option we had involved walking in the middle and hoping the cattle didn't spook and gore one of us. This at least gave all of us a shot of adrenaline.

Once the cattle were behind us, our energy sank again, and our feet slogged on. A whistling teenage boy came toward us at the next curve in the trail, sauntering as slowly as the cattle he was supposedly taking back to the barn.

La Faba oozed quaintness, and might have been considered beautiful, if we weren't all so exhausted. Andy was the only one who thought it worth noting. Even usually perky Camille looked drained, her sweaty hair hanging around her face. The trail got harder the closer we got to Laguna. Ben had made himself the rear guard, sauntering behind Bethany so she wasn't on her own at the end of our straggling line.

"I hate up!" I said to myself over and over, making a mantra of those three words: "I hate up! I hate up!"

No one was talking to anyone when we finally saw the first of the farming village's stone buildings where we'd be spending the night. Galician songs came through the open door and windows, an enticing combination of Celtic and Spanish music.

I slumped in a chair set against a wall by the single lane road in front of the albergue, too tired to even cross the street.

"I'll get you a drink," Ben said to me. I was working hard to hold back tears. He reappeared quickly with a bowl of peanuts and a cold coke and pulled up a chair. I rarely drank soft drinks, but this one contained a much-needed sugar boost. We'd finished walking for the day, I was sitting down, the sun was shining, and Ben was close by. Maybe it hadn't been such a bad day.

A stunningly beautiful African American teenager with a halo of shoulder-length curly hair appeared at the top of the trail. "Can I join you?" she asked and sat down before I answered. She too looked exhausted. All she had with her was a tiny bag slung over her shoulder.

Jules came back from the albergue, took the last chair, loosened her bootlaces, and pulled out her feet with a sigh of relief. Only then did she notice the American girl's small bag. I could see Jules immediately dismiss the American as a "wannabe." She asked in a sweet voice, "Is your backpack being delivered?"

"No. Hi, I'm Lani, from Chicago. I got robbed in León. Lost everything." She gave a dismissive wave of her hand at our obvious concern. "Best thing that could have happened to me. Sure, I don't have a passport or money, but you know?" She stretched. "I feel light in a way I never imagined possible. I'll need to get a new passport in Santiago. People have been kind. My experience must have gotten on the albergue grapevine because I've had *hospitaleros* offer me clothes and backpacks—you know how there's always stuff left behind? The only things I'm carrying are toothbrush, shampoo, underwear, and a t-shirt. And I've been offered free room and board." She pointed to my bowl of peanuts. "May I?"

"Of course," I said.

Lani took a handful and ate them quickly.

Suddenly sore feet didn't seem like such a big deal. I wondered how I'd react to losing everything. *I had my parents and Grams, and even Gerry, who would immediately come to my rescue if something like that happened to me.* I looked over at Bethany, who looked more frightened than horrified by Lani's story. *What would Bethany do?*

"Do you need anything, right now?" Ben asked.

Lani shook her head. "Nope. Doing great. I'm meeting up with this cute cyclist at O Cebreiro." She gave us a big grin. "He's going to buy me dinner. I'll see what happens next." She hopped up, refreshed, and strode down the trail toward her dinner destination.

A few minutes later, Ben and I pulled ourselves out of the chairs and went across the street to get our *credentials* stamped. The albergue was better than expected: modern, clean, and friendly, with a welcoming husband and wife who were the bartenders, cooks, and *hospitaleros*. The pilgrims' rooms were on the second floor over the combined albergue/bar/restaurant.

The music playing in the background seeped into my weary bones. It was exotic and familiar at the same time and left me feeling a mixture of sad and energized. I pointed to the speaker on the wall and asked the man behind the bar: "*Musica*?"

"*Luar na Lubre*," he said, nodding enthusiastically. "Good. Very good!"

I wrote the name down, planning on buying a CD if I could find one in Santiago.

After my shower, I did a quick hand washing of t-shirt, underwear, and socks. I heard a cowbell as I was hanging up the last wet sock on the clothesline behind the albergue. When I looked around the corner of the building and down the street, the scene in front of me could have taken place 100 years ago. A middle-aged woman, wearing the standard below knee dress over pants, was leading an ambling herd of cattle. A farm dog was barking and running between the much larger animals' legs, but neither the dog nor the cattle seemed bothered by the other. The barn and food were around the corner, as they were every day, and I guess that was all that mattered.

It was foggy when we started walking the next morning, but the skyline quickly cleared and from our mountain height we looked out at an ocean of clouds. Not long after leaving Laguna de Castilla we came to the stone marker telling us we'd entered the Galicia region.

"We are now in the land of hills, isolated villages, ocean coastline, and the birthplace of the Spanish dictator Francisco Franco, who shut down the Camino trail in his desire to keep foreigners out. The Camino didn't get going again until after his death in 1975," Andy said, paraphrasing from his guidebook.

"My book says only ten *Compostelas,* the certificates we'll get for walking the Camino, were given out in the early 1970s," Camille said, looking up from her book. "A Julio Iglesias song calls Galicia 'the country of a thousand rivers.'"

"Who's Julio Iglesias?" Bethany asked.

Andy coughed or snorted. It was hard to tell.

"Father of Enrique?" Jules said. "Basque terrorists kidnapped his grandfather." Trust Jules to know something obscure like that. She could be as bad as Andy.

"What are Basques?" Bethany asked.

"The Basque National Liberation Movement wants a separate country," Andy said, giving Jules a warning look. "They've been at war with Spain and France for a long time. But we're out of Basque country now. Logrono was near the edge of their disputed territory, so you have nothing to worry about."

Bethany didn't look convinced, and kept close to Andy for the rest of the day.

Everything combined to make it another beautiful walk: an easily managed dirt path, occasional shady trees to walk under, and ever-present stunning views of the surrounding mountains and multi-coloured green valleys. The air smelled damp and fresh. The heavy moss covering many of the tree trunks reminded me of going for hikes in the mountains around Vancouver.

We saw the first of what would become regular Camino stone markers every 500 metres the rest of the way into Santiago. After 20 minutes of climbing we entered O Cebreiro, a traditional village of ancient stone buildings made up of one large albergue, hostels, bars, and restaurants, all existing solely for Camino pilgrims and visitors. We passed a group of tourists taking pictures of everything, including our hiking group.

Another damn three kilometres hike up meant the walk was no

longer enjoyable. The tops of table umbrellas were the first things visible before anyone crested the steep path. We stopped at a bar for cold drinks, running into several people we'd shared a communal meal with in Pamplona. Or was it Burgos? Our stops were blurring in my memory. We stayed longer than planned, but it was fun to share Camino stories. A cyclist appeared, and everyone at the bar clapped in appreciation that he had made it up the slope.

"Remember that tall bronze statue of a pilgrim, the one leaning into the wind holding his hat?" Jules said.

"San Rogue, maybe?" Andy replied.

"And remember that windy day in—where was it?" Jules said.

"Maybe you could be a little more specific," I said. "We've had a lot of windy days, met a lots of pilgrim, and passed a bunch of Saint Jacques statues. The Meseta?"

An animated discussion followed, no one's memory of a specific windy day the same.

"I used my scarf to cover my head during one windstorm," I said, "and it almost blew away—the scarf, not my head," I added, seeing Jules was about to quiz me. "Andy caught it." Bethany now wore Grams' scarf all the time and I felt a rush of pride at my decision to give it to her.

"Did you ever lose your scarf, Ben?" Bethany asked, passing him a watermelon-flavoured Sour String.

"Almost, several times. I know it's kind of goofy looking." He removed his scarf, shook out the dust, and then rewrapped it around his neck. "My sister found it in an old suitcase. Leia was wearing it when...." He stopped, took a breath, and started walking again.

For the rest of the day, we took turns walking beside Ben and keeping him company, our way of showing support and sympathy.

"It's mostly downhill from here to Triacastela," Andy said,

"though my guidebook mentions that some areas are steep enough to make your knees hurt. Funny."

"I'm not laughing," Jules and I said. "Jinx!"

"All the town names and road signs will be in Galician from now on, rather than Spanish," Andy continued. I stopped listening and joined Ben, Bethany, and Jules. The three of them were sharing Bethany's bag of Zotz Fizz Sour Strings, a long candy with a sour-tasting fizzy centre. It had been Gaby's favourite, and Bethany said eating something Gaby liked helped make her feel closer.

We all nodded, happy someone had finally said Gaby's name.

After hiking for 12 kilometres, we paused at Fonfria to take off our boots and socks. The path was often so deeply worn into the ground we could barely see the blackberries growing along the stone walls above us.

Later, standing on the now ground-level trail, we looked down into the valley below and listened to church bells ringing. The green rectangular field's border walls of stone and shrub made the rolling hills look like a quilt pattern.

We walked through patches of heather and two hours later, stepped off the trail for another short footrest and nap.

It was a quiet and early night, all of us knowing tomorrow would be a 28 kilometre hike to Barbadelo.

It was hard to keep our energy up the next morning. The trail was beautiful—tree-lined, in the country, birds and farm animals were visible everywhere, and ancient stone buildings lined the path—but we were bored, and it showed.

We were also unsettled by something one of our dorm mates had said to us as we were packing this morning.

"We're almost there!" The enthusiastic Australian man who'd slept in the bunk above Jules was almost bouncing in anticipation. "Sarria next, where the Camino will crack a fruity, all those tourist pilgrims." He sounded like he was spitting the last two words.

"Then it's only 100 kilometres over five or six days and we're in Santiago!"

Bethany was still trying to work out what "crack a fruity" meant. The rest of us had been reminded of how close we were to the end of our Camino hike, a thought that left us anxious about the future and snapping at each other during breakfast.

We walked silently in single file until we came to a part of the trail where the four of us could walk side by side.

Bethany broke the silence. "Only five or six more days? Then what will we do?"

No one had an answer. The Camino was a tough daily grind, but being in the thick of it made it easy to forget about our lives in Canada. I'd looked at Ben after Bethany asked her question, but he looked calm and untroubled. I felt a flash of irritation. I didn't think Andy and Camille had any worries either.

Andy had been talking to Gaby every day, having insisted she keep in contact, regardless of the circumstances of her leaving. I suspected Gaby wanted the contact as much as we did. She either phoned him or he phoned her.

She was now living with Grams, and I had to admit I'd felt jealous when I heard how happy she sounded. Grams had worked her charm, and although Gaby could still only hobble, she was helping Grams fix up the back garden shed. They'd even gone to an outdoor Blues and Roots Festival concert at Deer Lake Park and heard k.d. lang. Grams and Gaby were obviously enjoying each other's company. I wasn't sure how I felt about sharing my beloved grandmother with Gaby. I'd need a haven when I went home.

I was dragging my feet, and Bethany and Jules weren't much better. Ben seemed tireless and was getting irritated glances sent his way by Jules. Andy had been trying to boost our enthusiasm for the world around us, but nothing worked.

"What is it with all these spooky villages," Jules said as we made our way through deserted streets and abandoned stone buildings in the hamlet of A Balsa. Many of the roofs had caved in, while other buildings' crumbling walls looked like a swift kick would knock them over. "Next time I'm bringing a video camera and making a film with these locations!"

"Next time?" Bethany said in disbelief.

Every time we passed a Camino marker, Bethany was now piling two and three stones on top, pausing for a moment of silence. She would go still in those moments in a way that almost made her invisible. "I'm running out of time," she said, aware of Jules' impatience. "There's so little time left."

The only thing I was doing with stones these days was kicking any I found in my way. Ben was back in my life and Camille and I were friends, but things were all screwed up with Gaby, and there were other things that still needed fixing.

I'm running out of time too. I need to find answers, make plans, sort stuff out!

23

PALAS DE REI'S YELLOW BRICK ROAD

From the top of yet another hill, we looked down and saw Sarria spread out in the valley below.

We'd been getting warnings about Sarria from anyone who'd walked the Camino before. Apparently thousands of people begin their Camino pilgrimage there.

"You're telling me that people who walk from Sarria get the same piece of paper, the same *Compostela,* that we're getting? That's not fair!" This news infuriated me. It seemed like a big-time injustice that 100 kilometres were considered equal to the 798 kilometres we would have walked by the time we reached the Santiago Cathedral.

Ben shook his head. He was getting used to my grumbling and had told me he'd realized my complaints usually only lasted as long as my feet hurt so he just ignored them.

"And I hate friggin' stairs!" I yelled at a dog stretched out in front of a doorway. It thumped its tail but otherwise didn't move. Maybe it was used to emotional pilgrims who had to climb the hill up to Sarria's main town square.

Bethany bent down as best she could with her backpack and

patted the dog. Its tail began thumping again against the stone step. "I wonder what happened to that man and his dog, you know, from Grañón?" she asked. Like so many people we'd met along the way, we'd never seen him or his dog again.

The Camino route took us by the Monasterio de la Magdalena, a 13th-century albergue that Camille had hoped to check out. Unfortunately, it was closed, like most albergues during the day. She had to be content with standing in front of one more place named after Mary Magdalene and admiring the building until she could no longer ignore her restless travelling companions. She added the name to her growing list of Mary Magdalene chapels, churches, and statues.

We left the town and walked down a hill toward a medieval stone bridge.

"The one problem with going down," I said, "is that it means—"

"You have to go up!" Ben, Bethany, and Jules finished the sentence, making me laugh. Who could stay mad with friends who like you even when you're grumpy?

Soon we were climbing through farmland. The uneven rock and stone trail was hard on our tender feet. "We're going to feel this," Bethany said. She held out one of her boots. "My soles are aching already."

That's all Camille and Andy needed. They started singing "These boots are made for walkin'/And that's just what they'll do!/One of these days these boots are gonna' walk all over you." Then they sang the chorus again.

Ben didn't help matters. "Again, please," he said, and started singing along.

We sang the chorus to that silly 1966 song, our six voices sailing out on the trail ahead. We were still singing when we walked around a big gnarled chestnut tree and came upon Diona sitting on the side of the dirt path. Her face lit up.

"I was getting bored and lonely," she said. "When I heard you singing that Jessica Simpson song, well...I'm so glad to see you."

"Nancy Sinatra," Andy corrected.

"Both," Camille said, reaching out to help Diona stand up. She walked with us for the rest of the day, telling us more fascinating and occasionally horrifying stories about being a female judge in Romania. It sounded like sexism and gender discrimination was rampant in Eastern Europe.

It turned out the new Barbadelo albergue was another oasis and worth the long walk, even if it appeared to be in the middle of nowhere. The front lawn had seats, trees, and sheltered areas with flowers where it was easy for tired hikers to rest. Charlotte and Andrea, the two women we'd met at the convent in Carrión de Los Condes and at several albergues since, were sitting at one of the outside tables.

Once we'd showered and washed only the absolutely necessary clothes, we joined Diona and the two women on the front lawn. Charlotte blushed when she shared the news this was their anniversary. She and Andrea had been married for one year though this was their official honeymoon.

Diona stood up and said, "I am the most senior, and of course only, judge at this table, which gives me the happy job to get a bottle of wine. We will all celebrate this wonderful occasion. Maggie, help me carry glasses." We were quickly back at the table, but Diona had bought two bottles, not one, and several cans of pop and iced tea.

As she began filling glasses, the newlywed Spanish couple from Logrono appeared. The plump husband had slimmed down since we last saw them. His tiny wife looked healthy and happy.

"Come! You are in time. Look," Diona said, "this couple is on their honeymoon too! We have lots to be happy about! Sit. Jules?" Jules sighed and got up to add two more chairs to our table.

I wasn't the only one who caught the swift glance between the

Christian newlyweds. It had been romantic to see how sweet they were with each other, but they were also deeply religious and had met at the Catholic High School where they both taught.

The Spanish husband and wife didn't immediately sit down as invited. Charlotte saved the day by getting up and starting to help the Spanish wife take off her backpack. Whatever she said made the couple laugh, and the tense moment passed. The table space expanded to include two more bodies.

Our communal meal became both a post-wedding and first-year anniversary party. It turned out Diona loved to cook, and she lamented the lack of a kitchen, saying she wished she could make a feast. She kept having drinks delivered to the table, while Andy paid for snacks for everyone. "This is the kind of event and night when we should splurge," he said.

"You're right, Andy," Jules replied, grinning. "It's a doozy!"

Andy rolled his eyes, but he was grinning too.

They assigned the Spanish newlyweds two bunk beds in the same room as Bethany and me. We were almost asleep when the couple finally came back. They'd learned that Charlotte and Andrea had also been to Israel and we'd left them comparing experiences about floating in the Dead Sea. They were quiet in their nighttime preparations. They always used the top bed to set out their toiletries and clothes for the next day and then spooned together in the lower bunk.

"*Buenas noches*, Maggie," the wife whispered.

Her husband popped his head up from behind her and called out to Bethany in the top bunk, "*Buenas noches*, Bethany!"

The four of us started to giggle. My feet still hurt, but my heart felt full.

Although we all started out at roughly the same time the next morning, everyone's walking pace was different. Diona and the Spanish couple charged ahead, while Charlotte and Andrea lagged, leaving our group of six in the middle. Within minutes we found ourselves behind or overtaken by more hikers and pilgrims than we'd seen in all the weeks we'd been on the trail. There was even a mother pushing a stroller with a crying baby in it while two whining four- and five-year-olds pulled on her arms, demanding to ride too.

"His feet will be a mess tonight," Bethany said, nodding toward the man in front of us who was wearing jeans and regular leather business shoes. He was alternating yelling, "*Si!*" and "*No!*" into his cell phone as he strode past us.

"His inner thighs are going to sting too, from his jeans rubbing his skin," I added.

With Camille in the lead and Andy at the rear, we worked our way around what we assumed was a church group because the man in the lead was a priest. Three of his male flock shared the weight of a large wooden cross, while several women prayed in loud voices, their hands clutching rosaries.

But the most bothersome were the boisterous bordering on obnoxious groups of 20- to 25-year-old Spaniards.

"I can see they're bugging you," Andy said to Jules and me, "but Spain has an unemployment rate of 27 percent and most of the unemployed are young people. A *hospitalero* told me it looked good on your resume if you've walked the Camino."

"It helps them get jobs?" Bethany asked. "Wow, I never thought of this as something I'd tell anybody about."

"I've worked hard enough that I want everyone to know what we did!" I said.

It was so easy to tell the experienced hikers from those who had started their pilgrimage within the last day or so. The newbies wore clothes that were too white and didn't have any underarm sweat stains that never went away when you could only hand-wash your clothes in albergue sinks. They wore sandals but didn't have tanned ankle lines. Their backpacks were overweight. The rowdy groups often had full wine bottles sticking out of their packs.

"Wait untill they find out pilgrim meals come with as much wine as you want to drink," Jules said. We were all feeling proud of our smudged, worn-looking backpacks, the still-damp socks drying over one of Bethany's backpack straps, and our tanned and sunburned faces, arms, and legs.

"This must be what veterans feel," Jules said, "when they see untested soldiers on the battlefield. You wonder who will last and who will give up at the next café."

As the trail began a steep decline down into Portomarin, Andy told us to be on the lookout for eucalyptus trees. I looked at Jules, but she shrugged his shoulders. "I only know Latin names for flowers."

My memories of Portomarin would be forever coloured by the very long bridge we had to cross before reaching the 52-step ancient stone stairway that went up and into the newer part of town. "What is it about stairs leading into city centres?" I asked. "Didn't any of the guys who plan these things walk the Camino? Don't they realize how sore and tired pilgrims are?"

"They built French towns on hilltops," Andy told me, "for safety's sake."

We stopped for what turned out to be a very unpleasant lunch, which didn't help any of our moods. Andy had read that *pulpo* or octopus was a Portomarin specialty and he wanted everyone to try it. We arrived just as most restaurants were closing for the afternoon and would not be reopening until the late Spanish dinner hour. The owner/waiter/chef at the third restaurant we checked out grudgingly agreed to make us *patatas fritas* and *pulpo*. His grumpiness must have impacted his cooking because the fries were cold and the *pulpo* too tough to eat.

"Chewy," Camille said, removing a piece from her mouth and

grabbing a handful of fries. We wanted to get out of the town as quickly as possible. The Camino route took us on an old footbridge, different from the one we'd crossed to enter Portomarin. Gonzar, where we would spend the night, was only five kilometres away, but Bethany and I moaned to each other about our aching feet, especially knowing there was still more than an hour of walking to do.

We were soon sweating from the steep uphill climb getting out of town. The path turned into another stretch of the *senda* along a highway.

The new albergue in Gonzar was a small building in a tiny collection of houses, but it was clean. Camille walked through the two streets of the tiny hamlet holding up her phone looking for unlocked access to WiFi but came back without having checked her emails or sent messages that we were all fine.

Diona, the Spanish newlyweds, and several other hikers we knew arrived throughout the afternoon. At six o'clock we pushed tables together and shared yet another story- and laughter-filled three-hour dinner. Everyone included us teens in their conversations. Ben and I sat beside each other, not touching but the air felt electric between us.

The resident waitress/bartender was a young Romanian woman who chatted happily with Diona about their home country. Apparently, she and her cousin, from the same Romanian village, did everything at the albergue but cook. They cleaned the rooms, sold drinks, registered hikers and pilgrims, and waited on tables. How they'd ended up in this isolated village working for the summer was a mystery. They hoped to eventually make their way to Britain, where over 100,000 Romanians already lived.

Diona shook her head as she shared the woman's story with the rest of us at dinner. "It's not good for Romanians in London," she said. "Everyone thinks all Romanians are gypsies, and lazy. She and her cousin will find it hard to get safe work." But Diona also understood why the two 21-year-olds had set their sights on

London. They'd be able to make six times more in wages than they could in Romania.

Ben got into a discussion with the chef who had worked at several Michelin-star restaurants in Spain until he got fed up with the hectic pace and of having painful feet, legs, and back from spending long hours on his feet. He'd walked part of the Camino and decided to find work in restaurants along the pilgrimage route to use his love of cooking in a less demanding environment.

"I also used to eat too much of my own cooking," he said, patting his Santa Claus belly. "It is no different now," he laughed, "but I am happier using my cooking skills in service to pilgrims." He was pleased to have someone interested in listening to his stories, and he and Ben stayed up talking long after everyone else had gone to bed.

My feet felt better when they were out of my boots. They had tingled refreshingly after I'd rubbed in Camille's peppermint foot cream. My feet smelled lovely, but the cream did nothing to stop the aching. I'd taken two Ibuprofen before dinner and another one at bedtime before trying to find a comfortable place to stretch out my sore legs.

Penance. Atonement. Amends. There are so many ways to say, "I'm sorry."

Getting up was torture the next morning. Thankfully, it was a short day by our usual standards and was only 18 kilometres to Palas de Rei. We walked in and out of one hamlet after another, through scrubland, by a field of mustard, and at one point had to walk single file to avoid the prickly vines and bushes that lined both sides of the path. It felt claustrophobic on the trail, with people behind and in front of us. We had to wait for an elderly woman and her granddaughter to amble up one short incline.

The paved road into Palas de Rei provided a broader walking space for everyone.

"It's like the yellow brick road," Bethany said with delight.

Our albergue that night had a back patio, and although we had to wait 30 minutes for the front door to be unlocked, we were content to sit and wait. Ben fell asleep leaning against the outside albergue wall and woke revitalized as the door opened.

Once we'd been assigned our bunks, Ben and I wandered around the town before returning to the albergue to spend a restful afternoon sitting outside reading, writing postcards, and napping in the sun.

I didn't want to think about the next few days, or after that. Vancouver was far away and, aside from Grams, nothing was drawing me back.

A phone alarm blasted out an Italian rock song at 5:30 a.m., again at 5:35, and for a third time at 5:40. The Italian owner of the phone turned over, shoved his cell phone under his pillow, and went back to sleep. By 5:45 everyone in the dorm was wide awake, whether or not they wanted to be, and the Italian was getting killer looks sent with Irish, French, Spanish, and Canadian curses attached.

His embarrassed girlfriend, who was in the bunk below him, got up and gave him several ineffectual nudges. He brushed her hand away. She turned to all of us and shrugged as if to say, "What can I do?"

Jules was already climbing down from her top bunk, her irritation evident, but I got there first. I stood on the edge of the girlfriend's bunk, put my head beside the sleeper's ear, and yelled, "Get up!" The guy almost jumped out of his top bunk in shock. I reached under his pillow and grabbed his phone. Finally, his girlfriend felt the need to draw the line somewhere and tried to take it out of my hand. I twisted around and threw the phone to Jules, who caught it and marched out of the room, quickly returning empty-handed. The Italian man started swearing at Jules and me as he jumped down and rushed out of the room. Jules and I shook hands.

"Job well done, Mulder," Jules said to me.

"Couldn't have done it without you, Scully," I replied, our actions and *X-Files* character references resulting in several people in the room clapping in appreciation.

The Italian man stomped his way back into the room, having found his phone from whatever shelf Jules had tossed it on, and began yelling at the two of us. Jules put her finger to her lips and mimed "shh," which only made the man angrier. Jules casually turned her back on him, gathered her things, and went to the bathroom.

"*Americana puttana*!" the Italian girlfriend hissed at me.

"*Italiania stronza*!" I hissed right back. Another thing about going to a school with lots of international students was you learned to swear in a variety of languages.

The day got worse when we discovered there was no toilet paper in any of the albergue washrooms. This wasn't a new problem, and we'd learned to make sure we always had a wad of toilet paper in our pant pockets and backpack, but it added to the albergue irritation already hanging in the air.

Andy, Camille, and Ben had been in another dorm room and didn't hear about the "Italian Job," as Jules called it, until we'd stopped at a cafe and were enjoying our first *café con leche* of the day.

"Dare I ask what she said, and you answered back?" Andy asked me.

"I had an Italian friend in one of my classes last year. And no, you don't want to know, though I feel sort of bad she thought I was American."

"Go Canada!" Jules said.

There were ups and downs during the day but most of the trail went through forests. We walked over the Rio Seco on the stone Maria Magdalena Bridge. Camille took more pictures, adding to her Mary Magdalene photo collection.

"I'm going to fill a wall in the store with these pictures," Camille said, making a quick note in her book so she'd remember the name of the river and where she'd taken the photo.

I'd lost count of the number of Mary Magdalene chapels, churches, and bridges we'd stopped at to let Camille take a picture. She had initially said she would pick four or five of the best ones and frame them for her store, but now, on day 30, she had expanded that vision to be a whole wall.

We walked into Melide, the midway point in our day and the largest city since Sarria, hungry and looking forward to our standard chicken or tuna *bocadillos*. Knowing our stay in Spain was nearing an end made our typical lunch food even more appealing.

But Andy had another plan. "Look for a *pulperias,* a restaurant that specializes in *pulpo*. I want you to see how delicious octopus can be and to remove the memory of that terrible lunch in Portomarin." When he found what he wanted, the *pulpo* arrived on a wooden platter flavoured with paprika, olive oil, and salt. This time, the octopus was delicious: tender and juicy. Bethany refused to eat it and ate another plate of fries. All of us were full and content when we began walking again.

Eucalyptus trees grew alongside our below-ground level trail once we were out of Melide, the path again worn down by millions of feet over the last millennium. Camille was the only one who said she could smell the eucalyptus.

In Castaneda, we saw a yellow arrow made from painted scallop shells on the wall of a house.

We stopped again to take pictures of each other standing beside the "K 55.5" Camino stone marker with the word "Magdalena" on it. It made me angry to see the marker covered in graffiti. "Don't people have any respect?"

"Most of the monuments look like that, Maggie," Jules said. "What's the difference?"

Camille started walking again, and we fell into step behind her.

After lots of up and down trails and more downs and ups through villages, we passed a road sign that said, "52 Santiago." We four teens looked at each other. It was obvious by our sighs, tight lips, and clenched hands the others felt some of my conflicting emotions of excitement, fear, and sadness. I reached out for Ben's hand and probably held on tighter than I needed to.

"Check this out," Andy said, skimming through his guidebook. "This city has a population of 7,000 but more cows than people." Having walked 30 kilometres, none of us cared who lived in Arzúa as long as there was a bed available somewhere.

"I am so done with 30 kilometre days," I said later, rubbing my throbbing feet. We'd picked our hostel solely for its name, Ultreia. White plastic tables and chairs covered the sidewalk and drinking pilgrims filled most of the seats. Camille had been hesitant, not wanting to stay some place that might be noisy but Andy had talked her into it. So far, everyone had been well-behaved.

Jules had left her boots at the bottom of the stairs. She'd stepped into a pile of cow dung somewhere on the trail, something she hadn't realized until the *hospitalero* stopped her from going through the front door. She'd emptied her water bottles washing the dung off.

"Remember the fuss you made in Roncesvalles?" Bethany said, laughing. "You were so afraid someone would steal your boots and look at you now, not thinking twice about leaving them at the hotel entrance to dry off."

"And after Fergus stole yours," Jules said to Andy.

Andy quickly corrected her. "Borrowed, they were borrowed, not stolen."

"Pinched, pilfered, scrounged. What ever."

"I'm happy none of us has to do 30 kilometres again too." Andy was also massaging his sore bare feet. Camille tossed him her peppermint foot cream.

"Sharesies," she said.

"Sharesies," he echoed, giving her such a loving smile, I knew I'd better be prepared to accept a new family member once we returned to Vancouver.

The beginning of the path the next morning was so far below ground level and bordered by such high dirt walls that it was impossible to tell if the day was overcast or if the sun was shining.

We hiked into and out of many hamlets and river valleys, passed lots of stone buildings and farms, and this time we were all aware of the minty-smelling eucalyptus trees. Occasional noisy stretches along busy roads left us exhausted after the relative quiet of the forest paths. Or quiet at least until we would hear soccer songs—Jules impatiently reminded us it was called football in Europe—being shouted out by another group of inebriated walkers.

"Bet they started in Sarria and are feeling so proud of themselves now that their five-day hike is almost over," Jules said sarcastically.

"Tourists," Bethany said, dismissing one particularly wild group who were playing a version of tag that required them to bang each other with their backpacks. They had already knocked over one unaware hiker.

Our group reached Arca in good time. By now, 22 kilometres a day was a breeze, regardless of our sore feet and the ongoing irritation at all the people on the trail with us. We agreed to leave early tomorrow to make sure we covered the last 20 kilometres into Santiago in time to attend the noon Pilgrim's Mass in the Cathedral. After the mass, we'd get our official *Compostela* certificate from the Pilgrim's Office.

"Both are ending rituals of your Camino," Camille said. "We have to go to the Cathedral. If we're lucky, they'll bring out the *Botafumeiro,* this huge incense burner that dangles from the ceiling and requires eight monks pulling on a rope to get it to swing from one end of the transept to the other. They initially used to do it to cover the smells of the pilgrims."

I had a restless night, waking up repeatedly, my mind busy with thoughts of my mother and father, of Grams and Gaby, of Ben, and questions about ways to make things different when I got back to my regular life.

My sleeping brain worked overtime, and I awoke with a "To Do" list:

#1) Apologize to my mother.

#2) Figure out a way to pay back Camille.

#3) Keep Ben in my life.

#4) Not be such a bitch about things.

#5) Make sure Bethany was safe, maybe see if she could come and live with us. Our house was big enough. Bethany could become Mom's next project since Gaby seemed to be Grams.

#6) Figure out what I wanted to do in my life.

No answers yet, but at least I had a plan.

24

SWEET SANTIAGO INCENSE

On that final morning, Camille would only let us drink a cup of *cafe con leche* before insisting we eat our *tortillas de patatas* while we walked.

It quickly became clear many other people had the same plan: arrive in Santiago in time for the noon mass and hopefully see the *Botafumeiro*.

Every signpost with a Camino symbol or the word "Santiago" on it had people standing beside it getting their picture taken.

"Sightseers," Bethany muttered under her breath. In Amenal, a community less than an hour out of Arca, we came to another bollard, one of the stone markers.

"I don't care if we look like sightseers," Andy said smiling at Bethany. "This is a special moment." He looked at Camille, who gave him a quick hug. The next person who came along—which meant waiting all of 45 seconds—agreed to take a picture of our group standing around the stone marker. Andy put his hand down on the flat top, Camille set hers down next, and on we went until there was a pyramid of scraped, tanned, and sunburned hands resting on each other.

Bethany made sure her hand was resting on all of ours. She closed her eyes, something that caused the photographer to ask her to open them for the photograph. The man handed back the camera to Andy, but when we started to remove our hands, Bethany made us stop.

"Wait," she said, closing her eyes again. Her small hand got hotter and hotter until it seemed we could feel a pulse of heat radiating down from one hand into the next. She opened her eyes. "Thank you. Now we've all got each other's energy inside us."

No one moved. Or scoffed at her comment. It went with the mood of the day.

"One for all and all for one," Camille and Andy said in another one of their telepathic flashes.

"Bethany, you look positively peaceful," Jules said when we were back on the trail. "You were a frightened mouse when I first met you. Now look at you! You're like this friggin' enlightened being!"

Bethany gave her a playful push. "I think I've inherited my mother's healing hands. Maybe I'll do some kind of healing, like Reiki. Or become a nurse, like your mother. Think she'd talk to me about what I need to do?" She was so caught up in her thoughts she wasn't aware of the sudden appearance of the Santiago de Compostela Airport on her left until she heard a plane take off.

Ben and I had already noticed the links in the airport fence filled with handmade wooden crosses left behind by pilgrims. "Don't even think about it!" Jules said when she noticed Bethany slowing down. "We don't have time to stop and find the right size pieces of wood to make some sort of yin-yang Taoist symbol to add to the fence!"

Bethany nodded reluctantly and kept walking but turned back for a final look before we lost sight of the fence artwork.

The next stop was on the Monte del Gozo, which Andy said meant "Mount of Joy." For the first time, we could see the city of

Santiago. Although both guidebooks said we'd be able to spot the Cathedral spires, none of us could.

"Pilgrims used to walk barefoot for the last 4.5 kilometres into Santiago. Any takers?" Camille asked. No one bothered to answer her.

While we made our way through the outskirts of the city by following the last of the yellow arrows, strangers smiled and wished us "*Buen Camino*!" It added a surreal element to the final 30-minutes of our Camino hike.

Busy sidewalks boarded the wide city streets. There were traffic roundabouts everywhere. As we neared the city centre, the cobbled streets became narrow and packed with other hikers and pilgrims.

Some hikers we passed must have arrived a day or two earlier but were still hanging around, maybe unable to separate from the Camino experience. Most were wearing their Camino clothes, unwilling to give up their hats and hiking boots. Some were limping and wearing elastic knee supports.

Others already looked out of place. They still had their Camino ankle tan, but now they wore makeup and freshly pressed shorts and shirts.

One glitch in our welcome was that the familiar yellow arrows suddenly disappeared. Now we had to pay attention to markers set on the sidewalk. At one point, a man stepped in front of us, making us bump into each other in a clumsy domino effect that would have looked funny if it had been a slapstick movie scene.

"Cathedral?" the man asked. When Andy nodded, he pointed to the next narrow street, not the one we were on, before wishing us "*Buen Camino*!" and disappearing back into his store.

"That was embarrassing," Jules said. "We walk almost 800 kilometres, get lost only once on the trail, and then get lost trying to get into Santiago? It's like a final test."

We were also passing a multi-national selection of tourists:

Americans, Europeans, Asians, and even an Arab man in a designer suit followed by several women who wore black chadors covering their heads and bodies.

"They must be hot, having to wear all that stuff," Bethany said.

"Imagine what they think of us," I said, looking at my sunburned arms and face and scratched bare legs. "Wait! I know what I think of us! We're all friggin' fantastic!" I exchanged enthusiastic high fives with Jules, Bethany, and Ben.

We exchanged big grins and "*Buen Camino*!" with every hiker we saw. We'd done it! We'd walked 798 kilometres, survived sore feet, bad weather, repetitious food, a group shake-up, and shared accommodations with sometimes pleasant, sometimes not so much, hikers and pilgrims from all over the world.

Gaby was on all our minds, though no-one said her name.

And even more important: we'd built a bond that would always be there, no matter how many miles or years would eventually separate us.

My feeling of elation was disturbed by the sounds of a screechy violin being played. The music got louder. We walked down a short series of steps into the shade of a covered archway. I felt bombarded by the piercing sounds of the street musician's instrument as his music bounced off the archway stone walls. We went down two more small sets of steps and came back into the sunshine, entering the large and open Plaza do Obradioro, with the Santiago Cathedral on our left.

It was too much—our emotions had been on a rollercoaster ride for weeks, and the end had arrived much too quickly. I felt Ben take my hand. I grabbed Bethany's small fingers and entwined them in mine. She took hold of Camille who reached out to Andy. Only Jules was initially reluctant, but even she eventually slid her hand into Andy's. We held on to each other in silence, staring into the faces we'd come to love and trust. We let go, but stayed close.

"This is it? I'm here?" I said as we walked across the plaza. At first, I couldn't take in all the people surrounding us. One group of hikers was sharing a bottle of champagne, passing it from one laughing person to the next. Other backpackers were in a huddled group hug, or taking selfies, or crying, or lying on the plaza square resting on their backpacks, looking dazed and unsure where to go next.

It was the gawking tourists taking pictures who looked out of place.

Before we got halfway to the Santiago de Compostela plaque set into the centre of the Plaza's stone floor, I heard my name.

"Maggie May!"

"Maggie!"

It sounded like my father and mother, but it couldn't be.

Other voices began calling out "Andy! Camille! Heh, Ben! Bethany! Jules! Maggie!"

My father and father were suddenly hugging me. Diona, Charlotte, and Erika had surrounded the others. Everyone was crying and laughing and clapping and shaking hands and hugging.

"But? How? Why?" I felt incapable of making a complete sentence.

My father had his arm around my shoulder and didn't seem to want to let go. "Your mother asked Camille if it would be ok because we wanted to be here to welcome you at the finish. We're so proud of you, Maggie May!"

Now it was my mother's turn to hug me. When she let go, I looked down and saw that her fingers were nervously drumming against her pant leg.

That small motion shocked me. *Was my mother nervous?* I'd never seen or imagined her to be anything other than in complete control of every situation and person she dealt with.

She and I finally made eye contact and stared at each other for what seemed like a long time. She began to cry, and I felt a shift inside me—it was like an internal avalanche took place and all the anger I'd felt for so long just slid away.

"I'm sorry," I said and meant it. Now we were both crying, holding on to one another tightly.

Mom was babbling. "I was so worried about you and I wanted to meet you at Sarria and walk the last four or five days with you but your father reminded me this was your trip and so we waited and I am so proud of you and you look so healthy and...." She ran out of words and stood back, embarrassed by her emotional state.

I gave her another hug, not caring if I was dirty or smelled and wasn't colour coordinated. My nose was peeling again, and my hair was in desperate need of a cut, let alone a wash. My left leg had a line of dried blood leftover from a scratch I'd gotten from a bush on the trail this morning.

None of that mattered. I felt a bubble of happiness rising inside.

"Maggie, we did it!" Hearing Ben say my name like that brought out another wash of tears. He stepped forward, took me in his arms, and kissed me. In front of everyone. Camille shrugged, threw her arms around Andy, and kissed him as intently as I was kissing Ben.

My parents had shifted all their attention from me to Ben. He smiled at them but didn't let go of my hand.

Diona was urging us all to get moving. The noon Pilgrim Mass was about to start. In a chatting, crying, and laughing group we headed toward the Cathedral, pausing to stare up at the recently renovated and repaired ornate facade and decorated spires.

The action in the plaza also distracted us. A mime was dressed up as St. Jacques, standing perfectly still on one side of the Cathedral gates with a gold bucket in front of him for donations. A group of cyclists were taking big gulps from a bottle of wine before passing it on to the next rider. A begging gypsy woman with a baby in her arms moved from tourist to pilgrim, but most people ignored her.

Led by Diona, my family and friends climbed up the elaborate Renaissance stairway to the cathedral entrance, we pilgrims still carrying our backpacks that felt as much a part of our body as our clothes and boots.

Near the large doorway, Ben pointed to a sign in five languages that said, "NO backpacks allowed inside." It turned out we had to go to another part of town and leave the bags there.

I heard Diona say, "*O asemenea prostie*!" which sounded suspiciously like a Romanian curse. "I meant to tell you. I'm sorry."

"There isn't time!" Bethany's voice quivered. "We'll miss the Pilgrim's Mass!"

A gypsy stepped out of the shadows. He smiled, showing dirty teeth. His pants were clean but rustic. He said something to Diona, having heard her swear in Romanian. She replied, and he switched to basic English. "Me. I watch," he said, pointing to our bags.

Out of habit we teens turned to Andy, but it was Dad who stepped forward and pulled out his wallet. "I'll pay you ten Euros per bag, plus the same again when we come out to collect them. Agreed?" He already had 60 Euros in his hand. The gypsy paused. Dad added another ten Euro note. The man nodded. We immediately yanked off our backpacks, and the man began moving them over to a corner away from the door.

Ben held out his hand and Dad shook it. "Thanks. I'm Ben." Dad held on a little longer than necessary, giving Ben an intense once over. When he let go, he was smiling.

"Looks like Ben passed the test," Bethany whispered to me.

"Mom and Dad, I want you to meet my friend, Bethany. She needs a place to stay." My parents didn't even hesitate. They both gave Bethany a hug and Mom had her arm through Bethany's when we walked inside.

The interior of the Cathedral was noisier even than the outside square. Hundreds of people filled every pew and aisle, sitting, squatting, and standing shoulder to shoulder. They were singing, praying, talking, laughing, crying, or upright in stunned, exhausted silence

Our group found space along one wall, allowing us to stay in visual range of each other.

A middle-aged nun was singing a hymn in as pure a voice as I'd ever heard. I felt an ache in my heart, of happiness and joy, and at the same time a bone-deep sadness this was the end. I leaned back against Ben and he put his arms around me.

Looking over at my music-loving father, I saw he was staring in wonder at the singing nun. I began to cry again. It was all too much, too wonderful, too hard. For the first time in over a month, it was my eyes that would hurt tomorrow, not my feet.

Camille leaned over and kissed my cheek. "Thank you. The past five weeks have been the best!"

She was thanking me? This day was upside down and backwards!

The Mass we attended didn't include the *Botafumeiro*, the giant, silver incense holder that could only begin swinging when eight monks pulled on a huge rope. Today, it remained hanging from the ceiling.

"Tomorrow you can see it," Diona said as she began moving us along again, this time back out the doors. "Time to get your *Compostela*. There will be a lineup. Come!" We grabbed our bags, Dad paid the gypsy the rest of his money, and we all ran down the steps and into a side street that led to the Pilgrim's Office.

Diona had been right. There was a line-up but it wasn't long, by Santiago standards apparently. Or so Diona told us. It was like this day had lucky fairy dust sprinkled all over it, and there were only 60 people in front of us, but unlike that first day in St-Jean, no-one had shiny, clean boots or clothes. People were sunburned, limping, and possibly thinner than when they'd started.

Once we had pulled our numbered ticket from the machine to

give us our place in the lineup, we waited in exhausted silence for our turn. To our relief, it took only 20 minutes to make our way to the Reception Area, 20 minutes we spent smiling and nodding at others who knew how challenging, how long, and how fantastic the Camino had been.

Still in a daze, I finally found myself standing in front of a long desk. I handed over the required three euros to the bored young Spanish woman.

"Your *credential*!" the woman demanded.

I fumbled in my search for my now battered *credential* booklet. A wave of panic rushed through me and I hesitated at handing it over to her. "I'll get it back?"

She nodded impatiently, and I gave up the proof I'd hiked almost 800 kilometres from France into Spain on the Camino Francés.

"Did you use any other forms of transportation for the last 100 kilometres?"

"No."

"Why did you walk the Camino?"

I heard the question repeated by other clerks to Andy, Camille, and Jules who were nearby. Ben was too far away. My mind went blank.

Why did I walk the Camino?

"To pray," I heard Bethany say. "For my mother, who is sick."

"Because I needed to think in silence and community," Camille said.

Jules was leaning over the counter, flirting with the man on the other side. She laughed at something he said as he began filling in her *Compostela*. When he handed the paper to her, he held on to it a moment longer than necessary. Jules winked, turned around, and hurried down the stairs, whistling.

I thought of Gaby and felt a wave of longing that she too could have been here with us.

An impatient sound of a throat being cleared brought my attention back to the woman behind the desk.

"I'm still caught up in the Camino. It's so amazing, you know?"

For the first time, the clerk smiled. "I do. It's good. Hold on to that feeling. It will disappear. Now, why did you walk the Camino?"

"For penance," I said, surprising myself. "I hurt someone, two people actually, that I love, and I needed to get their forgiveness. And forgive myself." Those last three words were the final piece in the puzzle of how to make changes in my life.

The Spanish woman gave me a nod of appreciation. "As it should be," she said, making it sound like a benediction. She immediately took a blank *Compostela* and began writing my name on it in Latin.

I stumbled as I walked outside but several people waiting in line steadied me. I was trying to read the black, ornately scripted words: *Margarita Emilia Mackenzie*. "I guess there is no Latin translation for MacKenzie," I said. I realized I'd spoken out loud. A hysterical giggle threatened to pour out, then another, but if I started, I might not be able to stop.

Jules was waiting for me at the front entrance. She held out her *Compostela*. I took it without thinking, glanced at it, then looked again.

I couldn't believe it.

The name written in black ink wasn't hers, but read, "*Gabrielle Alexandria Marchetti*." I looked at her, shocked. "What did you do?"

She didn't say anything, just gave me a grin and did a silly happy dance.

Awareness dawned. "You took those things. And you stashed them in Gaby's bag? That was the sneakiest, meanest—"

Jules held up her hands. "I know," she said, holding out her hands as though she expected me to put handcuffs on. "Gaby knew. She still didn't say anything." She shook her head. "Why? It's been bugging me. I don't like it when people, like you and her, know things about me but don't say anything. Are you waiting for something, for some special payback time?"

"Conscience at work?"

She shrugged. "Whatever, I felt like I owed her, had to make amends, so I took her *credential* out of her bag and used it in there instead of mine. This will help clear things up between us." She suddenly looked less sure of herself. "Won't it?"

I stared at the paper in my hands. "But that means you don't—"

"My bad. My tough luck. Come on."

My parents were waiting on the other side of the street guarding our backpacks. I had to say that in my head a second time to make it real: *My parents*. Mom was trying to repair her tear-damaged eye makeup. Dad was swaying to the music of another street busker.

Jules' word popped into my head: "Amends."

I had some amending to do.

But first, plans. Maybe I'd walk the Camino del Norte next, which begins in Irun, France, and follows the northern Spanish coast. Kata and Kodek, the Polish couple I'd first met over 30 days ago, had said the hiking trails in the Tatra Mountains on the border between Slovakia and Poland were like nothing else in the world. Or maybe I would go to Nepal, or India, and take Mom up on her offer to work in our family owned factory. Bethany and Grams could come with me.

Or Ben. Ben and I could plan a trip that would let him expand his cooking skills and let me experience more.

More of everything.

"Why did you walk the Camino?" The question still haunted me. It was ricocheting inside my head. Yes, for penance, that was one answer, but I realized there were others.

Because I needed to complete a task, to wake up every morning and walk for six or eight or ten hours putting one foot in front of the other, rain or shine, over mountains and across a desert, when I was tired, sad, happy, angry, and homesick.

Because I had to discover there are good people everywhere, people who would like, even love me, in all my cranky, snide, arrogant gloriousness.

Because I had to learn there was—is—always the possibility of making changes in my life, regardless of bedbugs, blisters, or boys.

I, Margaret Emily MacKenzie, will be fine. I can't wait to tell Grams. It seems such a simple lesson: If you take just one step at a time, there's no end to the adventures you can have.

Buen Camino!

BOOKS

Camino de Santiago (95 pages) and ***A Pilgrim's Guide to the Camino Francés*** (319 pages), both by John Brierley, considered "the" books to use by many pilgrims and hikers, with maps and short paragraphs of information about each day's hike.

There are too many Camino reference books to list. ***The Way of St James***, by Alison Raju, for example, is small and easy to pack. Most bookstores and Amazon sites will offer you a wide selection. Some books have maps and route information, and others have albergue phone numbers and addresses for each town you'll pass through.

What the Psychic Told the Pilgrim, Jane Christmas. You'll get a good sense of how tough the Camino Francés can be by reading this personal travel adventure.

FILMS & MUSIC (samples only)

The Way. This film is probably familiar to many of you. It's not 100% "true"—who wears jeans on the Camino like the character Sarah did?—but it will give you a visual teaser for the countryside and the eclectic range of people you can meet on any Santiago de Compostela Camino hike.

Saint Jacques, La Mecque [***Start Walking***], A hilarious film, highly recommended—in French, but with English subtitles—about three alienated siblings who find out that in order to inherit their mother's millions, they must hike the Santiago de Compostela trail together.

Walking the Camino, Six Ways to Santiago, documentary. Six Camino pilgrims hike Maggie's route.

Strangers on the Earth, Dane Johansen, an American cellist, hiked the Camino with his cello and gave concerts of Bach music along with way. When I hiked the Camino Francés for the second time in 2014 with my daughter, Emily, we kept meeting up with Dane and his film crew.

YouTube has thousands (!) of Camino de Santiago films uploaded by hikers. There are also maps to download.

WEBSITES & BLOGS & MUSIC (samples only)

Santiago de Compostela Camino Organizations. Many cities have their own Camino organization that arranges regular local area training walks and bring in speakers to share their Camino stories, plus there are the national organizations. Here are two:

Canadian Company of Pilgrims, https://www.santiago.ca

American Company of Pilgrims, https://americanpilgrims.org

Don't forget to read Santiago de Compostela **blogs**.

Luna na Lubre, Spanish Folk Music Group

Oliver Schroer's Camino CD, recorded in churches along the *Camino Francés* route.

ACKNOWLEDGMENTS

Hugs of appreciation to my readers and editors: Meave Wilde and Quynn Stafford of the P.I. Teen Writers Group; Young Adult novelist Ellen Boyd; and Camino hikers Emily Thierry-Gray, Gay Paige, Carol Davis, and tween Elise Harrel. Thanks also to Kate Conway of Wicked Whale Publishing for her skills, patience, and goodwill.

A "CHEERS" to my marvellous Muddy Lotus Writing Group who read drafts and provided feedback, tea and cookies, and nudges when needed: mythology & magic realism author Zoe Landale, poet & memoirist Kate Braid, artist & children's book author Andrea Spalding, and writer & movement teacher Barbara Stowe.

ABOUT THE AUTHOR

Joy Llewellyn has spent much of her childhood living in an isolated fly-in bush camp in northern Canada where she developed an appreciation for wild spaces, mosquito repellant, and adventure books. She promised herself that when she grew up, she would feed her rebel adventure yearnings and voyage around the world. Joy has travelled to over 30 countries and herded goats in France, lived in a Tibetan Buddhist Monastery in Kathmandu, Nepal, and hiked thousands of kilometres on different Camino routes in France and Spain. She was a newspaper journalist, has had fiction and non-fiction articles and stories published in anthologies, and wrote and story edited film and television scripts for many years, work which led to her teaching screenwriting in Canada, India, and China. Joy now lives on a small island where she hangs out with real and imaginary female rebels of all ages and writes stories about them.

You can learn more about Joy at www.joythierryllewellyn.com

instagram.com/joyonpender

ALSO BY JOY LLEWELLYN

Hi, I hope you've enjoyed reading the adventures of ***Camino Maggie***. Please consider leaving a review on Amazon.

If you would like to be on my email list, send me a note at joyteenrebelseries@gmail.com. This way you will learn more about the ***Teen Rebel Series***, including getting notices when the next two books are available. My initial "thanks" for joining my mailing list will be an inventory of the gear and clothes Maggie packed for her Camino hike. It's something you can use for a future backpacking trip (that doesn't require a tent).

Have you hiked any of the Caminos? Or gone on another big adventure? I'm interested in hearing about it.

I will be publishing two more ***Teen Rebel Series*** books in 2019-2020. Here's what I can tell you so far:

Spark Rebecca

Rebecca's first foster parent was from another planet, her second is an eccentric meteorite hunter, and the guy she's attracted to has put them all in danger. Now it's up to Rebecca to keep her Alien foster mother from being sold to the highest bidder.

Gator Boarding Ariela

When a raging typhoon strands Ariela in the Louisiana Women's Prison, she must outwit escaping prisoners, a revenge-seeking guard, and a cranky grandmother while avoiding marauding alligators and keeping her young brother and inmate mother safe.

Cheers to you and all your future rebel adventures. — Joy

SNEAK PEEK OF JOY LLEWELLYN'S NEXT BOOK

SPARK REBECCA

1/Let Me Out!

My voice echoed in the shadow-filled cave. "Please, Linsss! Just for ten minutes. Five minutes! Let me go out!"

Linsss ignored my plea and continued to groom itself.

I tried again, aware of how whiny my voice sounded. "Please! I've been good."

The alien shook its head. My burns and wounds had almost healed, but it just kept saying, "Too sssoon," and ignored my pleas to go above ground.

Being told "No" again left me with little choice but to be devious.

Sitting in the far corner of Linsss's underground cave, I forced myself to think of Mom. Usually, I didn't let myself because it made me too sad, but "Some days call for desperate measures," my father used to say. I thought of Mom baking bread. Of her reading to me as I snuggled under the patchwork quilt she'd hand-sewn for my fifth birthday. I closed my eyes and imagined the two of us shivering on the dock every May 1st, counting down from 20 before jumping into the lake when we came to my age number.

"Painsss, Mite?" Linsss said, finally looking over at me.

I kicked my feet out, making my soft hammock bed swing back and forth. It was made from the same sturdy material as the translucent curtain-like sheets that dangled from the ceiling. I wiped away tears with my sleeve. "I miss Mom," I sighed. "Do you know where she is?"

Linsss ignored my question for the gazillionth time.

I didn't want another day of lying in my hammock, of watching the twirling, see-through strips twist into a unique pattern, then fall in a cascade of wispy white material. At first, I'd thought the strands might be alien art, but Linsss had shaken its head when I asked and said, "homesss." I still didn't know what that meant. One end of every hanging piece stuck to the cave roof like it was Krazy-glued. I'd discovered I could stand on the grooming platform, take hold of a strand, and swing myself out, without my weight pulling it down.

One hanging strip gave off a light that dimmed at night and brightened in the morning, as though it knew instinctively when day and night changed. The daylight version was more candlelight than electric bright though.

How did Linsss manage when it was outside in the desert during the day? Having so many eyes packed together in two bunches on each side of its forehead must make it sensitive to light.

Or did it? I had so many unanswered questions. *Maybe it had alien sunglasses.* That made me grin.

Oops. I need to stay sad looking.

It was time to do something, even if that involved lying. "I missed my birthday. It was the week after the accident, and that was a long time ago so I must be 13 now, and I never got to celebrate!" I rubbed my eyes and sniffed, at the same time knowing my attempt to look miserable would only confuse Linsss. It found my human emotions baffling, intriguing, and complicated.

Running my fingers through my long red hair felt good but months without a brush meant my fingers touched mainly tangles. I sighed loudly again, waiting to see how Linsss would respond.

The alien squatted beside me. I was always impressed by how fast it moved, and how elegantly it crouched. Its long willowy legs bent at two different places, making it look like it had two knees. With long arms, bent legs, and bulbous head, I thought it looked like a combination of a dragonfly and praying mantis. But dragonflies on Earth didn't glow sparkly under their skin. And Linsss didn't have wings.

"Birth-daysss. Daysss of birthsss."

"Yes!" I said, sobbing as dramatically as possible.

Linsss was smart, but one thing I'd learned over the long time —one month? Two? Three?—that I'd been underground was the alien could not lie. Because it wouldn't fake feelings and stories meant it believed everything I said and did was true. I felt a twinge of guilt about my tears, but if I stayed underground any longer, I'd go crazy.

I had tried to escape once, waiting until I thought Linsss was asleep, but the alien had suddenly appeared in front of me in the tunnel. It didn't say anything, just pointed a long thin sparkly arm back toward the cave opening. I had pretended to be sleepwalking and turned around slowly and kept staring straight ahead as I retraced my steps and climbed back into my hammock. It had taken a while to calm my breathing.

I buried my face in my hands, watching the alien through my fingers as it tilted its bald head and pondered this new information.

"Humansss do? Birth-daysss?" The hissing, lilting voice echoed off the rock walls.

I wiped my eyes with my sleeve again and took a deep breath. "Birthday parties are to celebrate a new year in a human life. They take place on the same day each year. You get a cake." I drew a three-tiered cake on the cave floor but doubted if Linsss would know what it was.

Linsss tilted its head, which it always did when it was thinking.

"And you get gifts," I continued, "things that are special and just for you." Not that I'd ever had any of those things even when I was living with my parents, but I'd read about them and had always dreamed of a party with friends and presents.

"No bakesss."

I laughed, which may have been the alien's intention. It was trying to understand human humour and occasionally attempted a joke.

"My mother and I used to cook together," I said, but eying the bare cave reminded me how silly a comment that was. Aside from my soft material hammock, the only things in the cave were the hanging silk-like strands, the grooming platform, and a pyramid-shaped pile of rocks that Linsss added to occasionally after one of its desert runs.

Plus, there was that all-important—to me—sack of alien food that hung from the wall near the door. It was filled with blobs that looked like chocolate cupcakes baked by a bad cook: lopsided, lumpy, and burned on top. They tasted ok. The sack never seemed to empty; it was like an alien Mary Poppins Magic Bag.

My drinking and washing water came from a rivulet of water dripping along a groove in the rock wall and falling into an eroded sink-like stone. A deep hole in the back of the cave was my toilet, with torn-off pieces of the dangling fabric my toilet paper.

Linsss unfolded its long legs and stood up, towering over me, but I no longer found the alien frightening. Its many black eyes blinked rapidly as it stared down at me.

I took this as a good sign and remained quiet.

I had no idea if Linsss was male, female, or a bit of both. *How had it been born? As an egg, in a test tube, or from a sac like spiders and tadpoles?* Even though I wasn't afraid of Linsss, a sac breaking open and alien after alien spilling out was gross.

Its seven-foot tall body gave nothing away. It didn't have body parts as human men and women did. Now that I was no longer afraid of Linsss, I loved watched the sparkling lights that seemed to float around under its skin. I'd seen a picture of a house decorated in twinkling Christmas lights once and that's what Linsss looked like. Even at night when it was sleeping on the grooming platform, the floor of the cave filled with fluttering shadows made by its moving skin-lights.

Maybe it was the creature's regular morning grooming and its kind and patient nature—things I always associated with Mom—that made me think of it as female most days. When it was moody and disappeared for hours, it reminded me of my father, though Linsss never hit me, which my father had done. A lot.

Staring up at the creature, I searched again for its nose. *Did it even have one? Or ears? Maybe it smelled or heard through its skin. That would be cool.*

The silence lasted until I couldn't stand it any longer. "I've got ants in my pants, as Mom used to say. That's a good sign. It shows I'm better. 'Ants in my pants' means I'm restless," I added, knowing Linsss found English expressions confusing, but we'd talked about "restless" before.

I stretched my legs, enjoying the feeling of my muscles tightening and then relaxing. There was hardly any pain today. The injuries that should have killed me were healing well.

I want fresh air! Peanut butter! A hairbrush!

I want Mom.

I didn't bother saying what I was thinking. Linsss had heard me complain enough today.

"Giftsss." The alien took one long step then another before

pausing at the opening of our cave, where it waited for me to follow.

I stood up, wiping away my tears, and walked as quickly as I could. *Don't let Linsss see me limp!* I thought, afraid it might change its mind.

The path we took meandered through a long dark passageway. *Had Linsss found it or made it? Maybe it led to an abandoned mine?* Prospectors had been working these mountain mines for over a hundred years before they all closed. We'd been able to see the mountain from our cabin so maybe I'd know where I was if I could get outside and look around.

It was a steep hike. Although most of my injuries had healed, my left leg was still weak and quickly began to ache. The alien silky material Linsss had wrapped me in after finding me must have alien medicine in it too. It had still taken me a long time to heal enough to get out of the cocoon and walk around the cave. Linsss had expected me to mend faster, and later I realized it just proved its belief that humans were weak.

I wished I could show superhuman strength or a superpower to prove we weren't frail. "Humans are not delicate, we're just different from you," I often said, a comment always met with polite alien disbelief.

The burn scars on my face hadn't gone away though, and I could still feel them when I ran my fingers down my cheek. Linsss had left my face uncovered but wrapped up my damaged body until I l probably looked like I was in a cocoon. *Maybe if Linsss had covered my burned face in cocoon material, there wouldn't have been any burn scars left on my cheek.*

I put my hand on the tunnel's rough rock wall and followed the winding passageway in darkness. Sudden dips in the uneven ground jolted my injured leg, and when I stumbled, I bit my tongue to keep from crying out.

At first, I could see Linsss's outline ahead of me and hear the patter of the alien's feet, but the creature walked faster than I could hobble. I was getting farther behind. I was sure Linsss had an eagle-like vision because of its bunched multiple eyes, and its long legs probably meant it could travel tirelessly anywhere, day or night.

The tunnel was quiet except for the drip, drip, drip of water, and the occasional sound of rocks sliding down the earth walls. At least, that's what I hoped was making the sound. *Please, let it be falling mud or tumbling rock, anything but a snake slithering toward me.*

I'd hated creepy-crawly things ever since I was six and woke up to find a Yellow-Bellied Racer snake curled around my metal bed frame. Mom had smacked the snake repeatedly with the broom, and when it uncurled and slid to the floor, she chased it out of the cabin. She said it probably came inside seeking the sunshine-warmed iron bedpost.

I'd told her when I was an adult I would make all my furniture out of wood. She'd laughed and hugged me.

I missed being hugged.

My breathing quickened, the beginning of panic making my stomach go tight. I wanted to be outside so badly, to see the moon or the sun, to smell the desert and hear birds, anything but the sounds and shadows in this gloomy tunnel.

Then I heard rushing water. *What if I step off the path?* I couldn't see the alien and called out, "Linsss!"

It was quickly beside me. "Sssorry, Mite." It ran one of its hands along the rock wall and, like a piece of flint striking a steel knife, a spark appeared, giving me a small flame to follow.

"Badsss," Linsss said, pointing toward the nearby ledge that led down into intense darkness. "Farsss." Linsss kicked a nearby stone to prove the point. It was a long time before I heard the soft "plunk" of the stone hitting the underground stream.

When we began to walk again, I hugged the wall until I could no longer hear the running water.

It wasn't an easy trip to the tunnel entrance. We climbed over piles of rock, a simple task for Linsss with its long, spindly legs, but not for me. The alien couldn't even offer to help—a lesson we'd learned the hard way at the accident site. If I touched its skin directly, or it touched me, it burned my skin—a reaction Linsss still couldn't understand. "Humansss sssoft," it often said.

When Linsss had found me, I was unconscious. I'd been tossed from my father's truck as it rolled down the ridge, but bushes had broken my fall. Linsss had picked me up just before the truck exploded in the gully. As Linsss ran away from the flames, I'd started to wake up and my face had flopped forward and brushed its shoulder.

I'd screamed in pain, but it was too late and the damage was done. Linsss saved my life, and in the process left me with a facial scar that ached when I was tired.

The alien had taken me back to its cave, wrapped me in a cocoon of silky material, and left me to recover. Whatever made up that alien stuff had healed the cuts on my body, my broken leg, and my internal wounds.

If it had only slathered it on my face too. I began each day feeling the scar, but without mirrors or shiny surfaces in the cave, all I had was my imagination. When I tried to explain to Linsss what a mirror was and why I wanted it, the alien was first puzzled, then impatient. Physical appearance was another human thing it thought ridiculous.

It never occurred to Linsss a scar would upset anyone. It had many jagged marks on its legs and back, which, for all I knew, could be old battle injuries, or tattoos done for beauty, or marks that showed its social status. Just more questions on my ever-growing list.

"Lassst." Linsss scampered up an eight-foot-high rock wall and tossed down a rope. "Tiesss," it called down.

I wrapped the rope around my waist and wondered if Linsss had found it or left it there just for this purpose. Maybe the alien had been waiting for me to insist I was well enough to go outside. *Maybe it was a test.* "I'm ready!"

Foot- and finger-rests were few and far apart. I searched for any grooves in the rock wall. The climb quickly exhausted me. I paused, letting my tired body drag on the rope. "I need a minute," I said, my voice echoing in the chamber. "That means I need a rest."

"Ssstill." Linsss's round face looked down from a short distance away. I re-checked the knot on the rope around my waist and forced myself to relax.

I'm a rag doll, an empty shirt, a net as light as air. I repeated the lines over and over. They were from a poem I'd written one rainy afternoon while I looked out the cabin window waiting for the summer storm to end.

Feeling better, I called out, "Ok!" Linsss pulled me up on the rope, though I tried to help by pushing off the rock face with my feet. "You could have hauled me all the way!" I said when I finally swung my weaker leg over the ledge, not caring if I sounded angry, and forgetting I wanted to appear like a tough human.

"Need ssstrong. Ssstretch musclesss," Linsss said, its head tilted and black eyes blinking.

I wanted to stay mad, but I could see a glow outlining the entrance hole. I felt a rush of adrenalin. *Freedom!*

Linsss's long body briefly blocked the light before it went through the opening. Now it was my turn. Gingerly, I put one foot then the other outside and stood on the flat rock ledge jutting out from the mountainside. I bit my lip to keep from calling out, "Mom! Mom!"

I'd never knew a person could feel sad and happy at the same time.

The view would have been beautiful even if I hadn't been underground for such a long time. The ghostly glow given off by the full moon cast shadows on the bushes and cactus in the valley below. The wind brushed my tangled hair and caressed my skin. An owl hooted in the distance. If my leg hadn't been so sore, I'd have danced.

"Glad birth-daysss."

"We say 'happy birthday'."

"Happy birth-daysss, Mite."

We stood together in silence looking out at the silhouettes of light and dark fluttering on the land. I turned to Linsss, tears appearing with no prompting this time. "Thank you. This is the best birthday gift ever."

Linsss made a noise I thought of as a "snortle," a drawn-out snort and laugh combined.

We stood together listening to the sounds of the desert at night: the wind rustling through cactus, an owl's two-note cooing, followed by the musical whistles of a canyon wren. After a few minutes, Linsss turned and motioned for me to go back inside.

"Not yet, please!"

"Leg sssick. Ressst."

Linsss knew I was in pain. I had to admit I was not looking forward to the return journey to the cave. My leg was throbbing from the jarring it had experienced on the trip up. I thought I'd hidden it well. Obviously not well enough.

If I was allowed out once, maybe I'd be allowed out again. "Tomorrow?"

"Sssee leg."

I gave the canyon a long final look, storing up the memory. I'd known from my first glance that nothing in any direction was familiar, which meant I didn't know how to get home from here. I had been depending on my ability to get back to our cabin on my own. I choked back a howl of despair.

As I stepped into the tunnel, I looked pleadingly at Linsss. "Tomorrow?"

The alien grunted, which could have meant "yes" or "no." I'd learned the grunt changed meanings, depending on its mood.

Happy birthday to me. I struggled to keep hold of the rope and slowly made my way down to the lower level tunnel.

Linsss's shadowy figure was barely visible above me as the alien waited patiently for my feet to touch the lower tunnel path.

I hope being 14 will be better. Now it was my turn to snortle. Next year couldn't be any worse than this one. *That was a stupid thing to say. After all the things that had happened to me?*

Things could always get worse.

I landed on the lower tunnel floor with a thud that jarred my tired body.

Soon I can get away and....

I stopped and concentrated on moving one foot in front of the other, feeling the path, making sure I didn't trip on a fallen rock or stumble into a hole.

I need a plan.

Heal. Explore. Escape.

I repeated those words as I entered the cave and, feeling bone-weary, went straight to my hammock.

Heal. Explore. Escape. I would have to find someone to help me.

Heal.

Explore.

And then escape.

Made in the USA
Columbia, SC
05 December 2019